VACATIONLAND

VACATIONLAND

Sarah Stonich

UNIVERSITY OF MINNESOTA PRESS
MINNEAPOLIS

The University of Minnesota Press gratefully acknowledges assistance provided for the publication of this book by the John K. and Elsie Lampert Fesler Fund.

Published by the University of Minnesota Press
111 Third Avenue South, Suite 290
Minneapolis, MN 55401-2520
http://www.upress.umn.edu

Library of Congress Cataloging-in-Publication Data
Stonich, Sarah.
Vacationland : a novel / Sarah Stonich.
ISBN 978-0-8166-8766-4 (pb : acid-free paper)
I. Title.
PS3569.T6455V33 2013
813'.54—dc23   2012048343

Printed in the United States of America on acid-free paper

The University of Minnesota is an equal-opportunity educator and employer.

20   19   18   10   9   8   7   6   5   4

CONTENTS

short days that dawn cold, colder, and, as the hand thawing on Meg's floor mutely suggests, life threatening. Besides a boreal starkness some consider lovely, the area is unremarkable save its record temperatures, most recently an axle-snapping minus sixty—the type of statistic that only provides fodder for grizzled locals who boast that the meek wouldn't want to inherit this bit of earth. Fetching her Sunday paper from Pavola's Diner the day before, Meg had watched the old boys mimic the latest hypo-thermia victim, a Chicago bond trader found on the Wikawashi Portage, speaking into a chunk of pine bark the size of an iPhone as if calling for a quote. Wheezing with laughter and the gunk of Camel straights, they put on such shows when tourists are within earshot, debating whether January is more dangerous than July, usually calling a draw, for there is peril year-round here on the wrong side of the Laurentian Divide, where straight-line winds toss pine trunks onto sleeping campers like Scottish cabers, flash floods dissolve trails from under hikers' knobby soles, and drownings are so routine their mention might elicit a shrug. And since there is water, water, everywhere, canoeists go right ahead and drink, inviting parasites to rue their days from the inside out, when even the toddlers over at CubCare DayDen know bet-ter, having been taught, along with the alphabet song, the rhyme about moose poop soup. Things that do not look dangerous are. Wide-eyed does nicked by cars have been known to kick-box through windshields, and while only two hunters have been fa-tally hooved, both were from Minneapolis and perfect examples of why one might think twice before just showing up here.

Linger over the weak coffee at Pavola's, or the venison chow mein at the Boon Dock on what Arno calls Chink Night (don't ask for chopsticks) and realize these natives are merely discourag-ing outsiders who might grow too fond of Hatchet Inlet—a place as grungy as the cabs of their pickups and frayed as the collars of their Pendleton's. Miners and laborers who limped home from Korea and Nam to face union squabbles, strikes, and pit closures blanch at rumors of a new espresso bar or bookshop. Few of them blink at such local place names as Jap Island, Squaw Creek,

Polack Swamp, or Krautville, leaving such gnashings to tourists who drive up in hybrids quilted in left-of-left bumper stickers, wearing zip-off shorts and thirty-dollar quick-dry underpants.

Hatchet Inlet has been sprucing—the fish hatchery is now a gallery, and two "partners" have opened a B&B in the old rectory. Poured footings for an organic food co-op only portend more riffraff to come.

Meg blinks at the hand, wondering what those men welded to their stools at Pavola's might make of it. The knuckles are embedded with grime the color of local clay. It's entirely possible she has watched this hand rev an ATV or hoist a twelve-pack counterward at Walt's Bottle Shoppe.

In the next room, Jeremy drops a corner of his paper. "What's your precious mutt done now?"

Ilsa is Meg's dog at times like these and Jeremy's when his feet are cold, or when tourists in town crouch to pet, commenting on her white coat and gin-bottle blue eyes. In private he complains she couldn't pull her own weight in Purina, grousing, "She's just so *decorative.*" Where he comes from dogs earn their kibble; Border collies herd, hounds hound, and Corgis drape the Queen's arm like overbred handbags.

Ilsa had delivered the hand in her manner, tentatively and hopeful of praise. In the past, there'd been numerous waterfowl and occasional mammals—some dead, some literally hanging on, like the wolverine pup swinging by a fang-pierced ear. A white mink with deep canine punctures wasn't as fortunate—Meg laid that beautiful creature on a newspaper and whimpered along with Ilsa as it breathed its last. Now this.

Jeremy's voice cuts through the pulse in Meg's ear. "Sooo, Margaret. What's she brought us this evening?"

" 'Sssa . . . ," Meg is just able to mutter, ". . . human h-hand."

Newspaper rustles. "Is that so?"

She crouches. Snow has melted from the fingertips to expose lavender nails. The cut wrist resembles the butt end of a dainty roast, its pink bone marrow the texture of ice cream. When she touches it, a clear gloss tips her finger. Her stomach coils.

"Jer?"

Meg only calls her husband "Jer" during monosyllabic moments of illness or panic and, though it's been awhile, desire.

Jeremy's tone shifts. "Yes?"

"Cawldasherf." She would repeat "Call the sheriff" but is pitching toward the kitchen sink to bang her temple against the porcelain ledge and vomit. After rinsing, she holds her fingers under scalding water.

In the periphery, Jeremy's khakis scissor across the linoleum.

"Okay, Pooch-Face, what've we here, another mangled bunny?" He barely glances at Meg. "Really, Margaret, if you're going to keep this sort of animal, you should acquire a stomach for such things." When annoyed his accent grows more clipped.

Meg cannot warn him fast enough. He's already down on one knee and in the time it would take her to say, "It's real," he's realized.

"Bloody *hell*!" His elbows and knees pump in reverse until Jeremy is pressed to the beadboard. He lobs his gaze between the hand and Meg, who can only shrug and wipe her mouth. Ilsa sweeps her tail, still holding out for praise, but Meg only points to the corner, insisting, "Go." With a pained look, the dog toenails to her rug. They both lunge for the phone then, but Jeremy is longer-armed. He begins jabbing numbers.

"What is it you call over here again, 411? *O* for operator? What?"

"911." Meg grabs something to cover the hand and Ilsa whines as it's draped with a novelty tea towel from Turin printed with a blurred Jesus face. As the call connects, Meg stands on her tiptoes, nudging closer to the receiver. A bored female voice clicks on, "Fire and police. What is your emergency?"

"It's, um, a, a hand," Jeremy clears his throat. "We've a human hand here."

A stretch of silence precedes, "Your name, sir?"

"Jeremy Hoyle."

"Hoyle. Like *According to*?"

"According to, yes." To Meg he mouths, "Brilliant."

"Mr. Hoyle, where are you calling from?"

"Crow Point." He tries to jerk away to pace, but Meg holds fast. He recites their fire number and the county road. "You know where that is?"

"Yes. Please state again what your emergency is?"

Jeremy looks at the dish towel. "Christ."

"Sir?"

"A hand." He speaks slowly. "The dog has brought it to our cottage . . . a human, severed hand."

The voice is matter-of-fact. "You're sure it's severed?"

He touches his forehead. "Well, by definition if it is not attached it's severed, now isn't it?"

"Sir, does the hand, if that's what it is, appear to have been *cut* off, or, separated from the body in another manner?"

"Another manner?"

"Wrenched, or possibly chewed?"

Jeremy's face goes milky, and the receiver rolls into Meg's waiting palm.

"Hello?"

"Now who is on the line?"

"Meg Machutova."

"And your relationship to the caller?"

"Wife," she says loudly to be heard over Jeremy's gagging. "I'm his wife!"

"But your name isn't Hoyle?"

Meg answers in the tone she reserves for tiresome students. "No, not all women change their names just because they've chosen to marry, Miss." When Jeremy makes a slashing gesture across his throat, she turns away, plugging her free ear.

The operator asks, "Mrs. Machutova, can *you* look at the hand?"

She lifts the towel. It's less blue now, leaking watery blood. The cut is so precise the wrist hairs are lopped clean. "It's severed. Quite severed."

"Okay, then." The line is static filled. "Does the wound look fresh?"

"Fresh? Would that matter?"

"It may help determine whether the party or parties involved are in the vicinity."

"Vicinity?" Meg glances at the door, at the eighty-year-old lock that could be bitten through. "It seems pretty fresh. Would you like me to smell it?" Meg dodges a scowl from Jeremy, who disdains sarcasm in others. During the long pause, she suspects the operator is considering it, but then she only asks, "Male or female?"

"Male."

"Any distinguishing marks, wedding ring?"

Jeremy budges in, pressing his ear next to Meg's. She recoils at his breath, realizing he's rinsed with Petite Sirah.

"No ring."

"Okay, then. I'll patch this all through to Sheriff Janko. In the meantime, can you please put the hand somewhere cold and away from your dog? In your fridge maybe?"

"Our fridge?"

"To preserve it. Put it on ice to keep it cool. But don't let it freeze. Can you do that?"

"Sure, but . . ." Meg suddenly doesn't want the operator to hang up, doesn't want to lose the tether of a voice from a lighted, peopled place, even if it's just a room above the local fire hall where there are no horrors on the floor.

"Yes?"

"What's *your* name?"

"We don't give out our names, Mrs. Machutova."

"But . . . you've got mine."

"Yes, I do. Take care now."

Take care? But the voice had clicked off.

Laying the phone down, Meg wonders if they should pack up the hand and attempt the drive in to Hatchet Inlet, but peering out the window she can barely make out their Subaru—now a soft lozenge of white buried to its wheel wells. Meg had seen her first SHIT HAPPENS bumper sticker in Hatchet Inlet, applied upside down to the back of a muddy Rover. She learned to drive on these very roads in an equipment truck her grandfather bought at a mine closure—a vehicle that could fjord a creek, boasted six studded tires, and was best driven with earplugs. As their driveway disappears behind horizontal snow, she longs for such a truck, forgetting the many Hummer drivers she's flipped off.

Remote perfectly describes their location—ideal for an ax-wielding lunatic. Naledi is not a place one passes by; it's where one ends up. She backs away from the window, asking the ceiling, "Why don't we own a gun?"

"A gun?" Jeremy peers over the rims of imaginary glasses. "Survivalists and assassins own guns, Meg. Criminals and those millions misinterpreting your Constitution own guns. Writers and painters tend to not."

Meg sighs and hangs her head to see the tea towel has absorbed a pink stain, as if Jesus is blushing. They toss a coin to see who will handle the hand. Jeremy loses and lifts it with a spatula onto a bowl of ice. She slides the bowl into the refrigerator next to the lasagna thawing for dinner. When something falls from the freezer door to the molded egg compartment, she pries it out—a plastic magnet shaped like a steak, embossed with letters to suggest grill marks: KUKANEN'S MEATS: PRIME CUTS AT CUT PRICES! The bubble that has been forming in her throat pricks open and she shakes with the sort of laughter that eventually makes her back hurt.

Jeremy turns. "Are we amused?"

Bending to blink into their refrigerator, her laughter trails off. In any marriage, along with the good comes the rest, and there, crowding the bowl of hand are Jeremy's staples: jars of marmite, HP Sauce, an open tin of kippers, piccalilli relish, and cloying jams made of fruits she's never heard of. A new jar has appeared, mercifully opaque, of jam made of something called pluot. They are approaching their tenth anniversary. Meg remembers her Grandfather Vac's joke about a couple that had been married so long they'd gone through two bottles of Worcestershire sauce. Squinting at their own, Meg cannot say whether it's half-empty or half-full.

"Amused?" Meg closes the refrigerator and braces her back against the door, slowly plowing down through lines of magnetic poetry. "Hardly."

They look everywhere but at the puddle. She turns away so Jeremy cannot see her chew a cuticle. Perhaps the hand's owner has simply had an accident—a logger being careless, a butterfin-gered chainsaw-sculptor trying to make Momma Bear just right. Maybe some indignant wife teaching her man with roving hands a severe lesson, a *sever* lesson . . . .

Jeremy's moving out of the room.

"Where're you going?"

"Perhaps you're right. We should have a weapon."

Meg gets to her feet and casts about for the phone, eventually pressing the Find button on its base to follow the sound to the fruit bowl, where it beeps among bananas. In the living room, Jeremy is wobbling on the couch cushions, reaching for an an-tique handsaw hung on a log beam because Meg likes its patina of rust. She rests the phone on her collarbone. "That's your idea of a weapon?"

Meg once assumed that where intelligence flourished, so too would common sense. Watching her husband wrestle the saw, she thinks of the local boys who once pursued her—capable, rug-ged boys who would have become the sorts of men certain to own guns, even gun collections. The saw is displayed above two canvases from Meg's new series, *All That's Underneath,* images re-flected across the mirrors of memory and water. One painting shows a wedge of water between the prows of docked aluminum boats, sun refracting from every surface to suggest heat, boat license numbers shimmering upside-down and backward. The other canvas is water alone, but with reflections of birches shrug-ging shoreward under a sky stirred with scraps of bird wing and thin cloud.

Once upon a time, Naledi was Meg's entire world, a place hemmed on every side by water in all its incarnations—stream, swamp, puddle, or lake, the most elemental of elements, in which nearly all of her early instances of awe took place: the moats around her sand pail, the shallows where she dog-paddled while buoyed by bleach-bottle water-wings, the bubbled depths and the dark shock of her first cannonball, the silver surface where grace visited her in the moments of finally mastering the Australian crawl. Her paintings evoke glossy mud, cattails poking, gasoline rainbows floating over the fishy sluice between wooden boat ribs. Meg has re-created these visceral memories in so many brush-strokes, sealing her past under the hard varnish of the present.

She looks up to see Jeremy wobbling on the cushions like a young John Cleese. Clumsiness, Meg reasons, is an affliction, just like pattern baldness or psoriasis, and so shouldn't be held against a person, surely not so brilliant a person. She shakes her own less crowded head, feeling a little sorry for Jeremy. His gifts —an ability to quote the Magna Carta or fluency in Mandarin— simply prove useless in places like Hatchet Inlet.

The saw comes off the wall with a twang and Jeremy's arm windmills as if he is in a skit. Her husband is a struggler— cannot light the gas pilot without shrieking like a Brownie, wields a canoe paddle like a tennis racket, and suffers an irrational fear of deer ticks. So while he's indoors burrowed into some paper or manuscript, Meg is free to spend her daylight hours in peace, running the Brushmeister or chainsaw, or grading the road. She catches all bats and relocates any wolf spiders before Jeremy has any inkling. Chopping kindling keeps her arms toned. He has never darkened the door to the cellar, where pipes freeze and ver-min thrive, and where Meg often takes her morning coffee, firing up the old wood furnace and bringing a lantern when she plans to read. Recently, Meg has come north a few times on her own, leaving Jeremy in Chicago where all the civilization he desires is within a stone's throw from their brownstone duplex, where it doesn't matter that he cannot throw.

She exhales. "What time is it?"

He turns his wrist to look at his watch, nearly combing an eyebrow with the saw blade. "Seven."

"God, is that all?"

Neither mentions dinner, lasagna.

Ilsa follows Meg up to the bedroom, where they both circle to find comfortable spots. Meg turns on the radio to see if there's any news—any mention of a lost hand, but the only clear station is airing the *Polka Peggy Show*. Between songs, Peggy reads travelers' advisories and windchill updates. In a sudden shock of volume she hollers, "I'm now gonna announce a public service announcement! Jig Jorgenson up at the fire hall needs volunteers with snow machines to help fetch folks from their cars in ditches and deliver pills from the drugstore. Whoever's game, just give Jig a holler!" Peggy doesn't bother with a phone number, following up with the weather report and a pitch for the White Tail Supper Club, her up-north nasal accent somehow rounding and truncating words at the same time.

Meg's own accent is less definable. Before her art school years in England she boarded at St. Agnes in Chicago, where Polish nuns taught French and her roommates included a Kiwi and a Scot. At Naledi, her Grandfather Vac spoke mostly Czech and the radio was permanently tuned to the CBC because he could not abide American news broadcasts. Thus were Meg's aural influences, lacing her speech with odd inflections and vernaculars to comprise a patois Jeremy calls Meglish.

From her perch on the headboard, Meg uses the cordless phone like a bat, bunting rawhide pretzels to the space between Ilsa's paws. After Jeremy comes upstairs and changes into pajamas and his night socks, he sets the rusted saw within reach of the bed. Once under the duvet he props a literary journal as thick as a phone book on his chest.

"You can read?"

He only nods. Meg taps a rhythm on her knees and half-listens to the staticky drone of accordions. Though she actually knows the difference between a polka and a mazurka, such observations only make Jeremy feel more foreign than he already is. Meg cannot help that this place is home to her. She barely remembers the house in Oak Park, sold after her parents' accident. Summers and holidays were always spent at Naledi. Winter break was her favorite, when the resort slept and her grandfather's only chores were clearing roads, raking snow from roofs, and making indoor repairs. At Christmas they'd chop down a balsam and make a great fuss of decorating it with woven straw ornaments and crystal icicles, a few of the scant possessions Vac brought with him from Prague. During these holidays, he endeavored to teach Meg things he enjoyed himself: carving, brewing beer, and snaring animals for the hobby he sincerely encouraged her to share, taxidermy. She carved copies of balsa fishing lures she found in catalogs, and the rest of the time, most of the time, she drew. And so they passed their evenings at the big trestle table, whittling and sketching and skinning little carcasses. Vac sternly tutored her in chess, but cribbage or penny ante poker was played for fun and nickels. He plowed clear the bay and taught her to ice-skate in a contraption he'd welded from the chrome tubing of a kitchen chair. For half of each year the resort was snugged into a cottony hush, winter spanning darkly from Halloween to Easter. For six months, every lit bulb was a beacon.

Summers were a flip side of sunlight, simmering green movement, with Vac popping up everywhere like a gopher in a tool belt, armed to attend to the next thing, the next guest, the next problem. The long, rushed days of summer blurred with noise and people so that it seemed Meg could nearly hear the ticking speed at which they were spent.

She was expected to do her share around Naledi, so that by the time she was ten, Meg was manning the dock pumps, mixing gas, pounding dents from canoes, and drying spark plugs on her T-shirts. By twelve she was trailing the Saturday maids, hardworking girls Vac recruited from the nursing program at Laurentian. They taught Meg how to make a bed with hospital corners crisp as origami and how to remove stains from sheets Swiss-dotted by mosquito victims or rusty with menstrual mishaps; she learned a dozen uses for bleach and vinegar. In their sweeping, the girls rivaled champion curlers; they fearlessly stuck their hands in drains and scrubbed toilets flushed with water the color of Tang, all the while swaying their backsides to the transistor strapped to the housekeeping wagon—singing to Neil Young or

Fleetwood Mac, smacking rugs against tree trunks raising dust clouds while yowling to Aretha Franklin. They whispered things about s-e-x Meg did not understand. She wondered, of course, and curiously pondered the by-products of sex on sheets and in wastebaskets, deducing that adults simply oozed. She'd seen dogs paired in painful locks, knew about spawn and how fish and frogs reproduced, but when it came to her own body Meg knew as much as any girl raised by nuns and an old man. One distressful, cramp-filled afternoon, a maid named DeeDee gently explained to Meg what the sisters of St. Agnes and Vac had not, then drove her to Hatchet Inlet for supplies and her first dose of Midol. DeeDee offered to answer any questions, of which Meg had many, so that by the end of the long drive back to Naledi she knew everything. In ensuing summers other Laurentian girls would teach her other useful lessons, like how to apply eyeliner, roll an airtight joint, where to get the pill, and that *boner* meant much more than a mistake.

Meg juggles the phone from hand to hand. "Why isn't anyone calling?"

Polka Peggy singsongs, "That was 'Polish Sausage Polka,' sponsored by Yeti Deli, sending this next one out to all you shut-ins, 'specially youse up at Senior Cedars or over in the Section Eight housing. Nothing like a hot foot-long on a cold night!"

Normally, Jeremy might chuckle. She smacks his shoulder. "We could call the radio station! Like, to dedicate a song, only we'd tell Polka Peggy we've found a hand. She could announce it."

Jeremy snails a brow. "She'd think it was a crank call." Seeing Meg's look, he softens the set of his mouth slightly. "All right, then."

But the request line is busy. She holds the receiver so he can hear the buh, buh, buh.

"It's Friday night in Hatchet Inlet, after all." He pats her leg. "Just press redial every few minutes. You're bound to get through."

"What if the sheriff tries us? We don't have call waiting." They rely on the landline here, their own cell phones useless, with the nearest reception a quarter of a mile up the ridge. She decides not to dial again. When she turns off the radio there is the shock of silence before the underlayment of sound fills in—shifting beams, shuddering panes, gulping pipes. In such weather the lodge seems to slowly tense up before harrumphing back onto its foundation stones, as if trying to get comfortable. To Meg, Naledi merely sounds as it always has—not only alive but moody. Most guests over the years assumed the name was Ojibwe or Lakota for something in nature, something woodsy or serene. In fact, the name had welled up in Vaclav Machutova's native tongue the instant he saw the resort, a word that had emigrated with him, fluid enough to sound restful to a tourist, yet a singularly efficient description of these grounds he'd trudged one April day in 1940. After taking down the For Sale sign and surveying his future—all in need of repair—Vac shook his head and muttered, "Naledi." A scrap of frozen ground.

Abandoned by his wife, Magda, and certain that Prague would fall to the Germans, Vaclav had taken his only child and fled Czechoslovakia for the piney vastness of Minnesota, where he dug in at Naledi to raise Meg's father, Tomas, and to manage the resort with an immigrant's zeal. In America, Vaclav grew old quickly and remained old for a very long time. His few acquaintances were fellow émigrés as world-weary as himself. At the Sokol Hall, Meg learned to dance on the feet of such men. During these socials Vaclav was sometimes known to smile. Under his cronies' accents, deepened by swigs of Becherovka, her grandfather's name hardened, aptly, to Fucklove.

Meg had been his lone soft spot. By never speaking of this, it remained their secret. Even when dying, Vac never caved, never said aloud, "I love you." She'd been oddly proud of him for that.

Jeremy nods into his pillow, sliding into sleep. She holds out her hands, turning them like paddles, considering the paint-stained fingertips Jeremy used to hold like petals and kiss while quoting Tennyson: "Perfume and flowers fall in showers, that lightly rain from ladies' hands." Every couple has their differences—small chafings that eventually scab over. Nothing to lose your head over. Nothing to lose a hand over. Meg scans Jeremy's profile through the lattice of spread fingers. Asleep, he seems nicer, like he used to be.

Suddenly it occurs to her why the hand seemed so familiar.

Rolling from the bed she edges away, careful not to wake the dog. Downstairs, she slips into the porch that doubles as her studio. Stepping over a space heater, she avoids the still-wet painting clamped on the easel, the self-portrait she can't seem to finish: her girl-self, with Annie hair and freckles spattered over her nose, poised over the fishing dock like a bowsprit. The point of view is one looking down from just over her shoulder, looking into the water along with her—her face reflecting a halo of ripples that delicately warp her features, though not enough to soften her gaze, wary even at twelve.

She grabs her tackle box of drawing supplies and backs out of the porch, but not before turning on the outside floodlight and scanning the snow-covered slope for tracks that aren't animal. In the living room she shuts off the many lights Jeremy has left burning. Tiptoeing into the kitchen, she stares a moment at the bloody puddle, then sets down a few layers of paper towel to soak it up. Now, she thinks, there's a commercial.

Reaching for the fridge door she sucks her teeth and opens it before there's a chance to change her mind.

Pulling the tea towel away, she nearly smiles. It *is*. Practically a replica. The bronze hand she'd seen in the Rodin Museum in Paris. Only once in person, but again afterward many times in art books and as scale copies. Meg had desperately wanted to stay and sketch the bronze, but Jeremy, unable to resist or digest the rich Parisian food, suddenly developed diarrhea, as he had every previous day of their honeymoon.

Setting the bowl on the table she arranges fresh ice under the hand. Touching it isn't so bad—somehow it doesn't feel dead. The nails are broad and pale, the skin soft. Younger than she'd first imagined. Meg digs in the compartments for pencils and charcoals. Since able to hold a crayon, she's obsessively sketched.

Because there was nothing interesting to draw at Naledi, she drew what was at hand: minnows in a bucket, water weeds twisted by currents, fish-egg goo on submerged logs, a rusted stringer still attached to the skeletal jaw of a pike, her own feet half-afloat and terraced by the optical distortion of water. In the process of documenting such things they eventually grew interesting, and once she went away they became more so. After discovering oils, her path was set—fluid and malleable, oil was the only medium to properly portray water, but she was nearly out of art school before even beginning to understand the properties and complexities of it: how oil and pigment and beeswax reacted to the swings of temperature and humidity; how its own refractive capacities helped reveal the layers of intricate translucency trapped within a single liquid drop, ripple, puddle, lap of surf, or whitecap.

She would paint on her free evenings after dishes were cleared, when Vac was bobbing into some book. Often working past sunset, which at their latitude was around 10 p.m. in July, she was forced to stop with the light. Antsy yet, she'd lift Vac's keys from their hook and drive rural roads in the old truck, often to township bars with names like Chainsaw Sally's or Without a Paddle, using her fake ID and feeding the jukebox with her tips, not choosy about the boys she danced with. Sometimes she made out with forestry students or mechanics, rookie miners— the kinds of boys who hit their sisters.

Meg was nearly one of them once, not just a lake person. But for moving away and marrying a foreigner, she's gained a vague notoriety in Hatchet Inlet. For being Vac's granddaughter, she is grudgingly respected. She spots a few of those boys still around town, men now, mellowed some. They are just ahead in line at the grocery store with their kids, or pumping diesel into their large-axle vehicles, crossing streets in their steel-toed boots. They know who she is, of course, with her tangled mop and the white dog plastered to her side.

The hand could belong to any of them.

Looking at it, Meg simply decides she will not think about what she's drawing, just draw. After taking up a soft crayon she lays down a few tentative strokes before falling into the familiar rhythm of hatches and arcs, using the heel of her palm to smudge in shadows. She draws the hand from a long angle, then from above. Her shoulders drop, and her exhalations slow as she finally relaxes into the third sketch. It's only a hand, after all, and just as the nude models in her life-drawing classes are only breathing structures, the hand becomes a structure, too. The index finger has a gouge healed to a polished dent. The thumbnail is misshapen, with a white scar spiraled around to the pad. The hand has had its share of mishaps. Mirrored perforations on the heel of the palm indicate the ubiquitous fishhook snag, a rite of passage in walleye country. A wince tingles through the faint white scars on Meg's own middle finger. She'd been seven, maybe eight, running full speed into the lodge trailed by a bobber and a few yards of twenty-pound test, so awed by the color of blood—not really red, more like cooked bacon, bright rust, or the drooping sumac in autumn—the pain seemed incidental. At the threshold of the bar where no one under twenty-one was allowed to pass, she stopped and filled her lungs. The howl made Vac spill the beer he was tapping. He rushed over, scooped her into the room and onto a barstool.

A few guests gathered to gasp and mew at the hook sunk deep into her fingertip. Vac handed her off and backed through the swinging kitchen door, returning immediately with a toolbox, which he pawed through for the needle-nose and a wire cutter. He looked Meg in the eye and told her to holler all she wanted because it was going to hurt like goddamn Dickens. As Vac had pressed her hand open on the bar, the man who'd been waiting for his beer and on whose lap Meg was now ensconced gently canted Meg's head away, holding her firmly under his arm. Someone groaned, and someone else held her wrist, but Vac was fast—pushing the barb through and snipping the eye end to yank the hook free—barely enough time to gather the breath to scream.

He doused her finger in whiskey and made a bandage of a Hamm's Beer napkin and electrical tape. Meg swallowed and palmed her wet eyes, then held her middle finger up for all to see, lying. "It didn't hurt a goddamn bit!"

There was applause for her bravery and a few dimes and quarters. One of the rich sisters in Cabin 2 who smelled like gin gave her a five dollar bill and cried. Vac made Meg give it back, which made her cry. Until that afternoon, Meg had never heard herself referred to as an orphan.

The knuckles of the hand are rough as small knees. Meg traces the hand's contours, the eddies of each fingerprint, the moons of cuticles—it's a sturdy trowel of bones padded in muscle, upholstered in skin. When shifting the hand from one position to the next, she notes its long life line and offers, "There's years left on your meter, if you believe in that sort of thing."

Jeremy wouldn't, of course. He doesn't believe in many things. The hand, for instance, seems to Meg to have some life yet, as if its motor is only idling, not shut down. She wouldn't go so far as to suggest spirits exist, but perhaps a body's energy takes a while to fizzle out. There are places around the resort where she encounters pockets of air weighted by something, inexplicable moments in the cedar grove when she feels shouldered by a human emotion not her own—one she cannot quite pin, but it's something akin to benevolence—something unconditional. She spreads the cold fingers by lacing her own between them, then sets to drawing this bizarre union. The twined pose is awkward to maintain, holding the page down with her forearm and managing to twist her charcoal to blacken the cave of space between the two palms, hurrying so the hand doesn't become overwarm. In hurrying she employs long, loose strokes and hastily smudged shadows, the result being more spontaneous and interesting than the other drawings. There isn't much time. And what if Jeremy were to walk in to find her in this strange congress? She can imagine the drop of his jaw, the sort of reaction he might have upon discovering her in flagrante delicto (as only Jeremy would put it) with their electrician, Rory, a scene she has imagined. But her husband is asleep upstairs, his snore ruffling through the open heat grate in the ceiling. "Poor Jeremy," she yawns, "so disengaged . . . ," she nods to the hand, ". . . a bit like you, really."

When the clock chimes, she looks up to see the window has grown light and the storm has sidled off, promising one of those sun-shot, frigid days Meg takes personally. She settles the hand back in the bowl and adds fresh ice, hoping she hasn't harmed it. A dozen drawings account for the night. Kneeling, she slowly orders them in a stack, noting the various angles: the hand at rest; upturned and expectant as if waiting for coins or rain; palm down to trap a handful of air; on its side, as if drifted to a pillow. Few suggest it is severed, and only one shows the bone end, the finality. Just as Meg closes the drawings into a folder, the telephone rings. It doesn't startle her, tired as she is, so used to the hand she's forgotten it's a mystery to be solved.

"Hello?"

"Ya, hi. Sheriff Janko here. This Meg Machutova?"

"It is." She clears her throat.

"Cripe. Did I wake you up?"

"Oh, no. You've heard, Sheriff? About this hand?"

"How 'bout *that*? Listen, what kinda shape's it in?"

"Ah . . . ," Meg grimaces, ". . . good, I suppose."

"Those radial saws make a nice clean cut, don't they? I hear the torque threw the thing clear past the fence. We'd about given up finding it anyway, then one of the EMTs said he saw a white wolf just before the ambulance took off, so we pretty much wrote Hal's hand off as dinner."

"Hal?"

"Hal Bergen. Owns the lumber mill out past Juttala's? You maybe don't know him. Moved here from Michigan about the time you went away. You got a extra cooler?"

"Sure."

"Good. We're gonna airlift it to the Twin Cities and see if they can sew it back on."

"Back on?"

"Ah-ya. Hal's down at St. Sebastian's, 'coptered him out before the worst of the storm."

Meg sits. "Is he all right?"

"Oh sure, 'cept his arm's a little short. You can maybe put it in a Ziploc or something and pack it tight with plenty of ice? I couldn't get one of the EMTs to come out to you with so many other accidents, but close enough—the vet over at Greenstone's on his way out now, shouldn't be more than forty minutes. I got him on radio. You knew the Lahti boy, didn't you?"

She swallows. "Pete Lahti?"

He'd been her first. The same July night that Meg lost her virginity to Pete Lahti, Pete lost Vac's johnnyboat to a submerged rock, high on homegrown and speeding through the Encampment Narrows. When the boat canted and the hull screeched, Pete cursed and Meg yelped, but once the boat righted, they shrugged it off as just a bad scrape. Within minutes of dropping anchor, they peeled off their clothes for a second go, so intent neither realized the boat was sinking until water lapped a frigid interruptus over them.

To pay for the damage, Pete did extra labor for Vac the rest of that summer. If her grandfather had known how Pete actually spent most of that time on cabin beds that Meg was supposedly changing, or in shower stalls she was supposedly disinfecting . . .

"You must've had quite a time out there."

She fumbles the phone. "Pardon?"

Sheriff Janko booms, "I said, you must've had quite a time, taking care of Hal's hand."

"Oh, yes." Meg props herself back up. "It's been a night."

"Sure has. Listen, you won't be plowed out 'til tomorrow or later up there, so if you need anything, you just let Pete know."

"I will."

"Okeydoke, Meg. This is one for the grandkids, huh?"

"Sure is."

She fills the small cooler with ice. Glad to at least have a name, she tsks, "Really, Hal, how careless of you." Once Hal's hand is settled in and the lid ready to close, she crosses the index and middle fingers, still pliable—rigor mortis staved off by the chill. After tucking the drawings into her portfolio, Meg scoops

coffee and runs water and sits with an empty mug watching the
glass knob, waiting for the first perk, waiting for Pete.

He'd been different from other boys. They'd had more than
just sex. Pete had stuck by her the summer she was so panicked
about her future, had been there the night she knocked back a
shot of Jagermeister for each art school that declined her—he'd
helped burn the rejection letters and held her hair when she threw
up. When she got accepted to a school in England, he'd encouraged her to stand up to Vac, who wanted her to stay in the States.
After leaving, she wrote him long letters, to which Pete replied by
postcard, which was more than she'd expected. He even called
a few times. Longer and longer gaps widened between their cor-
respondences as they veered toward separate futures.

When Vac fell ill the following September, it was Pete who
called her Chelsea flat with the news. And though he'd been dat-
ing another girl by then, he drove hours to gather Meg at the
airport and then leaned along with her in the green tile halls of
the hospital for the days it took Vac to finally give in. The funeral
had been clergy free, at Vac's request. A bottle of Becherovka
was poured into the water after the ashes, and while Rudy Mack
played his accordion, the Vittorio brothers carved a pig and everyone got hammered. After the guests had gone, Pete picked a
bouquet of the state flower and made Meg toss it from the dock,
holding the waistband of her skirt so she wouldn't topple. That
was when she finally cracked, tears falling over the illegal flotilla
of lady slippers. Pete had been the only one to see her cry. They'd
slept together one last time, but both knew the end was the end.

Meg's chin slides lower until it berths in the soft crook of her
arm. It feels nice. Some memory or other curved away just out of
reach. Pete.

A distant gurgling could be Jeremy snoring, or the furnace
kicking in, but as Meg sinks deeper, it grows from a gentle purr
to a distant buzz saw and is finally audible as a snowmobile tearing the flannel of silence. Meg imagines a yellow Arctic Cat cutting through the drifts like a Norelco razor whooshing through a
Burl Ives Christmas special. The snow is so white! Pete would be

standing like a rodeo rider, wearing a fox-trimmed parka, speeding toward the cabin. Of course he'd be older. Forty by now, but surely still handsome in a rugged, *GQ* sort of way, threads of platinum in his hair and fine wrinkles broadcasting the gleam from those blue eyes . . .

The snowmobile reaches the back porch and moans down to a low rattle. He will be inside in a minute. A minute. Meg floats, drifts. Less than a minute . . .

A sudden bang jolts her upright. Peeled from her arm, her cheek is damp with drool. Too groggy to take in much besides the smell of coffee burning, she rubs the sting from her eyes. A man in goggles and an anorak stands outside the porch door, hitting the glass with a leather mitten. She flinches at the brightness behind his silhouette and waves him into the porch, then turns off the flame under the coffee. With bent pinkies she mines sleep from the corners of her eyes, shaking with cold. When she turns to open the door, Meg is so startled to see him directly in front of her she sits back down, hard. She'd never locked the door!

His mustache is snot-cicled and ski goggles obscure half his face. From across the table she can smell stale gasoline. He mumbles through a ruff of acrylic fur, "Heya, Meg. I'm here for the hand."

"Pete?"

He shoves the goggles up over his forehead and pushes his hood back. "Who else?"

A version of Pete's eyes stare from a stranger's chapped face, his once-fetlocked forehead is a shiny slope between bumpers of Brillo fringe. As if to make up for the hair, Pete has grown thick mutton chops that bookend his now plump cheeks. His nose is angry with telltale capillaries. It is him, but if not for his eyes . . .

He nods at the cooler. "That it?"

"Yes, but . . ."

"Sorry, Meg, no time to chat here."

"Oh, right. Of course . . ." She holds out the cooler like an offering. "How weird is this?"

Pete gingerly takes it, meeting her eye. "Yeah. Hey, we

oughta . . . at least, ah, grab a beer sometime?" He was looking at her hands, each knuckle creased with charcoal, her fingertips graphite-gray from rubbing shadows, yesterday's ochre paint still under her nails.

"Sure." She lets go of the handle, pulls Jeremy's old cardigan tight around her, folding her hands in. "A beer. Why not?"

"Right on." He's already backing out the door but pauses, giving her a scan. "Hey, Meg. You sure held up."

Meg nods, wondering how to respond and is saved when Pete slams the kitchen door. She winces when the glass rattles and he crashes shut the outer storm door.

His engine revs loud as a chainsaw, and he launches away. The roar slowly sputters down with distance, as she frowns, drinking scorched coffee, staring at the table, at the charcoal smudges and the evaporating ring of water where the bowl holding Hal's hand had been. She rubs the marks clean with her thumb.

Cold air left in Pete's wake is the only evidence anyone had been there. The chill and the coffee bring Meg around wide-eyed in the acrid air. After she rinses her cup, she scrubs her hands with a nailbrush.

In the living room she pauses at the foot of the stairs leading to the bedroom she's shared with Jeremy during summers and holidays for so many years. She drags an afghan from the back of the rocker and heads for the couch.

Curling her toes beneath a pillow, she hears the tip-tap of the dog descending the stairs. Soon she feels Ilsa's cool snout on her shoulder and smells the familiar fishy breath. Meg nuzzles Ilsa back, then presses into the pillow as she falls asleep, wondering if the surgeons will reattach Hal's hand with her wedding ring still on his pinkie, or if they will screw it off.

GINA FLATTENS THE ARTS AND ENTERTAINMENT SECTION and pivots it so Ed can see, tapping her finger over a photograph of a woman standing next to a large painting. The painting is of water, as far as Ed can tell, or at least reflections over a wet surface. While he's no connoisseur, he can see there's merit in the composition. The colors are pleasant, but the painting is a little abstract for his tastes—he hopes Gina isn't thinking of it for their own décor.

They've recently moved into their new condominium after thirty years in a tall, cramped townhouse. The last of their children and their detritus are gone, along with the futsy, comfortable upholstered furniture, including Ed's favorite chair. Gina is finally living her single-level dream of Danish modern.

Ed shrugs. "It's okay."

"Yes, but the artist—read her name."

"Machutova." He must know it, for the syllables ease around the silent *c* as he says it: Ma-hoo-toe-va. As he repeats the name, a face wells and Ed stutters. He clears nothing from his throat.

"Sounds familiar."

"It should be. Remember that resort we used to take the boys to?" Gina pulls the paper back and thumbs her reading glasses higher. "Listen: 'Margaret Machutova, former Lecturer of Fine Art at the Institute of . . . something -thwaite'—I can't pronounce it—'opens her exhibit, *All That's Underneath,* tonight at the Forbes Gallery.'" Gina reads the rest of the paragraph silently, lips moving, until the last sentence: "Oh, and a list of collections her paintings are in . . . goodness, the Getty? You remember her."

"How would I? She would have been just a girl."

"Sure you do, she was all arms and legs, looked a little like Orphan Annie. I even heard her called that once."

Ed frowns, "Was she an orphan?"

"I think so, mostly. I know that old workhorse who ran the place was her grandfather. I never saw anything like a mother, and she went to some boarding school, down here, in fact. You really don't remember?"

"There were a lot of kids there, Gina." Ed rattled open the business section. "Why would I remember one?"

"She was a bit odd." Gina absently squeezes her teabag. "Might be fun to go to the opening . . ."

"Ah, *no*."

"Well," Gina flops the teabag onto her saucer, "who woke up on the wrong side this morning?" She stacks her own breakfast dishes, leaving his, and heads for the kitchen.

Ed watches his wife walk away, noticing one side of her skirt is hitched higher on her broad hip. Spider veins broadcast upward from the pale crook of her knee. Once she's out of sight, he pulls the *Trib* closer to examine the photograph.

An artist, just as she'd claimed she would be. And certainly looks the part—her Japanese jacket is held together with a pin that looks like sculpture, and her hair is corralled in a loose braid. He wouldn't have forgotten the eyes. She's wearing the sort of pants Gina calls Capris, and Converse high-tops. Ed stares at the shoes until a door opens and Gina approaches. He slides the paper away with his elbow.

Her skirt is smoothed, lipstick applied, her purse slung. "I'm off."

"Where to?"

"It's my day at Silver Falls. Friday?"

"Right." One of her volunteer days—Gina's Fridays are spent ferrying seniors to the library and grocery store and back. She'll be home by six, smelling like them.

"There's a Lean Cuisine for your lunch." When she leans over to peck his forehead, Ed responds with a tic that could be mistaken for a grin.

He listens while she goes into the foyer to put on her heels. They do not wear shoes in the condominium, only soft clogs and slippers to lessen the din of footsteps on marble and parquet. Once the door clicks, Ed reaches for his bifocals and tilts the paper toward the light.

It's been twenty-four—no, twenty-six years. She'd have been around twelve then . . . fourteen at the most. Funny that she's the one he remembers best.

After lunch, Ed walks to the station to catch the 2:10. It's foolish to go all the way into the city, as Gina repeatedly suggests, especially when there is a lovely YMCA so close, definitely more convenient, and much less expensive. But Ed is adamant and hangs tight to his membership at the downtown health club. The ride in gives him time to read, and once in the city he's among familiar sights, walking down avenues he knows among people who move with intent. The honking that used to annoy him now somehow does not.

As soon as he settles into a forward-facing seat, three girls wearing academy uniforms burst into the car, giggling and backing into each other when the train starts. Before they can sit, Ed gathers his gym bag and newspapers. All three are the Machutova girl's age.

He sways into the next car, where the only free forward-facing seat is on the wrong side. Ed likes to shift sides going to and from so he's always on the lakeside, but now, to avoid a crick he will have to sit on the wrong side both ways. The train gathers speed as it leaves the haven of Lake Forest and begins what Ed subconsciously thinks of as the descent, traveling through towns less contrived, less like movie sets.

Unaware he's still wearing his reading glasses, Ed squints out the window. Speed loosens the lines and shapes of the landscape until all appears a mass of streaks, interrupted by colored ticks of blurred houses and cars. The distortion makes him think of the painting in the newspaper picture—if he were to take the elements of a still life or, say, the interior of this train compartment, shake them free of outlines, lay them flat, and then pour syrup over them, the result would be similar.

He wonders if abstract painters think up such methods before glopping the paint, or if they occur in the heat of the creative moment. Are they so unsatisfied with reality that they need to bend faces beyond recognition, make landscapes of blotchy dots, or sculpt statues with square breasts? He'd seen that in Spain.

As the train swales toward the city, he drifts, his forehead lolling over the glass, cooling the flush that ebbs and rises as memories nudge his sleep. When he finally shakes himself upright, the train has nearly reached his stop.

It's eight blocks to the gym, where Ed scans his card and passes Hector without saying hello, absently taking his towel. Once in the locker room he shrugs out of his sport coat and polo shirt. The mirrored wall confronts him so that he quickly stands straighter and sucks in his stomach. He swims and lifts weights three times a week but cannot fight gravity—recently he's developed pectoral sags, man-boobs, what his daughter calls chesticles. He shouldn't complain—he's fit enough for his age. But back during those summers, Ed was ripped, didn't carry an extra ounce; there must be pictures somewhere of him at that old resort . . .

The saddle of flesh spanning his lower back has thickened. On his way out he'll ask Hector if there's a trainer with an open slot for next session. For now, he supposes, he could ramp up his routine to four days a week, forgo the carbs. The waistband of his Speedo digs.

This time of day he has the pool to himself. He spits on his goggle lenses before prying them on. Diving in, Ed's lungs seize for a second—he's never quite prepared for the cold, but easing in isn't an option. You either do a thing or you don't. The water's every bit as frigid as that damn lake . . . what was its name? Something sharp sounding.

Hatchet? Yes, Hatchet Lake. Ed seldom swam there, never was one for lakes, always loath to speculate what was beneath the surface. He's reminded of what the grown-up girl has called her exhibit, wondering what she means by *All That's Underneath*. He plows forward in a breaststroke.

During those family vacations he usually left the water sports to Gina and the twins. She'd had her hands full in those years yet would insist, "It's your time, after all," hauling Eric and Paul out of the cabin so he could sleep late. Gina would feed the boys at the picnic tables then hike around with them to look for cocoons or to poke at spiderwebs or nests. They brought things back to the cabin for him to wake up to—bugs in jars, fish eggs, slick frogs, and once even some sort of hairy turd Gina mistook for an owl pellet. The rest of the time they crawled over slopes of stone and dug for hours on the tiny beach that was no more than a sickle of coarse sand.

He'd occasionally scoop up the boys for a round of ball toss-ing or a tussle, but being twins they were such a world unto themselves—better observed than interrupted. Since swimming and fishing didn't appeal to Ed, he mostly occupied himself with paperbacks in a lounge chair. When bored with the formulaic plots, he'd do chin-ups on the monkey bars—dozens—and as many push-ups on the dock. He repeatedly jogged the half-mile of road that looped to the many cabin driveways, a route Gina called his habitrail.

Evenings picked up when he'd have a few beers before his one daily duty of grilling whatever meat they were to have for dinner. After the boys were down, he'd have a few real drinks while Gina had a soda to mark the end of her day, and maybe he'd have another after she went to bed. By the end of the two weeks, just when Ed would begin to relax, he'd have to start gird-ing himself for the twelve-hour drive home.

There was a bar in the lodge, nothing fancy, a wide porch with a scuffed notice painted on the threshold—a black line with one side lettered Over Twenty-One and on the other, a red, em-phatic No! Obviously, an exception was made for the Machutova girl, who tended customers between the hours of 5 and 7 p.m. There was no service during the day, just a cooler full of beer that operated on the honor system with a slotted can for folded dollars. A plastic holy water font was nailed under the opener to catch bottle caps. Either the proprietor was sacrilegious or thought himself witty—Ed could only guess, since the old Czech never said more than six words at a run and feigned poor English when approached with demands or complaints. His name was Vaclav, Ed clearly recalls, but the girl . . . she hadn't been called Margaret then. Some derivative, but not Maggie.

The bar was quiet, a place to catch up on week-old newspapers and months-old magazines. The girl made her rounds, wiping down the few tables and emptying the plaid beanbag ashtrays after each use, which unnerved the smokers. She arranged matchbooks in fans and clipped the bags of chips and pretzels to the rack by color. Schmidt's Beer coasters were stacked in careful spirals. When she wasn't at these tasks, she sat on a phone book on a stool behind the bar, scrawling into a sketchbook shielded with her curled right arm. Meg, that's right. Like her grandfather, she wasn't much of a talker, responding mostly with nods whenever Ed requested a bag of peanuts or tonic for his gin. Once he commented, "So, you're a lefty, huh?" Without looking up, Meg slowly lifted her fist and sighed, "Cor-*rect*."

Displayed above the bar was a noteworthy collection of taxidermy—besides the usual jackalope rabbit with antlers was a trio of baby raccoons clutching musical instruments, a wolverine with a naked Barbie in its jaws, and a bass yawning through a set of human false teeth. An electric Hamm's Beer sign informed Ed he was in The Land of Sky Blue Waters, while a continuous waterfall fed a pool where a bear was poised to grab a fish. Ed must have been watching for a while one day because the girl actually spoke without prompting,

"He never gets one."

There was only one other girl at the resort, an older girl. *The* girl. Lilith was seventeen, a fact Ed only determined well after he should have. Lilith looked at least twenty-three and possessed the jaded nonchalance of a triple divorcée. She wore denim cutoffs so short that the fringe didn't cover the ramps of flesh Ed imagined would so perfectly fill his two hands. And while her breasts weren't large they were perfect, presented in crocheted halters and skimpy undershirts purloined from her brothers. At the beach, Lilith loosened the strings of her bikini so that when she was propped on her elbows, her plush breasts rested over the nap of the towel or the glossy pages of *Vogue*. A sudden turn or a slap at a mosquito afforded the rare sight of pink, the full deal, if Ed was patient.

The flawless length of Lilith seemed always slick with coconut oil, yet anyone would have to wonder, as Ed did, just how it got so evenly applied between her shoulder blades.

While out on one of his afternoon jogs, he nearly tripped over her. He rounded a corner and there she was, propped against a tree with her feet budging out into the path. A sweating bottle of Bubble Up was clenched between her thighs. She looked up and giggled.

Ed jogged backward a few steps, out of breath. "Ha-hello."

"Ha-hello back." She was absently twisting the ends of her blonde hair while watching his bare chest rise and fall. "You're in Cabin 11, right, with the little boys?"

"Uh huh."

"We're in 1, 2, and 3. I'm Lilith."

"I know."

"Is that your wife's real hair color?"

Ed chuckled. "Ah, no . . ."

"My mother said your wife might think about shaving. My aunts think you must be Italians."

"Do you always go around telling strangers everything you hear?"

"I'm rude."

"Yes, you are."

She cocked her head. "How old are you?"

"Thirty-three." Even as he spoke, Ed couldn't fathom why he had answered at all, let alone lied. He added, "And you can tell your aunts my wife *is* Italian."

"My mother's almost forty. We're all some sort of Scandinavian. I'm nineteen."

"*Are* you."

"Mmhm. I go back to college after I escape here. In Boston."

"Lilith. That's a dark name for such a fair girl."

"You mean blonde? I know. I hate my name. Call me Thilli."

"I should," he said.

"No, seriously, if you change around the letters of Lilith, I'm
Thilli. That's what I want to be called this year."

"You just might."

"Now you're making fun of me." Lilith somehow extracted
an airplane-size bottle of vodka from her cutoffs and poured half
into the soda bottle.

Ed leaned against a birch. "You're too young to drink."

"You think so?" When she offered up the bottle, her tube top
slipped to reveal a tan line over a bosom that looked to be of legal age. He watched as the hand he no longer seemed in control
of reach out to accept the vodka. After he gave the empty bottle
back, Ed folded his hands over the front of his running shorts.
Later he would recall her voice, realizing it was one of several
attributes that made her seem so much older—a Lauren Bacall
rasp, complete with attitude.

There were eleven days left of Ed's vacation.

After swimming, Ed works out with free weights, careful of the
rotator cuff he's ruined playing squash. In the locker room afterward, he sees a fellow he knows. The advertising firm Ed had
managed is only blocks away, and many of his former colleagues
are members of the gym. Sometimes Ed will briefly chat with
those who trickle in after five to begin their workouts as he's finishing his. They never fail to ask how it's going, meaning retirement. They feign envy and rib him about his idle time but do not
ask how he's filling it—perhaps like him, they cannot imagine
fifty hours of freedom each and every week. Ed still braces him-

self each Sunday night after *60 Minutes,* though no longer at the thought of looming deadlines.

He slips out through the door past the second row of lockers.

Ed and Lilith took great care to avoid any of the places other guests might turn up, assuming guests were who they should watch out for. Ed chose to believe Lilith's lie about her age—she was no virgin, that much was certain.

Never used to having him around much anyway, Gina and the boys cheerfully waved Ed off as he embarked on his long, frequent runs—as many as three a day. His family had their own set routine, happily clomping off to look for bones or wolf crap, or hanging around with other kids and other mothers whose husbands fished all day.

The three most secluded cabins sat well apart from the rest of the resort, clustered on a steep hill. This was where Lilith and her extended family spent each July. Her mother and two aunts had been coming to Naledi for so long they had a standing reservation. The women did not mingle with the other guests, preferring to play bridge at their own picnic table or sun themselves on their own hump of granite. They were friendly in a mannered way, always seemed privy to some inside joke, and were a bit bitchy, Ed thought, as well-to-do women often are. When he lurked on the piney slope waiting for Lilith, he sometimes heard them arguing politics or volleying scraps of French back at the static-filled radio broadcasts from Ontario.

Lilith had about ten cousins and brothers, all boys and so close in age they might've been mistaken for a scout troop. Lilith said her mother and aunts had become simultaneously pregnant several times, as if in some sort of synchronized leg spreading. The boys were a tanned gaggle who fished long hours and seemed to get on well. At the fire ring they made productions of roasting their morning catches in tin foil, or charring their hotdogs or marshmallows. Ed rarely saw them without some kind of food in hand—always sucking Tootsie Pops, their pockets blooming with licorice whips or Slim Jims. He'd thought the shared, sloe-eyed squint was genetic until he considered the constant snacking and the faint aroma of something familiar and realized they were often stoned. Luckily for Ed, the boys all pointedly ignored Lilith.

By necessity their couplings took place outdoors. The first time was against the very tree where Thilli (as he'd begun to call her during moments of inarticulation) had lain in wait for him, knowing the routes he ran. There were several sheltered spots, old mining blast sites that were rocky bowls ringed by trees, so far off the paths no one would wander near. They made almost no noise and were alert to the tiniest snap of twigs—soon enough both could discern a ruffled grouse from a partridge, or a running deer from a running boy. Their comings and goings were tributes to stealth. Ed, ever the adman, always with a slogan, tag-lined their sessions "furtive forest fornications," which Thilli laughed at a beat too long, as if she didn't quite understand.

In spite of Ed's aloofness during their brief meetings, Thilli soon imagined herself to be in love. She imagined out loud what their lives might be like if Ed left his wife and children and moved to Boston. He responded that she had quite an imagination. To her credit, she did not act predictably and threaten to tell. She claimed that with a family like hers, she was used to keeping secrets.

Sitting in a shaded Adirondack, Ed thumbed a copy of *Rabbit Redux,* occasionally distracted by thoughts of his own next romp with Thilli. By chapter 2, he began squirming under the theme of infidelity and decided to find a different book. He'd seen a ragged paperback of *The Carpetbaggers* somewhere, but besides the old Czech fellow, there was only one other person able to locate any given item around the resort.

Ed ambled to the bar and fed the dollar slot for a Pabst. The underage bartender walked in a minute later with a bucket of fish heads and heaved it to the rear counter. Meg spread newspaper over the bar, sat, and commenced paring out the fisheyes from their skulls with a grapefruit spoon, plopping them into a coffee carafe of water.

When she wasn't drawing or tending bar, Meg made novelty jewelry—post earrings and necklaces set with milky orbs—displaying them atop the candy case with a sign that claimed "Fisheye pearls!" Ed had assumed they were plastic, that the claim was merely a marketing ploy.

He leaned in, fastened to the procedure as Meg explained. "You boil the eyes and the pearls come out. Vac taught me how. You want something besides beer?"

"Yeah, ah . . ." It took a moment to remember his mission. "I'm looking for a book . . ." the title eluded him, ". . . by Harold Robbins."

She sighed. "Hang on." After wiping goo on her shorts, she scooted through the swinging doors and thumped unseen stairs.

Ed watched fisheyes simmer on the Bunn burner until she came back with the paperback and a handful of petite drill bits. She pulled a Dremel case from under the bar.

He thanked her for the book and began idly skimming pages, nursing his beer and sneaking the odd glance to check her progress. Once the eyes were boiled and cooled she held the pearls between dainty pliers and drilled a hole in each. Now and then one would split and she would exhale a Czech word, *proklate,* brushing the shards aside.

She shrugged at Ed. "I'm not allowed to say *shit.*"

Ed and Thilli had stumbled onto a perfect trysting place, an abandoned test mine with a wheelhouse almost a mile from the resort. Inside, the mouth of the fallow shaft was blocked with boulders. It was one of the few places Ed and Thilli felt safe enough to get almost naked or make any sort of noise at all. During their seventh meeting (she kept track) and their third trip to the old mine, they were finally caught.

He was on his back on a pallet with his shorts pooled around his running shoes. Thilli was astride him, chewing gum and swaying the blonde broom of her hair over his chest, pinching his nipples between coral nails. "Harder . . . ," he was urging, "*harder.*"

When a female voice echoed from the shadows, all of Ed went rigid and he reached up to slap a palm over Thilli's mouth. The words were repeated—in a rather glib tone, Ed thought, given the circumstances.

"Yooo'll get ca-aught."

Ed quickly scanned the darkened corners. Thilli's eyes followed his. The voice had come from the shaft, each word plumped by an echo.

"Who's there?"

Ed detected movement coming from a black shelf of space just inside the shaft. There, a set of thin legs hung from the shadows, a pair of Converse high-tops meeting and parting like windshield wipers.

Thilli had seen, too, and pried Ed's hand away from her mouth to hiss, "It's that little shit from the lodge. I'll kill her!" She abruptly uncoupled from Ed so that his penis slapped wetly and loudly against his stomach. There was a snort from the shadows. Thilli yanked her tank top down and began tripping into her cutoffs.

By the time she made it to the shelf, the dangling legs had disappeared. Thilli scrabbled up and jumped, trying to see into the shaft. She picked up the closest thing, a rusted cog the size of a frying pan, and heaved it up and over. Ed bolted from the pallet as the heavy cog scraped down around the shaft as if circling a very long drain, thudding when it hit bottom.

Outside, light footfalls padded away from the wheelhouse, Meg's laughter receding.

Ed spun Thilli hard. "Are you insane? If she'd been in the shaft, you might have killed her!"

She stuck out her tongue.

He stared at Thilli, half-dressed, panting, and looking just then young enough to spank. Ed hitched the waistband of his running shorts and looked over at the grubby pallet where they'd fucked. The absurdity of the situation struck him. *Who* was insane?

He found Meg in the bar, beading fisheyes onto monofilament. She looked up, poker-faced. "Peanuts?"

Ed sighed and shook his head. "Will you tell your grandfather?"

"Oh, he probably knows."

"Jesus."

She shrugged. "Well, maybe not. But he usually knows stuff. You haven't been very careful."

As if on cue, Vaclav Machutova walked in and nodded to Ed. He said something to his granddaughter in his language, and she slipped from her stool to go off on some errand. The old man picked up a rag and eased Meg's sketchbook aside so he could wipe the bar. The book lay open to a woodland scene done in pencil. Ed blinked at it sideways while the old man was occupied. The drawing of slim trees cleverly camouflaged sets of limbs twined amid the trunks and branches. Naked, birch-white arms and legs in unmistakable, biblical poses.

At least that's what Ed thought he saw. He picked up the closest newspaper and dropped his face into week-old baseball scores.

After leaving the gym, Ed stops at his bank to make a transaction that is more complex than seems necessary. Taking his multiple signed forms and packet, upon leaving he realizes that he'll be passing the pharmacy anyway, so he stops in to get his Lozol refilled.

A block past the pharmacy is a piano bar he'd frequented during his agency years. He checks his watch and calculates the time needed for his next two errands. Inside, he sets his athletic bag on the stool next to him as a buffer against anyone friendly. He flags the bartender. "Do you have Hamm's beer?"

"I'd say nobody has Hamm's anymore, sir." He steps aside so Ed can see the brand names on the draught pulls.

"Pilsner . . . that's Czech, right?"

"Yes, sir. Excellent choice."

Once Ed is served, he takes the newspaper article from his breast pocket and unfolds it to reread the last paragraph: "Having resigned her teaching position to relocate to a family property in a remote region of Minnesota, Machutova now paints full time. Her first show in five years, *All That's Underneath,* is a body of work begun in 2000." The article is brief, nothing of any personal nature is revealed. He wishes he'd thought to Google her before leaving home.

He did not have sex with Lilith again (he'd immediately stopped thinking of her as Thilli) and after the wheelhouse incident saw her only twice—once to tell her a lie, saying that the old man knew and had confronted Ed, threatening that if he didn't stay away from Lilith, her mother and aunts would be told, and both families would be banished from the resort.

She burst into tears and stomped up the steps to Cabin 1 as Ed watched, nearly unmoved by the perfect jiggle of her backside. Once out of sight, a door slammed, and then another, which Ed could guess led to Lilith's bedroom, where she would remain for the rest of her vacation, penning a tortured, multipaged letter to him.

Ed stayed close to his own cabin, managing to finish *The Carpetbaggers* and discovering his sons knew how to play both Chinese Checkers and Go Fish.

He approached the lodge only once, with the idea of finding Meg. He encountered her halfway up the path where she was pulling a red Radio Flyer loaded with cleaning supplies, a mop slung over her shoulder, on her way to clean a cabin abruptly vacated after the woman encountered a nest of baby voles.

He reached for his pocket. "I have something for you."

When Meg put the mop down, Ed held out two twenty-dollar bills. She frowned at him. "What's that for?"

"Just some extra spending money, like . . . like a tip."

She chewed her lip. "I don't really need it. I got money from my parents' insurance and from the airline—in some trust thing. Vac says I'll be able to go to any college I want, and that when I'm old enough to really be in the bar, I can buy everyone a hundred drinks." She leaned from foot to foot, looking longingly at the bills. "Forty dollars is a lot. Vac would ask about it."

"Okay." He began to slip the bills back into his pocket.

"But right now I don't get much allowance or anything."

He offered again, but she shook her head. "I have a better idea." Meg extracted one of the pencils that held her hair in an unruly twist. On a sanitary napkin disposal bag from the supply wagon, she wrote a few lines and handed it to Ed: "Windsor and Newton 36 tube oil set (in the tin case!)."

Underneath was the P.O. box of the resort and the zip code.

"A paint set?"

"Uh huh. Could you have it sent here right from the art store?"

"Won't your grandfather wonder?"

"Sometimes I win prizes from mail-in contests. Once, I got a little easel, so . . ." She toed a pinecone off the path, launching it into the brush with her high-top.

"Well, sure. If that's what you'd rather have." Ed folded the waxy bag and tucked it into his pocket. "Maybe you *will* become an artist one day."

Meg frowned. "Not maybe."

Lilith ambushed Ed for a tearful good-bye, handing him an envelope fat with the letter she'd wept and agonized over. He said he was sorry he didn't have any real gift for her, then suggested she might buy something nice for herself and handed her the two twenties that Meg had refused, plus three more to make an even hundred. He knew the money would go to her oldest cousin, whom she owed for a month's worth of marijuana and tiny bottles of vodka. Lilith took the money and sniffed, claiming she would swear off married men forever.

He gave her a quick, fatherly hug, careful to keep his groin clear, then turned and walked away.

From the picnic area, Ed could see the station wagon in the driveway. It was loaded to the point of scraping the hump, and Gina was half inside, corralling the boys into the backseat. With a quick look in opposite directions of Gina's rump and the path to Lilith's cabin, he stopped at a grill with a few red coals and roasted Lilith's unopened envelope, poking the pages with a stick until each was black.

And that was that.

Ed squints at the clipping, sliding it clear of the beer rings and the snack dish on the bar. He wishes there were more light— certainly there's more detail in the actual painting than any newspaper reproduction could show.

After his second pilsner, Ed checks his watch, stows the article, and tosses down bills to cover the tab. It's nearly dusk as he jogs the last few blocks, arriving out of breath to the store that's about to close. What he needs is easy enough to find, and he pays with cash so it won't show up on his Visa bill.

Walking along, he feels the bulge of bills against his thigh. He has no idea how much he will need for this next purchase. His final stop of the day is on an unfamiliar street. The reception is in full swing, the spare, white gallery space is full of types you'd expect—smug, with interesting clothes and tiny eyeglasses. He skirts the crowd, moving directly along the wall until he finds the painting from the article. It titles the entire exhibit, *All That's Underneath,* and is the largest of the twenty canvases. According to the catalog, it's also the most expensive.

Ed sees nothing but color at first, but with each blink and each step back, the canvas slowly reveals a shore that might be the one at Naledi: familiar, if only suggested. Shallow ripples reflect granite and what might be canopies of branches. Glimmers of possible windows wink. Shapes that might be boats float, and trees meet themselves at the shore, wavering and doubled in the mirror of water. There is a definite hour to the painting in the hues that suggests stillness of a day finishing—the entire canvas spattered with the melon light of evening. The picture in the paper hadn't done the painting justice.

Ed grows quite still, unaware of the people moving behind him.

Surely the place she has captured on the canvas isn't precisely as it is, or was. But it is the girl's interpretation, not his. Each eye, he supposes, has its own lens to the past. And while his own is a pinhole, he can see now how Meg might have seen it—a succession of laps and ripples hemming and expanding the borders of her summer days. And while it is impressionistic, it's also visceral; he can imagine that if he reached out to touch it, his fingers might come away dripping lake water.

He thinks he understands the shocking price of the painting (several times that of the others): it can only mean Meg Machutova does not want to sell it. She's at the far end of the gallery, deep in conversation with an older couple. Others mill about, waiting for their turn with her. She glances once at Ed without a glimmer of recognition, turning back to smile and nod at her patrons.

Ed locates a gallery attendant and voices his wish. The girl steers him to the director, a Joan-someone who brings him to an office. He hears only about half of the woman's chatter—she's excited about the growing reputation of the artist—and when Ed tells her which painting he'll be purchasing, she nearly claps.

"Ah, you are a connoisseur!"

When he begins counting bills from his roll, the woman takes off her glasses. "Cash?"

"I hope that's all right."

She nods, but her eyebrows knit as she watches him count out hundreds in neat stacks of ten, pushing each thousand forward until he finally nears the price and she begins filling out his receipt. She looks up, pen poised over the blank for Name.

"Ah." He hadn't thought past the actual purchase. How he would handle things afterwards. "Anonymous, please."

"Oh. I see." The eyebrows go again, the woman tapping her chin with the pen. "Well. The show hangs until May 10th. Will you be picking it up then?"

"No. I . . . can you ship it?" Ed doesn't know how these things work.

"Certainly. Where to?"

Ed takes the pen and writes the name of the place, the township, and all he can remember of the rural route. For good measure he adds the name of the lake. He turns the form facedown on the desk.

"Okaaay. I imagine you'd like to speak with the artist now, Mr. . . .?"

"Anonymous," Ed reminds her. "Thank you, but no." He unzips his gym bag and pulls out the thin, gift-wrapped package. As it meets the desk the package makes a *ting*.

"But please, after I've gone, can you see that she gets this?"

A T MIRIAM'S INSISTENCE, ESTELLE HAS SCHEDULED HER
flight so they can meet at the concourse and cab into the
city together. Given the nature of their mission, there
is the likelihood one of them might back out. More important,
neither should be alone as they approach the business at hand,
the crime.

Estelle is the first passenger up the ramp, calf-sueded and
cashmered as usual, with colorful dashes to complement the
dyed-fur trim of her coat. Up close, Miriam sees the fur is real
and sighs. It's not as if they haven't had this conversation. Estelle
is practically a spectacle next to Miriam in her woolen car coat,
tan slacks, and tan cardigan—an ensemble that could be tossed
into a dustbin should there be any need to dispose of evidence.
Similarly nondescript replacements are in her overnight bag.

The sisters bump cheeks, each quickly commenting that the
other is looking well. They turn down the vast concourse, and
for a dozen yards Estelle watches her sister in the periphery.
Miriam has faded some, Estelle thinks. Less like herself, more
like a widow.

Miriam can feel the deceptively soft gaze Estelle employs.
She turns and they make real eye contact. "You hardly look the
part, Estelle."

"What do you mean?"

"I mean you hardly look like a killer." It comes out much
louder than intended.

Estelle's gaze swivels to the family of travelers just abreast—
a couple with two beefy teens in varsity jackets with athletic

patches on their sleeves that look like Oreos. She squeaks, "Well, neither do you, Miriam."

As the family moves ahead, Estelle sees the patches are embroidered hockey pucks, and though they pass quickly out of earshot of the family, she attempts small talk, pointing out the many shops and kiosks along the concourse. "Airports were never like this back when Roger and I were traveling. They're like malls now, aren't they?"

To Miriam, the airport seems identical to the one in Boston—the same Starbucks and Cinnabons situated on the same corners so that she must concentrate to place herself in Minneapolis. As they walk, she fidgets with the bangles that had set off the metal detector at Logan and wrecked her nerves for the morning. She hesitantly tells Estelle about her run-in with security.

"Do you think getting rid of them might be more prudent than risking more trouble on my return flight?"

Estelle picks up her sister's wrist then drops it. "I'd toss them."

Miriam sniffs. "You would."

"You asked."

The silver bangles are souvenirs from a trip to Mexico with Dennis, but Estelle wouldn't know that. Rearranging them, Miriam notices a new liver spot on her wrist and frowns—they are definitely multiplying in spite of the expensive cream she'd ordered from an infomercial. The guaranteed two-week trial period has already passed twice. Suddenly ashamed for her brief flight of vanity, she shoves her hands in her pockets, deciding to keep the bangles and throw away the cream.

Estelle trawls for conversation. "Is that coat new?"

"No." Miriam stops. "There's nothing about me that's new."

"Well, you look fine, Miriam. Very nice." The hairstyle could easily be fixed. "By the way, did you get my birthday present?"

"I did. Thank you *very* much."

"Did you get the joke? The amount, I mean . . . a hundred for every year?"

"Of course, I *got* it, Estelle. It's a lot of money."

Estelle shrugs. "Well, my kid sister only turns seventy once!"

"I'm seventy-*two*. Since you started fudging your own age, you can't keep anyone else's straight."

"Oh. Well. Remind me to send you a second check."

Kid sister. Miriam inhales as Estelle starts humming her self-conscious hum. With her young face and lollypop voice, Estelle makes an unlikely elder to her, and to Penny, their in-between sister and the reason they are in Minnesota. Miriam looks hard at Estelle—her skin is taut with procedures and peels, any worry lines buffed away. If her sister worries at all, Miriam thinks, it would be over the sorts of things other people only dream of worrying about.

They will visit Penny. If it's as bad as all that, if she's doing that poorly, they will say their good-byes. If things seemed stalled and Penny really needs their help, Estelle and Miriam will fulfill the pillow pact and kill their sister.

Miriam whispers, "Maybe."

"Pardon, Mir?"

"Nothing." Penny could live for weeks yet. Months. Her sons seem to think so, anyway.

They move on, scanning open storefronts, making full stops to look at cleverly displayed bags of wild rice, plush loons, and novelty snacks. Estelle examines such items as if they are necessities, choosing packages of Gummy Mosquitoes and Viking Bobbleheads for her grandsons, a flickering blue night-light shaped like a bug zapper, and a pair of trout-shaped oven mitts for her day woman, Francesca.

A shop in the far periphery catches Miriam's eye. "What time is it?"

Coming from opposite coasts, each is hours removed from the other's time zone. Estelle pulls back a fur cuff to reveal her jeweled Omega. "Only 10:15!"

Miriam is out of the novelty store and charging toward the other shop, which sells Sleep Number beds. She's never seen such a store in an airport—in the window a mattress is sliced in half to show its innards slowly expanding and contracting as if breathing. She watches for a few huffs before heading inside to a fully made bed roped off against children or anyone else naturally inclined to lie down when tired. Miriam steps around the barrier to perch on the duvet. A lamp glows pinkly on the nightstand next to a water glass and digital alarm clock—she could be in someone's bedroom.

Appearing with her packages, Estelle's shoulders slump. "Oh no. Miriam, really."

"What? I need a bed." She lifts the price tag and makes a tiny noise. "And I have all that birthday loot burning a hole in my pocket." As she lowers down onto the pillows, a groan escapes her. Not bad. Squeezing her lids to feign sleep, she can hear Estelle breathing, and soon enough pacing commences next to the bed. Miriam is just beginning to drift along to the rhythm of footfalls when they stop. She opens one eye to Estelle staring down, very near. With a twinge, Miriam realizes she is in the same position poor Penny will be in an hour or so—prone, trapped, and at the mercy of sisters—those who love but have no obligation to like.

"I'm so tired, Estelle. A two-hour drive to Boston and two flights." She pauses before adding, "Both in coach."

When Estelle sits, Miriam shifts over, believing her sister might kiss her forehead. But she only clucks, "You should have said something, Goose. I would've upgraded you."

Miriam rises to her elbows, suddenly fighting tears. "I really did not sleep a wink."

"Of course, you didn't. I only got six hours myself."

"I might not have the energy for this, you know."

"But Miriam, you *said* . . ."

Miriam knew what she'd said. That she possessed the required detachment to do the Kevorkian thing, if it came to that.

She'd actually had some practice over the autumn, albeit on a dozen easy victims. When the eaves of her house were invaded by the very squirrels she once fed, Miriam lured them with peanut butter into Have-a-Heart traps purchased at a discount with her PETA membership card. In the beginning, she drove them to the next county and released them. But when the carpenter

took her on a crawl of the attic and handed her the repair esti-
mate, Miriam quit ferrying and filled a wheelbarrow with water.
After lowering the traps in, she'd look away for the time it took,
singing to drown out the bubbles of distress—usually something
upbeat, like Sinatra or Bobby Darin. "Longer than always is a
long, long time."

Yes, Miriam could kill—squirrels, anyway.

"You do remember, don't you? That night we promised?"
Estelle is staring at her.

"The actual pact? No."

Miriam sees a sales clerk circling, working up momentum to
either chase them off or begin his spiel. She sits up and quickly
reaches for her purse. Pulling out a pocketbook as the man nears,
she presses a forefinger into the mattress, declaring, "I'll take it."

She hands over her credit card, but when he begins to open
his mouth, Miriam shakes her head as if regretting he won't be
allowed to speak. He slowly backs away to get his forms and run
her MasterCard through his machine.

Blow-up mattress—$1,979.00. She considers the look on
Estelle's face.

"Priceless."

"What?"

"Never mind."

"Miriam, stop doing that."

"Doing what?"

"Mumbling things and then refusing to repeat them. It's
rude."

"Sorry. Where were we? Do I remember the pact? Frankly,
I don't. I remember being at Naledi and all the strange weather
that year . . . but one particular conversation?"

Estelle sighs. "Selective memory?"

"No need to snipe. I'm not backing out."

"But you must remember something."

"That it was just after Mama passed."

"And precisely why we agreed to spare our own children the
same sort of awful death watch."

One evening thirty years before, between one highball and the next, back when they could put them away, Penny draped herself in a rocker on the porch that smelled of ozone and mice and came up with the pillow pact. Miriam tries to recall Penny's words, tries to conjure her voice, but memories form stubbornly silent as old super-eight movies. She can *see* Penny as she was—tan and boyish in her Capri pants, one espadrille swinging loose from a toe as smoke from her Virginia Slims gave shape to her stories and dead-on imitations. Had Penny spoken the words of the pillow pact in her own voice? A born mimic, she seldom used her own.

Penny loved to do the cranky Czech who ran the resort, and guests that arrived each Saturday provided her with fresh material for the week. That year there'd been a high-strung minister in Number 4 who Penny imitated in stuttering, irreverent sermons. And the couple from Georgia whose fisticuffs always ended in noisy lovemaking, the husband bawling, "Who's your Big Bear, Sugar? Who's Sugar's Big Bear?" The dog-crazy opera singer from Ontario whom Penny did not try to emulate, preferring to wag her bottom like one of the soprano's Dachshunds, yipping and howling the score of *Die Fledermaus*.

"Miriam, are you even listening?"

"Uh huh."

What words and phrases Penny spoke that Miriam cannot recall, Estelle is unable to forget. Conversely, Estelle struggles to remember Penny's face, but not one feature will surface: she cannot envision the mouth that formed those eradicable words.

Estelle begins again, nearly word for word, her voice enough like Penny's to be haunting: "What if one of us was struck by lightning or stunned into a vegetable? What if one of us catches something fatal?"

Miriam envisions Penny's curls bouncing as she did her Harpo act. The minute something physical needed doing around the cabins Penny would perform, growing mute to teeter atop tables to change flypaper, or leap to tennis-racket bats, or puff air into swimming mattresses. Penny's cheeks always went apricot in the sun, and she never wore a dab of makeup at Naledi. They called her Pretty Penny. To her many nephews she was Aunt Pretty and is called so still, when she is decidedly not. Miriam's vivid screen of memory blurs as Estelle insists, "You remember her saying, 'I'd do the same for you. If two of us do it together, like a firing squad—if two are pressing the pillow or feeding the pills . . . neither can really be responsible. That's not murder.' "

In the echo of Penny's words, they turn to see the clerk frozen in midstep like a mime. Miriam motions him forward impatiently and takes the papers. She fills in an address form, signs the delivery order, and folds away her receipt.

Once outside the shop, they roam to the moving walkways, glad to be carried along rather than rely on their legs. They falter some when approaching the ends, stepping off and on with trepidation, neither quite able to take the other's elbow.

"It's discombobulating."

Miriam frowns. "Is that really a word?"

"I think so." Estelle squints. "I'd been searching for a word for us . . . for today. There are names for such things you know—*infanticide* or *matricide*. But what about a sister? Is there such a word as *siblicide*?"

When Miriam doesn't answer, Estelle looks up to discover they are gliding alongside a great span of windows, revealing her first glimpse of snow in years. It looks like plastic flakes swirling in a souvenir globe.

At the taxi queue, a digital sign loops the time and weather. As they mine their bags for scarves and gloves, Estelle shakes her head. "Five degrees! It's too cold for jewelry." She pulls gold clips from her ears, wincing. "I'd be dying, too, if I had to live here."

Miriam secures her collar. "Is that your idea of humor?"

After they give the driver directions, Miriam closes the Plexiglas slide. They are well out of sight of the airport before she rallies the courage to open the overnight bag on her lap, tipping it carefully to expose the white, zippered bag within. To her horror, Estelle plucks it out and opens it. Three syringes roll onto her palm along with one of the vials.

The liquid is a deep amber—the color of Penny's stained fingertips. "Oh, my. This is how? I thought they would be pills. You mean we have to . . . ?"

"Inject Penny? Not directly, just her IV." Miriam gently takes the vial and syringes. "You've no idea how hard it was to get all this. I had to drive to Quebec."

"No. I didn't know. Goodness. I guess I thought there'd just be some plug to unplug if it comes to that. Some machine to switch off."

"For God's sake, Estelle."

Estelle begins absently tracing circles on the glass. "Oh, Mir . . . I wish we could go back."

"Back?" Miriam considers her sister's far-off expression. "Oh. You mean summer."

They both mean Naledi, where their parents first took them during the war, and where they returned every July, eventually with their own children in tow. They sometimes wondered what made them return—the resort made no claims in its brochure other than being clean, which it was, freakishly. It was miles from the nearest town, Hatchet Inlet, and the lake itself was so far north the swimming raft often drifted to Canada. It was also remote enough their husbands were not inclined to visit.

The summer of the pillow pact, the sisters had eleven children between them, all boys but one, ranging in age from ten to twenty. Estelle's Max was the eldest, on break after his first year at Berkeley and supposedly keeping an eye on the younger teens. But by then the boys didn't pose many dangers to themselves—all could dog-paddle and make their own sandwiches, and two had Red Cross certificates. Miriam's daughter Lilith had a driver's license and could be more or less trusted with a grocery list. During these vacations, the sisters read fat paperbacks, boned up on their French by listening to the Ontario stations, and played bridge. They made occasional forays through cabin kitchens to put away mayonnaise or sweep sand and tossed coins to see who would venture to the lodge basement to launder beach towels in the shuddering aqua Maytags. For a full month they were happily idle.

Sometime during cocktail hour—when supper either burnt or didn't, depending on whose night it was—one of them would aim the binoculars toward the dock or the beach for a headcount of Lilith and the boys. One thing about Naledi, there wasn't much trouble to get into.

They learned differently only a few years ago, when Lilith, after her second stint of rehab at Birchwood for dependence on codeine and Zinfandel, embarked on her twelve-step program with zeal, skewing Step 4 to include others in her fearless moral inventory. She ratted out old digressions on behalf of cousins and brothers—revealing that all the boys had smoked copious amounts of pot and even hashish at Naledi. Max, in fact, had supplied his minor cousins with dime bags bought from a state employee who nurtured his crops among pine saplings in a DNR greenhouse. Such revelations were a bit of a shock to the sisters, but it *had* been decades ago, and boys being boys . . . They were a good bunch overall, and all had earned the requisite diplomas, married wives who produced mostly tolerable grandchildren, and settled in acceptable neighborhoods of decent cities.

The marijuana would have been water under the bridge, except for Max. Max, as expected, had progressed from golden boyhood to golden adulthood—dean's list at his law school, headhunted into a prestigious firm, and partnered by his thirty-fifth birthday. A few years later, Max's temples prematurely silvered as if on cue, and he nabbed a state senate seat, where one of his first votes was against legalizing medicinal use of cannabis, inciting Lilith to tattle. Like any politician, Max adroitly deflected any culpability. Since stones were being thrown, he said, he had plenty on Lilith regarding those summers. He also suggested that Aunt Pretty was likely more angry over his running on the GOP ticket than over a little weed.

Penny became incensed. Max, foolish and spoiled and smart enough to know better, had been *dealing,* selling to his underage cousins and others at Naledi—the Saturday maids, the dock boy who pumped gas, and God knows who else . . .

Estelle wouldn't admit outright her son was a hypocrite, and

Penny wouldn't let it go. After Penny threatened to leak information to the press, the two stopped speaking.

Initially, Miriam was a neutral go-between, passing along
pertinent news and family gossip between Estelle and Penny.
But when Penny took ill, Miriam nearly scripted her phone call—
smugly informing Estelle that one of the medications Penny most
needed—the one that might help her keep food down during
chemo, was difficult to procure and a crime to use, thanks in part
to Max.

"And you know she has glaucoma, too, on top of everything
else? Have you any idea how *that* might be treated?"

"I've done my research, Miriam."

Both lean back, hands resting on the bags in their laps.
Estelle sees Miriam no longer wears her wedding ring. Since
Denny's passing, her sister seems to have become more austere.
She wonders if Miriam isn't a bit relieved though, as widows so
often are. Her hands make small static movements. Of the three,
Miriam is the bustler, nothing if not practical, especially now,
when it's easier to do than to think. Her nails are trimmed and
clean and bare of polish. There's a tension in Miriam's hands that
matches the held-in quality of her face—the skin over her knuckles has mottled with age spots, a sight that bothers Estelle more
than it should. She makes a mental note that once back home she
will send a jar of cream from that spa in Marin.

Why is traffic moving so slowly? Estelle cannot recall a longer
cab ride. Her own fingers, weighted with platinum, idly paw the
eel skin of her shoulder bag.

Miriam watches the slow movements of Estelle's hands. She's
always found diamonds gauche herself but realizes now just how
well they suit cool, elegant Stella. It's been a long time since she'd
been called that—ages since the boys stood on the mossy steps
leading up to the cabins and shouted "Stelllaaahh!" in their best
Marlon Brando voices. Estelle had pretended to hate that.

Stella, Miriam shakes her head. None of it—nothing she owns,
none of the ease or luxury she's so accustomed to could have
made those last months with Little Roger any easier. And Big

Roger walking out so soon after, leaving Estelle to go it alone, just she and Max and that pile of blue-chip stocks—a period Penny crassly referred to as Estelle's abject prosperity. Miriam sighs. No wonder, really, that Max was so spoiled.

At the hospital curb they split the cab fare to the nickel, tuck pocketbooks away, and gather their things. The pavement is icy, and they balance while watching the taillights recede into the snow until the car is too far to call back. Estelle minces several yards to the salted safe zone and turns. "Come *on,* Mir."

Remembering an unsavory phrase that Lilith utters when faced with something difficult, Miriam looks to the hospital entrance and straightens. Indeed, she thinks, just cunt-up and do it.

The doors are centered by a statue of a martyred saint run through with spears. When Penny was told she had cancer, she chose St. Sebastian's for its proximity to her sons and for the irony—Sebastian being the patron saint of dying people, diseased cattle, and enemies of religion.

"Perfect for an atheist, really," Penny had joked to Miriam over the phone while making a doodle of an arrow. "Just shoot me."

Once through the revolving doors and in the lobby, Estelle inhales hugely, as if she cannot get enough hospital air. She breezes through to the gift shop where she buys a large bouquet of lilies and, inexplicably, two Mylar balloons on sticks that say Happy Today. She hands one over. "Here. One from each of us."

Miriam holds her balloon low, nearly stumbling on it as she trails Estelle and all her swinging parcels into the elevator. As the door seals them in, Miriam tsks at the mirrors on every surface. There is nowhere to look and not see a crowd of themselves. "Why? In a *hospital,* of all places . . ."

Miriam maintains there are two kinds of people—the kind who will paint over a piece of tape rather than bother peeling it up, and those who do things properly, thoughtfully. She makes such distinctions so regularly that her sons roll their eyes before she can finish, no matter the topic. Kyle, her youngest and most patient, has observed that one's defining traits tend to exacerbate with age—the nitpicker picks more nits, the self-absorbed become ultra-absorbent, and the mean become nasty.

She resents the suggestion. It's not that she's judgmental; it's simply that there's no reason not to take proper care with things, including oneself. The Surgeon General warned Penny on every pack, but did she listen? It's difficult for Miriam not to be angry when she's supposed to help ease the way. And Estelle hasn't begun to comprehend the seriousness of Penny's illness, certainly not the finality of the pact. She's brought fudge!

The elevator bell tings, and for an instant gravity lifts the weight from their heels and a fleeting lightness rises through both sisters. Each looks quickly to the many reflections to see if the other has felt it, but just as suddenly they are set down again onto their bones and the doors chug open to slide their many images away.

The hall is a tunnel of pistachio tile. At a station at the far end they find a nurse chewing a pencil, engrossed in the daily Sudoku. When Estelle says Penny's name, the nurse straightens. She turns her monitor so they can't see and taps her mouse. "Right. Dr. Bell's patient . . . Lancaster, P."

"Lancaster, *Penelope,*" Estelle says firmly.

"Yes." The nurse comes out of the station. "You can follow me."

With an offer to find a vase, she takes the lilies from Estelle and leads them down another hall, remarking how the Minnesota weather can make traveling such a trial, as if knowing they've come from the airport.

They are taken to a small, overheated waiting room. After shedding their coats and shaking their scarves, they pile their things in a corner. They circle a small table before sitting to wait. Who knows for how long? The nurse hadn't even offered coffee. Estelle watches the closed door a moment before dragging her shoulder bag close.

She waits for Miriam's attention to make its way back to her before pulling a package from her shoulder bag. It's an old gift bag from a trip to London, embossed Marlbey's Teas, Ltd. Inside is a pillow-shaped package wrapped in tissue.

Miriam frowns. "Tea?"

Estelle lowers her voice. "Well, not quite." She peels layers of tissue to reveal a large Ziploc bag packed tight with smaller bags filled with a dried, dull green herb.

"That's isn't . . . Estelle, that's not . . . ?" Miriam stifles a yelp and her eyes dart to the door.

"I should hope it is, considering what it cost."

"You carried that on the plane?" The package weighs at least a pound.

Estelle shrugged. "I could have FedExed it, I suppose. But since Penny needs it now, and since I didn't have any trouble flying from Negril with it . . ."

"Negril? Jamaica?"

"Well, goodness, I wouldn't know where to get such a thing in Palm Springs. I thought of Mexico, certainly closer, but Lord knows what sorts of things go on down there. I just decided to visit the Robertsons—you've met Kitty and Earl. They have a winter place there, and their driver, Eddie, is such a nice young man, has those deadlocks, though . . ."

"*Dread*locks, you mean?"

"As I said. How they keep those clean. Anyway, Eddie took me to a special plantation where a woman gave me some lovely tea, very relaxing, and sold me this." She rewraps and stows the package.

Miriam sucks her teeth. "Well."

Estelle leans back. "Well."

They look around, scanning the tank of lazy angelfish, the stack of *Highlights* magazines, and the crocheted wall hanging shaped like a crucifix, just the sort of thing Penny would make fun of. Once they've taken everything in, there's nothing to do but wait. One of the Happy Today balloons ticks against the wall just above a heat vent.

It seems an eternity yet can be no more than a few minutes before the door opens. The nurse wordlessly ushers in a white-coated woman and quickly backs out.

They stand.

"I'm Dr. Bell."

They shake hands and peer at the tiny letters on the doctor's name tag until she offers, "Melissa Bell, Oncology."

She's pretty, like Penny.

Once they sit, the doctor wastes no time. She gives each of them a pinched smile and says in a voice of practiced succor, "Your sister took her own life this morning."

The air in the small room shifts and collects to thicken just over the table.

Dr. Bell takes three empty prescription bottles from her lab coat and places them on the table. Two envelopes with their names written in Penny's hand are eased from a folder and slid forward. "I'm so very sorry."

Neither sister moves or speaks. The doctor presses a palm over each of their hands. "As you know, it was only a matter of time . . ." After a full minute she rises. "I'll be right outside, if you have any questions. Your nephews are waiting in the room, in case you'd like to view . . ."

They both shake their heads and Dr. Bell nods, edging away, taking the prescription bottles. "Of course. I understand. I'll have the floor nurse tell them where to find you."

The door bumps shut. Miriam and Estelle do not look up, do not acknowledge the envelopes or each other. For the second time during the long morning, the sisters' gazes settle on hands—this time their own, focusing where the doctor's hands had pressed and warmed theirs, imprinting them with the news.

Estelle blinks and stares at the facets of a large ruby, Roger Junior's birthstone. She spreads her hand flat. *Well, that's that. Aunt Pretty's coming to join you, RoJoe.* She hadn't thought before, but now she's suddenly glad that Penny and Little Roger will be together—that her boy will no longer be alone. That Penny won't be. Just then the thing Estelle has struggled for all morning comes to her with more clarity and vividness than seems possible—Penny's face, her girl-face, bolting into focus. A scene fills in around her. They are all on the porch of Cabin 2, she and Miriam are cross-legged on the floor and Penny is on her knees, laughing and pressing a raw hot dog through the mesh of the screen door. On the other side, Dandy, the resort's old chocolate lab, frantically laps and scrapes his teeth against the metal. Sunlight cast from his tail flickers across Penny's nose and chin. That face. That sight, Penny's face, her voice—even smells cut through decades to rush at Estelle, bringing scents of rain, of mice and hot dogs, the rays of sun hatching over Penny's brown arms.

Estelle's eyes close like shutters to seal the moment. *How could I have forgotten that?*

Across the table, Miriam is examining her thumbnails. On her husband's last night, she'd fallen asleep in the uncomfortable chair next to his bed. When his breathing had stopped, she'd started awake to the lights of the monitor flashing once for each second of silence. Miriam cannot know what became of Dennis at that moment—probably nothing—likely nothing, if she thinks about it in any rational way. And now, she cannot know what will become of her sister Penny besides ash. She doesn't share Estelle's faith yet cannot quite embrace Penny's lack of it.

Will their sister just dissolve away to silence? Even as she's wondering, Miriam's thoughts are cut short by a shriek of familiar laughter—a shriek that pricks the cotton wool that has muffled any recall of Penny's voice all day. Miriam hears Penny perfectly now, as if the volume from the past has suddenly swelled, as if her sister is right next to her, snorting and hysterical.

She can hear Dandy, too, the gross squelching noise—the rasps of tongue, muzzle, and teeth. She can see and hear it all—all of the sounds of that summer afternoon, breeze through the screens, quick little waves smacking the beach.

Squatting in front of the two of them, Penny can barely catch enough breath for one small word: her exhalations are hooted out.

"See?" Penny says. The pitch of her voice is high and nasal with allergies.

She pivots toward Miriam and Estelle, her sneakers making rubbery squeals on the painted-blue floorboards. The hot dog is gone, the wax wrapper crinkled under Penny's heel. Her palm is still on the screen, but she's only teasing Dandy now, enjoying the tickle of each desperate lash of his tongue. She looks squarely at her sisters as if demanding an answer.

"See?" She insists.

Penny is eight years old, nothing important has happened to her—her big teeth aren't even in yet. Her legs are folded reeds with scabbed kneecaps and her eyes are fierce with this one moment. A bit of hot dog is caught in her bangs and tears of laughter lacquer her freckles.

This is not a memory. Estelle and Miriam both see her clearly, hear her perfectly. Penny is laughing the pure kind of laughter that can make her wet her pants. She is helpless with it.

It's infectious. They can hardly help themselves. Jeweled and mottled hands reach forward to blindly link as the small, smooth pair slips away.

From one grasp.

Then another.

V ESHKO SCREWS HIS EAR CLOSER TO THE TELEVISION as the excited talk show guest erupts in phrases that are obviously offensive and perhaps obscene. Veshko looks from Tyrone to Jerry Springer, wondering when the host might take matters in hand, but Jerry only stands mute in the aisle with arms crossed, cradling his microphone the way some men cradle bottles. Jimmy, the brother of Tyrone, shrugs at the camera, basking in the attention as the crowd hisses and shouts. There is some trouble having to do with a fat woman seated between the brothers, but Veshko can find neither *bonin'* nor *ho* in the *Webster's* pried open on his knee.

While watching television is only slowly improving Veshko's English, an abstract sense of his new country is clipping into focus.

Much livelier than those on *Ellen,* certainly more so than those on *Oprah,* many of Jerry's guests are distraught, angry, and often related. They argue using words Veshko cannot look up fast enough; full sentences slip past his ear as if greased. Now they are trying to hit each other, these two brothers who have dressed in matching shirts for the occasion, but bald men in jackets emblazoned SECURITY press them back to their chairs. Tyrone and Jimmy glare at each other over the head of the woman, whose name is Anita. Anita is the hue of a Sacher torte, with great painted lips and metallic moons of eye shadow that shimmer like her outfit. Nowhere in his new home of Hatchet Inlet, Minnesota, has Veshko seen women wear such abbreviated clothing. Anita's cleavage forms a holster of flesh deep enough to conceal a weapon. Ethnic Americans sometimes carry guns, Veshko knows, although the characters he has met on *The Cosby Show* would never. Or should he say would *not*?

There are no black-colored people in this small Minnesota resort community, which makes Veshko suspect they must live in places like Chicago, where many talk shows are taped—a place he visited during his long layover at the airport of O'Hare, where he saw many different sorts of people, many colors. Still, America seems less like the melting pot he'd imagined it would be and more like his own country, where people settle near and stick to their own. In America, immigrants even have their own villages tucked inside cities, such as the Chinese. This he has seen on cable reruns of *The Streets of San Francisco,* the program about two detectives, one handsome and young, and the other grandfatherly, with a nose resembling a penis. Veshko is amused by this program's portrayal of uncorrupt police.

His finger lands on what he is looking for, *skank,* which, amid the many bleeps, is one of the many words Tyrone repeatedly shouts at the woman. Veshko reads the entry and sighs, "Of course. A whore—a *kurva.*" He puts the book down and rises from the sofa, crossing through the dining room into the kitchen, where his footsteps land on linoleum squares in sync with the chant "Jer-ry, Jer-ry." Yellow-green, yellow-green. He opens the fridge and lifts a can of Budweiser from the door, a beverage that somehow shares an identity with the real Czech Budweiser. The beer is as pale and subtle as the people of his new home. He heaps cold meatballs and potato dumplings onto a plate, leftovers from his dinner at the Tuomala's. Since coming to Hatchet Inlet, Veshko has had dinner each Sunday with a different family, alternating between parishioners of the two churches that sponsor him. St. Heikki's tiny congregation did not have the resources to get their own refugee, so they teamed with St. Birgitta's to pay Veshko's airfare and provide him a home. One Sunday Veshko has dinner with a family of Finns; the following week he is fed by Swedes. Oddly, the parishioners of both churches are so similar looking he can barely tell them apart. They seem to make no distinctions themselves and greet each other mildly, as if any history between them is forgotten, though they are only a few generations removed from brutality. Veshko has observed that in America, the past can be just water under some bridge, as they say. Hatchet Inlet's citizens mingle peacefully and have many bumper-sticker sentiments in common—many are pro-life *and* pro-war. They share other similarities as well, all housewives, for example, seem to have an aversion to spice yet embrace salt. He reaches for the paprika just as the microwave beeps.

After his meal, Veshko returns to the couch, but *Jerry Springer* is over. He switches channels to a program about a small-town sheriff in a place called Mayberry where a woman named Aunt Bea is acting out matronly hysterics in black and white.

Veshko fiddles with the rabbit ears, but no color emerges. Assuming there must be some problem with the satellite dish, he climbs to the second floor, then takes the rickety steps to the attic where he forces open a dormer window.

The dish is anchored next to the chimney. He climbs out, clinging to the window sash, and immediately experiences a wave of vertigo that tugs from his diaphragm to scrotum. He attempts to get better footing, and once secure he hunkers down, breathes, and looks out over the town. Spread before him is a broad view of the north. He can count seventy-seven houses, five bars, and three churches. There are two canoe outfitters, a bait shop, the IGA supermarket, three motels, the food co-op, post office, and a windowless library that looks like a power station. A new Pump-n-Munch sits directly across from the Holiday station on the piney road that leads south to the interstate that leads to the rest of America. Just as the freeway sign promises, much of what a person needs in life can be found in Hatchet Inlet: Gas Food Lodging. But if Veshko wanted to buy a parakeet, or see an ophthalmologist, he would have to travel fifty-seven miles to the first large town. He looks down to the T of the clothesline pole where the red bicycle leans, his only form of transportation.

Many roofs in Hatchet Inlet have satellite dishes. Many yards have dogs, but the owners are either inside or gone, so that the animals pace yards fenced with metal mesh or lay in hard hollows of dirt. The house next door has no dog, no dish, and a closed air, though Veshko knows his neighbor Pete is home because the back end of his Suburban sticks out from the garage not deep enough to house it. Pete works long days, and when he's not out tending sled dogs, inseminating cows, or stitching them up after a wolf tears into them, he sits in what he calls his rumpus room, reading Larry McMurtry novels and drinking Dewar's from a coffee mug that says "#1 Dad." Pete is divorced and dislikes two things; one is his job. When Veshko politely asks how was his day, Pete sometimes makes a certain lewd gesture, wriggling his fingers and saying, "Up to my elbows in cow, buddy, up to my *elbows.*" Often he repeats himself for Veshko's benefit. After a particularly harsh day he might say, "Mud, shit, and blood, pal, *that* is how was my day. Mud, shit, and blood."

If Veshko peers past the trailer park and its slope of spangled poplars, he can see over the expanse of the lake and the horizon of water, where, if he had binoculars, he might glimpse the province of Ontario. Balancing on his heels, Veshko feels the house shift minutely under him. Canadian breeze scours his ears. While taking in the highlights of Hatchet Inlet he has nearly forgotten his mission—to check the satellite dish. The wires are connected and nothing appears to be broken, so he eases back through the window, shivering.

Downstairs he watches the screen as black and white switches abruptly to color the moment *The Andy Griffith Show* breaks for a commercial. "I understand," he says, understanding. After the commercial, a new episode begins. Now, not only is Aunt Bea afflicted with some brand of anguish, so too is Floyd the barber.

Ready to begin his practice, Veshko kneels near the coffee table, shrugs deeply, and shakes his arms like a swimmer before a competition. He rhythmically shakes his wrists and quickly rubs and squeezes each finger before setting his hands on the inert torso lying on the coffee table. He presses his palms to the sternum and begins. He would prefer a living body, of course, but Jessica will have to do. It is no good for a masseur to let his hands forget their trade. Soon after Veshko moved into the tall yellow house, he and his good neighbor Pete made Jessica together. As they sewed and stuffed her, Pete pointed to the crotch and jokingly growled, "*Es ist verboten!*" and they discovered they had some language in common. While Pete's German is an old dialect learned from his grandmother, it is adequate. Veshko is shamed by his own poor English in spite of Pete's encouragement. Besides German and his own language, Veshko can speak Italian and Polish, a few Serb and Croat dialects, and some pretty morsels of French.

Pete knows some Finnish from his father and teaches Veshko words that are hills of vowels interrupted by brusque consonants. He learns a few unsavory phrases, mostly regarding sexual intercourse with one's mother or sister. Their German conversations are less crass and become nearly fluent as empty Bud cans accumulate on the carpet of Mrs. Kubich.

Mrs. Kubich had abruptly passed into the afterworld the week before Veshko came to Hatchet Inlet. Stroked out, he was told, but since both church committees had planned he would live with her, the family offered the use of the house until they could settle the estate and sell. On the day of Veshko's arrival, the old woman's belongings were much as they had been when she was removed by the ambulance—a load of delicates in the dryer and a saucepan in the sink. Veshko gently moved support hose, cardigans, and lavender sachets from enough drawers to put away his own things, then shut the doors of several rooms and settled in to live under the watchful stares of Mrs. Kubich's people. They gaze from gilt frames hung high on walls or set on bookshelves that hold no books—dozens of sepia eyes watch over as he practices his massage, eats, and sleeps. They are Slavic faces with wide cheekbones and high foreheads. He doesn't much mind them, even feels an odd kinship, sometimes acknowledging them in no particular language at all.

Veshko has not placed any of his own family photographs out for display, assuming they would only elicit curiosity from his few well-meaning visitors.

He works over Jessica, kneading outward from imaginary ribs, his concentration breaking only when commercials blare and blast color into the dim room. The dummy, which Pete has named, is fashioned from a leotard and several pairs of tights filled with flaxseed. She has comically large breasts formed by bags of millet, with the knots centered to suggest nipples. As Pete sutured Jessica's torso, Veshko confessed that Jessica Simpson was not known in his home country. Pete only shrugged and told Veshko his own wife, The Ex, had small breasts. The Ex lives in Duluth with his two children and her new husband, Needle Dick.

On the screen, Floyd the barber is now in full flummox. It turns out he has lost a sum of money Aunt Bea had entrusted him with. Aunt Bea won the money playing bingo and is wracked with guilt over her sin of gambling, so has vowed to give her winnings to charity before anyone can find out. But Floyd is weak and confesses to the men of Mayberry, who rally to help him. Floyd slumps dejectedly near an open cell in the sheriff's office. The police in this program do not close the cell doors; instead they play checkers with their prisoners and serve them homemade meals with cloth napkins.

The big-eared sheriff says to the troubled barber, "Now, think, Floyd, *think*. Where's the money?"

Veshko repeats, "Sink, flood, sink. Ver iz za mawney?"

"I uh, uh . . ." Floyd hangs his head. "Oh, d-d-darn it, Andy!"

The other actors speak in slow drawls he mimics while massaging Jessica's calves and legs. She has no hands or feet, and Veshko has considered filling pairs of Mrs. Kubich's gloves and socks with flax to make her whole. Seeds in Jessica's midsection make a faint *scritch* when he presses with his fists.

Aunt Bea's money is found, and there are sly smiles all around, including a rodent-like grin from Aunt Bea herself, who had known all along that her money had been misplaced. When the program is over, Veshko changes the station and flips Jessica facedown for her second hour.

Her spine is a length of plastic chain stitched into the back of the leotard—his hands move upward from imaginary coccyx to imaginary shoulder blades and to the wobbly neck and occipital ridge.

Nova has a special on dingoes.

At midnight Veshko turns off the lights and goes to his bed, where the sheets smell of bleach and dust.

Pastor Dan, the Swedish minister, was the first and so far the only person in Hatchet Inlet to attempt engaging Veshko in any sort of political conversation. At the counter of Pavola's Diner, Veshko was deep in his textbook, conjugating verbs, and Pastor Dan was reading his newspaper. The pastor rattled his page, poked it with a finger, and asked Veshko, "In your opinion, Veshko, where do you think Šlobodan Milošević should be buried?"

Opinion. Almost certain he understood the meaning of the word, Veshko rose from his stool and closed his English book, slowly annunciating each syllable of his response: "I have not an opinion in this matter." He smiled and left a tip for the young woman who'd brought his eggs and so much bad coffee. Once outside, he glanced back through the window to see Pastor Dan adding several more coins to the pile of tip money.

In the afternoon, he finds a package in his doorway. It's a video from Mrs. Jorge, the town librarian. There is a note, easy to translate: "I haven't seen this myself, but thought you might like it!" The video is *Welcome to Sarajevo*. The incongruity of the title puzzles him. A travelogue? From before the siege, surely? He will watch it once he's figured out what's wrong with the VCR. Pete comes after work with a twelve-pack and examines the machine, which turns out to be not broken. He demonstrates to Veshko how he need only switch the input cables, explaining that Mrs. Kubich must have let her grandchildren play Nintendo on the television. Pete begins to describe Nintendo, but Veshko excitedly interjects, "I know this Nintendo! My nephews back home has it . . . *had* it." Veshko repeats, "I know this video game."

He forgets *Welcome to Sarajevo* and goes to rummage through cupboards and closets, searching for the Nintendo, as if a child might leave such a thing behind.

On Saturday Pete hooks a trailer to the Suburban, and they pull an aluminum boat far out of town to a closed-up, oddly named resort, Naledi, where, Pete explains, he once had a girl in another life. Veshko asks if he believes in—the word takes a minute—*reincarnation*?

He doesn't. Pete expertly backs his boat trailer down to a narrow beach between two docks. Next to the dock is an old building for boats only, a water garage built on cribs. Pete takes a key hung in the eaves to let himself in. He comes out lugging an outboard motor.

"This is not trespassing?"

Pete snorts. "Hardly."

With the motor sputtering blue, they zoom from the dock and travel halfway across the lake at full speed. Veshko closes his eyes against the sting and feels his hair parted by the wind, first one way then another. When the boat stops, it lowers itself slowly, like a big animal sitting. Veshko nearly asks Pete to do it again. After skirting the shore they turn into a narrow channel that leads to a marshy bay. Pete explains the water here will be choked with tall weeds by August, but for now the bass swim under the boat in the new growth, begging to be caught.

Pete teaches him to cast. At first Veshko holds the rod too tightly, certain he will fling it from the boat, but after a while he is able to relax, and the reel buzzes and the balsawood lure glides through the air. Veshko is a quick learner, and once he comprehends Pete's phrase "all in the wrist" and makes a few practice casts, he can throw his line and swat black flies at the same time. He catches two fish, one resisting so wildly he expects some giant by the time it's pulled to the boat, but it is only a slender pike. Such fight in only an average fish, he marvels, asking Pete, "This is an American fish?"

"I guess. You don't fish back home?"

"Sometimes in rivers. Not like this."

Pete catches many perch and three bass too small to bother with. They troll near the reeds for several hours, not saying much. Pete makes a few jokes about Veshko's fishing hat, borrowed from the closet of Mrs. Kubich but at least freed of its silk flowers.

"I wouldn't wear that on the street, pal . . . ," Pete advises. "That faggot down at the B&B might just ask you out dancing."

"Faggot?"

"You know." Pete flops his wrist. "Homo."

"Ah, yes."

Pete offers some history of the area, telling of the fur-toting Voyageurs, tough little bastards who were not always French; some were natives, some Russians, and even bohunks like Veshko. "They were called Pork Eaters, *mangeurs de lard,*" Pete adds, "so probably there weren't many Jew paddlers."

After a beat Veshklo still doesn't laugh, so Pete urges him to guess what the leading cause of death among the Voyageur bastards was. Since Pete has described them paddling rapids and portaging for miles, shouldering loads weighing more than themselves, Veshko guesses drowning and hernias.

"Nope. Constipation!" Veshko doesn't know the word, so Pete pantomimes, scooting his bottom over the edge of his seat to grunt and clutch his stomach before falling dead against the oar.

By early evening the beers are warm but taste better. Veshko discovers he can urinate off the bow while still fishing, simply by trapping the rod in his armpit.

"You got the hang of it now," Pete says to his back. "We call that double-poling."

Hoping for one last fish, they troll the entire way back to Naledi. Approaching the land so slowly like this makes it feel like a real voyage. Veshko leans and watches the branches of white pine move like dancers' arms above the roofs of the log cabins, sees how the late sun bounces from the water to spray the resort windows with gold reflections, making even the saddest little buildings glow.

In English Veshko says, "This is one beautiful country, my friend."

Pete glances to where Veshko is looking and shrugs. "I 'spose."

Veshko realizes the talk shows knowingly exploit people's dramas and anguish to sell commercial slots—commercials that have expanded his vocabulary to include many conditions: pattern baldness, erectile dysfunction, vaginal dryness, and a cornucopia of terms for alarming side effects. Still, he is drawn to the talk shows and has his favorite hosts. He knows instinctively not to trust the small-eyed propagandist Doctor Phil, and half of the women on *The View*. He likes Ellen very much, an open-faced, seemingly humble person Pete refers to as a carpet muncher. Pete has suggested Veshko should get out more, away from the idiot box. He invites him along to inseminations and sheep castrations.

He politely declines but takes the advice to heart. Veshko packs lunches and takes long bicycle rides. He follows the roads Pete had steered them over to reach Naledi. One day he makes it the entire way. Though the bicycle is sturdy enough, the going seems more difficult the closer he is to the resort. When he finally arrives, Veshko realizes the tires had leaked, one nearly to flatness.

Huffing, he shrugs out of his Spiderman backpack and soaked shirt. Down the hill from the lodge is a little beach where Veshko wades in to wash his face and underarms. Splashing in the shallows he looks up at the few old buildings. Perhaps in one of them is a bicycle pump. He takes the key from the eave and opens the boathouse, where there are only boats and oars and cans of gas and a cupboard full of fishing gear.

Other buildings also have keys in their eaves—one houses a rusty truck and snowplow and a number of tires leaning against a wall, but no pump to fill them. He eventually finds one in the shed nearest the road, hanging from the rafters next to an old blue Schwinn with no seat. After inflating his tires, Veshko borrows a rod from the boathouse. The two bass he catches from the dock are enough for a meal. He pierces his fish with long metal tent stakes and toasts them over a fire of smoking birch. After settling on the warm sand he closes his eyes, only for a moment it seems. But his sleep is so instant and deep that when he wakes the sun is in a different place and the tight scorch of sunburn stretches across his brow. Now he will have to hurry to get home before *The Price Is Right,* which Pete sometimes comes over to watch, having ruined his own television by pitching an ashtray at it.

Veshko carefully cleans and returns the few things he's used—the rod, a fillet knife, the pliers he'd used to unhook the fish, and the tackle jig. In the dark boathouse, he imagines a voice and freezes in midstep. It is only water muttering against the metal walls and the gunnels of the old boats, speaking in the same tone water does everywhere. He reluctantly backs out and locks the boathouse door. Next time he will bring worms.

Once home, he abandons Jessica to massage his own calves and spread butter across his face and pink shoulders. Veshko lowers his aching thighs to the couch cushions and is asleep before the anticlimax of *The Streets of San Francisco.* He doesn't hear Pete's tap on the door or his retreating footsteps.

By July, Veshko is stealing away to Naledi several times a week. He sometimes fishes from the dock but more often will liberate the wooden skiff from its slip in the boathouse and row nearly to the island—never landing, only skirting. Pete ribs him about the new definition in his arms and legs, asks if he's training for the Tour de France.

"Only getting exercise," he lies. By the end of August he knows the shoreline of Naledi well. A quarter-mile south is the Catholic summer convent, St. Gummarus. The bell that sounds for vespers is Veshko's cue to row back and pedal home, which places him on Mrs. Kubich's couch ten minutes before *The Price Is Right.*

A Saturday in September is set for the annual Swedish church supper. In the afternoon Veshko shaves and dresses with extra care. When Pete backs his Suburban into the driveway, Veshko is waiting with Jessica under one arm and his portable massage table under the other. Pete makes room in the back, moving ropes and harnesses and cylindrical metal coolers that hold bull semen. They strap the dummy upright into a seat and Pete places mirrored sunglasses on her flat, drawn-on face. Veshko climbs into the cab, still vaguely uneasy in the vehicle, which is the height of a military transport. On the way to the church, Pete sings along to Willie Nelson, thumping the steering wheel to the tune of *Don't Get Around Much Anymore.*

Heads turn when Veshko and Pete enter the church basement. Several young men hoot at the dummy, and there is a ripple of laughter when Veshko readjusts her blonde wig. They leave Jessica slumped on the stage and line up for the buffet. After pierogis and hot dish, Veshko nervously gulps his coffee black while people pour sugar and some sort of powder into their cups. He climbs to the makeshift stage and unfolds his massage table, and when he sees Pete nod, Veshko clears his throat and waits for Pastor Dan to join him. After the pastor introduces him, Veshko announces to the crowd that he would like to show the generous people of this good American village what his profession was back home. The demonstration is the idea of Pete and Mrs. Jorge. Only when Pete and the Jorge family begin clapping do others join in.

As Veshko arranges Jessica's limbs, it is quiet enough to hear plastic spoons scrape Styrofoam. He begins by rubbing the dummy's lumpy calves and explaining the large muscle groups, base anatomy, and the many health benefits of massage. This is a speech he has written out in English and practiced aloud while sitting in the borrowed boat. He rubs and kneads while he talks, looking up at the crowd often. There are sniggers from the back of the room where several teens are gathered, but under Pete's glare those quickly abate. Veshko explains that many male athletes have sports massage, such as the Vikings who play American football for this very state. Veshko eases Jessica from the table and faces the crowd, offering, "I can do this to you. Who would like?"

The parishioners grow still. Men at the long tables are faceless in the shadows cast by their billed caps. Since he can read nothing on these male faces, he looks hopefully to the women of Hatchet Inlet. As his eyes travel the crowd, girls giggle and women shake their heads or look suddenly to their hands. One old woman points at him and laughs out loud. Only after it is apparent no one will volunteer, Pete steps up and bows brusquely to the crowd. There is relieved laughter as Pete approaches the table, peeling off his jacket. His face is red, as if he's swallowed something large.

Back in his home city, Veshko's spa was adjacent to the national gymnasium and natatorium. There, he had directed seven masseurs, a hydrotherapist, a physical therapist, and a nurse specializing in sports injury. He thinks of these old colleagues while he identifies Pete's pressure points for the audience. The nurse, Magda, now teaches land-mine victims to balance on artificial legs and clasp spoons in their hooks. One masseur, Goran, lives in Sarasota with a distant relative.

Paper casings from straws shoot across the tables where younger people are seated. Women stand and begin to clear away paper dishes.

He does not know the fates of three of his coworkers, and the rest are dead. Stepan. Vanja. Zdenek. Carl. He is glad they will never know of this moment.

Pete coughs and turns his head away from the audience. "Hey, buddy. Not so hard." Veshko eases his thumb from under Pete's scapula. The crowd is the color of lake reeds, moving as stiffly, craning their necks in unison. Pete's name is wrapped in words of joking encouragement as Veshko finishes his upper back. When he kneads his way down either side of Pete's spine to his sacrum, guffaws ring. Veshko shakes his head and mutters so only Pete can hear him, "Fuck these people."

"Yeah . . . ," Pete whispers in agreement, ". . . fuck 'em."

He suddenly hates each face in the church basement. Hates

these people who have been so kind and giving to him. "Fuck *you* as well," Veshko says to Pete. He backs quickly away from the massage table to face the parish, takes a short bow, and smiles, saying in his own language, "You are not my people."

After fleeing Sarajevo, Veshko spent a year looking after his brother's children in the country, at the farm, the *majur* of his dead uncle. There his days were purposeful, taken up with finding fuel and growing enough food and keeping the cow safe from poachers. At night he attended his orphaned nephews, whose dreams were perforated with city memories—bursts of smoke and people scurrying under the weight of water jugs, trying to avoid snipers. To add to the boys' confusion, they had been told that those lying in the streets were asleep. Veshko had been more forthright. Often he woke to the cries from their beds, wet with urine and sweat. He would cradle their small skulls and massage their temples and necks, hoping to lull them to a sleep of better dreams. Veshko traded vegetables and well water for enough gasoline to run a small generator so that Gregor and Milan could have Nintendo. They could play a few hours each day, happily exiled into the screen. Just when it seemed they might all go back, that things had settled in the city, he was contacted by the family of Veshko's sister-in-law and her husband, the boys' other uncle. The nephews were taken from the farm with only a few days' notice so that these other relatives, *strangers,* might promptly adopt them.

He'd returned to the city alone, but there was little left for him. The family who'd taken his nephews had immigrated to Canada, but Veshko was unable to determine what town or even what province they had gone to. He applied for immigration himself. Now he is here, in the United States of America.

Just as he arrives at the tall yellow house, Pete is pulling into his driveway.

When Veshko opens the porch door, Pete calls out, his voice gruff, "Hey!" pointing to the dummy sitting upright in the backseat.

Veshko shakes his head. "You made her. You keep."

Inside, he places the six-pack of Bud within reach, opens a can, and crosses his ankles on the coffee table Jessica had occupied. He watches *Jerry Springer*. By the time the first commercial comes on he has gleaned the theme of the hour: mother-daughter team strippers. There is more breast-shaking and catcalling than he is comfortable with, and he's about to turn the television off when he spies the boxed videotape wedged next to the console. He slips *Welcome to Sarajevo* into the machine, thinking he will be viewing tourist sights and vistas of that city as it was. Instead, it is a drama about foreign journalists who come to report on the siege. There are a few British and an American, holed up in a damaged hotel lobby, arguing and drinking between missions out to gather stories of carnage. The drama unfolds into a moral dilemma about whether or not a journalist should rescue a young orphan from her current hell.

Laced through the film are bits of actual news footage, some he recognizes. One he does not shows a victim being helped from a bombed storefront—an elderly woman carried by two men whose arms form a chair under her bottom. She is in shock, looking down to where her foot sways loosely from bone and mangled flesh, the ankle destroyed. Veshko stops the tape, rewinds it, and watches the bloody dance of the woman's foot in slow motion. He looks at her face. He plays the scene over. The only light in the house glows blue from the screen. More news footage shows heads of state and politicians making speeches about The Problem. When the face of Milošević appears on the screen, Veshko launches forward so that his knees burn upon meeting the carpet. He ejects the videotape and reaches around the set. The cord is yanked with such force the heavy television moves several inches.

"Opinion," he says, breathing hard. *Opinion*. "Yes. I know this word."

There are no lights on in the hall, so he moves by feel along the paneling to the foyer. Climbing, he counts the stairs to the second floor, and then to the attic, taking one breath for each riser. There are forty-two, his own number of years.

Once in the attic, he pries at the window, stubborn and

swelled from a recent rain. He digs at the casement with his fingernails. Suddenly it is urgent he escape the stale air. He slams the videocassette at the glass until the pane shatters. He reaches through and tugs the sash from the outside until it gives.

He climbs to the crest of the roof in three strides and disengages the satellite dish by kicking it from its mooring. It spins along the slope and bounces at the gutter to sail to the grass below. After hitting the lawn, it rolls a few yards, connecting with the cyclone fence, where it dings to a halt. A light comes on in Pete's kitchen. A curtain lifts, then drops. The light goes off.

Vaguely aware of the blood running between his fingers, Veshko sits hard on the rough shingles. *Welcome to Sarajevo* is still in his hand, the cassette now cracked to expose its guts. He opens the plastic case like a book and shining brown tape loops to pool in his lap. He pulls out length after length of the tape, offering fistfuls to the wind. Tape billows and he watches it flicker, reflecting streaks of moonlight, fluttering farther lakeward, farther north with each gust.

North. He thinks of Naledi—of the quiet boathouse, where he will often sit in the rowboat that is neither red nor orange but somehow both, where light floats in on ripples and pricks through the corrugated tin skirting that is rusted like a hem of brown lace.

Closing his eyes he can imagine the slight motion of the boat and the lapping echo of water caressing the hull. There is a small door on the lake side that offers Veshko the view of the outdoors as if it were a room—a ceiling painted in blue daylight and clouds, the floor carpeted with water, like some Magritte painting.

The end of the videotape requires a firm tug. Freed from the reel, it sails up and away—he cannot tell how far in the darkness. Surely it will tangle on a tree branch or fall to some road, but Veshko chooses to imagine gravity defied, that the videotape might be carried high over Hatchet Inlet to ribbon over the bays and winking whitecaps to Naledi, perhaps even farther beyond the wild shore, where yet another country begins.

MODERATION

EVEN HALF-PARALYZED AND DOTTY, GRANGER'S FATHER still hounds him for the gossip and goings-on at Birchwood, rehab hot spot to the stars where Granger is a counselor. It's not just Oscar—everyone wants the scoop, the skinny, the dirt. Speculation flourishes, rumors swell and make print to blare from the racks at the checkout lines at Cub and Rainbow— *Lindsay Vomits on Costar! Two and a Half Men Minus One! Was Amy's O.D. Intentional?*

Granger knows that what happens at Birchwood every day is a far cry from what the tabloids report. Not that he could tell anyone what he witnesses, since he's contractually obliged not to, but the truth is that after a decade of strict adherence to the confidentiality clause, Granger is itching to spill and unsure why.

He's begun to feel less dedication during the hours he's paid to be there, and none when he's off the clock. Perhaps it's been too long since his own struggle. Granger was only twenty-five when he got clean, and after thirty years he's beginning to think longingly of the harrowing, lopsided days when he was using. Any successfully recovered addict—certainly any good counselor—understands how memory warps time and reality. Granger knows well enough that only the rosy, lying lens of the past can turn waking up in the woods wearing one shoe and your pockets full of salad into a fond memory. Take the shameless Birchwood alum who penned a novel of high fiction and peddled it as a junkie's memoir, pissing off scores of recovered addicts *and* Oprah.

He could surely tell his father a few juicy Birchwood tales, true tales. Since his stroke, Oscar has lost broad swaths of vocabulary, most of his memory, and all control of his bladder. What would he ever remember to repeat with words he doesn't own? And to whom? He's certainly made no friends since moving to The Falls (yes, really) where, despite his former Foghorn Leghorn command of oratory, he plays daft and dumb with the staff.

When Oscar does speak, he stutters, tongue-tied and angry about being tongue-tied, which only renders him angrier. Much of what he means to say simply sticks to his palate like peanut butter, placing Granger in a new position during conversations with his father, one of advantage. Now that Oscar is a captive audience, Granger could spew a lot more than celebrity trash. He could shout out all that he's kept to himself, but when he muses over where to start, all he can think is, "Katie, bar the door."

During one of their last truly coherent matches, before his stroke, Oscar claimed to have no regrets.

"Not a one."

Granger had stared. "You have got to be shitting me?"

Who, *who* gets all the way through with no regrets—owning up to nothing? Yet Oscar had even expounded, "I'd do it all exactly the same way."

Taking in Oscar's grin, Granger deflated. Back then, it was he who responded incoherently.

There is the occasional actor or rocker to endure at Birchwood, but every addict Granger counsels might as well be on stage for how dramatically their comedies and tragedies unfold. Every patient's chart is a playbill of shame and redemption, hope and despair. He still manages to pity some of them, just not as much as he's begun to pity himself for his grinding routine, the time wasted on those 70 percent who will statistically, invariably relapse.

After a full day of counseling, Granger drives the tedious hour upriver to the nursing home. He's late but has an excuse—has fetched another urgently needed item from Oscar's basement—

today it's the old army-issue binoculars Oscar's been pestering him for. Granger had spent a half-hour searching, then another half-hour hunting down the Armor All and rubbing mold and grunge from the leather case.

When he presents them, Oscar grunts at Granger, as if he's the demented one and says, "Skate oats. Why in hell would I w-want those?"

Granger pushes the empty wheelchair ahead, leading so that Oscar must shamble behind in his walker. He's not exactly the hare pacing a greyhound but goes fast enough that Oscar has to struggle to keep up. Granger's come to think of the skyway to the commons as his father's own Bridge of Sighs. He forges ahead to save a table near a window and gets a tray with cups of coffee and pastry from the courtesy counter.

Nurses' aides will feed Oscar to save time, but Granger will only cut up Oscar's food. He sets the plate of cubed pastry near his father's more reliable hand and plunks a straw in his cup. If he wants coffee badly enough, he'll bob for it.

Between bites of a lemon bar powdered with sugar that looks agreeably like cocaine, Granger takes some pleasure in repeating to Oscar some old news, in case he's forgotten that the fatuous radio hack he listens to has turned out to be a confessed drug addict, popping OxyContin like Tic Tacs, even while rabidly holding forth against drug-using scum and potheads.

At the mention of the name, Oscar looks alarmed, then confused. "Limb-who?"

"You know who."

"A patient in your b-barn?" Knowing the word is wrong, Oscar flails his lame arm, ". . . your clinic?"

"Yes." Granger smiles at his own whopper. "He is in my afternoon men's group."

"What's egg, *he* like?"

"What would that matter, since you don't know who he is?"

Oscar responds most lucidly when provoked. To raise his hackles is to rattle his memory and oil his tongue, so Granger does his best. He sticks to incendiary topics like Bush's bumblings, Oscar's fundamentalist leanings, and gun control. A successful visit nearly escalates to blows, with Oscar spitting and shouting in nearly full sentences by the time Granger departs. Other patients are often alarmed to see this father and son nose to nose, ready to go at it in the mezzanine or TV lounge, where no one but Oscar can hear Granger hiss, "Not such a tough guy now, huh? But then I'm not six years old anymore, am I?"

Anyone can see they are related—both are short, with blockish heads burred with gray crew cuts, both sturdy as wrestlers. Despite his stroke, Oscar is as strong as he is confused, making him one of the most dreaded patients in the south wing.

Oscar doesn't remember that today is his son's birthday. A few years ago this might have bothered Granger, but dates are not included in what sparse history is left for Oscar to scrabble through. Actually, Granger would rather not be reminded of his age, since statistically and genetically his father's state is a preview of his own. He hopes that when his own mind begins to snarl he'll have enough lucid moments that he might launch his car off the bluffs or cook up some nothing in his gas oven. He doesn't want to become someone he doesn't recognize, not again.

His first clean years were hard enough, and living under an assumed name in Winnipeg only complicated things. He'd learned to forge his new signature early on but was never comfortable with his new name, simply: Granger lacked the attitude and gunk in his throat to convincingly claim himself Tomas Milosz Machutova.

Letters his mother sent during those years implied that if Granger did return to the States, his father might just turn him in. Oscar believed Granger should pay for his betrayal, for more or less shitting on the American flag. He himself had served four years during The Big One and has the scars to prove it, nipped by a Nip to bleed his own blood to help preserve the democracy of the US of A, so that punks like Granger were free to yowl nonsense at peace rallies and light themselves on fire and date colored girls.

By the time Jimmy Carter granted amnesty, Granger was

still at loose ends. His mother had died while he was away, so there was no real reason to return. Fearing his addiction would be waiting over the border where he left it, he lingered in Canada another eight years, never once contacting his father.

Granger gets Oscar to his room and into his pajamas one leg at a time. As he makes to leave, Oscar mumbles, "Cork-dick."

"You're welcome," Granger says, closing the door.

In his Tuesday women's group, Granger includes an association game. He relies on such time fillers when he's not exactly on. Today's exercise is inspired by an old Chinese belief that personality types are based on an element. Participants are asked to choose one of the archaic elements—air, water, fire, or earth—and to choose it quickly, instinctively. The goal during group is that each person achieves a broader sense of self—even if the path to broadening is lined with New Age appropriations of age-old hooey.

Just by choosing an element, the women unconsciously reveal what they want and need, in responses that are achingly predictable to Granger. Ninety percent pick water, then talk about its soothing, cleansing quality. Those whose entire lives have been disasters often regress to their very beginnings, voicing their desires for submersion, baptism, or a dark, starless state of floating, obviously wishing themselves back in the womb. Then there are analogies of those choosing earth, and all its growth, tending its gardens, ad nauseam.

Today, though, one woman chooses fire, prompting Granger to sit up. Gail is new to group and, according to her chart, had been an ICU nurse in a pediatric burn unit until she was caught purloining morphine doses from patients. Gail is a CO, court-ordered, the sort who typically tests limits and tends to be uncooperative. Predictably, she is the last to verbalize, slumped in her chair and absorbed by the miracle of her thumbnail. She looks up reluctantly and sneers, "My element? That's obvious, isn't it? Fire."

"Why obvious? Say more, Gail."

"I might as well choose my fate now, before it chooses me. Anyway, I'm going straight to Satan's skillet to burn in hell."

Granger fights to control his face and inhales, "Well, if you truly believe in the devil, Gail, you probably also believe in a God, and to believe in God means to believe in forgiveness. Wouldn't you agree?"

"Christ. You're kidding, right? I stole pain meds from burned toddlers." The front rungs of Gail's chair lift off the ground and her shoulders meet the wall. For the first time during the hour, she looks around at the others, as if daring any to one-up her.

Granger jots "junkie pride" in his notes.

"How about you, Granger? What's your element?"

He looks up from his pad and chuckles. "My element . . . ?" To avoid such traps and questions Granger normally moves on, but Gail is the last in the game. She has the floor and has asked a direct question, and there are seven minutes left on the clock.

"My element? Well, if I had to choose . . . earth, I suppose."

Gail crosses her arms. "Why?"

"Because it's here beneath my feet, holding me up. Just under this institutional-grade carpet." It's meant to be a joke, but all he gets are a few weak smiles.

"Can you say more?"

"Gail."

"Hey, I'm just asking. Carpet's not much of an answer, is it?" Mimicking his tone she asks, "Please, say more about your element."

Granger meets Gail's eye. "Fine." As the room grows quiet, he says, "Earth, pavement, carpet. All are paths I follow every day. I'm held to earth by choice, by gravity. Over the earth I'm led here each morning to work with you. Then I follow another road to a nursing home, where my father spends his days terrorizing orderlies and pissing himself." Though Granger hears what he is saying, he keeps talking anyway. He weaves his fingers into a brim over his eyes, as if the lights have grown overbright. "Just once I'd like the road, the path, the carpet, to go *my* way. Back in time, maybe—sometimes, I'm tempted to go back to my using days . . ." He shakes his head. "In fact, I'd give anything for a line of coke right now." Before more words can escape he swallows and coughs. He's sweating, dripping.

When he looks up he sees twelve sets of eyes on him like a herd of deer. Even Gail looks concerned. Session is over. They all stand to link hands, but Granger steps quickly out of the circle as they start the Serenity Prayer, grabbing up his things before God can grant any. He's halfway down the hall by the time they're asking for the wisdom to know the difference.

He makes it to the staff room just as he thinks he will vomit. After locking himself in the toilet, he hangs his head and gags but nothing comes. He runs cold water and splashes his face, then stares at his reflection until someone knocks impatiently.

What happened in group cannot happen again.

Granger spends a jittery hour in his office juggling schedules and e-mailing colleagues, asking them to cover his sessions for the next three days. He goes to administration and requests four more days as emergency personal leave, using Oscar as his excuse. With the upcoming weekend added, Granger has nine days. Nine days away from Birchwood, and he knows where he should spend them.

His breath comes in hiccups of relief.

Though he is still a little unsteady, by the time he reaches the parking lot he feels high—a near rush—loaded with freedom.

Of course he knows all the symptoms of dry drunk.

Once at home, he packs as if for survival, cramming a rucksack with thermal clothes, boots, fishing pole, his Orvis wax hat. In the kitchen he fills a box with canned goods, pasta, and some vacuum-packed meals left over from an autumn camping trip. His cooler and tent are in the garage.

On the way out he plucks a list from the fridge—all items his father has insisted he find—slide projector, magnifying glass, Viewfinder, his Nikon. Binoculars is the only item checked off.

Just as he's about to crumple the list, he looks again and makes the connection—all are things to look through.

He rereads. What sorts of memories or visions does his father believe he might recapture through such lenses or a toy View-finder? Granger swears under his breath and lets the list float to the counter. He finds another box and begins to gather all the things Oscar has asked for. He'll have to stop at The Falls after all.

Once on the river road, he opens the sunroof and all the windows. He takes his time, pulling over whenever a few cars or trucks gather in the rearview. Even at this Sunday pace he gets to the nursing home in plenty of time for dinner. He buys a guest tray and sits with his father to eat coleslaw and turnips and some sort of baked meat. He retucks Oscar's napkin when it falls and talks about what he'd seen on his trip down—young eagles wheeling along the bluffs, a priest passing him on a sleek Italian motorcycle, and a dead deer stiff with rigor mortis that someone had propped up in the median facing traffic with a cardboard sign, "Eat me."

He describes these sights with such detail and unaccustomed animation that Oscar looks up from his tray and asks clearly, "You drunk?"

"Of course not."

His father scowls each time food falls from his fork. He stabs gray meat and points it toward Granger's wax hat and canvas vest, and asks, "Fish . . . ing?"

"Yup. I'm headed north."

"North? T-traitor fucker. Deserter."

"Not quite that far north. But c'mon, Dad, you can do better. Where's your repertoire? You're slipping—remember how you used to get Mom to cry with a single word?"

Oscar spits out a chunk of gristle, his lip tethered to the plate with a cord of saliva.

After their meal, Granger wheels Oscar to the lounge, where they watch a popular program about castaways on a Dr. Moreau–like island. The episode focuses on one character's heroin addiction. The ease with which the young man sails through his cold-turkey detox makes Granger laugh out loud. The boy sweats some, his stomach hurts, and little circles form under his eyes. Granger turns the volume down and edges closer to Oscar. "You think it's that easy, that's what it's like?"

"Dunno." Oscar shrugs crookedly. "You never tell anything about your pirates."

"Patients. You want stories?"

Fame itself often fuels the trajectories of celebrities that land in Granger's care at Birchwood. In rehab they are the brunt of curiosity for a short while, then their clothes get rumpled and they grow pasty and gain weight like everyone else, no personal trainers or stylists in sight. Soon enough they begin to blend in, so that by the end of their twenty-eight days they can walk the grounds all but unnoticed. In group they relay histories that are similar to everyone else's. Also similar are their patterns of use and decline, merely set in better locales with more expensive substances. Like everyone, they miss their real lives and come to rely on and despise the Birchwood routine of strict schedules and the platitudes that stitch the hours together. Regardless of how wealthy or adored they are, they have as many failed and bruised relationships as the rest of them. They suffer the same humiliations when no one shows up for them during family week. Often the only people still speaking to them are their managers, agents, or publicists. They relapse more often.

But Oscar wants stories, not reality. He wouldn't even recognize most of the recent celebrity addicts—not unless he reads *In Touch* or *Spin.* Granger thinks of a few whose foibles are noteworthy but decides to dredge up some more recognizable identities—to rename his addicts after the crooners and starlets of his father's day—people who couldn't possibly have been to Birchwood, mostly dead or old before the place even opened, though Oscar won't know that.

He starts big. "I only heard this secondhand, of course. But back in the day, Dean Martin came to dry out. Three times. Second time he knocked a janitor unconscious to get his car keys and drove himself to the first place that served alcohol. He didn't have any money on him, so he sang for drinks. Picture that, Dad, Dean Martin, singing for drinks at the bowling alley in Osceola." Feeling he should add some mundane detail to authenticate his lie, he adds, "Wearing pajamas."

His father's mouth hangs agape, but it often does. "Ossy-ola?"

"A town across the river, Dad. In Wisconsin." He has his attention, anyway.

Granger fabricates a scenario of a mafia moll who smuggled in tangerines injected with dope for Frank Sinatra.

Oscar's face reddens. "B-bullshit. Sinatra was never . . . there was never any hair. I mean *proof.*"

"I'm just telling you what I know." Granger's beginning to enjoy himself. For half an hour he details Grace Kelly's habit of Scotch and diet pills, Natalie Wood's detox from speed, and adds unsavory and unladylike details to Doris Day's smack addiction.

Oscar blinks faster, shifts.

Granger invents volatile and infantile behaviors and assigns them to men whose feet Oscar would've licked—Charlton Heston, Andy Williams, Patton. He doesn't bother including Joe McCarthy since everyone knew he was roaring.

Because Granger was always annoyed by Dick Van Dyke's aw-shucks, loose-limbed dorkiness, he gives him a nasty dual addiction to Heroin and aerosol.

As the windows grow dark, Granger works up to his finale. "Sit tight, Dad, there's one more . . ."

During this intermission, he fetches more coffee and some brownies. He opens a window so Oscar won't nod off in the cloying warmth.

Oscar juts his chin. "Liar. Lying liar." He squirms in the wheelchair.

"Now you're talking. Dad, you gotta pee?"

"Did."

"Perfect." To distract Oscar he holds the straw to Oscar's lips and feeds him bits of brownie, wary of his fingers so near his father's dentures. Granger ponders who he should cast—he needs a contemporary actor, a man of a certain age. As he wipes Oscar's lips, the perfect star pops into his head and he grins, the actor actually did have some history with drugs but had eventually overcome it, and now even has a son so mired in drugs he's a national joke. Not only that, there's even a resemblance, besides the hair and mutual lack of height. Not much older than Granger either. Delighted with his choice, he clears his throat and begins casually.

"Oh, yeah, and my friend Martin. Martin Sheen . . ."

"Sh-heen." Oscar sits straighter. "You p-pals or something?"

"Sort of."

"El . . ." He rubs him arm. "Elbow leaks."

"Just listen. I'll get you some aspirin if it's not better in twenty minutes."

Oscar grunts.

"This is a long one, Dad—a story Marty told me himself, in his own words, so I try to tell it word for word. You listening?"

"Igh."

Granger takes a deep breath, "Martin . . . Marty. Nice guy, by the way. Had a coke problem and a pretty good thing going with booze by the time he was twenty-one. Liked his junk, too, when he could get it. He was crewing on a freighter in those days . . . this was between acting jobs, right? Anyway, his ship pulled into Superior on a payday, and he had two months' wages in his pocket."

"You w-worked with him?"

"Sure did. So anyway, he cashed his check and picked up his mail and bought some shitty Dodge off a guy he met in a tavern. He had a car *and* a wad to blow so decided to quit the lake freighter and go on a road trip—a long one. He took his cash and split." Granger is pleased to see Oscar sitting straighter.

"Anyway," Granger continues, "you can guess Marty's road trip turns into a binge—a very long binge. He can't remember much, only that he traveled north. He pinballed from bar to bar, first in Duluth, where the last thing he remembers is being in a place called Matt's, where they were feeding a rabbit to a python named Dawn, the bar mascot."

"Martin *Sheen,* you say?" Oscar slit his better eye. "B-before he was puh-resident, right?"

For a moment Granger is confused. "Oh. Right. Quite a long time before he was president."

Oscar's fist comes down and brownie crumbs jump. "Gotta vote him out!"

"We will, Dad." Granger almost aches to tell his father they will likely soon have a black president, but he will save that delight for another day—he has this story to tell.

"Anyway, Marty couldn't remember much about his trip, but later he figured out a lot by the trash in his car—bar napkins and motel receipts and empties. At some point, he started north along the shore of Lake Superior, where he drank himself almost broke."

Granger gulped coffee. He was talking faster. "With the last of his cash, Marty stocked up at a liquor store and headed inland, thinking he'd camp out. He drove and drove, looking for a place, drinking along the way. Got about seventy miles until the roads went from paved to gravel. Halfway down one of those roads he realized he was as lost as he'd ever been.

"He was just about to stop and get some sleep when he passed a driveway leading to a resort. It was past season, but the place wasn't boarded up, so he drove in but couldn't see anybody, no cars, just empty cabins. Nobody at the lodge, either, but the chimney was smoking so he figured somebody must be around. Pretty soon he heard a chainsaw rev somewhere by the lake. So Marty went down to the shore to find a skinny old man cutting up a fallen tree, a big one. Behind him there was a pile of limbs already cut.

"When the old fella saw Marty, he nodded but went right on working so Marty had to duck flying chips. The old guy was wearing thick glasses with electrical tape holding them together. No jacket or gloves on, hands like roots."

Oscar sniffs, his nose running. "Rag."

"Sleeve," insists Granger. "So, anyway, Marty hollered, 'Where am I?' but the old man just nodded to the stump that was all chewed up and yelled back, 'Goddamn beavers eating dis place alive.'" Granger could do a decent accent.

"When he heard *eating* and *alive,* Marty remembered the poor rabbit at Matt's Bar—all the drunks crowding the cage, chanting for Dawn to swallow, fists on the bar. Swallow! Swal-low! The shape of the little rabbit still visible and moving just under the snake's skin. Marty could remember all that but realized he couldn't remember when it happened—whether it was a day, a week, or a month before. Anyway, he lost his stomach thinking about the scene. After he threw up, he slid down the nearest tree and passed out.

"He woke up sweating even though it was so cold he could see his breath. The old man was sitting on the woodpile with a splitting maul in his lap. The fallen tree was gone, all the wood split and stacked, so Marty guessed he'd been out awhile. The old man said, 'You were drunk before. But not drunk enough now, yes? When was the last time you ate food?'

"Marty's forehead hurt. He didn't know.

"The man said, 'I 'spose you got no money.'

"Marty went for his wallet just to make sure, but it was gone, probably had been gone awhile. 'Shit . . .'

"The old man said, 'No matter. There's work here, if you can work. You'll have a bed. Otherwise, I'll help you fix the flat tire on your car and you can go along.'

"'I have a flat?'

"'Yes.' He looked up to the sky. 'But you got little daylight, so maybe you'll stay this night.' He put down the maul and got to his feet and gave Marty a hard look. 'You won't steal from me.'

"'Steal?' Marty was offended. 'Jesus, man. Of course not.'

"The old man looked at him harder yet, like he knew Marty would dig up his grandmother's grave if it held a pint.

"He took Marty into the lodge and left him by the fireplace to warm up. Marty stood a long time, shaking and trying to focus on the stuffed fish and photos on the wall of the bar. The old man banged pots in the kitchen and eventually came out with two plates of scrambled eggs and something black. When Marty didn't sit right away, the old man reached under the bar and pulled out a bottle and nodded to the plate of food, saying, 'After you get that in you, I can pour some of this.'

"When he asked what the black stuff was he was told, 'Blood sausage.'

" 'You serious?' Marty's stomach rolled again, and he said, 'I dunno, old man . . .'

" 'Sit,' said the man. 'I have a name.' He poured a few fingers of liquor into a tumbler and held up his glass. 'I am Vaclav Machutova. Tomorrow, at breakfast maybe you can face real meat. I have moose, almost fresh.'

"You can probably guess that Martin stayed more than a night at the resort. He worked out a deal with Machutova for room and board. By the end of a week, he still knew very little about the old man—he rarely talked, never asked questions, just watched. Martin was left to do his odd jobs like pulling in the docks, draining pipes, shutting down cabins. He stacked wood every morning.

"Each morning the old man gave him a little glass of some sweet Czech liqueur at breakfast, then two beers at lunch, one before his sandwich and one after. Later, around three o'clock, when Machutova came around to check progress, he always had a flask of whiskey he never drank from himself. It always had the same amount every day, which Marty drained in two gulps. That was the routine. Around dinnertime, just when he was getting shaky again, Machutova gave him a glass of some high-octane stuff, and then a little more of the same just before going to bed. Marty was given barely enough booze to keep him from tearing the lodge apart looking for more.

"Besides, he'd already searched, but if there was any other alcohol it was either locked in the walk-in cooler or buried.

"During the second week he helped rebuild a run of stone stairs, which was a lot of work, and he wasn't feeling great, suspecting that the old man was watering his afternoon shot. His morning aperitifs were smaller.

"By Friday he was sure of it and was thinking about confronting the old man, but then Machutova beat him to it and admitted there was only the breakfast liquor left but none of the Czech booze, telling him, 'No more hard drink, only some few beers.'

"When Marty went to start his car, he found the flat tire was fixed, the trunk had been cleared of empties, and the gas tank had been drained. By the time he found Machutova at the woodlot, he was frantic.

" 'You siphoned the last of my gas?'

"The old man pointed to his log splitter. 'This needs petrol to run. And you need firewood for the stove in your room.'

"Marty was feeling panicky. 'Can I use your truck?'

" 'Transmission needs fixing. Town is twenty-six miles. I can make you a map, and you can walk or hitchhike. Once you get there you have no money.'

"Marty said, 'You're joking, right? You *are* going to pay me for the work I've done?'

" 'Compensate, yes, as I have done. Bed and board, as I said.'

" 'You're shitting me.'

"The old man smiled and said to me, 'I shit no one. But soon, you will be feeling sick? So get some sleep while you still can, or, walk to town to beg on the street for drink.' "

"Wait a minute . . . ," Oscar grumbles. "You said *me*. You m-mean *Martin*."

"Atta boy, Oscar, you *have* been listening." Granger pats his knee. "Sharp as a stick when you wanna be." Granger leans on the arm of the wheelchair. "Machutova was pretty right about getting sick. By Sunday night I was on the floor, sure I'd be dead by morning. I didn't know then it was going to get worse."

Oscar rocks forward, shifting in his chair. They are both aware of the smell but neither acknowledges it.

"The next part was . . . bad. I didn't have any sense of time passing. I sweated like a sieve, with cramps so bad I thought I was being stabbed. I had the runs, my heart galloped, and my hands felt like the skin had been torn off. Noise was something else—my ears were just holes—birds singing sounded like fingernails on a chalkboard, rain was like shots fired at a metal roof."

Granger paused long enough to flick something from Oscar's chin.

"One day, about in the middle of it, I just got up and walked into the woods, thinking it'd be easier to freeze to death, but it wasn't quite cold enough, so I even managed to fuck that up. By the time Machutova found me, I was hypothermic. He dragged me back somehow. That's when he took my clothes and locked the door to my room.

"It was a week before I could sit up straight. I was jaundiced and dehydrated. He made me drink water and tomato juice and eat oatmeal, a little more each day. The minute I could walk, he fired up the sauna and shut me into it with a couple gallons of drinking water, telling me it was good medicine. I must've still been a little out of it, 'cause I was sure he intended to steam me alive. I thought the door was locked, and that's how I broke my toes, trying to kick it out. Door didn't even have a lock—it just opened inward. I suppose the sauna was actually okay—after a few days I smelled normal, anyway, and could sleep some at night."

Oscar nudged Granger's knee, making a face. "H-hank-ie."

"Okay, Dad, but I'm not finished." Granger got up and found a napkin and tucked it into Oscar's fist, then closed the window Oscar had been leaning away from. It had grown cold.

"There was no real turning point I can put my finger on—I'd been drunk, and then for awhile I was in living hell, and then I wasn't drunk. But only for lack of booze. I didn't give a shit about staying sober. I just assumed I'd start drinking again once I was back in civilization—but maybe just now and then, like other people. I started working a little. Because of my toes he gave me easy chores at first. But by October I kinda got into it. Naledi wasn't a bad place to be. I even started feeling sorta good. I gained a little muscle from working around the resort. I started hiking up over the ridges—some divide, the Laurentian,

I think. Really pretty, you know? The very last part of autumn, when the woods were clear enough to walk in and the snow was just a skin. I didn't even know where I was on the map 'til later. Funny, it didn't seem important, and I never thought to ask."

Oscar was looking sleepy. Granger went on.

"But by November I *wanted* to stay. I went to Machutova's office behind the bar to ask if I could work through the winter, but he said no, it was time for me to go. I offered to fix the boathouse, build new cribs, but he just said, 'Not possible,' because his granddaughter was coming home for Thanksgiving from boarding school—he didn't really explain beyond that, just said it was time. 'Two days from now you go,' he said. 'It's arranged.' Just like that. I asked him where exactly he thought I was going, and he just pointed out the window across the bay.'

" 'That side, Canada. Where you were headed when you fell down here.'

" 'Man,' I said, 'if *I* didn't know where I was going, how could you?'

"He pulled an envelope from his desk drawer and said, 'By this.'

"It had my name on it. It was opened, and there was the letter, seal and all, looking like it had been read and folded a hundred times. It was all there: my numbers, where to report for induction, the date. I couldn't remember reading it before, but I must have. I mean, I knew, and I didn't know.

"Machutova told me, 'This is how you will go. We take small boat and fish until dusk. Then I take you to a launch at the border. My friend Carl meets you there, then we go our ways. Next morning I drop your things at the dock in a beer case—no backpack. Then Carl's wife drives you to Winnipeg.'

"He handed me another envelope. Inside were six Canadian fifties, a passport, and a fishing license. I looked at the passport, the picture of a guy older than me, and definitely taller, with a face that only looked a little like mine. I knew before I asked, 'Who is this? Who is Tomas?'

"Machutova shrugged, just shrugged. 'He was my son.'

"I didn't ask more, not that he would've answered. I found out everything later, looking up the name in old newspapers, finding out about the accident, reading the FAA reports.

"He took my stuff and packed it into one boat, then got a fishing boat all decked out with poles and tackle. We didn't talk much in the boat. We fished most of the day, all the way to some-place he called Lulu Island. It was freezing, but he said we had to keep fishing. There was extra border patrol in those days, so we just crossed and recrossed the line like we were fishermen who did it all the time.

"At dusk we docked on the Ontario side. Machutova seemed pretty anxious by then. He waved to this guy with a beard and told me to act normal. 'Bring him these,' he said and handed me the stringer of the pike we'd caught. Before I got out of the boat I went to shake hands with him, but he only put a thermos of cof-fee into my hand and said, '*Nashledanou.* Good-bye.'

"Once I was up on the dock I asked him, 'Why'd you do all this?'

"He shrugged and said, 'Once, someone helped me. Now I do.' Then he looked me in the eye and said, 'And one day *you* will.' And that was that."

Granger stares at the space between his knees, at the gray car-pet beneath. He takes a slow breath and looks idly at his father's slippers, crooked on the supports of the wheelchair. His gaze fol-lows Oscar's shiny ankle to his pants cuff, to his knee, then to the chrome armrest where his sore elbow leans. The old man's side moves in heavy, slow breaths, the breath of sleep. He sighs. "And that's my story, Dad." Now that he's told it, Granger knows it doesn't matter whether his father has heard or slept through the end, or even understood.

But when he looks up, he sees Oscar is awake, very awake, swallowing and struggling to make the dragged-down part of his face move. His father is nodding, making motions with his crabbed hand, and slowly working his mouth, almost as if he might say something to Granger.

EACH WORD MAKES A HUFF IN THE COLD AIR—WORDS Cassi and her great-grandma Bana set down playing Scrabble the night before. Inhaling *heft*, exhaling *cowl*, she swings her arms to stay warm. In, out, in. *Hasp, pucker, quiz*—each word brings Cassi another step into the bog, from hump to hump of squelchy moss.

Some words are less interesting in her mouth, like *jerk* or *pant*—the sounds they make only what they are, boring onomatopoeia. Of all three-letter words, she adores *fez*.

She hops the humps. Hop *keg* hop *mum* hop *sot*.

Hokum was laid down for a triple, but Cassi's not sure what it means, since Bana had only offered *twaddle* as a definition. She plans to consult the dictionary once she's back at the cabin. For now, she yells five-letter words at a trio of black spruce, *Comic pansy vomit!*

Anything goes as long as it's in the dictionary. Cassi had hooted when laying the *b* in front of Bana's *itch* to narrow the gap in their scores. Cassi's mother, Ara, grinding away at some countertop, only shook her head, but Gran Carina stopped stabbing forks into their drawer long enough to sigh one of her colossal sighs, saying, "Those two," which only made Cassi laugh louder and made Bana clack through her dentures, "And *those* two think fun is scouring the chrome off my taps."

Cassi blinks at the soggy ground ahead, wondering if she's very far off the path, and deciding, hopefully, not much, maybe. Tamarack needles stick to the wires basting her earbuds to the iPod in her hip pocket. She turns up the volume and squeals along to Joanna Newsom, "Svetlana sucks lemons a-cross fr-um meeeee."

She's a little thirsty herself.

High above, a hawk wheels as if attached to a maypole. *Hawk*—sounds more like something you'd cough up, Cassi decides, no name for anything so, so . . . *eloquently aloft.* Happy with that description Cassi blinks one eye, then the other, her lips moving soundlessly until a haiku forms and whispers itself out:

> Swooping for breakfast,
> Loop and pluck and swallow whole,
> Some unlucky vole.

Good or bad, normally she would stop to copy down such lines, to ease them from her head onto a page. Making poems orders her thoughts, and writing them down keeps them from piling up. But she's got no paper or pen. Her notebook, along with her hoodie, is in the backpack she believes she's circling toward, not realizing she's a quarter-mile from the path, that she's only aiming deeper into the bog. Bending, she reties the lace that keeps coming undone.

While not hungry or cold enough yet to panic or wish, Cassi merely imagines being back at Bana's warm cabin, watching from the vantage point of a ceiling tile, scanning rooms and halls as her family moves in and around them—some more slowly than others.

Why do some people seem old when they're not? Her mother isn't, only acts like it, crabby all weekend like her thong has ridden. And Gran Carina, who is not fat, wears pants with elastic anyway, and hums.

Bana, even with her face like bark, is ten times more fun—old as dirt, she says herself, tickled that she's lasted as long as she has. She was a beer-truck driver once and before that worked in a munitions plant as a mechanic. Bana can fix any kind of engine, built her own log splitter, brews nasty beer, and could care less about Cassi's grades or what Cassi says or eats or wears or doesn't. Bana's own appearance is unintentionally amazing: old dresses layered over long underwear, wrist warmers made out of old woolen tights, and a crocheted beret perched on the long braids crimped around her skull like pie crust—the perfect place to park pencil stubs and paperclips and fishing lures. Her cleated surplus boots ching with each step around the workshop. In winter these outfits are always topped with a ratty fur coat and doeskin choppers that hang from each sleeve by electrical wire so she doesn't lose them.

To the rest of the family Bana is Gran Ursa because Ursa is her name. But when Cassi was a baby, Ursa sped-fed her a jar of pureed bananas, which she immediately vomited back with precision. For the span of Cassi's toddlerhood, every sighting of Ursa incited her to scream, "Banaah!" and so she has been ever since.

In spite of their initial wariness, over the years Cassi and Bana have developed a somewhat smug bond that excludes the rest of the family—the sort of winking alliance strangers might share when sneaking out of the same bad play.

There's a tight corner in the workshop surrounded by shelves of motor oil and lithium grease and spray paint cans too rusty to read, where the two of them eat breakfast, smacking heads over the daily Jumble before settling into the *Times* crossword. Bana's chair is near the propane ring where the kettle boils, and she warms her knuckly hands, individual hairs of her fur cuffs sparking and filling the air with the smell of charred otter. Cassi's mother and Gran Carina are not allowed in the workshop because there's a chance they might start cleaning, and with all the power tools and blades it's too dangerous for the twins, so they have the place to themselves. Unmolested, as Bana says.

But this morning Gran Carina had intercepted Cassi on the path to the workshop and put the bucket in her hand, pointing down the road to the ATV trail, telling her to gather alder cones and baby cattails for one of her gluey craft projects. "Yes, *now,*" she had said, and "Don't take too long." That was hours ago.

Cassi thinks longingly of the sandwich in her backpack—rye

and cheese and the hard salami Bana had slipped in, warning Cassi to not tell Ara, who is vegan. Her mother loves to lecture Bana about her diet, warning that her heart is probably a time bomb because of the sodium, as if she might go off at the table. But Bana is stubbornly never sick in spite of living on ice cream and cured meats, usually undercooking things when she does rouse herself to light the stove. Her casual attitudes regarding refrigeration are alarming, but she is not ashamed of being a rotten cook in the way Gran Carina thinks she should be. No one suggests she start baking, but Ara has hinted that Bana might be a better great-grandmother if she maybe stopped acting like a weird uncle.

Hints. Always hints—no one ever dares say anything directly. It's true Bana doesn't make lemonade or like small children, but she will always drag Cassi along to chase the volunteer fire truck or ambulance to see where the accident is or what's burning. So it's not like they don't spend quality time, and she'll even teach Cassi something useful now and then, like after yesterday's unsuccessful swerve, when she demonstrated how to field-dress a fender-dented fawn with only a Leatherman and an ice scraper.

> Stupid-ass Bambi
> Bloody fur on my bumper.
> Pretty little lunch.

Bana's own words, barely rearranged, as they each grabbed legs and swung the carcass into the trunk of her Olds 88, leaving the pink pile for the crows.

Cassi regrets straying from the path. Just about now Vela and Lyra would be outside on their leashes to play. She wouldn't mind being there to toss them Teddy Grahams or pry them apart when they get started. Sometimes the twins will plunk down, clam up, and stick out their sandy chins in hopes of a story. If she's in the mood, Cassi might cave—on the condition she adds her own endings. The witch (craving protein) does eat Hansel—bones, hair, teeth, and all. The Grinch's heart shrinks even smaller with the stress of the holiday, ticking itself to infarction as all the Whos down in Whoville cheer. And back in the kingdom, the wicked stepsister snags the Prince after all, leaving Cinderella hip-deep in wedding reception mess. When they demand picture books, Cassi chooses only the grimmest of the Grimms'. Her favorite author, Edward Gorey, hardly needs editing: "A is for Amy, who fell down the stairs, B is for Basil, assaulted by bears." She changes the "C is for Clara" to "Cassi, who wasted away." "D is for Desmond, thrown out of a sleigh."

For generations, Olson females have been named in deference to some great-great-grandfather, an astronomer from Oslo, dead more than sixty years but still feared. Running her fingers across his old velum sky maps in Bana's den, Cassi has tried to explain to Lyra that while her constellation appears as a pretty bird, it's actually a vulture. Vela is eager for facts she barely understands—that she is named for the rippled remnant of a super nova adjacent to a pencil nebula. When told by strangers what a pretty name she has, Vela claps her jammy hands and shouts, "Penis benluba!"

Cassi's given name is Cassiopeia, which she is told she cannot give back.

Lined up young to old, the Olsons appear as versions of the same female, like the age-progression foldouts in a biology book. Vela, Lyra, Cassipoeia, Ara, Carina, and Ursa. All are sturdy and standard sized, with even features and thick, silver-blonde hair launching from canted widow's peaks. Each blinks filament lashes over ice-blue eyes, with Swedish complexions as luminous as their names; only their few freckles approach the shades of normal flesh.

The Goth girls in Cassi's archery club nod approvingly at the hue of her forearms and neck, awed to learn there is an SPF 90. In the recesses of family portraits, two dark-haired men appear as if Photoshopped: Grandpa Ray, Gran Carina's husband, and Cassi's father, Mark. Naturally swarthy, neither shaves when at the lake, making their Flintstone presences that much flintier as weekends wear on. Passing the fire pit during one of their brush-burning frenzies, Cassi heard them joke about the futility of flinging genes at Olson women, something about a clogged gene pool. She'd edged closer, but once they'd sensed her, both stopped chuckling and went back to toeing burning sticks and watching embers levitate.

At meals her father and grandfather are so quiet that Bana will put up with their stoniness for only so long before cracking, "Are you stunned?" And whether they are within earshot or not, Bana thumps her fist on the table when the subject of marriage or husbands comes up. Simply, they aren't necessary. She's done fine without for more than fifty years. Cassi's great-grandfather passed away while passing something on the toilet in the Vermilion Mine while reading a novel. No one ever knew what.

> Even mollusks have weddings
> Though solemn and leaden—

When Joanna Newsom's yowl stops in mid-lyric, Cassi halts to fish out her iPod and stare at the battery icon, flashing and flashing again like an expiring firefly. When she calculates the time she's been roaming against the number of hours her battery typically lasts, Cassi understands she is actually, officially lost. Battery's gone. She's gone. The sun, too, now hiding behind a cloud with tails of mist that follow, like the farts that trail her father. In spite of Ayurvedic remedies, acupuncture, and his dairyless diet, her father suffers from irritable bowel syndrome. He'd let one at the dinner table the night before, prompting Bana to drop the knife she was sawing sausage with and swivel, "Postcard from shit," glaring until he sprinkled his seitan with Beano.

Back in the city, Cassi's parents own a small yoga studio where they teach Iyengar and Bikram. Each evening they come home limp and damp after their long days of downward dog and upward dog. For supper her father makes some whole-grain veggie hash and serves it up in a flying saucer–shaped dish. Cassi has dubbed his meals UFO tofu, quite pleased by the palindrome. She suspects his cooking might have everything to do with the gas.

When he hogs the cabin's one bathroom or forgets to turn on the fan, Bana slaps his platitudes on the air freshener or pine candles with Post-its: "Practice lovingkindness!" "Mindfulness!" She leaves boxes of kitchen matches on the sill and plugs in the Glade persimmon night-light. She has trained Vela and Lyra so that when their father grabs a magazine and heads down the hall, one will shout, "Parcel post!"

Because her parents are married, same-race heterosexuals with 3.0 children, her family is supposedly normal, according to the current administration that Bana calls the Axis of Weasels. Most of Cassi's classmates come from blended families, some with two fathers or no fathers, step- and half-sisters, and rainbow mothers, and mismatched sets of brothers in every combination you can think of. Skin colors in her homeroom range from her own chalkiness to the tar black of the Ethiopian boy named Gur, who basically disappears when he closes his eyes. In between are the butter-skinned Vietnamese kids, and the shiny brown and coppery girls who roll their eyes at everything and scream at nothing.

When Cassi looks around the dinner table, she can only imagine what it might be like to have an interesting family—at least a more colorful one. She watches Gran Carina's spoonfuls of Coffee-mate meeting the inky liquid—remarkable only for those first few swirls before all goes beige.

Cassi pauses at an icy clear brook no wider than a run of Glad Wrap. Peeling her tongue from the roof of her mouth, she briefly considers drinking from it, then remembers all those tests her father had when he was hoping to be diagnosed with giardia. She moves on, smacking her dry lips, shivering.

Her fleece hoodie and fingerless gloves are in the lost back-pack keeping company with her sandwich. Besides jeans, she's wearing only her black Goodbye Kitty tee over a long-sleeved thermal undershirt.

This Easter holiday is the last family visit to the lake until Memorial Day. Since it's nearly afternoon, the cars would already be packed, with Bana itching to wave all but Cassi off. So, Cassi reasons, someone should start worrying soon, maybe come look-ing. Who knows, they might all be napping, dragging from too many chocolate eggs, having ripped into their baskets before the toast was even burnt. The air at breakfast was bad, nobody speak-ing to Bana after she'd stomped along the hall before daylight, rapping on doors and calling, "Christ is risen, how about *you*?" Bana's always finding opportunities to raise Christian hackles. The day before, it was defending the twins who got a time-out for saying *Goddammit,* when Bana insisted that it couldn't be blas-phemy if they don't believe in God and that four-year-olds simply don't because they are unpolluted, and that parents who do have no business brainwashing children with religious claptrap.

Cassi reads the glances over the table as bold as type. Her parents and grandparents are not just waiting for Bana to die, they are eager. But because she doesn't believe in second chances or any manner of afterlife, Bana is pretty well dug in to this one.

The sky reveals nothing of the direction Cassi might be go-ing; the sun, when it does appear, is weak and high. Not watch-ing her next step, her foot is suddenly sucked down as if some-thing has it. The rush of cold water into her boot is a shock. She wobbles and pulls, pulls again until her foot emerges with a sch-kuck. Cassi stares at bubbling muck and her wet, striped sock. Dropping to her knees, she plunges her arm in. Too late—her boot is gone. She watches the bubbles get smaller, get muddier, then stop.

Three weeks of babysitting money—that's how much the Doc Martens cost. Her mother had warned, "Every pound of shoe equals five pounds on your lower back," but Cassi bought them anyway, pushing aside the awful foam Crocs in toy colors.

Now her knees are wet and her arm is soaked to the shoulder. Suddenly everything feels . . . *seized,* the air colder, damper. She would just as soon plop down and cry, but losing the boot has triggered some instinct; it's urgent that Cassi get up now, get out of the bog. Because she must.

For a while she half-hops, limping over the moss and peat that had felt soft under her boots but is actually riddled with twigs and crusty ice. Heading to where the brush is thicker, Cassi breathes in, "cabin cabin cabin," hoping the stand of tamarack might open to one, where she could break in and find paper, pencil, water, maybe some food. She'd give her other boot for a blanket . . .

But when she emerges from the thicket, Cassi sees only more bog fanning farther and wider. Turning to go a different way, through the clumpy alder, she trips and scrapes her arm. It doesn't hurt much, but the sight of blood acts like a switch. She limps faster, passing but not recognizing the little pool where her boot went in. It takes twenty minutes to slog an eighth of a mile, each step an effort, though her foot hurts less now that it's numb.

She officially hates the bog now, remembers studying those tar pits in California, full of dead things sucked down and petrified. The peat beneath her could crack open any second with Indian skeletons or dead animals popping up. That Discovery Channel special about the potted mummy children? Scientists with tweezers picking at the raisiny face of a sacrificed boy, sending his body through scanners and poking around his insides to see what his last meal was . . .

> Maya mummy boy
> Had maize and milk for supper,
> Dagger for dessert

Food themes are seeping across her lines. Surely there are edible plants in bogs. She scans the ground for anything that looks soft enough to chew, reaching for plants she doesn't know the names of: leatherleaf and false lily, Labrador tea. She moves along, hunched with her head down, forgetting what she's looking for, losing the thread of where she is. She stops to watch a cattail that seems to be breathing. Reaching out to touch the velvet cylinder, Cassi marvels—Bana will want to know about this, that cattails can breathe. There are other not-quite-explicable things happening, but as in a dream it seems silly to question. The brown liquid that squelches up between her toes appears to be coffee. It feels warm, too, which is a great relief. At least she was lucky enough to get lost in a coffee bog. And where there is coffee there is food, so she anticipates passing a deli case any second, thinks of crusty sugar-topped muffins. Who knew? A Starbucks in the bog, and Bana has never even mentioned it!

When spindly tamarack open onto yet another clearing, she looks up, confidently expecting a barista and people hunkered over laptops.

Cassi stifles a yelp. She closes her eyes hard, hoping that when she looks again, what she has seen will be gone, that they will be gone. She squeezes her lids until all is white. Her rope of words is so far out of reach she can't even braid a rhyme. When she opens her left eye, they're still there, as if getting lost could have gone any more wrong.

A bear and a wolf—so over-the-top it eclipses any fairy tale she might use to alarm the twins. The bear is propped on sticks, with its back to Cassi. At the bear's side, the white wolf rises from its crouch to sniff, easily catching her scent at twenty yards.

Her own howl has no sound. Suddenly she's the story—the lost girl clawed and gnawed to death, her frozen corpse left for trolls or whoever to make soup with, her bones sinking muckward . . .

When the wolf begins to trot toward her, she rushes inward to her blank page. Blank Page is where the lines usually emerge. Please, Cassi thinks, knowing she cannot possibly get to Starbucks without one, just *one* poem, please, because sometimes words come out as solutions. The scrap forms quickly and she frowns even as she says it:

> Shit. He will eat me,
> fangs on my white neck, red meat
> down his toothy hatch.

The bear begins turning on its bundle of sticks and says something to make the wolf stop. Cassi's throat fills with something like a hot sponge.

The bear stands and shades its eyes, land-ho style, calling, "Hullo?"

Of course it's a momma bear, the most vicious kind. When Cassi doesn't respond, the bear takes a step, motioning for the wolf to stay, which, by the way, it does not. Cassi is suddenly shaking so hard she cannot raise her arm. The bear's eyes grow rounder as she lumbers closer.

"You okay?"

This is no normal bear. It talks, has a human face and a head of wavy, red-bear-colored hair, and is wearing a bear coat, but with buttons. The wolf has a collar and is wagging its tail. *Perplexed* (one of Cassi's favorite words ever, it has everything going for it), she hangs her head to see pink blood on her wet, flopping sock. Headphone wires trail down her leg, the earbuds torn away.

"You're lost?"

When Cassi closes her eyes, the bear sounds nearly human. She whispers, "No," meaning yes. If only her neck worked, she could nod.

"I w-wan B-B-Bana."

Just as she begins to pitch sideways, the bear catches her. She's dragged to the folding stool she thought was just sticks and is made to sit. The bear unbuttons her hide and pulls off her sweater and puts both over Cassi, trapping her arms. Pokey fur tickles her chin.

"What's your name?"

"Cah-cah-ca . . ."

Bear inhales. "Okay . . . later, then. How long have you been out here?"

She's trembling hard but manages to wiggle five fingers out from the waistband of the sweater.

"Hours, right, not days? *Please* open your eyes." Bear digs in a bag and pulls out a water bottle, but after Cassi has only one gulp, it's pulled away, Bear saying, "Damn, that's too cold for you." Bear scoops up the thermos at her feet, pours coffee into its chrome top, and tips Cassi's chin.

This *is* a Starbucks! Her teeth clank against the hot liquid so that most spills over the sweater and fur that are not hers. "The water was too cold . . . ," she singsongs to the bear, "and the coffee is toooo hot." Now that she thinks about it, Cassi realizes she has no idea what porridge actually is. How can she not know that?

"Hey," Bear speaks softly, "you've gotta drink this."

Sure, if her teeth would open. One of her wrists is dug out and Bear holds it, checking her pulse. Bear peers into her eye, trying to lift an eyelid with her paw. Cassi rears back, falling off the stool. When Bear leans over her, Cassi sees little golden hairs on her bare-naked, bear arms. Pitiful coat, she thinks. She looks up and laughs to see Bear shivering in her little undershirt and bra. There are freckles and goose bumps smattering her cleavage.

"B-boobs. I have those. Getting them, anyway . . ." Cassi shudders, reminded of the single, bristle-like hair that's recently sprouted at the edge of her right nipple—a horsehair, a pube, a bear hair. There are no words for how it freaks her out. She looks down now to see it's much, much worse than that. She's grown a full, heavy coat.

"You remember your name?"

Cassi's eyes sting as coffee is poured though teeth pried open by the bear's thumb. She coughs. "Bana callsh me Lasshie Casshi." Suddenly struggling to get up, she says, "I left my notebook in the coffee swamp."

"You mean a coffee *shop*? Oh . . ." Bear looks around as if she too is lost. "I've got to get you out of here."

When Cassi's eyes close again, everything goes blue, thump-bump-bumpity-thump, like a pretty blue vein.

Cassi wakes up on a couch. *They* are on a couch: she's trapped by a blanket and quilt tucked into the cushions, her foot poking out the bottom, where a red-haired lady sits, holding her foot in her lap. The lady is squinting through a black eye and picking slivers from Cassi's heel. She knows her? She does. Tweezers flash.

"Ouch."

The lady looks up. "Oh, good. You're awake." She has a top on now.

"How'd I get here?"

"Not easily." She covers Cassi's foot and stands, looking relieved. "You'll be all right, I think. I'm Meg."

"I'm Cassi . . ." Saying her own name, she feels her stomach roll. "I'm way too hot," she says. "I might puke."

"Right." The quilt is pulled away. "Hang on, if you can . . ." The lady—the bear, Meg—hurries away into another, brighter room where cupboard doors squeal and slam. When her form fills the door again, she's holding a bowl. Cassi shakes her head. "It's okay, I'm not gonna now."

"You sure? 'Cause if you're really not, then I'll just make more tea."

"Yeah, I'm really not."

She feels her face, her cheeks. The rest of her is warm. There is a buzzing sensation in her limbs. She is a little dizzy, suggesting maybe she shouldn't move too fast, the nausea might come back. She can't remember much since losing her boot, which would have been, according to the clock on the mantle, about three hours ago. She blinks, realizing she has been in real, actual danger—that if not for the bear she'd probably be dying under some ratty spruce tree about now. She wills the tears from falling. Her foot hurts, but otherwise . . .

Cassi can hear water running in the kitchen, a kettle clanking. With a buzzing arm she reaches for the mug on a nearby table. Tea, sweet and almost warm, along with a saucer of stiff toast. As she chews she looks around. The wide room is dim in the late afternoon. On every wall are paintings—scenes either reflected over the surface of water or seen from underneath, some from a turtle's view. One is a fisheye perspective through the wire mesh of a live trap, with dozens of minnows like darting cough drops. Another shows warped weeds and an anchor; the one next to it has a sky reflected between the sun-shot sides of aluminum boats; another, wavering mirrors of shore-side birches. The paintings are calm yet contain a sense of urgency, each scene seeming tenuous, like real time does—as if a skipping stone or a boat's wake could ripple it all away in a blink.

A movement in the corner distracts her, and she pivots to see her own legs dancing a jig in a corner of the room. She quickly feels for her legs under the quilt and laughs—it's just her jeans draped over a chair, drying above a heat grate. Cassi slowly lifts herself from the couch and tests her tender foot, wobbling the length of the room in her underpants, slipping once on the salve smeared on her heel. By bracing against the wall, she manages to get one leg, then another into the warm denim. Her socks are on a rung of the chair. Meg must've rinsed out the muddy, bloodied one because it is less filthy and has dried to a pinkish-grey. Nothing feels as good as this sock.

Walking is possible as long as she holds on to something. She edges along a sideboard, where another painting leans. It features a metal shovel sunk to the shallows and a submerged snorkel mask aiming beachward through the water, framing blurred shapes of children in bright swimsuits. A small companion painting hangs next to it—one flip-flop caught under water in the crevice of a rock, the shadow of its floating mate cast from above. She slows, looks around at a few more. These paintings seem like captured moments to Cassi, trapped almost in the way she traps her thoughts on paper with words. She wonders if the paintings are painted to keep the moments, or to free them.

She sticks her head into a porch-turned-studio—one side is a run of windows, with blank canvases stacked under the sills. Outside, the lake is dull and pitted with the kind of rain that will turn to snow. The white wolf-dog is lying under a heavy easel, watching Cassi with eyes the color of her own, which Bana calls gin-bottle. As she limps closer, its tail thwacking speeds up, and when she reaches out, the dog rolls to offer its belly. Cassi kneads her fingers deep into its fur, saying, "Some wolf."

Looking up from her crouch, she is face-to-face with a girl— a portrait clamped on the easel—a girl looking over the end of a dock, staring down to the water at her twin staring back from below the surface through concentric rings, as if the water has just been disturbed, as if the girl has just spit into it.

The painting is a trick, a little weird. Cassi reaches out.

"That's Narcissus." Meg's voice comes from behind.

Cassi squints. "But it's you."

"Yeah. I was about your age there."

"Isn't narcissus a flower?"

Meg begins to explain, but Cassi stops her. "Oh, right . . . my Gran Carina tells me I shouldn't look in the mirror so much."

Meg hands her a cup of hot tea. "Speaking of, we need to call your family."

"No!" Cassi straightens. "I mean . . . can't we call Bana, instead?"

"Pardon?"

"My great-grandmother. *She* won't have a fit."

"Sure. What's her number?"

"I dunno. 2-1-8, and then 3-6 something, and a couple 4s . . . I think." She chews her inner cheek. "Numbers never really stick to me . . ."

"Okay. How about her name, then? Her real name?"

"Olson. Ursa Olson."

Meg looks up. "On Olson Point? In Jasper Bay?"

"Uh-huh."

"Wow." Meg seems surprised. "She's still . . ."

"Alive? Well, yeah, but she's like ninety-something. Do you know her?"

Meg hesitates. "*Know*-know her? Not really. Not well. She used to deliver out here when I was a kid—my grandfather knew her. She knew my grandfather . . ." Meg seems to be examining Cassi anew, from her white-blonde widow's peak to her pale hands. She says as if to herself, "I might have guessed."

Cassi edges toward the nearest chair, suddenly tired.

Meg offers a hand "Would you rather go back to the couch?"

Cassi shakes her head. "I'm fine here." She sinks into the wicker facing the window.

Meg nods. "Okay. Sit tight, then?" She takes a cell phone

from her vest pocket. "I just need to walk up the bluff to get a signal—I won't be twenty minutes." At the door she looks back at Cassi once, then is gone.

Seated, Cassi is again level with the painting of young Meg, thinking she's dizzy again, but then realizing the area surrounding Meg's face is intentionally smudged with soft brushstrokes, each leading inward to the center, until the viewer is drawn to the precise freckles smattered across the nose, the fine hairs of the eyebrows, and the photo-crisp details of the eyes.

Cassi unconsciously chips green polish from the moons of her nails. The longer she looks at the painting, the more she sees, or thinks she sees. This she knows for sure—the girl in the painting is impatient and maybe feels the frustration Cassi so often feels looking outward from some unfocused place.

Other kids get Ritalin. But Cassi's father claims that most teens, simply by dint of being teens, have some form of ADD. Forget that she was officially diagnosed with the actual test. Instead of a real therapist, she was taken to a homeopath, prescribed a low-sugar diet, and given tinctures and a retarded CD that's supposed to help her concentrate. So, basically, she's on her own. When the thoughts gnarl and merge, it's up to her to corral them into some form. Writing works best. Once they are committed to notebooks, her most rambling thoughts can be contained. The notebooks are all in a row, in order, on her middle bookshelf where she can see them. Even the twins know not to touch them. Losing one shouldn't be a big deal, but each holds a whole month worth of lines—thirty days of thoughts ordered. One notebook is a huge gap.

A door slams and a distant, "Cassi?" pipes from somewhere. "Here."

Boots thud to the linoleum and Meg starts making kitchen noises again—a crack of ice cubes wrenched from a tray, gluggy pouring sounds. A minute later she's in the porch, carrying a glass of Coke and a cloth twisted around a ball of ice chips. She sits and lifts the cloth to her bruised eye. "Ursa . . . *Bana* is on her way. How're you doing?"

"Kinda crappy." Cassi takes the Coke, shaking her head as if to clear it. "My *note*book . . ."

"I know, you talked about it in the boat. It must have been important."

"It had my lines." She points to her temple. "I need them for my . . . you know, my . . ."

"Your . . . ?"

"My navigation."

"Oh." Meg looks truly sorry. "Well, maybe I can look for it, go back tomorrow . . ."

"You won't find it." For the first time during the long day, tears blur everything. Meg makes as if to touch Cassi's arm but then doesn't.

"You can always write more?"

"Sure." The heels of Cassi's palms rock across her wet eye-sockets. "Easy for you. How about all these paintings? I mean, what if this whole place burned down—it looks like it might— what would you do then?"

Meg sits up. "Well . . . I-I'd make more." She winces, either at the thought or the pain around her eye.

"I gave you that, didn't I? I'm sorry."

"You remember?"

"Starting to." Static bits have come back—the flash of her sock flapping as they limped toward the shore; trying to vault from the boat; panic at being pressed onto the bench seat near the wolf; the outboard motor gargling; her arms and elbows everywhere . . .

"Hypothermia," Meg says, "makes people think and see odd things, say weird stuff."

Cassi feels her face mottle. "Like what? What did I say?"

"Not so much say . . . more like recite. Something about a bear peeling off its fur . . ."

"Oh, just a haiku, probably."

"Yes, I think so . . ."

Looking directly at Meg, Cassi's face crumples and she blubbers, "I did it on purpose."

"Did what?"

"Got lost."

Meg lowers the ice pack and looks at her. Water from the melting ice chips drip through her fingers in threes to the floor, like ellipses.

Cassi wipes her nose on her sleeve. "They needed something else to worry about. Otherwise, they'll just keep talking about putting her away in some home, some *facility*."

"They?"

"All of them. They say she's feebleminded."

"Ursa?"

"Yes!"

"But I just spoke to her, she sounded just fine. She still *drives* . . . ," Meg looks alarmed, "doesn't she?"

"Yeah. Exactly. She is fine, and she can do anything she ever did, but they just pretend she's senile to explain away the things she does."

"What things?"

"Just little things—like putting the phone in the double boiler. Her temper, like when she backed over the neighbors' mailbox because their giant new cabin ruins some of her view. She mumbles a lot, and she always 'accidentally' tosses Grandpa Ray's *Weekly Standard* into the fire—which everyone knows she does on purpose because she can't lie without doing that thing with her dentures. And some of the things she says . . . like telling Gran Carina, who's all Catholic and everything, that birth control should be a holy sacrament and the Pope should just go fuck himself."

Meg works to keep her mouth straight. "So . . . so, you got lost so that they would . . . what?"

"I dunno . . . worry about something besides her for a while, I guess."

Meg faces Cassi. "You know, if I hadn't been in that bog . . ."

"I know . . ." Her chin pocks. "I thought I knew the way out."

They sit for a long time, Cassi giving in, her shoulders heaving as she blindly trades wet, balled tissues for fresh ones. Meg silently holds the box.

By the time Cassi finally stops and gets her breath, it's growing dark outside. She feels emptied, but warm. She absently kneads her toes into the dog's ruff. Looking up, she sees nuggets of snow hit the window to melt down along the glass. In the reflection, she notices Meg's gaze is intent on the glass but unseeing, as if thinking about something, or trying not to, or maybe just watching the driblets on the glass. Cassi follows her eye until it focuses on a single drip, and in the time it takes them both to watch the line of it shimmy to the sill, a haiku forms, spoken toward the glass easily as a breath:

> "Raindrop jerks itself
> dripping, down a darkening,
> Shitty afternoon."

Meg smiles and their eyes meet in the reflection. Cassi shrugs. She's never recited in someone's company and certainly not *to* anyone before, not even Bana.

She might not always have her notebook, could lose it again. She could, she supposes, speak some of those lines that often seem so urgent, because it sort of works; for the moment there are no thoughts jamming, nothing to shift aside, no trapped lines.

Nothing to think about until Bana's Oldsmobile comes skidding down the gravel. For now it's only their reflections in the window—just her and Meg the bear.

K ATIE GETS WHAT KATIE WANTS, AND THIS WAS HER idea. She circled the ad for caretaker couple, and now we're living thirty hard miles from town, a long drive on a good day and winter's coming like a fist. I applied by mail, sending a résumé and two references to the address in Chicago, not exactly trying, but got the job anyway because of my construction experience and the two years at Hickey's Garage. Cars and engines are okay, but I'd rather stick to carpentry, even if it's tricking out log McMansion kitchens with granite islands the size of islands. As long as there are dot-comers spending, I've got work, and I usually get my winters off. Usually. But now Katie wants us to make more money for the house we're going to build and the baby we're going to have after she finally gets pregnant.

And that's how we ended up being caretakers at Naledi— *Vacationland,* according to one of the old brochures under the register.

I can tell you now: lots of people have pretty wrong ideas about what it takes to tend a resort. This one, without any guests even, is a ten-hour-a-day ball-buster. But people think, "We'll run a resort, it'll be fun!" I've seen the look—folks with out-of-state plates mooning at listings in the realty office windows, how they'll nearly skip around the grounds of any closed-up place with a For Sale sign. Katie calls it knotty-pining.

Take Wolftrap Lodge. Guy and his wife both quit decent jobs in Madison and sold everything, thinking they'll be living the good life up here in the fairy-tale north. People told them the septic was bad, but when you got a dream clogging your head,

I guess you literally don't hear shit. The kitty under the bar at Chainsaw Sally's has almost three hundred bucks in it and the dates we're all guessing they'll throw in the towel and crawl back home to Wisconsin. I'm a little far out compared to the others— my date banks the warmest weather against the busiest week of July, each cabin full of flushing guests and those shallow leach fields getting riper by the day.

Maybe sooner. I saw the cheddarheads in town last week, and they were already both looking pretty knocked back.

Katie gets up in the pitch dark and leaves here at five-thirty to make her shift at the hospital where she works in admissions. I worry about black ice and deer, but she calls me as soon as she's at her desk so I can enjoy my coffee. On the mornings her temperature is just right, we do it, then she lies with her hips up on a pillow for twenty minutes so it might take better. Lucky her smarmy boss is okay enough with it when she's rushing in at seven-thirty or seven-forty that he only jokes, "I see you're fucking late again" and slaps his knee. Those days Katie stays past three o'clock to make up the time, which means if she gets groceries or does anything at all in town, it's six by the time she's home. I tell her it would be nice to see her during daylight now and then. My point (that she misses) is that I'm out here by myself a lot. She says lamplight is more romantic anyway and wants to do it sometimes even before supper, after I've been up and down ladders all day or out in the freezing pole barn trying to get the plow running.

The owner of this place doesn't call, only sends instructions about what needs doing. The letters are signed M. Machutova, just like the checks, so I don't know if he's a Mark or a Marvin or what. If I had to write back it would be "Dear M," which sounds stupid.

This is a lot of work for one guy. I'm supposed to make sure the two good cabins are sealed up tight for the season and to keep snow off their roofs. The rest are nothing special, some with buckled beams, some leaning so hard M. has asked if I know anyone who would tear them down come spring. So now one of my jobs is to remove the plumbing, disconnect the wiring, and pry out anything of value, which is more than you'd think looking at these shacks; the old windows have heavy bubbled glass; there's nickel sinks, hammered iron hardware, some nice hand-hewn doors and cupboards—the sort of stuff the salvage yards in Minneapolis go apeshit for. The crappiest cabins are sided with cedar bark, making them bat shit central, so I put *respirator* on my to-buy list, but I've already inhaled enough guano to grow fangs.

Where we stay is nice enough but not as big as you'd think hearing the word *lodge*. What used to be reception is the living room with a fireplace made of stones that look like chunks of stacked Hershey bars—gunflint, if you can believe. The kitchen was pretty bad—all harvest gold and cheap Menards—so I swapped out some of the better cabinets from the empty cabins and pulled in the nicest old gas range to replace the electric one Katie was bitching no end about. Under the kitchen carpet—a stupid concept—we found decent linoleum, if you like old-old. The back office is mine, still has *Men's* stenciled on the door and a *cold* spigot just below the wall phone. On the lake side of the lodge was the old 3-2 bar, and a long glass porch, so drafty sometimes the willow rockers just start up on their own. I light a flashlight under my chin and tell Katie they're powered by ghosts of vacations past, "Mwah-ha-ha . . . ."

Up under the roof there're three bedrooms with single dormers. I'm supposed to tear out a wall to combine two of them into one decent-sized room, which should be no sweat with just the old framing and beadboard dividing them, but it's still work. Like I said, there's no end of what's next to cross off the list here at good old Naledi.

I got the two best cabins spruced up just before the first snow came, a week before Halloween so not all that early, but I'd barely got the plow working or the chains welded for Katie's Impala in time. Even though she's not pregnant yet, Katie's reading *What to Expect When You're Expecting* in bed each night. Every once in a while she nudges me back awake to read out loud something about episiotomies or mucus plugs. Just as I'm about to dream, right?

Mid-November had seven snowfalls, a few inches each, which I record in the log that M. has asked me to keep. These small snows make plowing manageable but constant—then the shit hit the fan the night before Thanksgiving and fourteen inches blew down from Ontario, so by morning we were socked in tight. Had to call the folks to say we couldn't make town for dinner. Katie had the mashed potatoes all made and that cranberry thing, so we thawed and stuffed a chicken and had our first and maybe last ever holiday alone, in peace. We ate by the fire on the floor like a picnic and watched it come down outside. It was nice, cozy, with none of Mom's Brussels sprouts to have to pocket, no Grandma barking old songs in Saami, and no wrestling Uncle Juri's car keys off him after he gets at the Aquavit.

They say there's only two seasons here, and both can kill you. It's a nasty December so far, cold enough to break records, so we're using up propane and firewood like crazy. Now neither of us comes inside without bringing an armload to the basement stove that's gotta be stoked hot or we'll have frozen pipes. Most of the stacked cordwood is seasoned but won't last if this keeps up. I burn a green piece for every two dry ones. Running a log splitter every other morning in minus-thirty windchill is just the sort of routine I hadn't counted on.

Plus, you forget how reflective snow is until you work outside in it. My eyes are so bloodshot I have to wear sunglasses now even on cloudy days. Katie says if I wasn't dressed in Carhartt, I might be mistaken for a rock star. But I tell her, "Just wait—it'll come into fashion one of these days."

We're having everyone out here for Christmas. Over the river and through the woods and all. I opened up Cabin 3 and heated it for a few days before I dared turn the water on. Katie's family will stay there, and my folks can sleep in our room, which is plenty big now with the wall gone. It has two windows, and the old hanging sinks in the corners make it like his and hers. I cut a tree and Katie made paper chains from pages of the old *National Geographic* magazines I've read and reread. I surprised her by spray-painting pine cones with silver tractor paint and hung them in the branches along with old fishing lures I found in the cellar that I know are worth an arm and a leg.

We go in on Saturday to shop for presents and visit the Living Manger at the hockey rink. This year Kelly Maki plays the Mary and shows off her new baby to Katie, who gurgles at it like an outboard and picks straw out of its hair. Afterward Katie cries into her hot chocolate, and I can barely get her to stop, so then I tell her the story about Kelly Maki during junior year, before she was a virgin, when she got biblical with Kenny Ojala under the bleachers where they didn't even notice me and Chip Heikkala hiding from Coach, toasted out of our minds.

Finally she laughs.

Both families show up Christmas Eve, and Katie bakes a ham. We play poker until midnight, then go out to aim a carol at the moon, but it's too cold to really sing much so we croak one round of "O, Christmas Tree," which is appropriate since that's about all there is here. Later, when me and her squeeze into the little room, I see the back side of the door has carved height marks next to the birth dates for two kids—one with the initials *TM* with dates from the '40s and '50s, and *MM,* with marks starting in the late '60s, making Mitch or Max or whoever he is about our age. There are kid stickers stuck all over the walls at knee height that I'll need to get off with turpentine, and little pictures painted right on the floor in nail polish. Katie says leave them be, then starts kissing me like she does all the time now.

I look up and see the outline of toads and mushrooms and mice carved right into the knotty pine, so I show Katie. "See what you're in for?" I tell her, swatting her hands from my crotch. "See how rugrats'll ruin your brand-new house? Think about that."

She pulls the covers over my head and says, "Now."

"No, sirree," I tell her, "not with my Mom a wall away."

Katie pouts. "But, hon, wouldn't it be great to make a baby on Christmas Eve?"

I lift the covers and point to what Juri calls wedding tackle and say, "As you can see, babe, not a creature is stirring."

Breakfast is cinnamon waffles and Dad's venison patties. Then we open presents. I get the fly rod I asked for, but then Katie gives me—in front of everyone—a three-pack of plaid boxers, complete with her explanation of how testicles need to hang naturally to maintain the proper temperature for healthy, active sperm.

I go outside and Dad follows, then my father-in-law, Ray, and we rake snow from the roofs of Cabins 4 and 5, then haul more wood to the cellar, where we can smoke without being ragged on. Ray, who knows his daughter pretty well, just hands over his flask and a gives me a look, like "I know, I know." Like I said, Katie gets what Katie wants. If you could see her, you'd know why. She can't go to the Twin Cities without being asked for autographs from people who don't believe she's not Kim Basinger.

Aside from the underwear, it was a good enough holiday. Like Mom said, Christmas doesn't get any whiter. Tommy complained there was no TV to watch the game on, then started snooping around, thinking I was bullshitting him.

"There's no reception."

"What in hell you do here without a TV?"

I shrug. "We have a stereo . . ."

"Yeah? But all night, all weekend?"

Katie whacks the back of Tommy's head and says, "We're trying to make babies out here, dipshit, what do you *think* we do?"

Well, that's not all. Besides the constant doing it, we play a lot of cribbage and read. Katie's been bringing me crime novels written by some an ex-lawyer, so I nod off to those each night. We snowshoe out onto the ice sometimes so we can listen to it ping and pong. You'd think the sound of ice cracking would sound like ice cracking but it doesn't—more like dolphins trapped under, or whales. We take saunas, too, birch whips, the whole nine yards, but I'm not about to tell Katie's snot-faced little brother that.

"Son," Dad pipes up from the couch, "if I'd known there wasn't gonna be no tube, I would've got you and Katie one of those VCR machines for Christmas."

Baby, or the lack of baby, is the topic that won't go away. New Year's Eve we drive to the Duckblind for dinner, and I see guys from my crew I haven't seen for months. One comes up to us and asks, all winking, "You guys knocked up yet?"

Eating like she already is, Katie says, "Oh, isn't this the best steak ever? I'm glad I didn't get the walleye." Pretending she didn't hear.

How does this happen? I cross my arms and stare at my wife. "Katie . . . ?"

Weeks before her birthday in February she says, "Don't you dare buy me a present. There's only one teeny thing I want, just a minuscule something down in Duluth." She books us a room at the Voyageur and takes that whole Friday off, saying, "It'll be a nice drive, hon, a nice break."

And half of it is. On the road we finally got clear radio stations, and I was glad to be near the things I'd missed, but at the same time kind of glad I didn't really want a Quarter Pounder or a game of pool. It perked me up a little to be driving into a city, even though the snowbanks are gray and the drivers are shitheads. I was thinking, too, how it would be nice to go have a beer at the Pilothouse, where there's a fireplace and a view of the lake, but then Katie reminds me we could drive back to Naledi and do just exactly that. Finally we head off to get whatever it is that Katie's wanting.

But there wasn't any shopping. It wasn't a tiny little thing she wanted at all. The surprise was on me, and not too pleasant. What Katie already had was an appointment with a fertility doctor. I find this out only after she tells me, "Turn here," and we wind up in the parking lot of the clinic. We argue in the truck until she starts crying—really crying—about how she needs to have a baby before she's thirty and too old. That's three years from now. Three.

A half-hour of embarrassing questions later, plus giving blood, the doctor tells me not to take any more saunas and puts me in a room by myself with a stack of tit magazines and a cup I'm supposed to jiz into. Unreal.

For a long time I just look out the window, watching a freighter snailing along behind an icebreaker. Then I try the magazines. After twenty minutes there's a knock on the door, so any momentum I had was shot. It was Katie, saying in that voice, "Honey, can I come help you?"

I open the door a crack and tell her through my teeth, "Don't you mean, 'Can I help you come, honey?' No." I shut the door.

So then she says loud enough those other poor fuckers in the waiting room can hear, "Well, gee, hon, it never takes you this long at home."

When I finally finish, I bring out the sealed cup and hand it to her. "Happy birthday," I say. "I wasn't thinking of you."

Maybe not the brightest thing to say. I'm sleeping in the kid's room now.

I tried turpentine on the Disney stickers and nail polish trees but only managed to take the old lacquer off, so now there's light circles around where the stickers still stick to the beadboard.

The test results say I'm not shooting blanks. Plenty of strong swimmers, millions. I know Katie wants me back in our room, at least parts of me. I'm not budging. I don't care if it is Valentine's Day.

The last few checks from the owner have come in blue envelopes with postmarks from London, England: M. Machutova is either on a long vacation or is too busy to write much in the way of instructions, so I just do what needs doing, which is still plenty, but now with most everything snowed over at least I have a little more time to myself. I cut a hole in the ice halfway across the bay and sled out a tent and kerosene heater so I can fish whenever. If it's dark I can look across to see the orange light in the upstairs windows where Katie's sitting in bed—maybe reading, maybe waiting, probably moping.

There is nothing quieter than a frozen lake at midnight.

I'm just about to cave when Katie goes alone to Duluth for more testing. I gave her a list to take to the Paperback Trader. She comes back late and plops a bagful of Grisham and Turow on the table and sits down hard across from me. "My pH and yours aren't compatible. My vagina is not a hospitable environment for your sperm. We need to try fertility drugs."

"Jesus H. Christ." I throw my hands up. "What's next?" It's almost twenty below, but I shove myself into a snowmobile suit so I can go to the tractor shed where there'll be something to weld. "Fer-fucking-tility drugs . . ."

She watches me pry on boots and says, "Please, hon? Just think about it?" Her chin's doing that thing it does when gearing up for a squall.

I remind her of that mother we saw at Costco being dragged by a brace of triplets on leashes. "I want to have a family, too," I tell her, "not a freak show."

Katie came home from work to find me asleep in the big chair by the fire wearing the reading glasses my Dad forgot here at Christmas. The thriller I was reading had fallen to the Filson shirt she gave me to make up for the lousy boxers.

She shook me awake, her face all wet. "Babe?"

I sit up quick. "What? What's wrong?"

"Nothing. I just walked in and saw you sleeping there, and at first I thought you were dead, but then I saw you breathe, so I just stood here looking at you, and I could just tell what you're gonna be like in about twenty years. And you know what? I think I'll love you even more."

So, I guess we've made up.

We're going to try something called in vitro. And that's it then. We agreed, no more science. Besides, that shit's unbelievably expensive.

Weatherwise, April is usually a bad month, and this one's no better. A little thaw, a little snow, and then thaw again. The first in vitro didn't take. Fish aren't biting either, and since the lake's covered in slush to my ankles I tear down the tent and pull everything back to the shore.

The stuff we've been doing—Katie's had her eggs *harvested*. And since timing is everything now, I have to give her the shots. There's her whitest curve, and do you think jabbing a syringe at it is something I want to do to my wife's backside? You know how, watching a guy get hit when you know it'd be easier to take the blow yourself? It's like that, even though she doesn't make a peep, and it's one big-ass needle, no pun intended.

True story. Listen to this. With all the freezing and thawing we got ice buildup on every eave, so I make the rounds in the afternoons knocking ice swags off the cabins and sheds and checking for leaks and dams. I was on the roof of Number 3 where there was a pine limb fallen on the chimney, so I crawl up to knock it off. Just when I get standing, I lose my footing. Just like that, one leg goes one way and the other goes the other way, and I twist and go down like Chuck Berry, dead on my basket—on the peak of the roof. Talk about pain . . . tears like a baby, and I'm rolled up all fetal, forgetting all about where I am, and forget all about the ice until I start sliding. Then it's all scrabble and claw, but there's no gutters on these places, so ass over teakettle I go, right?

I land feet first, pounded into the snowbank like a stake. I'm in the mother of all pain and have just slid twenty feet off a roof like it's a ski jump. So here I am, waist-deep in heavy snow, wind knocked out of me, balls on fire, and bloody lip running. That's bad enough, right? But when I look up, not ten feet from me, is what? One very large, very surprised moose. I shit you not. I'm as good as paralyzed, and there's a fifteen-hundred-pound animal staring at me with locomotive steam shooting out its nostrils.

With a moose, it's all about staying out of their line of sight. They got about the shittiest eyesight in the animal kingdom, bad at distance and peripherals. But when they are close enough you can smell their breath, they can see just fine.

So I'm screwed. Tears still coming from having the boys crushed, my knee feels busted, my breath is only just coming back, and I still can't move. Nothing to do but wait and see just how screwed.

When I can breathe again, I think about yelling to scare him off, but something stops me. We stare at each other a good minute. This moose is big, like big-big, and he sidles up closer to me one step, then another step, until I can see the gunk in its eye. What're you gonna do in a situation like that? So, I shrug, hold out my empty hands, and just admit it, "You got me, pal."

But nothing happens, right? When I try to move my legs, the moose moves his, lifting up each big knee like, "I'm free, you're not, ha!" You ever see a tree with a burl in the middle of the trunk? That's exactly what a moose's knee looks like, bigger than the Brunswick Pro Katie gave me for my thirtieth.

"Very nice." I'm not sure why I say this.

The moose blinks. Steps sideways and back, then forward.

"Shit," I say, "I wish I was you right now."

And I did. I'm not kidding—suddenly I wished I was that moose harder than I'd ever wished for anything. The moose blinks faster and tilts its head like it's actually listening. I mean, that it could even lift its head—did I mention the rack? Size of a love seat, I crap you negative. He was some specimen, that's for sure. The more I looked at him, the more I started to think he was kinda beautiful. I was getting used to the smell by then, and I got the idea that he maybe wasn't gonna charge me—cuz he would've already if he was going to. So I just started talking. A blue streak, actually, yammering about how I really, really wanted to be him right then, and asking him stupid questions, like, "So, a moose don't have to ejaculate into a cup to knock up the missus, do they?"

"Moose don't pay hundreds of dollars for tests to see if his splooge is up to snuff, isn't that right?

"And I bet you don't spend thousands to have the doctor—not you, but the doctor—try to get it in there centered just so into your wife where it will take?

"No? No? I didn't think so.

"And you don't have to take on extra work to cover all the extra medical. And live out in the middle of Bumfuck?"

I swear he shakes his head at that one.

"Oh, right," I say. "You *like* living out here . . . actually, this place isn't so bad, is it, Moose?"

His head moves a little, so I nod, too. "Thought you'd agree."

He still doesn't take his eyes off me. Seems as long as I keep talking, he keeps listening. The pain's still pretty good down there, and I'm still blabbing to keep my mind off it. Diarrhea of the mouth, I guess.

I can't even remember all I said, but I probably started to bore him. When he turned his back end to me, I saw each flank is as big as I am. Forget about what's hung between.

When he started to walk away, I actually hollered after him, "I'm not finished, fella! I bet *your* wife doesn't bawl every time she gets her period. I bet your old lady doesn't treat *you* like some rented bull?"

I laugh like crazy then—giggle almost—realizing yeah, actually, that's exactly how the moose's wife would treat him. She's an animal, right? And out here in the wild? What else do they really want from each other besides to keep it all going—to make little moose who will make more moose after them?

So there I am, jammed in the snow and left to think on that.

And I do. I think about how we're just animals—I'm an animal, and Katie's an animal, too, and is acting just like one, pulling out all the stops to make this baby happen. And I see that it's her instinct, that she can't even help herself.

Moose looks back at me from way down by the gate and snorts once, like, "You are one sorry fuck, you know that?"

Then he was gone.

By the time I got myself out of the bank and limped up to the lodge, I was feeling a little different about the whole baby thing and decided to tell Katie maybe I understand now why she's so dead set, that it's only biology that's making her a little nuts.

But I don't get a chance to say anything because she's got the latest test results from the final round of in vitro. Negative. She's dry-eyed, and quiet, which is the worst. And then she pours herself a drink, which she hasn't done for ages, sits down, and apologizes for the last months, says she's pushed too hard and is afraid of driving me away, and why don't we just get that Labrador in the meantime like we'd talked about, and if a baby comes it comes, and if it doesn't it doesn't, and besides there's always adoption.

She comes over and sits on my sore knee and says, "Let's just go back to how we were."

In May, Katie does get me the dog—a chocolate lab we name Sisu. The same day we got a letter from Naledi's owner, who decided to get married and won't be coming back 'til October, asking us if we'd like to stay the summer through September, et cetera. This time the letter was signed Margaret Machutova. So the Mark or Max was neither. The paintings on the kid room floor *were* a little femmy, when I thought about it. I asked Juri, who told us about her parents' accident and how the old grandfather raised her up here until he checked out himself. But who'd have guessed some girl barely Katie's age would own a place like this—inheriting this—just the kind of place that would kill you to have to sell, but still—what's the saying about the albatross around your neck? More like an elephant.

Katie was surprised I agreed to stay on. But I figure there won't be all that much work once my cousin Chim finishes plowing over the old cabins, and with summer coming, why not be on a lake? And I'd already started work on two custom jobs only a few bays down and can get there by boat, which is a helluva lot nicer commute than taking the road, and when there's time I can troll and cast for bass on my way home. Shit, yeah, we'll stay. Besides, our duplex in town can be sublet for twice the rent to summer waitresses or guys who work for the outfitters, so there's that.

The weather's been good and we have the longer evenings together. We'll walk Sisu through the woods to her favorite place to run—an old cedar glade with weird humps that might be burial mounds. I keep meaning to ask Danny Swifthawk or Jon Redleaf about the place, but I hardly get to town at all these days.

Sometimes, while Sisu gets busy scaring grouse or finds some dead-smelling something to roll in, me and Katie end up on some mossy spot, making out, sometimes more, which is a whole different story than trying to manufacture a baby.

I run into Juri at Pamida. He tells the same joke he does every year in July, banging my shoulder, "Don't forget to buy a fifth on the third for the Fourth!" We have the whole family and some friends out for a barbeque. Finally the lake is warm enough to swim in, but the fireworks make me a little nervous until I realize I'm thinking about the moose—that if he's still living around here somewhere, I don't want him or his family getting too spooked.

Spending August out here makes me see why maybe some people would drop everything and move north. The bugs are about gone, and I'm no poet, but last week, after a storm rolled through, it left all the trees wet in the sun and the sky all black in the distance, and I could imagine that sights like that might put words into certain heads. Katie gave me *Walden* to read, by that guy.

Anyway, he's not too bad, and for sure knows a hundred different ways of describing lonely. I turn to where Katie is cooking, looking good even in those plaid boxers, and I think, Why didn't old Henry just get himself a wife?

By Labor Day I feel okay about the shape we're leaving the resort in—with the crappiest cabins and outbuildings gone, there's a lot less maintenance. Things look damn good, actually.

The couple at Wolftrap made it through their first season, and it doesn't look like they'll divorce or go bankrupt. Since nobody won the kitty, Sally Pavola bought them a gas grill with the money as a sort of sticking-it-out gift with all our names on the card.

The birch and tamarack have turned, so the woods are all mustard colored under blue sky on the day we're packing up to move back to town. Katie's looking through a calendar set to go into a box and says, "Wow. It's a year to the day we came here, hon."

"Well, let's celebrate, open a bottle of something. Hell, it's our last day in Vacationland."

"You know, I never could find out what the word *Naledi* means," Katie says. "I even asked the librarian, and we looked at an Ojibwe dictionary and some Lakota phrase books." She shrugs. "Guess it doesn't matter, now we're leaving, but . . ."

"But what?"

She's suddenly not listening or looking up anymore, only following her finger over the calendar, tracing dates, back and forth, between the weeks of July and August and now.

"Babe?"

"Yeah?" I say.

But she doesn't answer, only gets that look she gets when she's calculating mileage or balancing her checkbook, chewing her lip, making that dimple happen. In a minute she'll figure out what I figured out about a week ago.

I set my load of boxes down and get ready to catch her.

ADODGE VAN ROLLS TO A STOP AT THE CORNER OF PIKE and Main, and the doors slide to expel a tumble of brides in full regalia. Once deposited, they wrestle their dresses and veils apart and line up single file to proceed to the stoplight. Holding hands they sway across the street making a string of bright bells. Each white gown is paint-spattered in Toucan Sam colors—orange, fuchsia, and acid green, some more splotched than others. After the last bride is safely across, they bump down the sidewalk to the entrance to the Duckblind Lounge. Horns toot, drivers call out from car windows. The brides wave gleefully and gesture obscenely.

Jon Redleaf shades his eyes, wondering which is the actual bride-to-be, watching the procession from the bench outside the co-op, where he's settled in the company of a dog he does not know, drinking a Green Machine smoothie, and smoking the last Camel from his pack.

The facade of the Duckblind is painted camo, its door half-obscured by a curtain of fake reeds and netting. The brides take turns holding the net aside and squeeze through, tugging along their skirts of stained tulle.

Like moving canvases, Jon thinks—the name of that abstract artist nearly tipping his tongue. Bald, dead—made the sort of paintings that museum visitors shake their heads over, claiming their grandkids could do better with pudding and a wall to fling it at. The name has *J* and two syllables, he thinks. Jon's ready to confer with the next person who emerges from the co-op, but it's

Bertie Kangas, who pauses next to Jon as another bride gathers her skirts to extrude herself from outdoors to in.

Neither Bertie nor Jon takes his eyes from the scene.

"Hey," Bertie says, "you're not working?"

"Nah. Not till Tuesday. Waiting on a load of slate." Jon nods toward the bar.

Bertie hooks a thumb into his holster as the very last girl jams midway in the doorframe like a foamy cork. Someone pulls her from inside, and she's sucked into the dark with a squeal. "That's Tammy Vidinovich's bachelorette party. They been down to the new paintball field by the rifle range."

"Yeah?"

"Since the guys started doing it now for their stag parties, they wanna, too."

The Duckblind door shuts on a hem, prompting a muffled curse.

"Goddamn is right." Bertie looks at his watch.

"What's wrong?"

The door opens a crack and the hem is yanked clear.

"Aw, just wish I weren't on duty. Didja get a look at Kelly Rantala?"

"Hard to say, with the veils and all . . ."

Bertie climbs into his patrol car. "The one shot mostly orange." He sticks his head out the window while backing up. "Under that netting she's fuckin' hot."

After Bertie pulls away, Jon turns his attention to the dog near the bench. The day seems to have a white theme. Bred for sledding, with maybe a streak of wolf, given the length of its legs. The dog is pure white. It's obviously waiting for its owner, looking at the co-op door each time a customer emerges, rising on its haunches in anticipation, then lowering and blinking in mute disappointment. It's irises are the disconcerting hue of fissured ice. Though at first glance the dog seems indifferent to Jon, he knows it's tracking his every move, and when he makes a click with his tongue, it's blue gaze locks on him. The leash isn't attached to anything, just coiled on the sidewalk.

It looks docile enough, but when he stands he backs away as if departing the company of royalty, fishing out his truck keys.

Locking cars is only a recent necessity in Hatchet Inlet. To the annoyance of the chamber of commerce, most of the tourist season had been paralleled by a long rash of thefts—grand and petty, mostly car break-ins, then in August the night clerk at Pump-n-Munch was robbed at gunpoint and pistol-whipped. All the crimes have been attributed to strung-out crank heads—two in jail now since the discovery of a lab they'd been operating out of St. Birgitta's church kitchen on weekdays. Ever since, dark sedans, clearly unmarked, edge in from outside the township to slowly patrol with city narcs behind the tinted glass. To buy Sudafed these days you must present a driver's license to Molly at the prescription counter, and there are even security cameras in the bait shops, but at least things are quiet again. A number of honor students, including the sheriff's daughter, have been sweating it out downstate at Birchwood Teen House: they are the victims, Jon knows. According to his nephew Bear, those making the profits are still around, just laying low.

Tourists are mostly gone anyway, trickling away as the last leaves fall, as Hatchet Inlet gears down and the north wind rears up to start lashing. A couple of guys in bird-hunting vests slow at the windows of Lefty's Bait, and a few late-season hikers with backpacks head toward Pamida. Gimp Wuuri works his way along the sidewalk, bent nearly double, wearing the same greasy parka he wears in July and January, now topped with a plaid cap. As Gimp rounds the corner a gust propels him faster, his fingers almost to the pavement like he's chasing dropped coins.

Wind is the bane of Hatchet Inlet. Everyone carps about the founding fathers who idiotically settled the town on the highest and windiest spot for miles. Just a quarter-mile down the hill is the protected inlet that gives the town its name, where Jon's ancestors were ensconced long before the lumber barons clear-cut their way north. The inlet is ringed with abandoned warehouses, boathouses, and a marina, all fallen on hard times. The shabby houses and buildings dotting the slope are the most sheltered and have the best views. It doesn't matter those views are framed between broken pilings and leaning warehouses: the wrong side of Hatchet Inlet would be a developer's dream, if anyone would agree to sell.

The wind has blown a scrap of white satin to the pavement near Jon's boot. He traps it and picks it up, spattered orange and green.

Pollock, he remembers now, stuffing the cloth into his pocket, Jackson Pollock.

A Halloween display in the video store window features a cutout of Boris Karloff, which lures Jon in. Roaming the aisles he idly picks up the cases, scanning the blurbs and putting the misfiled DVDs back in correct order. In the end he picks *The Iron Lady, Kung Fu Panda,* and *Live Free or Die Hard.* At the counter, a plastic jack-o-lantern with cardboard arms holds a sign offering a free rental to anyone dressed as a character.

"Do I count?" Jon jokes to the boy behind the counter.

The youth peers up through oily bangs. "What? As Geronimo?" He taps the sign. "See? It says *film* character."

"Okay, okay." Jon turns away for a moment. When he turns back his braids are rolled like cinnamon buns over his ears. "There. Princess Leia."

The boy snorts, unsmiling, but types a new-release credit into Jon's account.

Back on the sidewalk he cannot think of any more ways to stall, so goes to his truck and drives home. Kam's car will be gone. Of course, he knows this before the garage door rolls up to reveal her empty space and the oil stain. Still, something in his neck tightens when he walks in and sees her house key on the kitchen table. The only clock in the house is on the microwave. She'll have reached St. Paul by now, probably at her family's restaurant, maybe even helping with dinner rush. He walks through the rooms to see the last of her things have been cleared—her gold plastic shrine and candles are gone, leaving clean shapes in the dust topping the television. Thin lines of incense ash lay over the glass stereo shelf. The Vietnamese films are gone, along with all seasons of *The Sopranos,* making toothy gaps between his own collections of *X Files, Wired,* and *24.* In the bedroom a tangle of hangers are strewn on Kam's side of the bed. He gathers them and hangs them back on the rod, watching them sway a moment before pushing them aside and spreading his own clothes across to fill the space.

Stepping back, his calves meet the mattress and he sits. The bamboo plant on her bedside table leans in its glass vase like a straw, the stones dry. Jon takes it to the kitchen to soak in the sink. "Don't blame her," he tells the plant while running the tap. "I don't."

Kam has left poached salmon and bok choy with black sesame for his dinner. While the dish rotates in the microwave, he bends into the fridge scanning all that she's left behind: rows of jars of pickled things he didn't know could be pickled, sauces and fermented bean pastes and oils labeled in her alphabet. In the cupboards are cellophane packets of twig-like items, shriveled peppers and pods, schools of mummified minnows, fetus-colored curls that might be shrimp, dried weeds, and roots, and threads of utterly unidentifiable but edible things. The kitchen had been her territory, Kam happiest when going at some bit of fish or a rubbery brick of tofu or joint of meat most Americans would never consider. From his recliner in front of CNN or the *PBS Newshour,* he would be aware of the kitchen rhythms, the chopping and humming, the smells of scallions, garlic, knobby ginger—the cleaver sometimes stuttering along so fast it sounded like mechanical teeth chattering; the thwack of poultry being deboned just as some story of another suicide bombing in Iraq blooms onto the screen. She'd dice and soak and peel and marinate, oblivious to the news, sometimes adding what looked to him like dried ears or fingers, tossing it all at the sizzle of the wok, adding pinches and dashes to her alchemy while nattering her vowelsome language into her Bluetooth, talking to someone from home, tethering.

In the hall closet next to his waders are feed-store-sized sacks of rice and clay pots big enough to cook whole animals in. Her rice cooker is on the counter, intentionally left for him. She'd taken the time to stuff his *Diabetes for Dummies* cookbook with extra sheets of her own recipes copied out in English, her handwriting so light it looks faded, as if she's already long gone.

While his dinner is cooling, Jon pulls out each recipe and blinks at the ingredients for dishes he'll never make; he's not deft with a knife and is too impatient to marinate or simmer anything. Had she actually imagined his fingers frilling closed those little dumplings? He sets the recipes on the recycle pile. He'll clear the fridge and cupboards later.

To avoid sitting across from an empty chair, he eats at the kitchen island, standing, flipping through an old copy of *North Nations*.

After Jon rolls the trash bin to the curb, clinking and heavy with packaged food and jars, he stands and looks back at the house in the dimming light, hesitating. It's been his home for twenty years—fixed up now, decently furnished, with a new roof. It's pleasant and neat as a pin. He walks away from it at speed, telling himself he needs the exercise. Other houses strung along the road have also been improved over recent years. Several neighbors have remodeled or added on—a few have even landscaped their yards. Some places look better if only for having the hulks of old cars and appliances hauled away. At a few driveways, mailboxes still lean and litter pocks the ditches. In those houses the change of fortune is more evident indoors, as blue light from eighty-inch Sony flat screens flicker and windowpanes shake with heavy notes from Bose speakers. Multiple satellite dishes sprout at the edges of roofs like haywire mushrooms.

Once Jon would look down this road and see need. Now he sees Ramchargers and Hummers weighing down the fresh gravel driveways, many with dream catchers dangling from the rearview mirrors. After the first year the casino made a profit, small allocations were made to band members, just a few hundred now and then for each family. Steadily, the amounts grew and became a monthly allotment; eventually the money became enough to live on. Kids that Jon once coached in softball who hadn't had proper jackets now have iPhones and trick bikes. They own everything they think they need and see no compelling reason to learn much—half-believe they already know everything.

He looks down the road. It won't last. It all has a price; it's just that at the moment others are paying it. Jon has stood up in council to balk at services the casino offers—free day care, buffet lunches, and shuttle service in Lucky Feather vans. The takers tend to be mostly widows, single mothers, and laid-off miners who can least afford to gamble. Jon has suggested, and then implored, insisting there are better alternatives, like bringing charters in from Duluth or Fort Frances, leaving the locals alone. He's not making many friends these days, not by challenging elders in council meetings and raising his voice about shitting in their own backyards. Despite profits, Jon doesn't see the band is any better off than it was seven years ago. So far, money hasn't lowered addiction rates—though Bear has assured him that the Indian kids are at least taking better drugs than some white classmates who are mired in cheap meth. Some measures Jon has fought for have at least been implemented: a new drug and alcohol counselor has been lured away from Birchwood by a significant salary, and they are considering bringing in serious college recruiters and have promised to load another scholarship program. Nobody sees how tenuous the present is: the casino is overbuilt, profits are leveling and beginning to tip along with the economy—the whole endeavor is a gamble itself, unsustainable.

He walks fast for more than a mile, as far as the county road, listening over the past few hundred yards as a drone of distant sirens grows. A third siren starts up. By the nearness of it Jon reckons it is coming from the auxiliary garage where the township's second ambulance is housed. As he reaches the stop sign and peers down the road, the noise lessens, shifts, and his shoulders release. Whatever has gone wrong enough to warrant multiple rescue vehicles has occurred miles from the reservation. Jon checks his watch. Bear works lunches at the Lucky Feather and would have been off his shift hours ago, certainly home by now and off the roads. He fingers his cell phone, fighting the urge to hit speed dial.

Kam would say he's a mother hen. She would remind him the nest is empty now, adding her unique translation of an old adage, "Stop opening your blouse for the chick." And though she'd spoiled Bear some herself, she was right: he's grown, even has his own place in town, which he keeps clean enough. He hasn't driven his car into the Wikawashi or knocked up some white girl. He's doing fine. The thought of Kam on the road makes Jon even more nervous because she's a shitty driver, admitting herself that shitty Asian driver clichés don't come from thin air, tapping her forehead: "Maybe we got some crooked gene to make us lousy drivers." Hopefully she'd be home by now, too. She'd never given up her apartment next door to the family's restaurant—a one-bedroom that in her absence has been occupied by one of the chain of seemingly interchangeable ancient aunts. Ten of her cousins, a few aunts, and one uncle all occupy the apartment building the family bought after the restaurant took off. After it was awarded in *CityReader*'s best-of poll, the family took the honor literally and renamed it Best Vietnamese in a sort of unintentional marketing coup, for invariably the question "Where's the best Vietnamese restaurant?" is one often asked in St. Paul.

Jon met Kam the summer he was staying in the capital for several weeks, contracted to restore a spiraled chimney on a historic building near the cathedral. Each morning he stopped at the same place on University Avenue to get his iced coffee. Next door was the restaurant, and next to that was Kiki Nail, where Kam worked her second job, managing the place and keeping tabs on the young manicurists who sat outside on upturned plastic buckets when there were no customers. When he happened by, they never failed to tease him, calling out things like "Big Chief," or holding up their palms like movie Indians to say, "How," and giggle. He would only wink and raise his thermos in response. Kam never joined in, only rolled her eyes as if to apologize for her incorrigible employees.

One July afternoon when Jon was getting ready to head west to the annual Sun Dance, he'd come out of the coffee shop literally dragging his foot. Kam was outside the nail shop fanning herself with a menu. When she saw him, she let the fan fall, frowning.

"You limping. Why?"

"I'll be okay. Just dropped a brick on my foot."

Actually, it was a cornerstone, thrice the size of a brick. The injury was his own fault—eager to get on the road he'd changed from his steel-toed Redwings into cowboy boots, promptly fumbled, and now was paying for it. The pressure was tempting him to pour the iced coffee down his boot.

Kam stood. "How big?"

"What?"

"The stone. How big?"

He formed his hands around an imaginary shoebox.

"You better come in. Maybe some ice and a good soak."

He looked at the door of Kiki Nail, then down the street. "Thanks, but nah. I . . . have a dance thing I need to get to."

"Not *nah,* say *yeah.* How you gonna dance with a bad foot? Only ten minutes, anyway, and no charge for first aid." She had him by the arm then, and he allowed himself to be pulled inside and pressed into an aqua vinyl chair next to a churning footbath. When his boot was pried off they both winced at the swelling and the bruise spanning the top of his instep. Their heads were close, both looking down where her own sandaled, delicate foot was dwarfed by his somewhat hairy 13-D, the big toenail already darkening.

"No dancing with that."

"Not really a dance-dance. A Sun Dance."

"Wait here. I'm going next door for ice."

"Really, don't bother."

"Just there at our restaurant. No bother, because I insist."

When his foot was iced, it brought such relief his eyes misted. Once he was numb and his arches cooled with Tiger Balm, she swiveled him to the footbath, where she made him soak for half an hour with some sort of leaf that smelled like burnt hair wrapped around the bruise. He was half asleep when she talked him into a pedicure. When he opened his eyes, he couldn't stop laughing. His toenails were painted, each a different color: black, green, red, nearly the range of the beads on the chaps he'd be wearing the next day, a garment he reluctantly dragged out once a year. Jon always felt a bit like a gatecrasher at Sun Dance.

Well, if he was going to embarrass himself, he might as well do it in color. "Do you have any white?" He was thinking of the bleached porcupine quills on his vest.

She plucked up a bottle of Frosty Pearl. "This?"

"Perfect."

Obviously, there was no putting his boots back on, and Kam giggled while trying to stretch the largest pair of foam flip-flops onto his feet.

He shook his head. "I can't go anywhere like this."

"No, maybe not. You gotta dry. You hungry?"

Without waiting for an answer, Kam picked up his boots, and he had no choice but to follow. She was tall for an Asian, the top of her head nearly to his collarbone. They went out the alley door and into the next building, through a hall with crates of vegetables haloed by fruit flies, ending up in a glaring, steaming kitchen. A number of women in varying stages of old looked up incredulously at Jon while Kam yipped and yawwed at them over the din of chopping and frying and clanging metal. The women looked at his feet and held up their big spoons and dripping bamboo paddles to hide their tittering.

He was steered through the busing station to the dining room and into a booth. Kam slipped in across, and while the polish on his toes dried, she insisted he tell her about Sun Dance.

As covered dishes appeared from the kitchen, Jon described the fasting. Kam plucked lids to reveal deboned chicken wings stuffed with translucent noodles, broken rice with grilled shrimps topped with fried eggs oozing yolk, and little salt-crusted fishes roasted in banana leaves. The bowl of rice was enough for six.

He told her about the hours under the sun, the exhaustion

and hunger that trigger the visions for those who claim to have them. "Delirium, mostly."

"But why do they dance? For the crops? For ancestors?"

Her questions shamed Jon a little for his indifference. He told what he knew, and when he'd finished Kam nodded.

"Yeah, we have shaman, too . . . and a ritual in the mountains where the men drink hallucination tea made from root, but only the men get to drink it, which is really bullshit."

They both laughed. Before he left she made him bend to her level so she could compare the length of their braids.

That was three years ago.

Approaching the house he sees Bear's Grand Am parked in the drive. Jon stops in the driveway near the side porch and peers through the window as bats seethe in the eaves. Bear is at the kitchen table, studying recipes he's plucked from the recycling.

He lets the back door slam to let Bear know he's home. While Jon's clogging mud onto the mat, Bear leans back in his chair to poke his head into the hall, waving a recipe. "Why you throwing these recipes out?"

"Why are *you* reading other people's garbage?"

"Thought I'd come cheer you up. Besides, I got news."

Jon sees the envelope sticking out of the boy's shirt pocket. Bear grins. "I got accepted. I'm going."

Since dropping out of the vo tech catering program (because it was for morons), Bear had been working at the Lucky Feather. When not matchsticking root vegetables or whipping roux, he's glued to the Food Channel or experimenting with recipes for the sort of dishes Jon's diet doesn't allow. He'd applied to the Culinary Institute of America—the CIA, which gets a laugh every time.

"I'm going, man."

Jon eases the acceptance letter from the envelope and holds it up to the light to see the official watermark. "So you are."

He reads all three pages. The third requires a signature from a parent or guardian for students under twenty-one. He pats his pockets, and when Bear hands him a pen their eyes meet for a moment. Jon has been Bear's legal guardian since he was ten.

One winter afternoon, Jon's big sister June dropped by with Bear in tow and asked Jon to baby-sit. No biggie, he'd done it often enough, never really minding unless it messed up his own plans. Besides, he liked the kid a lot. But that time it did mess up his plans more than usual, with June promptly disappearing for two months. Cops were no help, and he heard a few rumors, but no real word until the call from Hennepin County Medical, where she'd been taken. As far as Bear has ever known, it was pneumonia. As far as explaining away the two-month absence preceding his sister's overdose, Jon had even less imagination, coming up with some story so awkward he can barely remember it. And though Bear has surely guessed, there seems to be an unspoken agreement to not dissect history—in much the same manner they don't acknowledge the eventuality that once Bear is off to California, his chances of returning to the reservation are probably nil.

Jon looks back over the second page, an invoice, reading the amount for tuition and whistling, though he's been well aware of the cost all along and has squirreled away most of his allotments for the past two years for Bear's education. Each semester at the CIA averages fourteen grand, and room and board is extra. "I guess that's the difference between a cook and a chef," he says, pretending to need the counter to sign the consent form, enabling him to turn away as he moves the pen forward.

"Yeah." Bear is out of his chair and bent into the fridge, frowning at the bare shelves. "Speaking of money, you ready to lose some more?"

"Cribbage? Soon as I sign off on you here. Maybe I'll win my dignity back after last week's skunk."

"Maybe you won't. Any Coke besides diet?"

"Nope." Jon sets the papers on the table while Bear pours soda into glasses.

"Two out of three, right?"

"Bring it."

While Jon deals, the far drone of sirens commences again—the return trip. Jon picks up his own cards and shifts in his chair, trying to concentrate on what to throw in the crib.

Bear taps the Formica. "Ah, *today?*"

"Keep your pants on." He thumbs a pair of threes until the sirens have faded. He slaps them facedown, immediately realizing he's made the wrong choice. "Dammit."

Jon loses the first game. By the middle of the second it's looking grim.

Bear doesn't raise his head when he says, "I went by Wok in the Woods after my shift. It's already cleared out."

Jon tried to sound casual. "New owner reopens next month. It's gonna be a pizza place."

Bear shrugs. "Maybe that'll do better."

"You'd think so." Jon plays a whole run to thirty-one before adding, "It's hard here."

"No shit." Bear shrugs. "Well, I have her e-mail, anyway."

"Yeah, that'd be nice for her—you two have that food thing going . . . she'll want to hear all about California." Jon rallies and wins by just two points after scoring a double run. "Looks like you owe me five bucks." He holds out his hand.

"Dumb luck." Bear already has his wallet out.

Jon pushes the bill into his jeans pocket, feeling the stained satin he'd plucked from the sidewalk that afternoon.

Bear squints at him. "Amused by my misfortune?"

Jon shakes his head. "Just something I saw today."

He follows Bear to his car with a fifty-pound sack of rice hoisted on his shoulder. When the sack thuds into the open trunk, Jon thinks of scenes from *The Sopranos*.

Bear crams the rice cooker in next to it. "You'll come visit?"

"Who wouldn't. Napa Valley?"

"Like, a ya-uh?"

"Please. When do you leave?"

"Three weeks."

"I can drive out with you. We'll get a hell of a lot more of your crap into my truck than this thing."

"But you'll still come out for Christmas, right? Sunny California—no snow?"

"Maybe."

Bear clips his seatbelt, nodding at the house. "You could move, you know. At least off the rez."

Jon shrugs and raps the half-open window. "You better skedaddle."

After Bear's car recedes into the dark, Jon pauses in the narrow space between the garage and house and looks up to the lane of stars showing between the eaves. One bat swoops out after another. He takes a pebble from the ground and twists it tightly into the cellophane from his cigarette pack, like a hard candy. He tosses it straight up into the darkening sky. From nowhere a bat arcs under it, then makes a tinny screech as if angered by the ruse. As his eyes adjust, Jon can see many more bats are out. He catches and tosses the weighted wrapper repeatedly, watching the bats navigate by echolocation—veering, diving, steering by the reach of their own sounds. Or however the hell they do it. He shrugs at the notion—of getting where you need to go, finding what you need to live by simply listening to your own noise.

Closing his eyes and slowly turning, he says, "Testing, testing," and turns back and does it again, experiencing a barely audible shift in the sounds—slightly deepened when he's facing the garage wall—lighter when he's facing the street. He plays with tilting his voice down to the pavement, then up to the sky. He tries to make bat noises, but they only crack comically in his throat. There was that program about a blind boy in England who navigated just like a bat with freakish accuracy, able to tell whether he was passing a lamppost or a tree, a bench or a bin. The Bat Boy . . .

He tries singing. There's not much music in him, he's never able to remember lyrics, and he is pretty much tone-deaf. But this one song his grandfather taught him—Jon can almost remember every word, cannot translate it exactly—something about the hunting moon. He nods, singing in a monotone, turning and keeping cadence at the same time—just able to keep his balance with both eyes shut. Jon listens hard to his own voice. It kind of works—he might not be able to tell how far he is from something, but he can tell when his song encounters something solid. Concentrating on the echo, he pays no attention to the words, of the hunter hampered by clouds, his faith flagging. After the hunter goes hungry awhile, he must humble himself and ask the night sky to open its gate of clouds—and it does, revealing stars and a hunter's moon, bright enough that arrows flung from his bow can find their marks as easily as in the wide light of day.

Ah, there, again. He knows he's facing the garage—listening so hard he can actually hear the wall. He can.

Huh.

In the morning Jon drives in to meet Rob and Tim Perla at Pavola's. They find a booth big enough to spread a plan of the construction site, and after their eggs and coffee they finalize details for a job up on Olson Point; an outdoor kitchen with a thirty-foot stone wall, a wood-fire oven, and a five-hundred square foot terraced slate patio. While Jon thinks the scale is way out of whack and the choice of stone is wrong for the site, he doesn't complain. He could use a concentrated bout of work. As they pore over the materials list, no one mentions the wisdom of spending thirty grand on a glorified barbecue pit. Contractors do not question the desires of summer people, for folly accounts for a fair percentage of income for Jon and the Perla brothers and others like them.

The job starts in a week, with a day or two of prep before the materials arrive. After laying out and leveling the site, Jon will set down layers of fine gravel and sand and roll them before the real work can begin—the part he looks forward to, which is hardly work—more like something he watches his hands do, the stone in his hands, his mind slowing to allow the line and contours of each flagstone or slab to determine his next move, allowing the material to take over.

"Okay, then." Rob nods and stamps Jon's bid and slides it across the table. "In the meantime, if you're up for a drive, I got a call from Naledi Lodge. Katie and me were caretakers out there the year before Kirsten was born. Rebuild on a flint hearth, and the owner's pretty picky, so I told her I'd get you."

"Flint? You don't see that everyday." Jon clamps the Post-it to his clipboard without looking at it. "Maybe tomorrow."

He's draining his coffee when Tim sits back. "You heard about the accident?"

"Last night?"

"About eight-ish."

"I heard the sirens. Bad one?"

"That railroad bridge on 77? Two girls who'd been over at the Duckblind all afternoon wrapped their van around the supports."

Jon stiffens. "Dressed like brides?"

Rob nods. "Yeah, that's what Katie said. From the look of the van they had to be going ninety. One of the Rantala twins and Jessica Wiirtinen. Both DOA."

"Jesus Christ."

"I guess their blood alcohol levels were to the moon, so between that and the impact they probably didn't suffer much. Katie says, anyway, if that's anything."

Tim sighs. "Something, I guess."

"But . . ," Jon shifts, "but still."

Tim holds his cup up so Sissy can see he needs a refill. "I guess Bertie Kangas went apeshit on one of the EMTs and broke his jaw in the ER. So he's on leave now."

Jon automatically primes his jeans pocket for his lighter before remembering that Pavola's, like everywhere else, is smoke free now. He shoves it back with the strip of cloth and thumbs the satin, rasping it along his calluses. They all sit a minute longer, and when Sissy drops the check on the table no one teases her, and she does not harp or shoo them like usual. In fact, now that

Jon looks around to the counter and other booths, he sees every-body's pretty well clammed up.

After adding his share of dollars to the pile, Jon stands, des-perate now for a cigarette. "Maybe I'll drive out to Naledi after all. I could use the air."

Once in the truck, he eases out the cloth to see he's thumbed most of the paint deep into the fibers and it's no longer white. Carefully smoothing it over the steering wheel, he rerolls it like a bandage before starting the engine and repockets it. He can feel the hard little roll at the juncture of his hip each time he raises his foot for the clutch.

He slips an Alison Krauss disc into the player and settles in. The drive up the northeast side of the lake is rougher than he remembers, though with the leaves gone it's easier to watch for deer, and he diligently scans the woods beyond the ditches on either side of the road. He passes blind driveways and memorizes mile markers where signs should be planted for CURVE or SLOW. Traveling at the posted speed, it takes nearly fifty minutes; by the time he turns onto the road to Naledi, songs have begun to repeat. Passing St. Gummarus summer camp, he notes that the cobblestone pillars could use some shoring up, the mortar's fall-ing out in chunks. Past the camp, the road dips close to the shore, the lake surface glinting through the trees. If he squints, he can see the narrows that open onto Ontario waters.

Just as he's thinking he'll run out of road soon, he sees the sign. He slows to a crawl and peers through a stand of pine at the peninsula where two old cabins sit—palisade log with sag-ging porches and cedar roofs in need of replacement. The lines are true enough, though, and both look like they've stood longer than expected. The drive leads slightly inland to a clearing, a cir-cular drive centered by a log gazebo doing duty as a woodshed. Down the path is the lodge.

When he takes the first porch step, a large-sounding dog barks from somewhere within. He doesn't bother knocking, just takes off his cap and waits on the steps as the tapping of claws approaches followed by the harder sound of footfalls. Through the porch windows Jon is surprised to see the white mixed breed he'd seen at the co-op the day before. On its own turf now, it seems more deliberate, clear-eyed, lanky as a timber wolf.

He's heard the lore about spirit dogs—the animal guide of the true teachers that have some connection to the moon and to all feminine energy of the natural world. Whatever the story, it was bound to contain some lesson and significance, but Jon's never much leaned to the plinky side of his heritage. This dog is just a dog—intelligent, but with a stare that might make someone believe something.

Owing to the name on his bid order, Margaret Machutova, he expects a widow and so has girded himself for a tedious meeting with bad coffee and unnecessary small talk. The inner door to the kitchen is suddenly filled by the face of a woman close to his own age, with a mop of curly, rust-red hair. She nods him into the porch and takes a firm hold of the dog's collar. Jon steps in and blinks at her white, paint-stained smock, wondering for a beat whether she has some connection to the dead wedding-dress girls, if she's paying some homage to them, but then he sees the wet paintbrush in her other hand and it clicks. Given her look of impatience, Jon can assume he's interrupted her work.

"Hello?"

"Jon Redleaf." He holds up his clipboard. "I'm the mason."

"Oh, right." Her face relaxes and the dog sits, cocking its head at Jon. He holds out his hand.

She wiggles fingers to show they are too paint-covered to shake. "Meg Machutova. And this is Ilsa." At the sound of the name the dog's ears pique.

He leans in to pet. "We've met, actually."

"Yeah?"

"You were in the co-op yesterday?"

"Yes," Meg nods, "we were."

Jon peers into the lodge. "Should we take a look?"

She leads him through the kitchen, stopping to set her paintbrush in the freezer. "Oil," she explains. They cross a dining area cluttered with boxes open to art supplies and books, pottery, blankets. Jon nods. "You moving in, or out?"

"Um, in-ish, I suppose, for now. I'm staying straight through this year." She seems tentative, as if still deciding. "I've never stayed a whole winter."

"Well, you should be all right. You've got quite a woodpile."

She's pleased someone's noticed. "I do. Took two months to split it."

"You have a plow? A snow machine?"

Meg gives him a curious look. "I do, and a rifle, and flares . . ."

"Sorry," Jon apologizes. "I'm told I'm a bit of a mother hen . . ."

"S'all right. There's probably some kitty in town wagering I won't make it."

He chuckles because there probably is. As she leads him to the hearth she goes on, half-joking, but not quite, as if running through the list for herself, ". . . generator, topped off the propane . . ." She stops and turns to Jon, "A car battery. Two weeks is about the longest anyone has ever been stranded out here. And this is the fireplace."

The hearth is wide and spans half the wall. It's chocolate gun-flint, not a common stone. Jon runs his hands over the surface, using a fingernail to chip a tiny bit of mortar. He sniffs the mortar before setting it to his tongue.

Meg toes a loose corner piece. "See?"

"Yup." A dozen or more stones are missing. He squats and pokes deeper at the mortar with a small retractable pick. "Where'd they go?"

"Who knows?" she shrugs. "Taken to use as doorstops or bookends . . . to weigh things down."

Jon shakes his head. "Too bad. It would be an easy job, I could do it in a day, but to find any pieces to match . . ."

"Oh, there's more. Just up where the oldest cabins were. I'll show you."

He follows her out of the lodge and along the shore where

they pass the two cabins he'd seen earlier. The first one looks casually tended, but the second has an air of abandonment, with roof shakes missing, the logs dry and gray. The support pilings barely hold up a porch that juts over the water like a pontoon. The cabin is canted north, with a view of the narrows and border waters.

"You letting that go?"

Meg shrugs. "I had an ad in the *Trapline* all summer, but nobody seems to want to live this far out, so yeah, I might have to. It'll cost less to tear it down than get it up to code to rent it. You know old resorts."

"I 'spose." He looks back over his shoulder. "Still."

They climb a steep path that opens to a plateau where the old foundations of three buildings embrace empty squares of grass. At a corner of each foundation is a pile of mossy rubble where the chimneys have fallen. The stones are roughly the size of egg cartons. He cleans one on his sleeve, digs out another, and nods. The flint is heavy stone that fractures squarely, with a natural sheen. "Yeah, these are perfect, actually." He sniffs a chunk of mortar. "Same mason as did your hearth?"

"My grandfather."

He looks up. "I could come tomorrow with the proper mortar."

"Great."

Her jacket is open to her paint-stained smock. He asks, "You know this painter, Pollock?"

"Jackson Pollock? Sure. Of course."

"You like his stuff?"

"Um. I do, actually."

Halfway back to the lodge she stops at a fork in the path and nods toward a spruce grove. "You want to go in?"

"In?"

"Shame to come all this way and not. Besides, you might get too busy tomorrow. It's been awhile . . ."

"Awhile?" He blinks at her.

"Since any of you have come out. Maybe even since my grandfather was around, so that's what . . . twenty years? Billy Longbow used to, maybe twice a year, and Ed Friday . . . but I imagine they're long gone, too?"

She has named elders dead for many years. He opens his mouth just as she nods again down the path. "Go on ahead if you want. Coffee's already made, so . . . just stop back to the lodge with your bid after."

He shrugs and aims himself down into the copse, thinking, "Whatever." Whatever is down this path that brought Eddie and Billy all this way would maybe be worth a smoke and a walk to stretch his legs . . .

After a quarter-mile of black spruce and a slow incline, the path rounds a hump of granite and ramps steeply downward. It's a descent into the shade of a cliff, the air as cold as the stone it parallels. At the low point of the path he is drawn by smells of cedar and peat, the air growing damper by degrees as he walks into a narrow space where outcroppings of stone nearly meet above his head. Jon crouches along, ducking to clear a brief funnel of darkness that opens to dim light and a view that stops him in his tracks.

Before him spreads a cathedral-sized glade, heavily shaded by old-growth cedar and white pine, with only a few streaks of sky breaking through heavy canopy. The absence of sound is so complete Jon wriggles his jaw, thinking his ears have plugged. Across the expanse, tree trunks thick as columns separate low hillocks. The burial mounds are covered by a dozen types of moss in as many shades, from pale pea color to dark billiard green, fuzzing up along curved cedar trunks like sweater sleeves.

A pileated woodpecker hops up the bark of a white cedar and latches itself on, looking as prehistoric as the glade feels, its red crest brilliant against the velvet dim. Making his way slowly toward the center of the burial ground, Jon knows he's near water—he can smell it, hears it trickling, and stops a few times trying to locate its source.

Noting the almost perfect uniformity of the small hills and the equal distances between them, he stops, turns, and turns again. He counts the mounds and measures them by walking the dimensions. Assessing the width and breadth of the glade, he ticks the information to memory and tries to gauge a reading of true north, but with so little sunlight it isn't possible.

Of course. He'd known there was such a place, that it was somewhere up this way, but his whole life the notion of a burial ground has never conjured up anything like the word *sacred*. To him, only *windblown* and *desolate* came to him, gray words painting their own picture. But this . . .

He leans into the silence, absently rubbing the satin in his pocket. Every sound is absorbed. Though his eyes are open, a second layer of vision overlays what he's seeing. The Dodge minivan's doors opening toward him on the street, girls dressed like brides in tulle blooming forth like peonies opening.

Jon smells the saturated green of the glade and imagines dusk, and a ribbon of black—the road the brides would have traveled, the tight curve. He feels something in his chest shift, thunk to the left, and settle. His eyes are wide, his view a panorama. The slow-motion spray of windshield glass and lace, veils and arms spread wide, wing-like as they burst from the wreckage. Virgins sailing, shedding glass like glitter in contrails behind them. They fly skimming through the copse of chalk-white birches with feathered sleeves, green garlands, and skeins of ivy twining from the trees to adorn them.

The moment is buoyant. Jon himself lifts as the flock of two girls take wing, aim skyward, break through the canopy, and are off.

He stands still for several minutes, waiting, but there is nothing else, only the green, the feeling of green, the smell of it—enveloping him. Jon's hand is fast in his pocket, tight around the cloth. He fishes it out and tears it into two strips using his teeth. Carefully, he lays the pieces down on the moss in a cross pattern because he supposes they might have been Christians. He makes sure the clean side is up, the white side—the color of forgetting.

He digs in another pocket for cigarettes and breaks open a Camel Straight, making a little pile of tobacco over the strips of satin.

Hopefully, they didn't know what hit them. He backs away from his small offering. Maybe they left themselves upon impact, maybe, Jon thinks, they flew from their bodies feeling only speed and cool air and the thrill of flight.

A PRY BAR CLUTCHED IN ONE FIST, THE OTHER PLANTED on her brand-new hip, Ursa Olson steps back to assess her handiwork, pleased by what she'd been able to accomplish with only a few tools and indignation. Stripping her kitchen to the studs wasn't something she'd thought through. Simply, she began doing it, and when it became difficult, or her limbs complained, she'd grab some lever or the sawsall or the tube of Bengay.

It began early, when she was supposed to be in town for physical therapy. She wasn't because Kip Karjala was supposed to drive her and called to say his car was making the same noise again. Ursa offered to limp the half-mile over to look under his hood, but Kip said, "Yeah, Ursa? That would kinda defeat the purpose, wouldn't it?"

No matter. She could drive herself, having finally found the car keys in the flour canister where Carina had hidden them. Clever on Carina's part, Ursa had to admit, given the odds she would ever bake anything. Her daughter was not usually clever—in fact, Carina was quite unformed in many ways despite her age, despite being a card-carrying member of AARP.

Ursa settles behind the wheel. The Olds 88 is an automatic, her hip is nearly healed, and she rarely uses the brakes anyway. But before she can even turn the key, a huge pickup coasts down the drive and stops in the loop, blocking her way. Its door is painted with a logo of a beaver clutching a handsaw, perched on a mound of wood shavings. Ursa hoists herself out and waits until Larry Perla's son, what's-his-name, walks over with a clip-board and a tape measure.

"Rob," he reminds her when she asks.

Assuming Carina had called him about the dryer vent, Ursa leads him back to the house and gets busy making instant cof-fee. It's already after eight and too late for the clinic anyway. She digs a donut from the depths of the breadbox while the kettle boils.

After walking all the way around the foundation, Rob bangs in and wipes his feet. She hears him set his tape measure down on the table, and when she turns she sees he's also spread flat a set of blueprints. Ursa sighs. Dummy. He'd meant to go next door, where an old cabin like hers had been razed and was being replaced by a new behemoth. She bangs the kettle back onto the hob. "Goddammit. Now I've missed my appointment because here you've stopped at the wrong place."

"I don't think so, Mrs. Olson." He holds out his clipboard. "You're fire number 3958?"

"That's right, but you're still wrong." Ursa hands him the do-nut and claps powdered sugar from her hands.

He pauses. "Look, here's the work order. For *this* house."

"What work order?" She elbows in next to him.

"For the remodel?"

"What remodel?"

He nods at the blueprints. "This one." First he points with the donut since there's no place set it, then slips it into a pocket of his Carhartt. He runs a sugary finger over the thin white lines of the blueprints, showing Ursa how existing rooms of the house would be expanded, how the thicker lines represented new rooms altogether.

"This house? You're certain?"

"Yes, ma'am. See?" He taps the corner where names were printed, Ray and Carina Olson.

"Carina?"

"Your daughter."

"Jesus wept, I know who she is." The vein near Ursa's temple thumps, reminding her she hadn't taken her Diovan. She leans over the prints and demands that Rob explain in detail. He does, tracing the blueprints as he speaks. The sunroom addition will poke out toward the lake like a glass ship: a new master suite with his and hers bathrooms added to the west side, along with a den for Ray and sewing room for Carina. With the great room/kitchen and mudroom, the expansion would bloat the house to three times its current size.

Rob puffs up a little himself. "Twenty-five hundred square feet."

"Oh?" Ursa inhales slowly through her nose.

He rolls the last blueprint away to reveal a colored rendering. In glowing hues, the expanded house along with the grounds appears wholly unreal and soft edged, as if the artist had been drugged with mushrooms, or was Thomas Kinkade. "That color," she taps a grouping of flowering shrubs, "does not exist at this latitude."

So that is Carina's dream house, Ursa thinks. A fairy tale house plunked down over her cabin like a pretty shell over a nut. Carina had promised the place would barely change a bit—that she and Ray might make a few repairs and maybe think of renovating in a few years. Looking at the blueprints, it is obvious they'd been at it for months—getting bids, having the plans drawn up. They would've had contractors crawling all over the place. But the only time she'd been away from the house was during her hip surgery and days in the hospital.

"Christ on a bike," Ursa mutters. "I've been hoodwinked."

Rob straightens. "Pardon?"

"This takes the cake."

Rob grins. "Doesn't it?"

She ignores him. Even at her bedside, Carina had repeated that things would be much the same—Ursa's bedroom, for instance, would be kept as is for when she visited. And she would visit. Not to see her shabby old house or her daughter, but to fish from the dock or sit with Cassi over the Scrabble board in the workshop.

Ursa doesn't see much of her great-granddaughter because the girl's mother is always too busy to bring Cassi up from Minneapolis. Ara and her husband teach yoga or *tie-chee* or whatever Buddhist-monk business they do that leaves her so thin and twitchy, and him so gassy from the Euell Gibbons diet and all those fermented teas that smell of compost.

Rob nods out the window to the stand of old growth pine. "Kind of a shame about those, though. Five, maybe six will have to come down."

Ursa blinks at him. "Say again?"

Between the house and the lake, several dozen red and white pine tower over a slope of orange needles and brown cones. In the sixty years since Ursa arrived at the cabin as a bride, she has watched these trees grow from impressive to stately. She had tracked their growth annually, using the old Swedish logger's method, multiplying the length of the trees' shadows by her height, then dividing the resulting number by the length of her shadow. These measurements are scratched in the wood of the boathouse door along with dates, a sort of diary of trees. Most had grown only an inch or so in the '49 drought, but over the wet spring and summer of '56 they shot up well over a foot, and so on. At the millennium, the last measurements taken, many were nearing ninety and a hundred feet. Curled photos of those struck by lightning or blown over in storms are tacked to the boathouse wall in memoriam, with the dates of their demise inked—eleven in total lost, five alone to the Fourth of July storm of '99.

The trees shield the house from the wind, shade the roof against heat, and wick humidity in the dog days of July and August. The breeze through the needles makes companionable hisses so precise in their varied tones that Ursa can practically guess the wind speed by the sound.

She looks suddenly to Rob but then realizes the groan had come from her. "Cut down?"

"Yeah. To MAKE room." He is employing that voice as if she were challenged. "For the SUNROOM," he repeats. "But this here kitchen where we're standing stays pretty much as IT IS. Ray tells me it's Carina's favorite room, so . . . we'll only just blow out that ONE WALL THERE."

Ursa looks to the wall he would "BLOW OUT" and turns back to ask flatly, "You got any kids, Bob?"

"Rob." He shrugs, digs for his wallet, and extracts a Sears portrait of a very pretty wife flanked by two equally pretty pubescent girls holding soccer balls and wearing shiny short-shorts and knee pads—the sort of picture a pedophile would go batshit over. Rob taps the photo. "That's my Katie, and there's Kirsten and Katrina."

"Well, enjoy them now, young man. Enjoy them now." She hands the photo back and eases the work order from the clipboard.

He begins to roll up the blueprints and color rendering. "It'll be something, don't you think?"

"It will," Ursa tears the work order in half, "over my dead body. This house and land are still my property, at least for the next ninety days." She opens the door. "You're trespassing now, Robby Perla. Vamoose."

She barely hears the truck door slam or Rob's tires spitting gravel, occupied as she is surveying the kitchen top to bottom. What might well be Carina's favorite room is still hers. Granted, to Ursa the kitchen is merely a place to collect meals that she usually eats elsewhere, either from the TV tray by her reading chair in the porch or the workshop, where her plaid lounger faces the Magnavox. Under the clutter and grime, the kitchen is a well-crafted room, so sturdy it could have been constructed by a WPA crew, built when *built* actually meant something. The maple cabinets, aged to a molasses sheen, are hand-hewn and have forged iron hasps. Next to them an *L* of windows with thick old glass that warps views of the lake in a dozen different ways. The copper sink with its sloped drainage ramps is deep enough

to drown a litter, and the black range has two ovens, six burn-
ers, and yards of chrome badly in need of polish. The oak floor
is half-covered with the original red linoleum rug, pinned down
by aluminum strips screwed tight with old floor wax and food.
Heavy nickel light fixtures were refitted from propane to electric
after the war, though Ursa rarely uses them since it's easier to flip
on the brighter fluorescents she'd hung in the '60s.

True enough, the kitchen was once Carina's domain. Since
she was seven or eight and old enough to hold a match to the
pilot, Carina had been the unofficial cook and bottle-washer in
the Olson household—even before Ursa had gone back to work
after Lars died. Carina still cannot be in the house more than a
few minutes before grabbing some sponge or the Comet, raising
her white eyebrows at Ursa's housekeeping, particularly around
the stove, as if grease were a personal affront.

Carina has recently retired from teaching Home Ec, which is
called something else these days, and now has ample time on her
hands—never good, Ursa thinks, for someone so uncomplicated.
She looks out to the scaly pine trunks, thinking of her daughter,
whom she supposes she must love but does not admire in the way
she admires the trees.

Her daughter claimed she wanted to preserve the cabin, keep
it rustic. And rustic she'll get, Ursa sniffs—she can build a castle
here, but there will always be a sand-point well, voles, and shallow septic.

When Carina hinted the diamond-willow furniture and
lamps wouldn't look right in Ursa's new apartment, Ursa agreed
for once and said, "Keep it all." Ray took her shopping for more
fitting replacements in Duluth, where she discovered Slumber-
land sold more than just beds. Never once lifting a price tag, she
chose a new dresser, a sleeper couch with a matching chair, and a
maple dining set for two—the old oak trestle table that had been
built for the cabin would never fit anywhere else. Her son-in-law
paid for it all and didn't bat an eye and didn't act like he was doing her some great favor either, so she gave him that.

Recalling Carina's nasal trill, "You can't take it with you, Mother," Ursa turns to the round-shouldered Norge. "Bullshit," she says to the refrigerator. "Just watch me."

She packs up the mishmash of dishes and cast-iron pans into milk crates, not bothering to wrap or pad any of it, dragging crates one by one to the garage, then comes back with a wheelbarrow. Drawers of utensils are emptied into a laundry basket heaped over with mixing bowls and baking tins. She carts out the toaster oven, the Mixmaster, and a waffle iron not used since Nixon. On the counter are a dozen Mason jars and Arco cans weighted with years of pocket miscellany—pennies, screws, string, rubber bands, lint, dead batteries, ticket stubs, safety pins, magnets, plastic barrettes, keys—utterly forgotten crap that makes satisfying splashes when dumped down the old well shaft.

Counters are cleared of the knife block, canisters, breadboard. She grabs a Bic and lugs the recycling to the pit and torches it, not even taking the plastic off the unread copies of *Real Simple* (a gift subscription from Carina). Once those are ash, she heaps on a dozen paper grocery bags with a year's worth of crossword puzzles, junk mail, coupons, credit card offers, and countless flattened Cap'n Crunch boxes. Flames leap in pastel licks, dyed by ink, black flakes rising into the pine boughs.

Contents of the Norge go into the wheelbarrow and are pushed to the workshop where Ursa crams it all into the old beer fridge, shoving aside quarts of home brew to make room.

Back in the kitchen she faces the empty cabinets, absently fingering a bristle on her jaw and recalling Carina's most recent labor of love, a weekend spent hand-burnishing the cupboard fronts with Danish oil and an old diaper. With a Phillips bit on her cordless drill, it's easy enough for Ursa to loosen the base cabinets from their moorings. She has to get a wrench for the rusted nuts, but once smeared with lithium grease they nearly spin off. The upper cupboards pose more of a challenge, but by positioning milk crates underneath for support, they don't crash down when she frees the last bolts. The doors alone are enough for a bonfire.

In the cellar she swims through spiderwebs and coughs into the fuse box, cutting juice to the kitchen lights. Too impatient to go get the ladder from the garage, she removes most of the old fixtures while standing on the table or on the counters, chuckling when she thinks about that old commercial with the geezer upended on his carpet like a turtle and yammering, "I've fallen and I can't get up!"

She paces in front of the gas range, eyeing its hulk. When she was a child in Sweden, a man had come to their house to move an enormous radiator from the parlor to the domed conservatory where her father's telescopes were. The cast-iron radiator weighed several times what the laborer did, and Ursa and her brother had watched, rapt, while he used pry bars, gravity, and patience to move a seemingly immovable thing.

Her old undercrib mechanics cart would surely be around somewhere, probably in need of a squirt of 3-in-One. A pair of oak oars would make sturdy enough levers. Extraneous weight could be stripped from the range by removing burner wells, knobs, racks, oven doors. Still, getting the cart underneath would take plenty of figuring and probably more strength than she had. Ursa rubs her shoulder. Besides, it looks just the tiniest sliver too wide to slide out the door. She's thinking about calling Kip Karjala, trying to recall if she'd lent him her arc welder, when the thud of silence falls.

The rhythmic fam-fam of pneumatic nailers from next door has suddenly stopped. Ursa has become so inured to the racket of construction that she only notices when it commences with biblical loudness, or when it stops, hurling blankets of dead air. The distant generators shush to a gargle, which means the crew is on break. Eleven-forty means lunch. Her own had been Slim Jims and string cheese, a meal barely requiring hands.

"Ah-hah," she says, patting the range.

Ursa walks the road, passing several dusty pickups and equipment trailers to a raw, wide driveway winding to the construction site. Her old neighbors had sold out to young dot-comers who could afford lakeshore taxes. They'd already torn down a perfectly good cabin to make room for a four-bedroom monster with windows in stupid shapes. She walks between pallets of lumber and cedar shakes to where several workers are sunk into folding chairs or perched on coolers, eating or smoking.

"Boys. Who is in charge here?"

All heads turn at once, and when their startled looks don't fade, Ursa realizes what a sight she must be—hands coated with grime, long johns tucked into work boots, her dusty white braids tucked like suspenders into the tool belt sagging over the hips of an old house dress.

The one with a crew cut and ear protectors stands. "That'd be me, ma'am. What can I do for you?"

"I could use some help moving a stove."

"Oh?" He seems relieved.

And should be, thinks Ursa, since she hadn't come to complain about the noise or the new ruts in the road or the pickups canted into her stretch of ditch.

He looks at his crew and nods at the two who aren't eating. "Guys?"

They don't look all that big.

"It's very heavy."

The foreman points to a third worker, an Indian fellow with hammy forearms covered in stone dust. He reluctantly rewraps his sandwich, and when he unfolds to his full height Ursa recognizes him as the boyfriend of the nice Oriental gal who runs A Wok in the Woods, where Ursa sometimes gets takeout on senior discount night.

Back in her kitchen, all three look at the stove. The two shorter ones glance at each other, then her.

"You're getting rid of this?"

"Yup. If you'd just put it on my trailer, I can haul it to the dump. The fridge, too."

One piped up. "Well, heck, I can take it off your hands." The other shoots him a look, saying, "And I could spare you the trip on that fridge." Then they notice the cabinets pulled away from the walls. "Not them?"

"Yesirree. All of it."

The two make little tick-faces at each other, as if colluding to keep such sudden luck to themselves.

"Sink and countertops, too, if you're interested."

"Whoa. That sink?"

"Lady," the Indian speaks up. "Those countertops are soap-stone." When his mates glare, he turns and nods toward the sink, asking, "You know the price of copper?"

"Listen, I know what I've got here. And it's all headed for the heap, so help yourselves, boys. Take the chairs and table, too, if you can get 'em out the door." She points to a corner where she'd tossed the wall fixtures. "Those are solid nickel. Now they are worth something."

"No shit?"

"No shit."

The eager ones are stronger than they look and spend the rest of their lunch break and then some prying most of the kitchen out of her house with plenty of good-natured grunting and ob-scenities. Trying to push the stove out the door, they discover the doors have to come off after one gets his motherfucking fingers scraped.

"I told you it was too wide," Ursa says, handing over a flat-head driver.

In an hour they've loaded most everything but the kitchen sink, backing their trucks up and down Ursa's long drive.

The phone begins to ring just as the Norge is strapped to a dolly and rolled out. She ignores the ringing and watches as the freezer compartment drips its way out, wondering if there might be some venison still frozen to the rack.

The phone stops and within a minute begins ringing again.

Once the men are gone, Ursa stands in the middle of the empty room. The floor is thick with dust and chaff and littered with mousetraps of various vintages. Hard outlines of old var-nish and wax indicate where cabinets had been. *Well, that's that.* She'll be moving in just a few months anyway. Her new place at Senior Cedars has interlocking rooms all on one level, spanking new carpet, a bright bay window, garbage disposal, and a toilet you could eat off of. It's a five-minute walk to the grocer and even closer to Pavola's, where she plays cribbage on Tuesdays and where her NRA chapter holds bimonthly meetings. What's a few months without a kitchen? It's not like she cooks. Until then, there's the gas ring in the workshop for tea, and the shop utility sink to wash her few dishes.

Where the fridge had been she notices a hole at knee height in the half-wall, made by something bigger than a mouse—and recently, given the fresh cone of sawdust on the floor. Chipmunk, probably. Normally she would investigate. It will be a relief to live somewhere she won't have to patrol with wads of steel wool and poison. But for now she is here, still mistress of the house she's occupied for so many years. While it's sturdy as a brick shithouse, the cabin itself is quite plain, really—certainly more so now with the kitchen gone.

The phone rings again. She rarely answers anymore since Daniel has begun screaming his head off daily from Minnetonka. Ursa reads the real estate section, knows what her son knows—that her peninsula and the twenty acres that back it are worth a million and maybe half again. But being rich at her age would only mean going on cruises with people she doesn't want to meet and buying new clothes in sizes she'd rather not. When Daniel had suggested she might be too frail to make such decisions on her own, she'd immediately gotten a lawyer and signed everything over to Carina. Daniel's got no argument. He has no children, no grandchildren, no heirs. Carina gets the property by default, if simply for having bred—even if was just neurotic Ara, who in turn has managed to produce those identical droolers Ursa can never keep straight, Vena and Lyra, or Vera and Lina, and Cassi, of course, who seems dredged forth from a different generation of Olson genes as if to redeem the line, coming along well after Ursa had given in to apathy regarding her offspring. The girl has her share of woes, and a bit of darkness, but also some real light like the constellation she is named for, Cassiopeia.

Removing the wainscoting has a rhythm to it, hook and

pry and *pop,* offering instant gratification by revealing wires and pipes and old insulation tucked between studs—the bones of the kitchen. Ursa merely braces herself against a chair and presses down with her good leg on the pry bar. Square-headed nails squeal. The fireplace poker and tongs prove especially handy—those will stay with the house, naturally, forged long ago by her dead husband. Like Lars, the tools are not particularly handsome.

After the walls are stripped, she dials her daughter's number, poised to act as if nothing's afoot, planning to give her every opportunity to come clean. Carina answers on the first ring.

"Mother! I've been trying you all morning."

"Carina, I'm looking around here. Are you sure all your furniture is gonna fit in this little place?"

"We'll find room, Mother. How did your therapy go?"

"Peachy-keen. Say, I was thinking of slapping a coat of paint over those kitchen cupboards for you, they're so old-fashioned . . ."

"Mother, don't! I mean, don't bother. *I'll* deal with them."

"Actually, it's too late for that."

"What? Please stop worrying about the house. And for heaven's sake, please don't do anything."

"But I want it to be shipshape for you. Now, when exactly are you thinking of moving?"

Carina pauses. "Maybe August."

"Oh. You think so? Because that'd be a real mess—what with all the construction that'll be going on here." She waits a beat. "The addition?"

Carina stumbles over a few words, but then Ursa begins speaking over her, steadily, without raising her voice.

"Cut down even *one* of those pines, Carina, and I will haunt you. I'll haunt you for as many years as those trees have lived."

"Mother . . . I was going to tell you."

"Can it, Carina."

"Okay, okay. Lordy, calm down. I won't cut any trees. Listen, I'm driving up there first thing tomor—"

Ursa squeezes the tin snips, silencing Carina and severing the phone cord, which she needs, actually, to bundle the wainscot piled on the kitchen floor.

All day Ursa has paid little heed to the time, hunger, even her aches. Earlier, knocking shelves out of the pantry, she'd found a dusty bottle of Aquavit and discovered it to be more effective than Anacin. The floor of the empty kitchen is pooled in light from a lamp dragged from the living room. Ursa scans the room—just where the sink had been is a rectangle of something caught crookedly behind a pipe just between the studs. At first it appears to be a slab of wood. Closer, she sees it's leather. A book? There is a petrified vole carcass next to it in the framing.

The book? When Ursa realizes what it is, a tight jab akin to pleurisy rocks her. She never expected to see the register again, had long ago given up finding it. Ursa gingerly eases it out and wipes off layers of dust and d-CON nuggets. It must have fallen behind the countertop . . . and had been there all this time? Jesus Christ Almighty, if she'd had a nickel for how many times she'd looked for the thing over the past forty years. After first misplacing it, she'd routinely conducted frenzied searches that Daniel and Carina had chalked up to episodes of change-of-life madness. Neither of them could find it either, or they certainly would have—she'd offered a twenty-five-dollar bounty. Later, she'd forgotten about it for years on end. The register was the only thing Ursa had ever stolen, and she'd never even had the chance to read it before it went missing, making its loss doubly unfair—nothing to show for her guilt, mild as it was.

The leather is mildewed and streaked, the cover tooled with the image of two birch trunks, with the letters of *Naledi Lodge* strung on a line between like laundry. She fetches a lawn chair from the porch just as bats start to scallop out from the eaves and dusk begins to suck away the color. In the middle of the kitchen, Ursa sits, takes a pull of Aquavit, anchors the bottle next to her ankle, and opens the register across her lap.

━━ ━━

To supplement her widow's benefits and Lars's measly life insurance, Ursa had fought her way into a job driving a rural route for a bottling company. The manager hadn't wanted to hire a woman, but Ursa stood her ground—they couldn't dismiss her qualifications: two years as a heavy equipment driver during the war in the same munitions plant where she later became lead mechanics assistant. It took months, but the manager eventually realized it wouldn't look good to deny a miner's widow, especially when the bottling company supplied canteens in mines across the Iron Range. She was grudgingly given a route other drivers dreaded—a meandering loop to border outposts, summer camps, and resorts on roads called trails for good reason.

Naledi was at the end of one of the worst, and Ursa quickly learned not to expect much of a welcome there. Most resort owners would have a boy to help with the cases and kegs, but not Vac Machutova. At first she wondered if he had some special dislike for her, or just women in general. She'd caught enough flak from the other drivers for taking a decent job from a man so was used to bellyaching, but Machutova was the silent type. At the end of her second season, she made it a point to tell him she would be driving his route the following summer as well, so he might as well get used to her. In the early years, she often had either Daniel or Carina in tow simply because there was no one else to watch them. Maybe Vac hadn't approved of that, but who could know? If he had opinions they were not uttered.

Anyone could tell he had no time for the sharp-faced Irish girl married to his son, Tomas. And if Vac had a wife of his own somewhere, no one knew diddly about it. Tomas and Anne showed up with a baby the third or fourth summer of Ursa's route, and she began to notice the change in Vac, a slight softening in the set of his mouth. He'd always have something in his pockets to show the little girl: a grouse feather, a minnow in a jar, a dragonfly pinned to a Popsicle stick. Her name was Margaret, but he called

her Marcheta and spoke Czech nonsense to her when he thought
no one was listening.

Carina was almost finished with high school by then but still
sometimes rode along in the truck, reading *Good Housekeeping* or
poring over Simplicity or McCall's catalogs. As soon as she was
at Naledi, Carina would scoop up little Margaret and make goo-
goo noises at her. Once, Ursa and Carina arrived just as a bad
storm was pressing in. The hue of the sky was the brackish green
that precedes a tornado, with that ozone smell in the air. Everyone was hither and thither, tying things down and pulling up
the boats and flipping them over. It started to pour just as Ursa
wheeled the last of the beer cases inside. Guests had rounded up
their children and retreated to their cabins, and little Margaret
was handed off to Carina, who took her to the thick-walled laundry room in the lodge cellar.

Once everyone was inside, there was nothing to do but wait.
Ursa found herself alone in the bar with Vac. Without a word, he
handed her a clean bar towel and nodded to her dripping hair.
After she'd dried off, Ursa asked for a beer. He stayed behind the
bar while she drank it, tweaking the radio dial, trying to catch a
weather report through the static. He shut it off finally, and they
watched as curtains of black rain began to swoosh from across
the lake. It didn't seem like conversation was an option, since
any questions Ursa asked were all met with one-word answers.
When she noticed a cribbage board on the bar, she challenged
Vac to a game, figuring there was no sense in being trapped
and bored.

When one of her first hands totaled zero, she slapped it
down, sighing, "What Betty shot at." This puzzled Vac, and when
she explained the saying, he told her there was a similar Czech
phrase, which roughly translated as, "What the man fishing with
hope caught."

He wasn't bad looking when he smiled, and up close she
could see he wasn't as old as his posture—he had maybe ten years
on her. In the time it took the storm to wear itself out, he won six
bits from Ursa and she learned a few more colorful expressions.

Vac wasn't exactly surly, more like taciturn. Not a terrible trait, Ursa thought. He *was* a man, and there weren't many of those around; the few bachelors her own age were war cripples, drunks, or Finns, and sometimes all three. And she did miss the one aspect of marriage one would naturally miss. She wasn't young, but she wasn't so old to have forgotten.

"You look a little like that Kraut," Vac said. "Dietrich, even more pale." She couldn't tell if it was a compliment.

"Well, I'm no German."

"Norwegian?"

"Swede."

"Yes?" Vac seemed relieved. "Swedes are very clever with steel—tools, bridges—I have an ax, made in Bergsjo, maybe you know the place?" When she laughed, he shrugged and gave in, joining her.

Before she left that afternoon, he invited her to sign his guest register. The registers were kept on the shelf behind the reception desk, recording the names of every visitor since the day Naledi opened for business. A single volume might account for a year or two, with spines labeled '40–'42, '54–'56, and so on. Any kid old enough to reach the counter signed the registers just underneath their parents' names. On the back of each pale green page were a series of columns written in Vac's small script, about half in English. Initially, Ursa assumed these were only mundane notes—logs of repairs or expenses, rainfall amounts, or lists and the like. But Vac never left a register open for anyone to find out, always weighting them to the blotter with a wrench or rock so no breeze or person might flip the pages.

A month after that storm (which took two of her pines) she encountered Vac in the checkout line at the hardware store. He mentioned in a friendly way that the bass were biting, and that he would be around the resort all weekend, which made the cashier snort, Vac being famous for rarely leaving Naledi.

On Sunday she packed a lunch and drove out. The season had wound down, only a few cabins rented by fishermen having a last stab. Ursa and Vac fished for a few hours but got skunked. When they stowed the gear and poles in the boathouse, she noticed an old Mercury outboard disassembled and laid out on a tarp.

"You're missing a pin here," she said, picking up the carburetor, turning it.

"Yes."

"I can bring one out next time I come."

That's how things began, in the way they do between people who by nature are guarded. Ursa can recall no distinct or memorable steps taken toward one another. They knew something might happen, and when the time came, they let it. And since both were too practical for passion, their physical couplings were straightforward and commenced with ease.

After September, when his son had packed up his family to go back to Chicago and all guests had decamped, Vac would settle in while most resort owners went south for the season or moved into town. Business at local gas stations and restaurants wound down to quarter-speed, so that Ursa was usually laid off until the few winter lodges reopened for skiing and snowmobiling.

Her personal visits to Naledi were mostly during this off-season. She and Vac didn't go out in public together or meet in Hatchet Inlet, not because they were hiding anything—it simply didn't occur to them. Nor did Vac visit Ursa's home, though he sometimes drove his johnnyboat over to collect her from the dock at Olson Point. Neither imagined the other in any context outside Naledi. Visits weren't planned. When Ursa felt like it she would drive out or troll over, bringing a quart or two of her beer, maybe some bait, a sack of cashews, a smoked chicken, or sausage from the bohunk butcher. Other times Vac would cook them a meal, after which they might play cards or go city-fishing, which meant casting from the dock. If they had an entire day, they might pack a cooler and tour the Canadian side. In winter months they'd ice fish or snowshoe to the ridge with its view of the divide and eagles wheeling. At night Vac might build a fire or stoke up the sauna. If the roads were icy, Ursa spent the night.

She can't remember now how she managed such absences, or what she told her children, but they were older by then and hardly curious about her life. She didn't lie to them exactly, just omitted information they wouldn't need or want.

"There's a lot to be said for conserving words" was one of Vac's unintentional witticisms. Back when she was freshly widowed, Ursa was sometimes asked by rude, well-meaning people how Lars had died. The sparseness of her response added its own drama: "In the mines." She didn't offer details—that he died well above ground on a company toilet while reading a detective novel. Let them think cave-in, is what she'd settled on—crushed or suffocated. And while she was sorely tempted to shock them, Ursa never said Lars died taking a crap.

Truth is, those mines are among the safest in the world. Truth was, Lars failed his physical when he'd first signed on, but the company doctor was a fishing buddy and so inked something other than *murmur* on the forms. Her biggest disappointment had been never finding out the title of the detective novel—she would've liked to know what plot twist or gruesome scene had held enough wallop to trip her husband's faulty valves.

Once (and only once) while walking through the reception area of Naledi, Ursa found the current guest register open—an uncharacteristic oversight. She casually read a page from the previous month while standing at the desk. A note was stapled to the register page, written by a minister in Cabin 8, complaining about the holy water fount in the bar, placed to catch caps falling from the beer bottle opener. The note had two words underlined in Vac's ink, *impious* and *blasphemous,* below which Vac had written *Look up.*

He'd written a paragraph about a soprano from Winnipeg—a regular guest, apparently, since Vac wrote that her repertoire had expanded over previous summers. She sang *rooster early,* so that other guests had complained, but Vac obviously hadn't seen fit to ask her to stop, had only moved her to a farther cabin. He compared her to some Czech opera singer whose impossible name was followed by a prewar date and the name of a Prague opera house where Ursa assumed he'd attended concerts. Below were several lines in Czech laid out like the lyrics of a song.

Last on the page was a dense paragraph sidled by a column of numbers devoted to Cabins 1, 2, and 3—all occupied by a family of sisters who apparently brought rafts of children each year: *Again, they demand the best cabins. Again, all driving new cars.* Vac had added steep charges for their requests for additional folding cots and bedding. The children were listed, too, a few with checks next to their names. One name, Roger, had a small, somber cross drawn next to it with a question mark.

Ursa was ready to turn to the next page when Vac walked in.

"Interesting," she said. "These are your . . . observations?"

"Yes, just that. Things I see here, about the people. A way to practice writing in the English."

"May I read more?"

"No." He eased the register away and closed the cover.

After that, registers were always clamped by heavy banker's clips. The fact that they were closed made them more tempting and more mysterious than they likely were. Still, Ursa's fingers often itched for how badly she wanted to pry one open.

Vac and Ursa continued in their fashion. Feelings were seldom mentioned, though Ursa sometimes felt a wave of gratitude, mostly for the physical, sometimes simply for having someone who actually listened when she told a joke or read something aloud from a newspaper or magazine. In many ways they were like couples their age who had been together many years, any nonsense long past.

On a hot August afternoon when she'd had more delivery stops than usual and was exhausted, Ursa pulled up to the parking loop at Naledi, turning nearly around in her seat when she saw the sheriff's car. Earl Janko was walking up the hill from the lake, looking grim, his cap dangling from his hand. Over his shoulder she saw Vac in the distance, sitting on a crate next to the gas pump. Vac sitting still was a rare sight. She got out and started down, but when she was a yard away from the sheriff, he gently caught her elbow and shook his head. They stood together, dumbly watching from afar as Vac rose and went to the sandbox, where he picked up Margaret, his Marcheta. The girl was about six that summer, maybe seven.

"The parents . . ." Earl Janko's voice droned on in details Ursa didn't entirely take in, only the gist. Vac was halfway to the lodge before he stopped and shifted the girl's weight on his hip. His cheek rested over the crown of her head, and with his free hand he brushed sand from her knee, then brushed again, slowly moving his fingers over the skin, as if feeling for any single remaining grains. When Vac suddenly slumped, Ursa took a few steps forward, afraid he might drop the child. It was a full minute before he finally lifted his head from the mass of the little girl's hair, and in Vac's next step, Ursa witnessed a change that she understood to be permanent. In the time it took him to lift one foot and force it forward, he stepped wholly away from one part of his life and into another. As if testing his new legs, he took the lodge steps slowly. When he opened the screen door, he turned and looked out once, blankly, before quietly shutting the door on himself and his granddaughter.

Just as Ursa and Vac began, they ended, gradually and with little fuss in the aftermath of the accident. A day after the sheriff brought the news, she received her first phone call from Vac, stiffly asking her to come run the resort for a few days and watch the girl. When she did see Vac after his return, he said little, barely offered up a word about either Tomas or Anne.

After a second trip, for the funeral, Vac grew preoccupied, submerging himself in the details. There was Margaret's education, a house to deal with, an estate to settle, insurance, the lawsuit against the airline, a trust fund to establish. Anne had a mother, of sorts—a martyred, fading alcoholic; the only other relative was Anne's much-younger sister, a girl named Cathy, not quite Carina's age. Ursa didn't know how the arrangements for guardianship had been settled but knew Vac was adamant that Anne's mother wasn't fit, and that he'd hired a lawyer. There hadn't been a will. For months he was mired in legal wranglings.

One of the more competent summer maids who had dropped out of the nursing program was kept on after Labor Day to help with Margaret. Other than Ursa stopping there on her route, there was no question of her visiting Naledi with the little girl there.

When Vac began taking trips to inspect potential boarding schools, Ursa gently suggested that with all the plane trips he'd been taking, and given his age, he might consider making his own will, some arrangement for Margaret, in case the next-worst thing were to happen. She knew she'd stepped over some line when Vac's jaw set, "*Nothing* will happen to me."

And nothing did. At least not during the years Ursa continued driving the route.

After he'd placed Margaret in a boarding school in a Chicago suburb, Vac rented a furnished apartment near it and stayed for much of the school term. Ursa was at a loss to think how such a person spent his time in Evanston, but he did, staying whole semesters and bringing Margaret to Naledi for holidays and breaks. After Easter, Vac would stay north, sending the girl back by train (wearing a tag that said "carriage") with an Amtrak escort. In that way he could get the resort ready for the season. In May, Margaret appeared along with the first guests and stayed until Labor Day and the beginning of fall term. That was the cycle.

By the time Ursa was poised to retire, the girl had turned into a gawky, somewhat intense teen, all chubbiness gone, with a face too small for her mop of copper hair. On the afternoon of Ursa's last delivery to Naledi, Vac was nowhere to be seen. She hung around the bar afterward to see how Margaret was getting on. Meg—as she called herself by then—seemed content enough to Ursa, well-adjusted, if not quite outgoing, but not as reserved as Vac. She usually had her nose in some sketchbook, drawing while she tended bar. She couldn't serve drinks, only mix, so customers paid for their Cokes or 7UPs and were given a glassful with just enough room for the slim shot they poured themselves. Beer from the cooler was on the honor system, a slotted can nailed to the wall.

When Ursa helped herself to a Pabst and started to fold a bill, Meg looked up from her sketchbook. "Mrs. Olson."

Ursa turned. "Yes?"

"You don't have to pay."

"Really? Why?"

"Vac says," she shrugged, "that you shouldn't."

"Well." Ursa's bottle cap bounced off the chipped holy water fount. "I wish I'd known *that* for the past eighteen years."

"Pardon?"

"Nothing. Just a joke." Ursa smoothed the bill, intending to leave it as a tip. She sat at the bar with a crossword puzzle, musing aloud over a few clues. The girl bit a few times, and together they came up with "bandolier," "tempest," and "mongrel." The expensive school was apparently doing well enough by the girl, although Vac had voiced a concern that she wasn't much of a reader. Ursa imagined Meg just wasn't *his* idea of a reader. And why would she be, Ursa thought, when she has her own form of entertainment there in her hand. Meg was composing a pencil drawing of a copse of slim birch when a customer came in and placed an empty ice bucket on the bar.

Ursa asked casually, "You take art classes at that fancy school?"

Meg chipped at the ice machine with a rat-tail file, loosening a jam. "They only have water colors and clay and stuff. It's Catholic, so we're not allowed to do figure drawing. And they're too cheap to let us have oils, so I only draw."

When Ursa went to use the ladies', she noticed a new sign over the towel dispenser, fashioned with several dozen straight pins stuck to the fiberboard, spelling out "Check Yourself!" Closer inspection revealed that each pin pierced a single wood tick—a few still squirming.

Ursa thought she might stay for second beer. She stayed for three. When Meg finished her drawing, Ursa asked to see it. At first Meg frowned, then offered the sketchbook, a curve of mischief edging her lip.

Bare human arms and legs were interspersed among the birch trunks and limbs, camouflaged to blend in; many were entwined in some way—limbs as pale as bark engaged in very human behavior, the faces obscured by leaves, fingertips twigging out to buds, birch knots of breasts, penises alert as branches. Ursa fought a grin, clearing her throat. "Well. You have a talent."

She stood and eased away from the bar. "Say so long to Vac for me." She looked around the room that she might remember it better. At the reception desk, she opened the glass case as if it were hers. Inside the guest registers leaned in order by year. She located the one she wanted and took it, not caring if the girl had seen her and not looking back to find out.

Outside, she saw Vac with one of the dock boys, both loaded down with heavy gas cans. She waved, but Vac could only nod back.

That was pretty much the last she'd seen of him, other than from afar sometimes in his truck, heading to the Sokol Hall or the lumberyard. She didn't see the girl for another five years, when they found themselves shoulder to shoulder at Vac's funeral.

*

Ursa tips the bottle and Aquavit warms the length of her throat. Adjusting the light, she shifts the lawn chair and opens the guest register.

She skims over the first entries to the pages of the week of the summer storm. On the dog-eared page there is an asterisk at her signature. On the other side Vac had written: *50 mph wind. Today the storm—we play the card game with pegs. The driver woman's name is Ursa—as she must know this is from the Bear? 10 cc of rain.*

She leafs forward.

Superior fishing—two walleye just from the dock, both over 50 cm, both taken by Ursa. One for me, smaller. Floured and fried. She laughs to be the one gutting while I cook. Snow soon. Ordered books from St. Paul. More visits, I think.

On his birthday in October:

Maybe less old this year. LP records and card from Tomas. Self portrait by crayon from Marcheta. Ursa comes out, not too much, sometimes too little. Hard frost. I will weld chains for her Ford.

About an odd, damp weekend when jagged peaks of frost formed on every surface, the low clouds and cold amplifying every snapping twig, he'd written:

Wind. Deer and wolves all night. Odd the sounds of one killing the other isn't too terrible. Wolves have one place and the deer has another as his meal. We have our place, too, falling asleep.

Ursa reread the paragraph, clearly remembering that night, of being disturbed and rolling awake to the sounds of a kill, being soothed back to sleep by Vac.

She flipped back and forth through the register. Vac had been as economical with his writing as he'd been with speech. Still, there was enough written to pull the gauze from a cache of memories.

After the December storm (everything prefaced by weather, it seems) that paralyzed the entire county:

Three days snow, nearly a meter—sauna stove is burned through—I will cut a barrel for new (buy acetylene). To sit with Ursa free of clothing is a ~~good~~ fine thing.

At the word *sauna* she vividly recalls running from its door to plunge into the lake, remembers the water feeling like cool oil, the steam rising from her breasts to mix with mist over the surface. As Ursa reads she is tugged back into her middle-aged body, when nothing ached, when there was nothing to hide.

And yet another storm, this one in January:

Watched the snow and watched more until the trees bowed under their armfuls. What others search for so mightily in churches is only here on fragile altars . . . .

Ursa trails her hand over the pages of the register, nearly nodding off but jolts when a car door slams. She looks out to see Carina's Chevrolet. Dawn has cast its lavender net through the pines.

The screen door opens and Carina forms as a silhouette

crossing the dark porch. "There you are, Mother. And awake at this hour?" Carina steps into the kitchen. "I'd been calling all last . . ." as Carina's eyes adjust, the rooms condition is slowly revealed. ". . . night. *Kitchen*?" She looks behind as if to check which door she'd entered.

Normally pale, as Olsons are, Carina blanches to a rabbity white, repeating, "Kitchen . . ."

Ursa follows Carina's gaze around the empty room. She sucks her dentures and with near remorse says, "Ah, *ja*. That." She pats the seat of the second lawn chair she'd been using to prop her leg on. "You've had a shock," offering the bottle of Aquavit. She says, "Here. Have a seat."

"Oh, my Lord . . ." Carina nearly stumbles. "Mother?"

"Here, Carina." She thumbs back to the first pages of the guest register. "Sit. I want to read you something."

I N THE THICK OF THE TRAIN STATION CROWD PATRICK braces, chin up, certain he's caught her scent. Her idea of a greeting—one she never seems to tire of—is to sneak up from behind and cover his eyes. She's done this since he was a toddler. Patrick has mentioned these early shocks to his therapist—the darkness, Cheerios flying, the fresh-grave smell of patchouli as his mother's palms steal the light. Even now, thinking he's prepared, he staggers when the sudden blackness clamps.

"Guess who?"

He laughs too loudly and pivots into an awkward hug. His mother's cheek is cool against his. They are standing where they shouldn't, in a stream of travelers rushing and adjusting their backpacks and laptop cases and gnawing at cell phones, oblivious. Still in his mother's grip, he baby-steps both of them away from the traffic. Something sharp presses into Patrick's sternum, and when they separate he sees an amethyst the size of a dreidel between his mother's tie-dye–covered breasts.

Taking both of his hands she leans back. The scan.

"You look wonderful, Patrick!"

She looks quite well herself, the few pale crow's-feet at her temples are accentuated by a tan, making her sea-green eyes greener. She's got that hale, windblown glow she always brings back from her travels. Patrick struggles to remember where she's come from, but then notices the many Hopi bracelets on her wrist and remembers—spirit questing or some other plinky pursuit in a desert near Taos with other menopausal women.

He can't really be expected to keep track of all the trips, to know at any given moment whether she is in Lhasa or at Esalen. He'd only half-read her latest letter, laying it aside when he reached the bit about "the waning of the blood tides."

"You look good, too, Mom—healthy." When she frowns, he corrects himself. "I mean Cathy." It feels unnatural to call her by her first name, but she insists.

"That's better. Now people can assume you're just meeting a friend. That way I won't embarrass you."

"You don't embarrass me."

"Not yet." She squeezes his wrist with a strength that numbs. The visit has just begun.

"Here," she says, handing him a tote bag with an ugly brass vessel poking out. "This is your Aunt Anne."

Before her desert sojourn, Cathy had been in Big Sur at a workshop titled "Shedding Earthly Anchors." One of hers, she'd discovered, was the urn of her sister's ashes, which rightfully belongs to her niece, Patrick's cousin, Meg. He barely knows Meg but clearly recalls her small wedding, and her groom, Jeremy, a very tall man with an accent—Patrick's first full-on crush.

Meg's mother, Anne, had been killed along with her husband in a plane crash long before Patrick was even born. Cathy had been only a teen when her older sister died but still will not fly, which is why Patrick often finds himself collecting her from bus depots or ferry terminals or train stations like this one, where unsavory types loiter and the floors are appalling, but where, she reminds him, there is always free parking, and that looking down is optional.

As they make their way to the luggage area, his mother billows a little, having readopted the wardrobe of her hippie days: capes, kimonos, and voluminous skirts, and in this case a caftan fit for a Grateful Dead concert. On her most recent birthday, Cathy had ritualistically burned anything in her closet that was clinging or revealing, claiming she was sick of being an object, was finished with presenting her boobs and backside on the sick tray that is, essentially, *fashion.* Her sexuality, she told Patrick, was hers alone, to be shared with what lovers she chooses. Cathy often tells him more than he wants to know. Besides, these clothes are comfortable, she says. "I can finally stop holding my stomach in." Patrick knows she's fit as a sylph under the layers, with her daily marches and the yoga regimen. Glancing sideways, he's startled to be at eye level with her.

Has she grown? He has imagined himself shrinking since coming to Minnesota, living among so many statuesque Nordic types. As if reading his mind, his mother flips up a heel, and skirts fly in a Martha Graham flourish to reveal her platform sandals.

Still. Lately Patrick's been suffering a Woody Allenesque hypochondria in which he imagines himself not only shrinking but dying. Despite his youth, he thinks of sudden aneurysms and strokes, lethal skin ailments, or freak accidents in which he is perforated or diced. He's grown wary of rich food and foreign travel and has recently passed over an opportunity to kayak in the Borneo. What if he were to capsize in some river where that rare parasite lives, the one that will zoom straight up the urethra of passing male swimmers? Because the creatures are barbed there is no wrangling them from that delicate channel, and because the pain is exquisite and since there are no vascular surgeons in the Borneo, there is only one option. Patrick can think of no better reason to avoid traveling to remote locations.

Kevin has suggested more than once that Patrick might be watching too much Discovery Channel. And as if Kevin's name has just flashed across his forehead, Cathy purrs, "How's your honey?"

He dreads this freakish mindreading she calls their "connection." Like a phone perpetually off the hook for her to pick up whenever she wants, she has a one-way eavesdrop on his brain. "He's not my honey, Cathy. He's my roommate."

"Well, whatever he is this week, he's a sweet boy."

Sweet, yes. And funny. But as his mother implies, they are on-again off-again, with Patrick slow to commit. Lately, Kevin complains about the difficulty of living under the same roof and never knowing what's coming next. In a nod to one of their favorite films, Kevin has hinted that Patrick pick a persona and stick to it by hanging a flip sign on Patrick's door lettered NORMAL on one side, ABBYNORMAL on the other.

His mother waves down the porter with her claim ticket. The man retrieves an absurdly bright tapestry duffle and heaves it into Patrick's arms, nearly toppling him.

Cathy presses a dollar into the porter's dark hand and nods solemnly, "Namaste," leaving Patrick and the porter blinking at one another over her deeply bowed head.

He struggles a moment with the weighty bag, wondering if it might be easier to drag it when Cathy impatiently relieves him, hoisting the duffle to her shoulder stevedore style, sighing, "C'mon, Mudpat, I'm starving." He gets ten feet before wheeling in horror, dashing back to retrieve the bag of Aunt Anne.

Because she is a vegetarian, they go to a new organic bistro where the chef is reputed to be a hysterical genius. Though Cathy knows Patrick doesn't like other's forks near his food, she talks him into sharing dishes. They order sweet potato gnocchi, eggplant souf- flé, and a bottle of Pinot. He insists on his own salad.

Between the main course and dessert, Cathy informs him cousin Meg is having some success in the art world. She takes an article from her purse and spreads it flat. It's from a big Chicago paper, has a photo of Meg standing next to a large painting.

Patrick scans the text. "Good for her." He taps the photo. "She doesn't look fortysomething."

"She's had a few other exhibits, major ones. And is selling work. Did I tell you she's left that stick of a husband?"

"Oh. The Brit?" Patrick tries to sound bored. "Why?"

Cathy shrugs. "She said he couldn't be bothered to recycle anything. Ever. He never peeled the carrots even though he knew she liked them peeled. I imagine there were real reasons, though."

"Ah . . . Jeremy, right?"

"Yup. Didn't he look a lot like the Monty Python what's-his- name? Never mind, you're too young. John Cleese. Anyway, Meg and I have started writing a little—seems she's been fixing up what's left of her grandfather's old resort."

"What for?"

"To live in, I suppose."

"Up *there*? Jesus. Why?"

His mother shrugs. "Who knows, maybe she's living her dream."

"Or nightmare. I remember that place."

"Oh, right . . . that's where we discovered your allergy to bees."

Why anyone would leave a perfectly civilized place like Chicago for the backwoods is beyond Patrick. "Maybe she's jumped the fence? I hear those outpost towns are big lesbian colonies."

"I don't think so, Patrick."

"You sure? They migrate north, where they can live openly with their Huskies."

"Oh, now . . ." She clamps down on a spoonful.

"They wear hats with fur flaps . . ."

She sputters through a mouthful. "'Nough."

Pointing his fork at the tote propped on a third chair, Patrick says, "So, that's my Aunt Anne?"

Cathy eases a rosemary needle from her teeth. "Well . . . mostly, I think. There were two urns, one went north with Meg and the old man. For some reason I'm pretty sure these aren't just Anne's—some might be Tomas. Not *all* of them, apparently fish had gotten to them . . ."

Patrick lays his fork down. "Mother."

"Sorry." She presses a napkin to her mouth. "So were you able to get Monday off?"

"Monday? Why Monday?"

"Well, it's an awfully long drive for an overnight."

"Pardon? You mean we're not meeting her here?"

"Patrick, the plan was to drive up and deliver the urn in person." Cathy crosses her arms and leans back. "You didn't read my last letter!"

One crème brûlée arrives with two spoons. One has a smear,

so he snatches up the other. "No one reads snail mail anymore. You really should e-mail me. So we're driving all the way up to Bumfuck?"

"Language, Mudpat."

"I wish you wouldn't call me that."

"Yum, this is good."

"Well, go for it now." Patrick withdraws his spoon at Cathy's advance. " 'Cause you'll be eating Canadian bacon and deer meat all weekend."

"The place isn't that backwards—Meg sent me some nice brochures. There are several decent restaurants, even a new co-op. And it's called venison."

"What is?"

"Deer meat."

Patrick leans in. "Tell me we're not staying out at that awful place?"

"I got us rooms in town, a new B&B called the Rectory."

"No."

"Relax, Patrick. You could use a few days out of town. And I'll do most of the driving."

Patrick scrapes the last spoonful. "You usually do."

Once she has brushed her teeth and neti-potted and is tucked away in Kevin's room along with her duffel and human remains, Patrick goes back to his room, resigned.

A suitcase is clammed open on the bed, A-list and B-list clothes in neat piles. Kevin is sitting cross-legged on the free side, picking through his choices. "This cashmere isn't the best color on you."

"You have no idea where I'm going."

"You'll have your iPhone—send me a few pics."

"Kev," Patrick straightens, "imagine where you'd land at the end of a very long sled dog race."

"Hmm. What about those loafers?"

"Nope. Something with tread."

Kevin grins. "How about a khaki vest with all those pockets? Aren't they all the rage up there?"

"Ha. Do you have a plaid shirt I can borrow?"

Kevin cackles, pitching sideways off the bed. Patrick steps over him and into the bathroom, where he stares at the contents of the open medicine chest.

"Have we got any sleeping-anything? I need to go to bed, like, *then*."

Patrick barely registers Cathy loading the car or buckling him into the passenger seat in the dark at the curb, but at 5 a.m. on the dot they pull away. For the first hour, he dozes but keeps jolting awake. Finally, he yanks off his sleep mask. "Have you been braking?"

"Maybe a little tap now and then—it's your cruise control. I'm not used to it. Here." She hands him a DQ napkin. "Drool."

He gives up on sleep and holds his thermos like a sippy cup, mutely watching the landscape change from fields to woods. He plays an Elliott Smith CD until Cathy balks. "The lyrics! He's so depressing."

"He stabbed himself in the heart."

"Good Lord. Why?"

"Tuh. A girl."

"Please find something else?"

"Okay, but we're not listening to any Dylan or goddess chants . . ." Patrick flips through the case and holds up Barber's "Agnus Dei." "This one doesn't have words."

Cathy presses a palm to her forehead.

Farther north, the highway cuts through bog land and spruce forest. Since they cannot agree on music, he fiddles with the radio, but the only clear stations feature eighties rock, polkas, or right-wing talk shows with commercials for Ensure and attack ads on liberals. When they dip into a decimated valley of open pit mining, even those stations crackle away to silence.

"We are lost." Patrick's head lolls.

"Such drama. We're nearly there, an hour maybe. Two at the most."

Patrick mimes cutting his wrists.

Closer to the border, the forest thins, pines struggle up from rock outcroppings like Dr. Seuss bonsai, all straining southward as if trying to go there.

Cathy points to a tottering fire tower. "Look. We're getting close." Mailboxes start to smatter, and Patrick tries to pronounce some of the names, giving up at Putzl. When they pass a rusted gate and mailbox with T. Kaczynski on it, he sits up, but Cathy shakes her head. "Montana, Mudpat."

They arrive, finally, in Hatchet Inlet. The town itself isn't quite as grim as Patrick remembers. As they circle looking for the B&B, he spies an antique shop with cabin- shabby-chic in the window, a hip-looking deli called Yeti, and an actual coffee shop. Many cars have out-of-state plates and canoes or kayaks lashed to their roofs. Anchoring one corner is A Wok in the Woods; with its soaped windows Patrick can't tell whether it's opening or closing. They pass the Borealis Tavern with its sign for Ladies Only Wednesdays committed to neon.

"I told you there'd be lesbians," Patrick points. "I'll bet they have wet polar fleece contests."

They find The Rectory, which is just what it claims, a brick house next to an old Catholic church. Patrick drags his roller bag in, ready for country tchotchkes and duck stencils, but the reception area is done in teak with Barcelona chairs and cowhide rugs. The proprietor's name is Ricardo. He and Patrick eye each other over the guest registry while Cathy's credit card is run through the machine. Ricardo's no native, Patrick decides. Not wearing Paul Smith.

They are given adjoining rooms. Patrick flops facedown on the astronomical thread count duvet while Cathy goes through their shared bathroom to unpack.

He wakes disoriented, his mother at the edge of his bed gently rocking his hip. She's showered and changed. "C'mon, Bunny. Time's a-wastin'."

"Hmm."

"Up, Petal."

"No need to pinch."

Once Patrick is dressed and his hair precisely tousled, they drive out to a popular lodge with a brass plate at the door claiming it is on the state's historic register, famous for never having burned down. The lodge is massive, built with the sort of trees you see in old pictures where whole teams of draft horses pull one log. The lobby is woodsy-posh with a walk-in fireplace, but more impressive is the collection of guests. The resort is hosting a conference of foreign journalists, many milling with their pre-dinner drinks. Cathy leads him past two handsome men in turbans, a German-looking man with a bow tie, and a raven-haired woman wrapped in a sari, reading from her iPad. He'd expected characters from *Fargo* and pull tabs, but the guests speak real English and none carries a tackle box. Patrick feels underdressed in his jeans and pullover. Cathy pulls him through the lobby to a bar where they settle at a low table in a corner and order drinks.

When his juniper mojito arrives, Patrick asks it, "Where *are* we?"

"Oh. There she is!"

He turns. Meg is prettier than he remembers. She's wearing a fawn suede poncho and knee-high boots. Her age is hard to pin—diligent with the sunscreen, he supposes. After a round of double-cheeked greetings, they all sit, and for a moment only smile at each other until Cathy hiccups into her martini and they all laugh.

"It's so good to see you both. And Patrick, you are all grown up!"

For a half-hour, he listens to them catching up. They talk about Meg's work, Cathy's travels. Like a house on fire, Patrick thinks, peas in a pod. He's unsure why their enthusiasm should bother him.

After Meg excuses herself for the bathroom, his mother gently urges, "She's just gotten divorced. And we're the closest thing she has to family."

"I'll be good. I'll converse." As Meg walks away, he notes her stride, the set of her shoulders. "She'll be fine. She's a lot like you."

Cathy grins as if she's received a compliment.

The moment Meg is back, he asks, "So. I kind of get it why you left Chicago, but England?"

Cathy pestles his foot with her heel.

Meg doesn't seem to mind. "I was never at home in London. Just like Jeremy never took to this place. Leaving Chicago was harder, but I never had time to paint there. I still miss it—some days I'd kill for a decent slice of pizza, or Thai." She nods toward the expanse of water out the window. "But there are so few distractions here, and I'm working well enough." She looks up. "Nothing says it's forever . . . but I guess we don't always love where we need to be."

"Need?"

As the hostess approaches, Cathy claps her hands. "Table's ready!"

In the morning, Cathy drives them north from Hatchet Inlet following Meg's hand-drawn map, decorated with line sketches of landmarks to watch for. There's a countryside grotto made entirely of taconite balls, a bait shop housed in an old caboose named the Last Chance. They stop at a wayside rest with benches carved in the shapes of moose racks. After they make the final turn, Patrick rolls the map and tucks it into his shoulder bag, not asking if he might keep it.

The last miles are rugged, the pavement giving way to gravel. The last sign of life is at a cobblestone arch leading to a camp called St. Gummarus, where an old nun with a quilted vest over her habit pushes a wheelbarrow of bleached antlers along the verge. Patrick wrenches his neck while craning back to make sure.

They reach two cobblestone pillars, where the road narrows to muddy ruts, and Patrick moans each time his Passat scrapes. "We should have rented a Jeep."

"I can't help it, honey." Cathy stops the car, and they switch. Over the last stretch neither says anything when the car bottoms.

Between gaps in the trees they see the lake before they see Naledi. The car descends into a tunnel of pine, and at a wide spot Patrick parks and they walk a path toward chimney smoke. Meg is on the porch to greet them. At her side is a large, wolf-shaped dog with light eyes.

Patrick stops. "What is that?"

"Ilsa? She's a mix, a little Malamute, a little Husky . . ."

"And . . . ?"

Meg shakes her head. "Not enough to worry about."

Inside the small lodge, she shows them her makeshift studio, a wide lakeside porch with skylights punched through, allowing splotchy light to filter down through the trees. The living area is broad and dim, with stacks of art books, rolls of canvas, and boxes shoved under tables, as if Meg had scurried to clear clutter. Upstairs are a few claustrophobic dormer rooms with paneling the color of stout. It's definitely up-north, very lived-in, Patrick observes. Meg has hung a few of her large abstracts and scattered modern Scandinavian rugs to brighten the rooms.

They have coffee in front of the fire, drinking from cups Patrick has admired in a Finnish design catalog. Looking around, he sees Meg definitely has taste, just maybe a little too much of it.

Cathy carefully takes the urn of ashes from its tote and hands it to her niece. "I didn't know if you'd wanted to keep these, or sprinkle them, or what."

Meg turns it in her hands. "Oh, both, I think. I'll scatter some here and there. I thought we might do it together. Not really a ceremony, but something, you know?"

Movement out the window catches Patrick's eye and he turns. He inhales, pointing to the large man quickly descending the hill behind the lodge.

"Oh," Meg says. "That's just Jon. Jon Redleaf. My tenant. He helps out with handyman stuff. Lives in the outpost cabin."

"Why the rifle?"

"I'm not sure, maybe to scare off the cougar. There've been a few sightings."

"Cougar." Patrick repeats: "Cougar?"

"No worries. Really."

Patrick edges closer to the spooky wolf-dog near his feet. As his mother and Meg burrow into another yakfest, he scans the bookshelves flanking the fireplace, noticing that his cousin owns every book by Polly McPhee—the Danielle Steele of lesbians who pens romances set in exotic locales. Just as he's thinking, *That nails it,* his mother sees him perusing the shelf and turns to ask Meg.

"How's Polly?"

"Okay. Her eyes are going, but otherwise . . ."

"You *know* her?" Patrick sets down his coffee cup.

"Well, sure. She was my guardian after Vac died. Polly's family, more or less. You'll meet her after her nap."

"She's here?"

"Uh-huh. Since last week."

Outside, they walk single file down the hill to the dock. Patrick lags, taking one step for each gray board. His mother carries a small bunch of what looks like bouquet garni, tied with a reed, and Meg has the urn. After she pours a handful of the bony ash into the water, Cathy tosses her little bunch of greens after them. They all watch as the ashes float, then sink. The women lean together, one shoring up the other, though he can't tell which. He digs in his pocket, relieved to find one of the ironed hankies Kevin had packed for him.

Of course he's seen Cathy cry before—he must have.

As it turns out, they aren't finished. There's more sprinkling to be done. They climb back up the hill and meet Jon Redleaf, who offers a jumbo hand for Patrick to shake. They follow Jon's back for a quarter-mile through the woods to a corridor of cedars to emerge at a weird glade of mossy mounds.

Meg sprinkles more ash while Patrick furtively tries shuffling bog muck from his heels. Jon says something in his language, then takes a filterless cigarette from his pack, twists it open, and scatters flakes of tobacco while he mutters. Ash and tobacco rise together in a vortex before settling over orange needles and moss.

The ashes rose before they fell.

He swears they did. Patrick holds up a palm, there is no breeze, not a leaf has stirred. He looks to the others to explain this failure of gravity, but they all have their eyes closed.

Once they blink themselves to, Meg twists the lid back on the urn and the women turn to walk back to the cabin. Patrick begins to follow, but Jon lays his hand on Patrick's shoulder and says quietly, "Let them go ahead."

"Pardon?"

"They're grieving. You're not."

Patrick blinks. "Oh. Well, I guess . . . right. I'm not. I never knew my aunt and uncle—Meg's parents, I mean."

They sit on the ledge of rock for several minutes, both gazing straight ahead, until Jon says, "You're two-spirited?"

Patrick straightens. "Pardon? You mean like two-faced?"

Jon laughs. "No. I only mean homosexual. *Berdache.*"

He stands, ready to run. "*Berdache?*"

"Uh-huh. In my culture you might become a shaman or a healer. That's all."

A shaman? He looks up at Jon. "No shit?"

"No shit."

Patrick sits back on his rock. Jon offers him a Camel, which Patrick only takes out of politeness. He's a Saturday night smoker. He leans toward the proffered flame and gingerly sucks the Camel, barely inhaling the unfiltered smoke, wishing it were an American Spirit Light. When he hands back the lighter, Jon tucks it away with his crinkled pack.

"You're not having one?"

"Nah." He shakes his broad head. "I quit."

Patrick waits, but the man adds nothing more.

As if the urn has a limitless supply of ashes—of cremains—his mother and Meg decide to take some out on the lake to sprinkle on some island. They will paddle to a place that had meant something to her father. "I'm not sure why, exactly," Meg admits, "but it might have been where I was conceived."

Patrick gently shakes the urn. "Aren't you gonna run out?" His mother volleys a look.

He declines the journey by canoe but holds the bow steady while his mother and Meg settle in, the white dog between them with the urn between its paws.

"How long will you be?"

"An hour, maybe?"

"Take your time!" Patrick shoves them off with more force than is necessary, nearly tumbling from the dock. After they paddle away, he walks along the shore.

There's hardly any resort left compared to what he remembers. Only two cabins. The rest of the little clearings have only broken foundations in tall grass and one old building used for storage. He peers in, but there's nothing but stacks of new floorboards and sheetrock. The cabin out at the end of the point is probably the Indian's—its roof bright with new shakes, a set of snowshoes hanging in the eaves, and an impressive pile of cordwood stacked nearby. The other cabin would be Polly McPhee's, a neon nylon rope strung tree to tree leading from the cabin to the lodge, which Patrick reckons is some sort of guide rope. Up the trail is a truck that must also be Jon's—a massive black pickup with bumpers like mammy hips.

Farther along the lake path is a sauna, unlocked—just a stove and benches, wooden water buckets and a barrel of birch whips. He's headed in the right direction anyway. When the trail opens onto the shore, he stops. The old fish house leans, just as it had, with a warped door that takes a few kicks to open. The interior is much smaller than he recalls. The screens are rusted, and enamel basins filled with dead leaves line the low shelves. In the middle of the room is a sloping table hacked with old knife gouges, including the ones he'd once made. At the end there's a chipped sink to catch entrails and drain the bloody water.

His father had given him a new fishing rod for his tenth birthday, and for months before their visit to Naledi, Patrick had watched *Big Rick's Bass Bonanza* each Sunday on Channel 7. For a full hour, the host and his sidekick did little more than sit and cast and talk about lures and lunkers and water depth and other hideously boring things. But something about the program drew Patrick, and he began to anticipate similar hours in a boat with his father, fishing like those men in quiet camaraderie, happy to do nothing but cast and float.

But once at Naledi things weren't as he'd imagined. It was unusually hot. The boat had a slow leak so that fishy water with a skin of gasoline soaked his sneakers. He was made to wear a life vest that hindered his every movement, and sun burned through his blond hair like a laser. The whole time they were out that first day, he'd had to go. By the time Patrick finally caught a fish, he reeled it in with anticlimactic relief. His stomach ached and he was experiencing the beginnings of heat stroke.

As he stands in the fish house, Patrick recalls the weight of the hammer in his hand. The pike had wriggled so that he kept missing its head. His father, who'd grown up on a farm, insisted the process was a lesson. "You should know where your food comes from—it doesn't just appear on your dinner plate, Pat." When the fish was finally still, his father handed him the fillet knife. "You've seen me do this enough times. Just give it a try."

The scales stuck to his hands and the knife handle was slick with slime. Sweat trickled into his eyes. When his fish was half-mangled and he was sure he was going to vomit, his father lost patience and grabbed the knife, muttering, "Goddamn pansy."

Patrick backs out of the fish house, slamming the door hard enough a splinter flies. He walks aimlessly, far inland and away from the resort, eventually meeting the path they'd all followed earlier to the clearing where the ashes had floated upward for no good reason.

He finds the spot and squats on a bed of cedar needles, leaning forward to stare at the tiny gray nuggets of bone, already darkening with moisture. He picks up a few.

They are very light. Just shards. Nuggets of Meg's mother, fractions of her father.

He'd often wished his own father dead, some days harder than others. On their last night at Naledi, Patrick discovered a wood tick attached to his scalp. He'd panicked at the dinner table, but Cathy had calmed him enough to inspect his head, parting his hair gently, saying she would just grab her tweezers and have it out in a jiffy. But the second she'd stepped into the bathroom to look for it, his father had gripped Patrick's head to see for himself. "You don't need a goddamn tweezer for that." He grunted, took a hard pull on his cigar, then touched the ember to the tick. When Patrick jerked, the burning cigar stamped his scalp. He screamed.

He still has the half-moon scar, can remember the smell of singed hair. Patrick dove under the table for cover, his father laughing and poking his lit cigar after him, calling him "faggot" and "queer." "Come here, you little fairy!"

He remembers his mother's banshee-like yell as she launched herself to fill the space between him and his father, and the silence afterward as his parents glowered, each daring the other to say even one word. He heard heavy footfalls. The screen door yawned, then slammed. After he'd crawled out, his mother held an ice cube to his scalp, then dabbed it with some minty cream.

Patrick smells the sharp cedar all around, realizing he has seen his mother cry—that night at the kitchen table, tending his burn and wiping her own eyes, annoyed as if the tears were flies, forcing cheer into her wobbly voice. He sits back on his heels to rest against a slope of stone.

They'd shut themselves into his room for the night, pushing the two singles together to make one bed. She lit the kerosene lamp and they stayed awake past midnight making shadow puppets. When that grew boring they made up a new story all about Brave Sir Patrick and the Knights of the Formica Table, a tale of how Sir Patrick had slain the Bog Monster and saved all the citizens of the little Kingdom of Naledi. They were still awake when the cabin door opened and closed, but his mother only tensed, barely pausing while telling her part of the story.

She was still in his room when he woke up, sleeping in a chair pushed up tight against the door. How could he have forgotten that?

Cathy left his father soon after. Had she known about the fish house incident, or the many others before it? He knew he had everything to do with their divorce, even before he fully understood why. Other than cards with checks on his birthday, they never heard much from the Bog Monster, who remarried and had two more sons, both straight.

He supposed it was natural for Cathy to overcompensate: she marched in Gay Pride parades when he didn't; she volunteered at an AIDS hospice, even subscribed to *Lavender*. When he joked to friends that his mother was gay enough for both of them, Kevin always gave him a look. All along, she had encouraged Patrick to celebrate who he was and to pity the narrow-minded. Because of her insistence, Patrick hesitated to do either.

Patrick rests against the same stone where he'd sat with the Indian. He leans back, facing the sky, feeling the ash between his fingers. Cathy is healthy and relatively young for a parent. Forget airplane crashes—there are snakes in Sonoma and cliffs in Nepal. Trains derail, and buses plummet into Third World ravines. The eventuality that has been only abstract in Patrick's mind suddenly gels. Even if his mother lives to be ninety, one day she'll be only nuggets of bone . . . ashes in hand.

Patrick is suddenly very tired. And it is so quiet here.

He dreams of nothing, aware that he's dreaming, but also aware that he's dreaming a full, rotund sort of nothing, which makes no sense, yet utter sense. He is also aware of where he is, certain he's only half-sleeping, but also sure that he is indeed asleep. Lucid dreaming. He'd read an article about it. This could be that.

Though he rests on stony ground, his body feels buoyed; his back feels naturally melded to the earth. His breath is precisely in sync with the cedar boughs swaying above.

I won't forget this, he says in his dream, not exactly knowing what *this* is, but knowing it doesn't need to be named.

When a twig snaps behind him, he slowly awakens, curiously

listening for what will come next, as if only eavesdropping. Then Patrick remembers the cougar and is suddenly very much awake. He slowly raises his head, elbowing up the rock inch by inch, barely breathing, heart thwacking. Instinctively, he makes no sudden movements. He turns his head as if it's on a pole, until his neck strains, barely allowing his shoulders to follow.

At first he doesn't know what he's looking at. Then he realizes the tawny, crooked fence he's squinting through isn't a fence at all, but the slender legs of a herd of deer—only yards away on the rise just above him are six, no, eight does with several adolescent fawns, all grazing.

His mouth molds upward into a slow grin and he whispers, "Hello."

Heads tick up in unison to look at Patrick. They have truffle-sized eyes with stiff, inch-long lashes. Their nostrils grow wide at his scent, and he feels a rush of gooseflesh sleeving over his skin. The hair on his neck tingles, and something he can only describe as a current of joy pulses through his body. When he laughs, he cannot help himself, hard as he tries. The deer scatter, showing him their white tails and hoofing divets of earth at him, making him laugh harder.

He laughs until he sees the last fawn is straggling—it has a bad foreleg. The herd breaks into factions, the older fawns with their mothers leaping over the mounds and out of the glade.

Without thinking, Patrick gets up to follow, jogging along on the path as the lame fawn plunges through the glade, urging him on. The fawn stumbles, and Patrick stops. One knee is awkwardly knobbed—struggling upright, it never takes its eyes off Patrick, even as it spreads its spindle legs and lowers its head, as if confronting him.

"Sorry." Patrick holds his palms up and steps backwards several paces, smiling. "No worries." He slowly turns to walk in the opposite direction, glancing over his shoulder to see the fawn still in its stance. When the path forks, he veers away from the disturbed animal and exits the glade, picking up his pace until he's running.

As he runs, Patrick's legs seem to shift into automatic. It's been a very long time, but it feels good to run, to pound a rhythm. He keeps it up, not wanting to break the cadence. When the path crosses an old logging road, he takes it up an incline snaking along a ridge. The hill is tougher—a full breath for each kick into the air. The half-mile stretch leads up out of the woods to a broad cap of granite, where Patrick stoops, panting toward the view, amazed to see how far away the lake is, how far he's run.

Once he gets his breath, he trots the mile back to the resort, all downhill.

"You okay?" Meg asks.

His mother steps out of the canoe to take his offered arm. "You look flushed, Pat."

"I'm fine." Patrick suddenly wraps his mother in a hug, lifting her a little off the dock, inhaling her familiar smell, the same old patchouli, but with something fresher, maybe the lake air.

"Down, Mudpat. You'll strain your back. Where've you been?"

"I went for a run."

"Really?" She looks at him and straightens her serape. "That explains your shoes."

He looks down. "So. A little mud?"

At the lodge porch he heels off his shoes and follows them in.

After he gulps water cold from the tap, they have more coffee and eat sandwiches in the kitchen, the one bright room in the lodge. Patrick remembers the room as it once was: the dark lounge that kids weren't allowed into. He looks up to where there was once a mounted row of silly taxidermy—a jackalope, and some trophy fish with a Barbie in its mouth, and a motley band of rodents holding toy instruments in their needle-sharp claws. He remembers that. The Hamm's sign with its glittery waterfall, the smell of beer. The old beadboard has been painted over in a glossy sea foam, and the taxidermy has been replaced with a shelf of midcentury pottery in cream colors. He eats three sandwiches.

After lunch they drink beer in front of the fireplace and have a sort of gift exchange. Meg opens the little box from Cathy and lifts a sterling chain that ends in a little silver claw holding a blob of red coral.

She's able to appear pleased while obviously puzzled.

"For women in transition," his mother explains.

"Oh?" Meg nods. "Oh."

The coral looks like something you'd drop from tweezers into a metal dish and promptly cover, but Patrick only nods too, saying, "Nice."

Meg gives Cathy a framed photo—a reprint of the last picture taken of her family, showing Meg at age six, leaning against her father Tomas's leg, her hair corkscrewing from her headband. Her mother, Anne, is pretty in an Irish-lass sort of way but sits with prissy straightness. The old man, Vaclav, stands behind with a look that suggests he would rather be gutting something.

Patrick is surprised when Meg holds out a small package to him. He unwraps a flat wedge of stone. He stares at it, afraid to respond.

"Turn it." Meg laughs.

On the other side is a nearly perfect fossil of a dragonfly wing.

"Oh." He looks up. "That's . . . really beautiful."

Meg drifts to the mantle where the second urn with its remaining ash has been placed next to its twin. She shifts the urns this way and that. "Funny how you can look at something for so long and not realize how ugly it is." The urns are etched brass and look like they were purchased at a cheap head shop. "Awful, aren't they?"

"Well," Cathy offers, ". . . it *was* the '70s."

"Maybe I'll go down to Minneapolis and choose one decent urn for both, something less hideous."

Patrick shifts closer. "There's this pottery co-op in my neighborhood—one of the artists there makes these cool urns . . . very . . ." He scans the room, its well-designed objects and polished floor. ". . . very *you*."

"Yeah?"

"I could take you there."

"Really? If I came down, you would?"

"Sure. There's plenty to do besides. You could . . . visit."

Meg nearly claps. "That'd be great—we could go out for pizza . . ."

"And Thai . . ."

"Be warned, Pat, I will take you up on that."

While he hates being called Pat, it doesn't sound so bad coming from Meg. He looks intently from his cousin to his mother and back, noting the resemblance—the springy hair that is auburn on Meg and tinseled silver on his mother. They both have the same green eyes and sharp little trowel chins.

Meg stands next to Cathy. "I was thinking of grilling tomorrow. Can you come out for lunch?"

They are both tall, with no-nonsense shoulders and jawlines.

Cathy looks hard at her son. "Actually, it's such a long drive, and Patrick works on Monday."

"Work? Maybe not . . . I mean, I can probably get someone to cover for me."

"Are you sure?" Cathy is still looking at him.

"Yes." Patrick leans closer. "I mean, we came all this way, we've hardly gotten a chance to hang out. I was even thinking, too . . . I mean, I don't even know if it's the right season, but I wonder, if there's time, maybe we could go fishing?"

Meg smiles. "Sure we could. If Jon's not busy, he might even start up the old Evinrude for us. I know where the walleyes usually are."

"That'd be cool. But, um, what do they call it when you just fish, but don't . . ." Patrick makes a slashing gesture across his neck.

"Catch and release?"

"Yeah. That." He looks from his cousin to his mother. "Can we do that?"

⤳ DISEMBARKATION

LIFE DOES INDEED FLASH BEFORE YOUR EYES WHEN YOU'VE only got minutes left, though not in any way you'd expect, not in any order that makes sense. It's been all hop, skip, and jump from when the lightning strike cut short the question, "Peanuts, sir?" to now, as the seatbelt sign shakes itself loose to land near my shoe.

It's been no more than half a minute since the oxygen masks fell from above, and fifteen seconds since our stewardess, Mandy, has given in to hysterics and buckled herself into the fold-down seat where she now sits with her face buried, opening and closing her knees as if flashing code. The unlatched door to the cockpit swings open and shut. The pilot is stiff, possibly in shock. The co-pilot works furiously over the controls and shouts into his mouthpiece to the tower in Chicago. He repeats a series of numbers and one word, "*Vector,*" over, and over.

Like the other women, Anne is screaming, her mouth stretched so I can see the crown that was replaced after the popcorn kernel incident—we'd been watching *Ben* with our daughter, Meg. For a month now she's been begging for her own pet rat. Oh, that *that* will be the last film I'll ever see . . .

So, there is the screaming, but since time has suddenly gotten quite precious, I pretty much hear only what I want. Anne's nails are deep into my forearm—four moons of blood, but it doesn't hurt. Adrenaline, "nature's pain inhibitor!" I'd probably read that in *Reader's Digest,* one of those "I Am Joe's Urethra, I Am Jane's Adrenal Gland . . ."

I disengage Anne's grip, hoping she might settle down once she realizes this is out of our hands. Now she's maniacally stomping the footrest with all her might as if it's a brake that might stop the plane.

The vibration is impressive—it's actually hard to focus with eyeballs quaking. A *Time* magazine I'd read cover to cover is jiggling itself out of the seat pocket. Just minutes ago I'd finished an article on solar flares and had begun another claiming troops will be withdrawn soon along with more lies from Nixon. There was also something on Jane Fonda, and a poem by Ho Chi Minh. Some trio. Seems we are all doomed, when you think about it. Before the magazine, I'd read the *Trib,* also full of the sort of the crap those of us on Flight 36 are about to be spared.

A woman is repeating the Lord's Prayer for about the fifth time while someone else roars at her to shut up. There are only about twenty of us. I look around to see different reactions to identical fates. Just behind us is a couple returning from their honeymoon—sailing the Apostle Islands in Lake Superior. I know this because we stood in line at the gate together. Neither of them has made a sound, and they are holding on—forgive my saying—for dear life, wrapped like monkeys around each other, eyes squeezed shut against it all. The businessman in 8A is weeping openly. There's an old couple, calm, tearfully attempting to talk to each other over the din. Two young women traveling together sob with their foreheads fused. The woman praying aloud sits in front of a guy about my age who is now punching the back of her seat, given in to rage.

We reach for the oxygen masks, boxing at them as they dangle and sway like marionettes. I manage to get Anne into hers—it dents comically into her cheeks, filling and emptying with hysterical steam. Once we all get them on we look pretty silly. In our plastic muzzles we are Yogi Bears or Boo Boos—Meg would laugh, anyway. Anne looks at me, her horror shifting for a moment to disbelief.

That's when I realize I'm laughing.

This is awkward. I clutch her hand and shout so she can hear over the roar of the remaining engine, "Not laughing at you, darling, laughing *with* you!"

But she's not with me. Not on this one. I'm not usually jolly—hardly lighthearted—yet somehow in these (surely) last moments, everything strikes me as funny, even ridiculous, as if making up for lost laughs, a life short on levity . . . absurd thoughts and memories burble up from somewhere. Why now?

Why anything? Meg was only two months old when we brought her north the very first time. My old man picked her up, held her high above his head, and jiggled her until she spit up, straight into his mouth. I didn't actually laugh, though of course inwardly I was howling, singing, "Yes, sir, that's my baby . . . ."

She's with him now, back at the resort. Meg follows Vac around, pestering him until he lets her help, handing him tools, ferrying empty gas cans to the pump at the boathouse. I don't like her too close to the motors and all that can go wrong on the docks, but at seven she believes she can do anything, and my father only encourages it, letting her sit on his lap to run the throttle of the Chris-Craft or steer the front loader. She has a canoe paddle carved to fit her small hands and her own tiny hatchet, Christmas gifts from the Grinch himself, the man about to become her guardian.

Jesus.

Oh, here's something you don't see in movie plane crashes. The cabin is bucking like a mechanical bull. Passengers' legs lash chair-backs and arms flail overhead. We jolt side to side as if on a Tilt-a-Whirl. Anyone with eyeglasses is shit out of luck—all have flown, lost.

I press Anne's forearm down so she can't backhand me again. She's button-eyed and mute now, probably thinking of Meg, if she's thinking at all. She'd be mortified at the thought of our little girl being raised in the backwoods by a disagreeable old man, who, according to Anne, lacks warmth or anything resembling humor or compassion. Vac never liked Anne either, so they've had that in common, and they stubbornly turn only their worst sides to each other. Anne's precise manners and reserve bloom in his presence. He takes it all in while pointedly ignoring her. But there's more to Anne than Vac knows. She's smart and reasonable, and, when she forgets herself, even sexy.

There's not much I could say now about my father that might reassure her . . . . I could suggest he isn't all that surly, that his expectations of others are only in proportion to their maximum potential. That he does have feelings, just not very many.

I've just now realized that the traits we most dislike in others are the ones we most strongly share, good or bad. I hate the inherited exactitude and discipline that make me so good at what I do. It's too late, of course, but I wish for spontaneity now, to have lived more sloppy days of sloth and gluttony and whatever other deadly sins I might have crammed in . . .

So Meg might not be raised in the warmest nest but will grow up as I did, independent at least. Some study, done by the Dutch I think, claims a child's character is formed by the time they are three. And who knows, the rest of her childhood might be quite pleasant. Vac does things with her he'd never done with me—they play card games, he carries her on his shoulders, and teaches her Czech words I was never allowed. And this one thing that gives me the most hope—I've seen them doing nothing together—just drifting along in the rowboat or mucking through ditches, or sitting close to stare at the flames of whatever pile of trash or brush they've set fire to. I came into the kitchen once just as he'd sat her down and said he was going to rub her feet. I was surprised enough to stop and watch. He took a saltshaker from the table and sprinkled the leech off her foot and tossed it behind and into the sink so she wouldn't have a clue. He did a quick rub, claimed, "Good as new," and gruffly sent her on her way. He used to rip them off me like Velcro. My father might mellow with an orphan in his care—which, considering my view out this window, will soon happen. I pull the little curtain closed so Anne cannot see how closely Lake Michigan looms.

I was a half-orphan myself until I got a long-lost mother for my twenty-first birthday. Vac had always claimed she'd died but would never offer how, or of what. Then I came of age and Vac gave me a hundred dollars, a quart of scotch, and the truth—confessed that my mother was only dead to him, probably alive somewhere in Germany with the man she'd gone off with. Prague was a grim place after two years of occupation when my mother fled. Vac said he found me in my crib in our flat with milk and biscuits, and a warning pinned to my sleeper written in first person, as if I'd written it: "Feed me no bananas!" was the translation. I was two.

As my father told the story, saying the word *flat,* I could see high, baroque plasterwork and doors with prism glass opened to an ironwork balcony. I remember a quacking toy on the parquet—a wooden duck on wheels with a string. Of my mother I have no memory, no clue. A few years ago I did find a photo from which her head had been neatly torn away. Her wedding dress was sleeveless, showing plump, white arms, one clutching the pinstriped arm of her groom. Along the bottom in white ink was "Vaclav and Magda 6.9.1936." So while my mother might not have a face, she at least has a name, one my father has never once muttered in my presence. "She was gone," Vac told me. "The war was coming. So you and me, we come here. That's all."

He won't keep our daughter at the resort all the time, I can hope for that. He'll send her to boarding school, like he did with me. I'll say this: he understands the value of education. The prep school he chose for me was not convenient or inexpensive, but it was heavy in math and science, and competitive enough I might have a chance at the best universities. He chose in the end, filling out the scholarship applications himself.

Besides his errant wife, my father also had a career I'd never known about, had been an engineer himself. I learned this only on the day of my own graduation, when he gave me the sterling insignia pin from Brno Institute, his own alma mater.

An open book he isn't.

You can see why I might be a little concerned for Meg, but he's all she's got now. Anne has a beleaguered, alcoholic mother she barely speaks to, and a much younger sister, Cathy, a late-life accident only about fifteen now, set on becoming a hippie.

Vac is sixty-four, almost sixty-five. He might live to witness a few of the many of the milestones I'll miss. I won't be attending ballet recitals or school plays. No paternal jutting of the jaw for me, no protecting of Meg's virtue, no teaching her to drive, no prideful smiles at her graduations. I won't be reluctantly sending her off to college, or feeling any misgivings at losing her to some horse's ass who will make her either happy or miserable. I'll not be jostling any grandchildren on this knee . . .

But I can envision these events, can imagine what Meg might look like, and even guess at the sort of life she might live. In spite of the chaos in this cabin, amid all the moaning and panic, the imagination soars. Snippets of the future flick through my head like so many movie stills. I can see Meg as a gawky teen, then I can jump a few years forward to her face in dim light of a dorm, hunched over some college textbook. She'll be a beauty all grown up, and handsome in middle age, perhaps with features less soft. Eventually, those curls will go gray and crow's feet will crease her temples, when *she's* sixty-four . . . . Now of course, *that* tune runs through my head . . .

A hawkish clarity makes me aware of the tiniest details—fine hairs caught in the band of the Timex on our neighbor's wrist across the aisle, the stitching on the shoes of our hapless stewardess. Every fray of the ratty upholstery of my armrest is distinct. The stain on the underarm of the pilot's white shirt is shaped like a Scottie. I'm trying to calm Anne as I observe such minutiae; I modulate my voice and repeat soothing lies: "It'll all be all right. We'll land soon."

More parts of my mind are at work here than I've realized could ever be—the scientists are right about this much, the brain is indeed underused. Had I only known what I know now, think of what I might have accomplished! Were I a betting man I'd wager a thousand that if you gave me a Berlitz kit right now, I could learn Portuguese in the next few hours, if I had hours. Give me the *Times'* Sunday crossword, throw it at me.

But I'm not a betting man—and wouldn't lay any odds on our odds. Not now.

The engine sputters and something cracks and makes a whirring sound, as if metal is spinning away from the plane. We are descending now. Our final descent.

Well.

There is something to be said for the relief—that all decisions about the future are suddenly made. We are off the hook, no more thinking, no more responsibility. I'm relieved of my duties, won't ever have to accomplish so much as buying a stamp . . . Shame I won't live to see the millennium, though, that I won't spend my retirement in the next century. My partner Paul predicts that by the year 2000 there will be computers no bigger than briefcases. Overpopulation will have us living stacked like cordwood, but cancer will be curable. In twenty-eight years, in 2000, Meg will be thirty-four, the age I am now. My orphaned daughter will be a grown woman driving an electric car and living in a cubicle.

What, if anything, will she remember of us? There are plenty of photographs for her to reference, and most have heads, but . . . I should regret not searching for my mother, though I did not think much about her one way or another until Meg was just beginning to walk, when one day I looked at my daughter and grew furious at the idea that someone could abandon a toddler. All I've ever wanted of my mother is to know why.

I look at Anne and feel few regrets, for without her there'd be no Meg.

She first came to Naledi as a nanny with a family from Milwaukee. I'd finished my third year at Urbana, ready to apply to Caltech as a grad student, and she was at a women's college in Illinois. She was lovely and ice-cool, and unlike other girls in that I had to chase her. Vac said nothing, only asked if she was a Catholic. We wrote each other, and she came back the next summer to be a waitress at a fancier resort closer to town. She made it a point to date others, to torture me. Sometimes I think I married her because I was jealous, or because my father didn't like the look of her. Sometimes I give myself more credit. We weren't unhappy in the eight years before Meg, and then, once she was born, there was something real between us.

We left Naledi this morning while Meg was having oatmeal and drawing with colored chalk. When she saw I was carrying luggage, she stood up on the chair and did her little dance and sang our farewell song, "Daddywog, Pollywog, off and away, Daddywog, Pollywog, back another day!"

I recently walked in on Anne trying to entice Meg into making a song just for the two of them, but Meg was absorbed in finger paints and stubbornly uncooperative. Anne was pouting a little, but when she saw me in the doorway, she was mortified. I shrugged, saying just the wrong thing, "Sometimes it's just that father-daughter thing." She snatched *After the Gold Rush* from the eight-track pile and pitched it at me.

We drove to Duluth and caught the Chicago flight, stopping in Minneapolis to pick up more passengers. It's the same flight we take on summer Sundays on the way home to our four-day workweeks. We can do this, fly unlimited weekends in July and August, because Anne works for the very airline that owns and operates this plane (which is about to crash or explode or both), in the PR department, no less. I don't expect she'd appreciate the irony of that right now.

I repeat myself, but, again, this is not at all like you see in the movies: there's no wind howling through the compartment, no debris flying. Just a shuddering and falling, and now and then a sudden bouncing up and gain in altitude that I suspect some of the other passengers might mistake as a good sign.

It's been eight minutes exactly—my second hand is precise, though I'd prefer one of those new digital watches if they didn't cost a grand. I'm the only one who can see into the cockpit when the door swings. I've watched the pilot, nearly catatonic with fear, come to life long enough to take off his cap and puke into it. The copilot has his hands on the controls, but he shakes like a leaf each time he looks at them . . .

I tell Anne again, it will be all right. And this time I'm sincere. It *will* be all right. We will die, yes, but it'll be all right. What a misused phrase that is, how flippantly we bandy it about . . . *all right* means all is right, right? All is certainly not right, but this is what it is. I've never believed in fate, or any crap like astrology or life after death, but the reality—the here and now—is not something you can argue, is it? The plane's been hit by lightning. That is a fact.

"My baby," Anne groans, clutching the ball of her stomach. Well, not everyone gets to be born. A son, I was hoping . . . . But I'm not even going there . . .

Anne keens, "Meg, Meg, Meg." I disengage her nails again, this time from my thigh, and clamp her hands between mine.

I peek through the curtain to see we are now paralleling the shoreline. Lake Michigan will take us in. It will be much, much colder than Hatchet Lake. What the impact doesn't accomplish, hypothermia and drowning will.

I've been nearly done in by both myself and have to say I can think of worse ways to go. Back when I still went to the Hatchet Inlet Middle School, Vac drove me five miles to the bus stop on the main road each morning, either on snowmobile or by truck. One day, I waited half an hour before I reckoned the bus had either broke down or I'd missed it, but in any case, it wasn't coming. It was a long walk back to Naledi at ten below zero, but I'd have made it, if not for making the stupid mistake of sitting down to eat my sack lunch. After two frozen bologna sandwiches, I couldn't, didn't want to get up—all my energy had gone to digesting the icy food. By the time Vac came searching he was lucky to find me curled up near a culvert, feeling ever so sleepy.

Drowning isn't a bad option either. When I was nineteen and home from school during a Christmas vacation, one of the local girls I used to hang around with drove out. Vac had gone to Eveleth to get a part for some pump, so we had the place to ourselves. The girl, Kari, had brought a bottle of Bushmills, which we opened in the sauna. She showed me a trick her uncle knew for getting very drunk very fast, mixing the booze with water and pouring it onto the hot rocks. We inhaled 120 proof steam and waited. And it was like being slugged. Kari took off her bikini top and ran from the building. I thought she'd only roll in the snow, but then she jumped into the hole cut in the ice, and I followed like a stupid seal. Between the cold shock and the alcohol, things quickly went bad. I took in a huge breath of water and began to sink. While Kari and her blonde hair floated just above, all backlit and oblivious, my muscles would do nothing I asked. It was almost too late by the time she realized I wasn't fooling. She managed to pull me up and out, but really, I would've been content to stay . . . it would've been a great last vision—a bare-breasted girl swimming through a ray of cold.

Maybe these moments are less frightening because of those. Death within reach is nothing so terrifying as death from afar.

Anne is trembling now and trying to say something, but it's stuck.

I squeeze her hands. "I know, Annie. Shush. It doesn't matter, now. Close your eyes."

As I said, I don't buy the idea of eternity, but I might entertain the notion that if there's anything out there—up there—it might just be some collective spirit, winking down on us with a bit of unconditional forgiveness and amusement for our foibles. To be alive is to be a fool. Surely those approaching death head-on understand that much, as do I, only now.

My father did his best. My mother did her best, too, which maybe wasn't so good, but she was human, so naturally weak when tempted with happiness.

I can smile now and realize that benevolence might be within my grasp, or whatever pure state that comes of losing everything—of having nothing to lose. The Buddhists have that shit down, don't they?

I take off my oxygen mask and kiss my wife's forehead.

Meg will be given what love as Vac has to give. She'll be taken care of.

I catch a glimpse out the window and inhale. My chest opens—possibly with the first full breath I've taken since this has

AT THE SOUND OF BOOTS SCUFFING GRAVEL POLLY McPHEE peers over the sill and sighs. It's him again, this time leaning on a spade with his stubbly chin propped on the handle. If it was only that, but he's directly facing her window, not quite staring, just fixed.

"Shoo!" she whispers, yanking the window shade hard enough to make another tear.

Polly would already have a good start if not for his lurking. She has traveled a great distance and is finally settling in, recovered from her road-weariness. But now, how is she to concentrate, let alone write? When it isn't Mr. Machutova, it's the wind. Neither has desisted since her arrival—he shuffles and loiters all day, and pine branches cuff the roof all night. And day or night, the slurp of surf makes Polly imagine she needs to pee every hour or so.

She cranks the volume on the cassette deck toted from Halifax. Maybe Rostropovich will drive the old man off.

There are few guests at the resort, only two other cabins have cars on their grassy slopes, but Polly imagines more will arrive soon. Then he'll have to quit his lollygagging to manage things, greet people, open cabins, and make them habitable. Hers barely had been, but Mr. Machutova had conveniently vaporized before she'd had a chance to inspect her lodgings. His negligence aside, Polly hadn't really minded her few hours of housekeeping—after her days in the car she craved physical activity. Cleaning was an unavoidable delay in sitting down to her task. As she shook mouse droppings from drawers and scoured rust stains from the basin, Polly looked around the rooms—if memory served, they'd once been particularly airy and gleaming. Could the place be so dulled by twenty summers? Or had memory put on a polish that hadn't been there to begin with?

She'd hung her cleaning rags on the line, but within an hour wind had jettisoned them to the needle-orange ground along with two hand-washed blouses. If it had been wind she was craving she might have stayed in Cape Breton, where Eleanor used to complain she'd have to turn herself every now and again when walking or be left at a slant.

When attempting to pin the laundry back up, the clothesline itself fell and the hook proved too high for her to reattach. He seemed to be everywhere yet nowhere when needed. She'd searched the grounds, finally billowing up to the lodge to find him bent over a peeling porch table, reading the portion of a newspaper not covered by the paint can set on it. A wet paintbrush poked from the back pocket of his coveralls, a mustard-yellow accident poised to happen.

When she asked if he'd see to the clothesline, his response was a grunt and he didn't move an eyelash, didn't seem to care a whit. Annoyed, she pointed to the window where aspen leaves repeatedly plastered themselves as if trying to get in. "And when might *this* be expected to stop?"

Mr. Machutova milked the loose skin over his Adam's apple. "Couldn't know that. Only know this day's weather. See here." He lifted the paint can, leaving a bright eclipse over the newsprint. "Forecast. Just arrived."

"Pardon?"

"Newspaper comes on the mail boat. Mail on mail boat is two days old—the forecast is for two days future, so, arrives with weather." While she absorbed this he added, "Maybe something working its way down from Manitoba."

Naturally, she thought, blame Canada.

After dinner Polly sits at the little enamel table with one of the blank Moleskine journals almost too nice to sully with ink. Somehow in the chaos of packing she'd forgotten her fistfuls of

pencils and a six-pack of legal pads. Now she has only the journals and expensive fountain pens that had been retirement presents. She stares out the porch screen where sun casts shadows
of spruce eastward like spears. The coolness of the tabletop
seeps into her forearms and raises gooseflesh. Finally putting
down the pen she shakes her wrist as if she actually has been
writing.

She has begun rereading her notes, pondering possible beginnings. Now all she needs to do is cobble her thoughts into sentences and those sentences into paragraphs to fill pages that will
form chapters. Of course she knows writing a book is no simple
matter, having written several on her dual subjects of botany and
geology, but memoir has proven more difficult than Polly would
have imagined. Every time she sits down to it, something just at
the front of her skull goes tight, leaving her squeezing her temples as if to extrude the words forth. In these few attempts, Polly
has learned two things: that memory is far from reliable, and that
a life, no matter how riveting, cannot be written out in a linear
fashion and still be riveting. Hers certainly isn't.

How is it, Polly wonders, that there are so few facts in a life?

There must be paper and pencils around somewhere. She
shrugs into her pea coat and walks the road, looking over her
shoulder before ducking down short driveways of ragged grass
centered between sandy tracks. There are two couples with children at the resort, but they are housed on the far side. Letting
herself into vacant cabins, Polly pulls drawers and opens cupboards only to find a few loose sheets of spiral notepaper, a score
tablet for bridge, a dry Biro, and a few colored pencils.

Back on her porch, she looks to the opposite shore blurring
in the dusk, can hear the surf break only a few yards from the
cabin—fast little waves pawing the shore as if trying to pull the
pebbles in. Polly closes her eyes to concentrate. Satisfied she
doesn't have to go, she sighs relief at avoiding the darkening path
to the outhouse.

She makes tea, opens a book, and after reading the same
passage twice nods away from the pages with a soft snore.

Arriving at the lodge out of breath with the knot blown out of her scarf, Polly finds Mr. Machutova at the reception desk, crabbed over a page of the same newspaper, working on a much-smudged crossword puzzle. The table is painted, save one leg. When Polly politely asks for paper and pencils, he frowns.

"Paper? Paper can be bought in town."

Of course it can. But her schedule is one Polly means to stick to, and her planned trip to town isn't until Tuesday. The drive isn't one she would relish making twice in one week.

"Please. You must have something?"

He ducks away, mumbling in his language. Returning, he stands behind the counter as if to remind her he is the proprietor and sets down a thin stack of construction paper, several sheets of lined binder paper, and two short pencils from the Scrabble box. Yesterday's paint is dried over his knuckles.

"Thank you."

When he fails to respond, Polly retreats the way she came. On a window ledge near the door is the mislaid paintbrush, its bristles mummified yellow.

At her "desk" she lines up what paper the old man has surrendered plus what she's found on her own. Sharpened pencil stubs are arranged over a dish towel blotter, and a cushion is pressed over the wicker seat of her chair. The kettle is on the hob and tea in the pot. Once everything is ready, Polly stands at the window for several minutes. The sun is shining steadily after a spotty morning of fast-moving clouds. Really, it's entirely too nice to spend the whole day indoors. Embarking on what she tells herself will be a short walk, just a quick tour of the grounds, Polly lifts her coat from its hook and lets the screen door slam behind her.

The road and cabins look about the same. Since her visit in the '60s the place has not been modernized in any way save the addition of a cinderblock bathhouse. She steps in to inspect two shower stalls and a dresser with an oil lamp. An alcove holds a

claw-foot tub facing two glass block windows. On her way out
Polly feels the gas hot-water heater by the door and leans, wrapping her arms as if around a shapeless uncle.

Much of the resort is pocked with neglect: a sack of mortar left leaning near a wall has hardened to its own shape, with
tatters of sack flapping; a tipped wheelbarrow has a maple sap-
ling sprung through its rusted hole. Flat stones from a run of
stairs have eroded to a jumble below, and high on the plateau
old cabins lean like a trio of gossips, their eaves and sills lushly
bumpered with moss. Polly takes a vaguely familiar path inland where it's less windy, walking in the manner she does most
things, with purpose—anchored on her immediate surroundings,
not on what might be around the next bend or what she's just
passed. Bunchberry has berried and the sumac has gone bright.
A fork in the path leads to a bog, where each footprint fills with
water and spindly tamarack drop yellow needles. At her feet are
colorful pitcher plants looking tropical and misplaced amid the
hair-cap and hornwort. Inhaling deeply, Polly recalls students'
faces going blank when she'd attempted describing the smell of a
bog. Water hyacinths, leatherleaf, bog rosemary—soft and woody
plants in various stages of growth and bloom and rot make for
a heady decay. Once through the bog, Polly forks away onto a
deer path. The first hundred yards are clear, but soon she must
press through thick alder bushes that close on her like curtains
of switches. The trail climbs the ridge, nearly to the crest of the
divide. Halfway up, it narrows, much more steeply than she remembers. Her walking stick is back at the cabin. She turns back
down and veers the wrong way. In the middle of a clearing she
looks down to see no path at all. Polly has always prided herself
on her keen sense of direction—what Eleanor had called her in-
trepid compass. She turns a full circle, sure the path was just here
but then sees it might possibly be over there. The sun is obscured
behind a bank of clouds so she cannot get a reading on north.
She walks almost the entire perimeter of the clearing twice before finding the path, and then nearly missing it.

Almost glad to be headed back into the nasty thicket, she

hurries back to the resort, feeling foolish that she of all people should be lost. She's only sixty-two—yet for a moment had felt the apprehension of an elderly person, experienced a sense of time warping, of having missed a step. She doesn't relax entirely until reaching the cabin door. Hand on the knob, she looks up to the hill to the woods she's just come from. It's been a very long time since she's been at Naledi. Surely, walking along with someone is a different matter from finding one's way alone.

The days feel truncated. Each is, in fact, shorter than the previous day, if only by a minute or two, the daylight slowly leached by the latitude and season. Polly welcomes autumn, welcomes the coolness of this corner of Minnesota, which is actually farther north than Halifax. On her long drive here, she'd been amused to find herself heading north from Canada.

Thursday she took a canoe ride and paid dearly for it. Skimming along as if pushed, she'd reached Ontario in only minutes, then had to fight the headwind for more than an hour to get back, getting down on her knees among the ribs for stability. Paddling continuously, she'd done something to her shoulder in the process.

Trudging back and forth to the bathhouse where she's taken to soaking in Epsom salts, Polly seldom encounters other guests—she's only exchanged pleasantries with the Mickelsons and Harveys—but at the sight of their cars being loaded, she regrets not having been more social. The rolling beach balls are deflated, life vests hung on their pegs, and the sand cleared of plastic toys. When they pulled away, Polly surprised herself by hurrying down the road to see them off, nearly trotting behind to wave at the small faces lining the rear windows. She tripped to a stop in her clogs and kept waving a little too long, like an abandoned granny.

On her way back, she sees Mr. Machutova heading to the fire pit, bent under the load of twigs on his back looking for all the world like a character out of Grimms'. Now it's just her and the old grump, who despite his own penchant for lurking seems to twitch at her every approach. Polly is curious about arriving guests, but not enough to ask. It seems the only other soul at Naledi is the young laborer always hauling something or passing by in his jeep, eyes shaded by a fringe of black hair and attitude.

In the lounge she casually looks around to see if the reservation book happens to be out or open. Polly leans over the candy case with its few Hershey bars and packets of licorice that were once red. Her gaze shifts from the candy to the glass and her own reflection. Faced at such an unflattering angle, there's little to be vain about. Her hair is the same pageboy she's worn for decades, gray now instead of gingery, cropped just beneath her ears, where her neck has gone to crepe. Her face has grown broader, as if to match the spread of her hips. She lines up one eye with the *o* in Salted Nut Roll, blinking along with the tick of the clock, time passing, she thinks, even as she stares at herself like an old fool.

Determined not to fret over wasted days (five!) and disgusted at her failure to produce one decent page, Polly loads the cassette player with Bolognini, breaks the seal on her inkpot, and takes up the best pen, the gold one etched with her initials. Not allowing herself a second to think, she dips into the ink and begins at the beginning, quite awfully.

When I was young . . . when I was just a young girl in a small town . . .

In our gray harbor town, ~~when I was young~~ where I was born. Polly sighs as she strikes words. "For God's sake, just write." Writing badly, she reminds herself, is better than not writing at all. She's taken to speaking aloud thoughts and the words she's writing; at first absentmindedly, but then reckoning that if she speaks she might hear herself actually say something. She has begun, at least, powering the pen forward with whatever comes. After a half-hour of battling the impulse to edit as she goes, Polly settles into something akin to a rhythm. The particular motion of setting ideas to paper reminds her she enjoys writing, not least the tactile elements—the scritch of the pen, the way pages polish the heel of her hand, her pen nib clinking the bottle in so many inky toasts.

Within the hour he is hanging about near the cabin, raking and reraking the same piles of aspen leaves, but this time she barely notices. Cello strains swell over the sounds of wind scouring the gutters and the creaks of the chair she's forgotten is so uncomfortable. When reaching the end of each page, Polly scans it, biting the gold fountain pen. Only later will she see the tooth marks and chuckle. Each dent represents progress, however slight. She inhales the blue smell of ink, ignoring the screen door that repeatedly yawns open a few inches before banging shut.

By afternoon Polly has half of a chapter describing her childhood home and the provincial port she'd fled at seventeen. Rereading, she winces at more florid sentences, quickly editing out such drivel as *urged, even by the waves that seemingly whispered . . . away away.* And *to follow a future I knew was farther than my young mind could travel.* She wishes for a red pencil, reaching for a burnt umber crayon to run through words like *provenance, fruition,* and *destiny,* stanching the sentimental ooze.

Outside, the rusted Orange Crush thermometer sways lightly on its hook, scraping the cedar.

Slowly, her words have begun to form into the paragraphs, detailed descriptions of the seaside, the eaveless shingled fishermen's houses, the village streets and the roads slanting down to the cannery and the docks, the cliffs and headlands jutting into the Atlantic like prows of decommissioned ships. Polly has yet to begin describing what happened in such places—hadn't actually anticipated that difficulty.

Polly understood early on that she could not flourish in Cape Breton, where blind faith bowed the McPhee family low before a harsh God. They belonged to a closed brethren, convinced that if they could just endure the suffering of this life—a given in their gray harbor town, swept clear of prospects by Polly's teens—they would be rewarded at the moment of the Rapture. The Rapture, Polly was warned, could occur at any moment. In some radiant flash the sky would wedge open and McPhees, tall and small, would be yanked heavenward, uprooted from their plodding realities, away from the suffering that seemed, at least to Polly, to be self-inflicted—the worst sort of poverty, in which they had enough to eat, but minds went unnourished. Radio, newspapers, or magazines were not allowed in the McPhee house. The list of acceptable secular books besides school texts totaled twenty. There was no music other than hymns, and contact with anyone outside the brethren—anyone interesting or curious—was discouraged. Schooling leaned heavily to scripture, and the only science class was rudimentary botany. At night, young Polly tied her ankle to the bedpost with a jump rope to avoid being sucked from her bed and through the roof lest the Rapture come for her. Lying sleepless in the sag, girded by hard-breathing sisters, Polly was wholly unable to imagine rising up among them, consistently failing to envision an afterlife. Each time she tried, the vision was no more than a void with little sparks, the same thing she always saw with her eyes scrunched tight.

After procuring her first library card (Polly somehow understood this to be her first subversive act) she began to quietly discover, volume by volume, that there existed a world beyond their raw cape. Initially she was drawn to other landscapes, climates populated with exotic natives: Laplanders or Mongols. Polly's mind was malleable, and she could imagine these other cultures were not so immoral as she'd been taught, only different—she'd been warned about heathens, but the more she read, the harder it was to believe that such people as the gentle Polynesians or Inuit were doomed to Hell. Questions accumulated, the sort Polly knew well enough not to ask at home, not that anyone there would have answers. The librarian often did and would lead her into the stacks to pull out this book or that. Polly read the science textbooks forbidden in school and became particularly keen on the laws of gravity and physics, which were proven indisputable, unlike faith. While the public school girls in town swooned to Frank Sinatra or James Dean, cutting pictures from movie magazines, Polly kept a tracing of Isaac Newton folded into her hymnal. Her limited contact with those outside the church and her instinctive avoidance of those within meant Polly was more or less on her own.

The one steadfast constant Polly found safe to moor herself to was her surroundings—the earth and sea and their innumerable mysteries. Even the weather, which was often brutal, at least made more sense than the wrath or benevolence of unseen deities. For companionship she sometimes sidled close to the seals loitering on the wharf, giving them names she might give dogs (there were no such things as pets on the McPhee farm). Fishermen grew accustomed to the pudgy girl sitting on coils of rope, feeding bits of her lunch to seals she called Rex and Freddy and Alice, sometimes reading aloud to them from the pages of *National Geographic* about their far-flung cousins in the Arctic or the Galapagos Islands, the coasts of California and British Columbia.

Her furtive studies expanded to include geology, botany, and biology. After reading Henslow she became interested in theories of evolution and Darwin. She asked Miss Smithwick, the librarian, for Mr. Darwin's books in a whisper and was allowed to read them in the tiny office behind the circulation desk.

Walking home from the wharf one afternoon, Polly was able to shrug off the brand of fear worn by her family like cloaks. She was released from notions of wrath, and indeed from fear of or belief in any god, in any form. It happened as she walked toward the headlands, as a soft rain began to fall, streaking the cliffs and pocking the bay. There was no sense rushing, she was going to get soaked in any case. As pebbles on the beach grew wet, the pitch of their sound underfoot deepened. Rain parted her hair, rivuleted to the tip of her nose, and launched in drips from her earlobes. As if coming awake after a long dream, Polly stopped and slowly took in everything around her, all more detailed with each blink, the added dimensions, deeper saturations, and harder outlines. In a few moments—and it only took a few— she came to understand that each drop of rain, each molecule of water and earth and those of her own body were of a whole, one inseparable from the other: that she and the cliff and the pocked sea and the wet beach were unified. Polly knew then that she belonged to *this* world, grateful for the knowledge she would never be snared skyward in the queer fate her family prayed so hard for. When her physical life ended, so would she—just as the beach pebbles would dry when the sun emerged. Rain trickling down her neck became a sort of reverse baptism. A simple cloudburst had solved the mystery of the universe for her—that there was no mystery, that life was the complex result, the stunning fusion, of all that occurs in the sum of nature and time.

Nearly fifty years later, that afternoon remains indelible in her mind, and occasionally she recalls her bolt of clarity on that shingle beach. One day she had walked into a tourist shop and saw a T-shirt with simple black letters, Life's a Beach. She'd chuckled while handing over her money and wore the T-shirt around the house and in the garden until it was baggy and frayed, the words nearly laundered away.

Polly was inspired to study harder, and her grades landed her a scholarship to United College, secretly applied for with the help of Miss Smithwick. Aware of what she was up against at home, she revealed her intention to go away to school only on the morning she was scheduled to depart for Winnipeg.

When she made her announcement, her father abruptly stood and her family rose in his wake instinctively like a flock of birds. In the ensuing silence, her eight brothers and sisters filed out of the kitchen, and Polly was left to face her parents alone. It was not as if they weren't kind or good people, they were. But predicting their reaction, Polly had stowed her suitcase and the vinyl clutch with her train ticket in a culvert near the main road. She didn't expect them to be proud or glad, exactly—aspirations weren't encouraged in the McPhee household. Hope for better was considered immodest and un-Scottish. Polly anticipated her mother's tears but was surprised by her father's fury. Of all things, to study science? She was an infidel. Standing before her father unbowed, she could see that ignorance doubled his anger and fear. One of his own flesh and blood would be damned to Hell, he roared at her.

Polly was almost amused by the irony and tried to reassure him: "But Papa, you needn't worry, because I don't *believe* in Hell."

Never having been struck, she found her shock eclipsed the pain when her father's broad palm caught her jaw. As she staggered to get balance, her mother did not reach out. Her parents stood together, eyes locked and hard. She rubbed her jaw and looked at each of them, awed by the depth of their faith. Nothing Polly could ever say or do would make them understand that it was senseless to condemn those who did not believe as they did. Filled with pity, Polly backed away and quietly stepped out the side door as if only to get some air, or perhaps fetch the mail. She didn't look back, just walked as steadily as she was able.

Arthur, her oldest brother, followed her down the drive and across the road, where Polly gathered her hidden things. He wordlessly took the burden of her suitcase, and they walked together as far as the crossroads, where he waited with her for the bus that would take her through the village and to the town beyond, where she would catch her train.

When the bus came into view Arthur shook her hand with a sad smile, insisting she take a few folded bills he'd earned crabbing. "Don't forget us, sister, and wear the McPhee tartan now and again," adding, "I'll pray for your soul."

She touched his sleeve. "I don't have a soul, Arthur."

"Oh, Polly, that's a bit of drama, now . . ."

"Just think of me now and then."

In town, Miss Smithwick met her bus and spoke excitedly, but Polly barely registered the words. She was the last passenger to board the late train. Outside the window, all solid forms—people, buildings, and streets—had dissolved in the dark wedge between sunset and moonrise. As the train began to tick along, slowly gaining speed, Polly could no longer clearly make out what she was leaving behind.

The steeple of a newly erected church came into view, lit by a bright electric beam.

"Catholic excess," she heard a woman mutter. The light shone like a beacon, and as the train drew nearer Polly could see it was beckoning more than souls. Several passengers stood suddenly, a few with mouths agape. The beam of light wrapping the cross had attracted tens of thousands of moths, all manic and swirling in a pulsing funnel.

A few passengers crossed themselves at the site of the phenomenon, believing they were witness to some miracle—a miracle Polly knew was nothing more than nature interrupted: the artificial light was brighter than the moon and so pulled and held the moths in thrall, derailing them from their true migratory patterns. Most would batter themselves to exhaustion soon enough. In the morning, worshipers would be greeted with a carpet of pale wings over the church steps, a few last flutterings in the weave. Were her own family witness to such a sight, they might believe it to be a warning or omen regarding their misguided daughter.

Polly rereads her pages and sits back in her chair, massaging her stiff hand. Now that she's actually written something, she understands that to write effectively means to degloss history— to remember what she'd rather not and enter those scenes that stretched most painfully across her past.

A crash of biblical loudness erupts outside. The notebook in her lap falls as she snaps upright. She's out the screen door and down the stairs in time to see the last of the glass bottles tumble to crack against stones. The rolling rubbish barrel clangs to a stop, then rocks to stillness. He's just up the hill, on his feet now and slapping dust from his knees with his cap. The old fool!

"Good Lord. Are you all right, Mr. Machutova?"

"Yes, yes." He waves her away.

Ignoring his gesture she rights the barrel and begins tossing in strewn glass. If she helps, he'll be out of the way sooner.

At university she studied a dual major of botanical science and geology, supporting herself by waiting tables at an Italian restaurant and doing odd jobs in the school lab. Keeping her grades at a level that would guarantee scholarships took every moment between work and sleep. Letters home were returned unopened during the first two years. Her third Christmas alone in Winnipeg, Arthur sent a card, wishing her well, with news that three of her five sisters had married and one had given birth, but that otherwise, the McPhees were as they had always been.

The following Christmas her brother sent another card, this time with a thin letter enclosed. Their mother had died—not unexpectedly, he wrote. Sisters had birthed more babies, and Arthur had gotten married himself. The letter was a simple chronology of events one might find committed to the pages of a family bible. Again, he promised to pray for her.

She went to the University of Manitoba for her graduate studies. Her thesis topics were the soils and crust formations of extreme regions of the Canadian Shield. Field studies were spent in harsh conditions in the muskeg and alpine tundra. On such trips she was often the only woman. She wasn't pretty enough to be bothered by her fellow students but was often sought to help make an identification or solve a problem. Polly had little interest in the young men she spent so much time among, digging alongside or trekking behind. They did not treat her deferentially in the way they might treat an attractive or thin girl—in the field, at least, she was an equal.

When Polly matriculated with honors, the aging couple that owned the restaurant, the Delveccios, proudly attended her graduation ceremony and even hosted a small party for her. Somewhere she has a picture of herself in cap and gown, wedged between two beaming faces much darker than her own. Rudy and Marina had treated her well for the six years she was with them, and on the back of the snapshot were words in Marina's pretty loop: *Piccolo Polly, a doctor of geologist. Stupendo!*

In the Hatchet Inlet grocery store, Polly grows nearly giddy to find a sprawling school supplies display stocked for the fall term. She buys blue-lined coil binders, ballpoints, #2 pencils, a three-hole punch, legal pads, and, ever the teacher, red pencils.

Back at the cabin, she tosses her groceries into the icebox and sits to organize, gathering the old notes she'd repeatedly pawed through during her first days at Naledi. She groups them by date and relevance, hole-punching and collecting all the loose papers into the ring binder—old trip itineraries and calendar pages; scraps old enough to have yellowed; scribbles with turns of phrases that struck her as either poetic or amusing; descriptions of places or people; snippets overheard; things she'd thought to be silly or profound; bits of wisdom, adages, anecdotes; memorable things Eleanor had said . . . . One Sunday they had been out walking in a poor neighborhood when the door of a very small house opened and an Irish family dressed for mass began spilling out one by one. Polly lost count as children kept emerging, laughing when Eleanor mused in her dry way, "Babes from the womb like Shriners from a circus car."

After graduation, Polly took the first post offered and happily discovered teaching suited her. Her students were not much younger than she, but most seemed a generation apart—certainly in regard to their experiments with drugs and what they called free love. She could identify with their urges to rebel and gained their respect by respecting them, even as deep chasms existed between other faculty and students. The syllabus for her geology classes contained both botany and biology, since she knew it was senseless to teach only one science when each was so intrinsic to the other. Her biology class was heavily peppered with meteorology, which made categorizing or crediting her courses difficult, though the courses themselves were made more instructive and illuminating with such inclusions.

Knowing that publishing would advance her career, Polly immediately began writing texts. *Basalt, Black Fly, and Blueberry* is still taught. Polly never tired of her work—of talking about it, thinking about it, reading, or looking at the earth, poking at chunks and shards, turning them this way and that, and connecting the workings of each to the other. She carried a retractable pick, a small chisel, and specimen bottles in her purse, since you never knew.

In nature things were rarely what they seemed; scabs of tundra over sedimentary rock and glacial rifts looked barren but hosted amazing life—the microscopic contents of a mud puddle revealed a gala of organisms. One simply had to look.

"In the sedge-moss marshes," Polly once wrote, "the spring black fly (*Simulium venustum*) does indeed have a purpose besides biting victims to suicidal distraction—they pollinate blueberries. The wild blueberry (*vaccinium*) has quite an anecdotal and interesting history itself. In the twelfth century, Hildegard of Bingen, German nun and composer, was allegedly bestowed of numerous visions and epiphanies, likely brought on by the chronic migraines she suffered. Hildegard was also a healer and herbalist who discovered blueberries to be effective in inducing menstruation, though if not dosed carefully, sometimes more. In this discovery, Hildegard, a Catholic saint, thus unwittingly imparted herbal medicinal recipes to future generations of abortionists."

Such inclusions, considered gimmicky by her fellows, were sometimes criticized as were her methods: letting loose a jarful of insects in her classroom might buy some trouble with the department head, but the value of such demonstrations was proven in her high grade averages at the end of each term. Her texts were cited for overuse of analogy by her peers, a lack in structure, and liberal employment of anecdotes and asides—too heavy with human elements and observations. Her classes were popular enough to always have a wait list. Polly needed her students to know not necessarily *how* but simply *why* each piece of what they learned fit into nature's intricate jigsaw puzzle.

When her book *Torn Continent* caught on in American universities, she was offered posts at prestigious schools, though the farthest she ventured was Ottawa. But after Eleanor, she retreated back to the Maritimes, spending years in St. Johns, as far away as one could get from Argentina, where Eleanor eventually settled.

Her long career had ended teaching in Halifax—with enough years in service to collect the gold pen with the crest and insignia *Lux et veritas.*

Light and truth. The same pen, now incisor-dented, holds the place in a book on the porch table while Polly walks the road to clear her head. Another day of pressing backward has effectively pasted her into history, so that she cannot help comparing then to now. Stopping to catch her breath and rub a heel, she thinks back to childhood, of how she'd wandered miles of coastal plateau in all weather. As a student she trudged all terrains; geological events were seldom situated in convenient places. She'd always been a hiker. She and Eleanor would practically walk their feet off scouring the hills, Polly trailing her lover, the avid birder who identified songbirds and mimicked them in her own singsong warble. Eleanor laughed over what an odd pair they must make—she so tall with her binoculars aimed at the sky, trilling like a fool, and Polly bowed like a grazing animal, searching out plants or rocks, hoping for green agate or a blunt-leafed orchid. "I would think," Polly mused, "that we make an odd sight in any case." Eleanor was dark and thin, Polly was short and soft, like something underbaked—an endomorph to Eleanor's ectomorph. Eleanor looked mysterious, and Polly, in her own mind, was dowdy, robbed of color, with coarse hair undecided between ginger and brown. Her freckled cheeks tended to pink up from excitement, wine, or sun. If she gained an ounce of weight, it showed first on her face. "Pig cheeks," she called herself in the mirror. From a distance, she and Eleanor might have been mistaken for a severe governess and her chubby charge.

Eleanor was a cellist with the Ottawa Symphony and had been married once. She'd kept the flat she'd shared with her late husband, a violinist who had died young in a taxicab accident in Vienna. Polly was never quite comfortable in the flat, its history reminding her that Eleanor could choose.

The cabin bed is soft and the springs beneath caw like gulls with the slightest roll or wriggle. She dreams of shorebirds wheeling, of her mother gripping her collar so she won't topple from the pier or slip away. Eleanor is below, holding the gunwale of a bobbing yawl, waving for Polly to come down. The boat has striped sails like none Polly has ever seen. The cement stairs down to the tide line have dissolved in the salt air so that each is no more than a bump on a steep, gritty slope. Each time Polly tries to move, she's held fast by her mother's grip on her anorak. Eleanor's boat is less a boat than a bowl, a round vessel with no aft or stern, no way to tell which direction it might go once launched. Words she tries to shout to Eleanor are blown back into her mouth. Polly struggles, twisted in her nightgown, trying to break from the dream.

A tree limb near the cabin cracks and falls to hit the roof, jolting her awake. Groggy and alarmed, she wrestles the window shut, growing awake enough to ponder getting paper and pen to write down all she'd dreamt. But Polly reasons that surely such images are too vivid to forget—the foil gray of a sky before a gale, Eleanor's dark hair blown straight like a banner, a fairy-tale boat with sails bright as foreign flags. Eleanor had been older in the dream, her face as it would be now, as angular as Polly's is round. Hardly a dream one could forget. Polly thinks of the adjectives she might employ in describing it in writing and drifts back into sleep on sentences that swell with eloquence.

Over breakfast, Polly struggles to remember some odd dream—of not being able to move forward, a code of words she could barely make out, called from afar . . . a vessel? The moment she picks up her pen even these few fractured images slip away like sinking bits of mirror.

⤳ ⤳

Polly reads through all she's written since arriving. She edits for hours. Weeds, she thinks, her pages half-choked with them. By Saturday she has completed her first chapters. Pitiful, she thinks, considering the effort.

After washing up the dinner dishes, she goes out to the deck only to step on Mr. Machutova's discarded sunflower seed husks, crunching. He's been around again! Likely while she was playing the tape deck and unable to hear him over the music.

At the lodge steps she pauses on the first riser, rehearsing in a whisper, "Mr. Machutova, I'd appreciate my privacy. Mr. Machutova, I do not need watching over, you needn't be . . . so attentive? So present? Mr. Machutova . . ."

Why he can't just knock on the damned door and ask for whatever it is he wants? She enters the lodge porch and moves through the old bar with its collection of taxidermy, much of it suffering mange or the loss of glass eyes—Eleanor had chuckled at the sight every time: a jackalope rabbit with miniature antlers. The sorts of things drunks and children roar at.

A chair scrapes in a far room, and the sound of a spoon to bowl draws her beyond the reception area, deeper into the lodge through a dark beadboard hallway ending at the threshold of a dim kitchen. He's sitting with his back to her, elbows splayed, looking through a magnifier at a magazine.

"Mr. Machutova?" The room is warm. Fruit flies circle a bowl, eyelet curtains hemmed in stains thrum at the window. Polly leans on the doorjamb.

He's running his finger down a column and moving his lips. He either hasn't heard or is feigning deafness. If she tapped his bony shoulder, who would jump higher?

The linoleum is laid over with newspaper caked with boot prints. The icebox door is not quite closed, and though Polly wants badly to step in and press it shut, she doesn't. From behind he seems older, more slumped, and in the quiet she hears his breath, vaguely wheezy. He's barefoot, a calloused heel tapping the leg of his chair as if hearing some remembered music.

Polly stands a full minute before backing away on tiptoe.

In reception she stops. She's being silly, should march right back to the kitchen. Turning, she faces the mantle, cluttered with magazines and matchboxes, cups of pens and pencils (he'd had plenty!) and a few framed photos—one is a family portrait showing a somewhat younger Mr. Machutova standing behind a handsome couple seated with their little girl. Hard to imagine him as anyone's father or grandfather, but there he is. Next is a school portrait of the girl, older and wearing a school blazer, springy hair barely subdued by multiple barrettes. One photo is of just the girl with her father, a man familiar enough Polly thinks she might remember him as a youth, bailing boats or hauling wood around the resort, a preoccupied but polite boy.

There are only the three pictures—a small family, a brief history.

She decides not to return to the grubby kitchen. As for his loitering, she'll simply confront him in the act. In the bar, Polly passes by dusty tables snugged to the paneled wall where old chimney lamps backed with reflectors have been converted from propane, the mantles replaced with bare lightbulbs. The place had been tidy as a ship—she hadn't misremembered that. Stepping out the screen door onto the run of rough granite steps she recalls how they'd been hosed off each afternoon, leaving cold puddles for bare feet in the heat of the day, remembers climbing them behind long-legged Eleanor, trying to keep up.

As Polly writes, she hums along with a concerto. The pile of cassettes are collected recordings of the same music that initially had been a gift from Eleanor, a thick album of vinyl records. After those albums had warped or scratched, Polly replaced the set with eight-track tapes; then a few years ago she replaced those with the smaller cassettes now heaped on the table. Soon enough the cassettes will be obsolete as well, she supposes. Polly has followed the strides in technology with great interest, though it's still hard to believe some of the wilder predictions—that soon computers will offer more than libraries at the press of a key, that everyone will carry those mobile telephones. And instead of bothering to cook, we will just swallow some nutritious dinner pill. Polly sighs, hunger driving her to her feet.

After dinner is eaten and dishes washed she backs out the door to toss dishwater from the basin and nearly trips over him. He's sitting on the steps, nodding as if to the echo of the music she's just turned off.

"*Mis*ter Machutova!" Polly inhales. "Really . . ."

He pulls himself up by the rail and pine needles fall from the backside of his coveralls. When he speaks, his voice seems different.

"Miloš Sádlo played it as well. Better, don't you think?"

It's a name she's heard, likely from Eleanor, but that's beside the point. "Pardon me?"

"I heard him in the Municipal, Nouveau Hall. Have you seen Prague, Miss McPhee?"

"Mr. Machutova, have you been lurking around here just to listen? For the music?"

His brow creases. "For what else?"

Polly laughs. "I see. Well. I've not seen Prague, Mr. Machutova. Is that where you're from?"

He nods.

"You have family there?"

"No. Not there." He pauses. "I have a granddaughter, just gone back to school at London."

"Ontario?"

"No, the real London."

"Ah. And your son? I may remember him working here."

"Tomas. Was my son," he says blandly, as if merely correcting her.

"Was? Oh. I'm so sorry."

When Mr. Machutova adds nothing, Polly herself shuffles a little. "I can't think what that must be like, losing a child . . ."

"No," he shrugs. "You have no children."

"Um?" She cocks her head. "How do you know that?"

He nods over her shoulder at the cabin. "So many needs you have—that everything be just so—the way women with no children or husband become."

"Become . . . ?"

"With only themselves to worry after."

He's grinning. Is she meant to respond? Still holding her basin of dishwater, she suddenly flings the contents over the woody slope, barely missing him.

He squints. "When you came before, you weren't unhappy, not caring too much about the small things."

"Surely you don't remember me being here. That was many years ago."

"Yes, 1963."

Polly frowns. "You looked that up."

"No." He thumbs his temple. "It's here . . . with the others. You had your . . . companion then."

He remembers Eleanor? Polly pauses, leaning against the rail with the basin on her hip. "Odd, why I don't remember you?"

"Me?" He shakes his head. "I'm only part of this place. Guests remember only what they miss. For you, maybe only your lady friend."

Recalling them as companions is one thing, but to call Eleanor her *lady friend* seems presumptuous. Maybe his English is wanting, maybe he simply meant *friend.* Polly and Eleanor never so much as brushed hands in public and would not have given themselves away anywhere, even at such a place as Naledi, around people they would never see again. When they played pinochle or cribbage in the little bar, they made it a point to engage other guests and always sat at least arm's length in their deck chairs or when walking.

"She was teacher, too?"

"No. A cellist."

"Ah. For her you play the music."

"Music? You mean the tapes? They were a gift . . ."

"Music is. Your friend, she was tall, yes?"

She nods. "Mr. Machutova, do you own a cassette player?"

"For the small tapes? Maybe yes. Perhaps in Marcheta's room."

"Marcheta? Your granddaughter?" She looks up at the lodge, trying to imagine a college girl living there.

"The girl, yes. Also called Meg, less lovely."

"Wait here, Mr. Machutova. I am going to lend you some music. Then will you stay away, please? Leave me to my writing?"

"Of course." He nearly smiles—only a sliver of tooth, but enough.

After their month together at Naledi, Polly went back to teaching, and Eleanor left on her long-anticipated journey to South America. She'd been planning it long before ever meeting Polly— her "pilgrimage," she called it—to immerse herself in the regional music of several countries, dance to the merengue and the cuarteto, to hear the panpipes in the mountainous provinces, to learn the tango. It would be a real trip, a real experience. She'd taken a three-month leave from the symphony and had letters of introduction to several musicians; she had a train pass and an expensive portable tape recorder.

Eleanor sent long letters back with details of the countryside, the mountains, the pampas, the people, the rhythms. Packages for Polly arrived from Chile, Peru, and Argentina: woven shawls, skeins of Alpaca yarn, packets of oily coffee beans. Eleanor mentioned guitar lessons for herself, that she had rented a casita. She invited Polly to Cuzco for the holiday break. But Polly had expected Eleanor would be back by Christmas, and it was such short notice—Polly couldn't manage it.

Eleanor asked for an extension from the symphony. Polly thought it reckless to risk her chair, but by late winter Eleanor began to sound reluctant about returning to Canada at all. She wrote that the weather was too lovely altogether, that February on the plains of Argentina was better than the best July in Quebec. At the end of each letter she wrote, "Won't you come?"

Polly puzzled over Eleanor's motives from afar. Was she reinventing herself? Running away? She seemed to be forgetting the life she'd stepped away from, the life she had with Polly. For herself, Polly adamantly claimed to be quite happy where she was, though she hadn't consciously considered what that happiness might entail. Eventually, Eleanor admitted she was low on money, casually mentioning in a breezy letter that she'd begun giving cello and violin lessons to children at a convent school. After extending her hiatus from the orchestra, Eleanor did lose her chair to a younger cellist but didn't seem to mind in the least—there was no regret between the lines on the thin blue paper that she used to write to Polly.

Polly's response was cool: "Are you not coming back?"

Eleanor implored, "Come for the summer, we could see the Galapagos!" Polly was annoyed Eleanor would use the Galapagos Islands as a lure—what scientist would turn down the opportunity to walk the same lava flows Darwin had, to see his finches up close, to watch the salt-spewing marine iguanas, the flightless cormorants? She was sorely tempted but held fast. Her excuse being a half-truth, "I have a deadline." An article for *Scientific American,* which technically only needed editing, as good as finished. Eleanor called her a terrible liar and stubborn Scot, which so infuriated Polly that she stopped responding. After a few unanswered letters, Eleanor went silent herself.

It was September before she heard again; this time the postmark was Buenos Aires. A slim package of Carlos Gardel's three-minute tangos, sent by way of an apology, or to ease the next bit of news: Eleanor had leased a small house, having decided to sell her flat in Ottawa. She was staying. "In Buenos Aires," Eleanor wrote, they could live openly, if Polly would come. Eleanor said she could find plenty of work as a musician, had already played a few receptions with a string quartet. "And what would I do?" Polly responded.

"Be with me," Eleanor wrote back. "Learn a new language. There are rocks here, too."

Eleanor's letters, when set out by date on the porch table, lay out the chronology of how things eroded, then ended. At this distance, buffered by years, Polly can track their parting with less of the old resentment. They'd both been dramatic and unyielding, but Polly even more so. It seemed simple in hindsight—she'd loved Eleanor, but Eleanor was in love with an entire country in another hemisphere.

Polly gathers sheets of thin stationery into a pile next to envelopes cast green by the light from the oil lamp. Eleanor will be the most difficult chapter to write.

For several days, Polly stabs at the words, going out to pace the deck and paths before coming back to scribble more—parry and retreat, each page a joust.

She sees little or nothing of Mr. Machutova but imagines him at his table, eating his tinned soups and listening to the cassettes. When looking out her window, Polly idly notes his absence and wonders if he's enjoying Eleanor's music. For herself, she doesn't miss the tapes in the least and realizes that the new silence forces her to fill it with her own refrains, forces her hand to write.

He'll be around soon enough. She'll ask then. He'll have outdoor chores to do, boats to scrape, piles to burn. Something.

She walks the back side of the lodge to where she thinks the kitchen windows are. On tiptoe, she cocks an ear. It's a solo this time—a dusky thread of cello strains through the screen, bow polishing strings in a bronze-dark sound. For Polly, blessed with synesthesia, music is a colored thing and she envisions these notes as dark ribbons in somber metallic shades, like strands of Eleanor's hair.

A clash of noises startles her—the sound of a pot set to the stove, a silverware drawer yanked and rummaged. She flattens against the side of the building, as if in a crime drama. Realizing what she must look like, she nearly laughs aloud—here she is lurking under his window!

On Friday there is leftover casserole that will go to waste unless she takes it to him. She wraps it in foil and knocks on the kitchen door like a caller. He's listening to Rostropovich but does not turn it off, only lowers the volume and motions her in. She stands in the door rather than trod on his newspapers. He's making coffee in the sort of pot she'd seen once in Italy, two chambers screwed together. When he sets out two small cups, she protests weakly, has only meant to bring the food, not interrupt. He doesn't acknowledge her reluctance, only pulls out a chair for her.

The coffee takes several minutes to cool, during which time they listen. Mr. Machutova seems turned inward with stiffness, making her wonder if he's entirely well, though in spite of his scrunched shoulders she detects a lifting of his countenance at certain interludes. His eyes widen slightly and he says, "We had music in our house when I was a boy. My parents and sisters. All played very well."

"Ah."

They sit silently for the duration, both settling into their own thoughts, both nodding along to music of the past. If he'd noticed her knuckle away a tear, he was tactful enough to not mention it. He made no comment on her hasty exit.

She cannot push the pen. Her ring binder is two-thirds full, two-thirds of Polly's life set down and accounted for. She has reached as far back as she can remember and wrung it all onto paper, from the youth onward. Learning, teaching. The shortest, worst chapter is Eleanor's. Their three years fit into a mere twenty pages that read like reportage, but she is too hesitant to write how it felt, how it really was, afraid she'd get too mired, say too much to herself . . .

On her way to the bathhouse, Polly notices Mr. Machutova at

the end of the dock, leaning against a piling. The lake is yellow with the reflections of aspen, the surface spangled like fish scales.

She would call out a greeting, but Mr. Machutova seems wholly absorbed.

Polly has her towel, a magazine, bath salts, and a new wick for the oil lamp. As the lone guest, she can indulge in hot water without guilt, fill the deep tub twice if she likes, crank the flame on the hot-water tank.

Eleanor used to say a bath wasn't a bath unless your nipples were covered. Soaking up to her neck, she blinks out the glass block windows at vague shapes of trees and sky beyond. In an hour of staring, in the time it's taken for her fingers and toes to pucker, she has dared admit to herself that the book is not working—the bits of her past that are easy to write are dull, the interesting parts are too difficult to write at all. The hot water is nearly depleted. In the steam it's hard to tell how much of the wet wiped from her face represents tears. Her upper lip tastes like the sea. Polly has never failed herself before.

Her reflection in the chrome spigot shows a puffy-eyed, fat seal.

"Truly," she asks the spigot, "who would be interested in the life of a futsy old professor?" The answer is a drip. "Boring old dyke," she sniffs at her image before covering it with her foot, deciding, just like that. She will quit.

Polly steps out of the bathhouse and over the stony path. Is she being rash? She could just take a break and come back to it in a few days, but her instinct tells her it's over. Her bathrobe puffs like a jib and pajama cuffs beat at her ankles. As she nears the dock, she sees Mr. Machutova is still out at the end but sitting in the same spot where he'd been standing earlier, as if he'd just slid down the piling. His legs splay in front of him like a child's and he's cradling his arm, head drooping to the left.

He couldn't be asleep? Just as she's wondering, he tilts sideways, moaning when he lands on the elbow he's been cradling. Polly drops her things. In rushing, one of her flip-flops sticks between dock planks and stays. The sun is lower, casting shadows at the same slant as the wind. His eyes are closed, but he is humming, his mouth knotted in a grimace.

"Mr. Machutova?" Polly wedges him up to sitting. He is shell-white.

He stops humming and says, "Marcheta."

"No, it's Miss Mc—. It's Polly."

"What?"

"Polly McPhee. Oh, Lord." She squints out at the lake. There are no boats out, and no cabins nearby, only the convent camp down the shore with a dwindling flock of nuns so old they couldn't help even if they could hear her shout. There's a phone somewhere in the lodge—she's heard it ring. "Listen, if I can get you up to standing, do you think you can walk?"

He grimaces but nods, eyes still shut.

"Okay . . . ," she says to herself, "on three." She counts one, two, three and heaves up with her knees bent. It's easier than she expects, thin as he is under the layers of plaid and thermal wool. Once he's upright, she ducks under his arm and his weight presses her shoulder. His ribs accordion against hers in hard breaths, and she hooks his belt loop with her thumb, lifting him like a sack. After several yards she rests and listens to them both breathing. When she starts walking again, his feet make attempts. Polly fits well under his arm and for once is glad for her lack of height, glad for once that she is indeed a little teapot, short and stout.

As they make limping progress over the dock, the magazine she'd dropped rifles its pages in the wind and eases itself into the water as if pulled by a string. Polly's towel and washcloth are blue squares plastered to far bushes.

They began to climb the stone steps, but after only three Mr. Machutova stops and begins to fold.

"Oh, my," Polly pants. "Oh, my . . ." She looks around. "We'll just get you to the bench there . . . two more steps. Can you make that?" He nods.

At the bench she slips out from under his arm and lowers him to sitting. "You won't fall." The words are more a plea than state-ment. "Please. I'll be right back. *Right* back."

In the lodge she dials *O*. The operator listens as Polly trips over her words and asks her to repeat until Polly shouts, "I have an accent, please listen!"

The operator tells Polly the ambulance might take a half-hour, as much as forty-five minutes.

Rushing the length of the porch, she plucks up cushions from willow rockers so that they lurch in her wake. Running down the hill, pine needles coat her bare foot.

"They're coming," she assures him, propping the cushions around his sides and hips to keep him from pitching. She dips away to her own cabin, which is closer, racing back with water and a blanket she tucks over his front like a great bib.

A half-hour!

His eyes have opened and he's sucking tight *O*s of air.

Polly crouches, watching his face for any change. Is it a stroke? Perhaps she should ask him the date? Or who is president? At the moment she's not sure herself and would be pressed to name her own prime minister. She holds the glass to his mouth, but he only shakes his head. Won't he say something? Absently, she drinks half the water herself. They are both breathing at his pace, quick shallow pants. "Are you in pain, Mr. Machutova?"

"Some . . ." He makes a face. "My knee."

Polly looks down and immediately unclamps her hand from his leg. "Oh! Sorry."

After several minutes his breathing slows to normal. Hold-ing his wrist, Polly can surreptitiously take his pulse. She fights to not show the relief she feels. His face grows less pinched and some color has returned. The worst could be over. He blinks at the lake as if thinking, as if gathering what he can of himself.

"Miss McPhee?"

"Polly, please. Yes?"

"Are you are a good person?"

She blinks. "A good person, Mr. Machutova?" It's not a ques-tion she's been asked. "Well. I haven't made much trouble, if that's what you mean. I've made mistakes . . . but yes, I'm good enough."

"Yes." He nods, recovered enough to focus on her. "Perhaps you are."

"And you, Mr. Machutova? You're a good person, too?"

"Vaclav. My name is Vaclav. Some would say no."

She follows the ambulance in her Rambler, just able to keep in sight of the red flashing lights. Unaccustomed to driving fast, she grow nervous when traffic picks up near town and lets the ambulance stretch out of sight. On Main Street she stops at the one light, but after it turns green realizes she has no clue where the hospital is. When a vehicle behind honks, she turns just as the young driver weaves around, giving her the finger. Pulling into the intersection, Polly cuts off a pickup making a left. The man leans out, "Lady! What the hell?"

"Sorry! Where's the hospital?"

The man looks at her, then at her provincial license plate and pulls up closer. He nods and calls out, "Follow me."

At the ER entrance she sees the ambulance already rolling away, the ER door open, and the end of a gurney as Vac is wheeled in. The man from the truck taps her shoulder.

"You with Vac?" he asks, nodding to the door.

"Yes . . . sort of."

"Well, you'd better go in then." He holds out his open hand. "Gimme me your keys. I'll park it for you."

"That's very kind . . ." Only as she steps inside to the cold tile does she realize her left foot is bare, her flip-flop gone. "Thank you . . ."

"No biggie. I was coming anyway."

Polly sits in admissions in her bathrobe and pajamas, looking like a patient herself, except that she's sitting stalk-straight with her purse in her lap.

The young woman from the desk brings a pair of hospital slippers and embarrasses Polly by holding each one out so she might ease her feet in.

"Any news?"

"No, ma'am, but when there is . . ."

Katie—according to her name tag—is a dead ringer for a movie star whose name Polly cannot remember. How Nordic-looking these Midwesterners are, she thinks, remembering how Eleanor had stood out during their few visits to this small town. Eleanor's mother was Armenian, her father English. "Horse-face with a tan," she would say.

Polly thumbs *Ladies Home Journal* and *McCall's*. The girl comes later with a cup of thin coffee and an egg salad sandwich but has no update. Polly closes her eyes.

Gently prodded awake, she peels herself from the bench seat and feels her cheek, embossed from the pattern on the vinyl. The doctor clears his throat again and perches on the arm of the couch opposite.

"Oh . . ." Polly props herself up. "And here I'm asleep. How is he?"

"Stabilized now."

"Will he be all right?"

The doctor looks tired. "Hard to say. His age is a complication."

"Oh, I see . . ." Polly realizes she wouldn't know if Mr. Machutova was seventy or ninety. Out the window, it's so dark it could be any time of night. Not knowing whether she should stay or go, she asks, "Will I see him?"

He shakes his head. "Asleep now. You should go on back to the resort." He nods out the window to the sidewalk, where the driver of the pickup paces, smoking a cigarette. "Alpo says he's going to drive out to Naledi and check on things, so you can follow him back."

"Alpo?"

"Alpo Lahti—his boy Pete works out at the resort?"

Pete, the boy she sees only from a distance, the one always

sulking under his shaggy hair. The last she'd seen him he was shutting down cabins for the season.

"That's kind, but I know the way."

"Alpo's glad to do it, Miss McPhee." The doctor yawns. "He's got plenty of time to kill."

"But what . . . what about the granddaughter?"

"Meg? She'll be called, if there's any need. Vac doesn't want her bothered right now."

"Did Mr. Machutova, did Vaclav have any message for me? Did he say anything?"

"He did, actually. That you should go back to the resort and do what you came to do. If that makes any sense."

"No. Maybe."

Polly dutifully follows behind Alpo Lahti's truck. Mercifully, Mr. Lahti drives slowly through the dawn. Once at Naledi, she offers to make him coffee but he refuses, though clearly he could use a cup. He coughs and digs a list from his pocket, handing it over. "Numbers you might need. Pete'll come back 'round this afternoon—button things up, get those boats in for the season, get you what you need."

"I'm fine on my own. Really." She takes a few steps up the slope.

"He won't be in your way. He'll just take on the work here 'til Vac gets better."

Polly begins to speak but is distracted by the view over Mr. Lahti's shoulder. The lake has calmed, finally. The surface smooth and glassy. No wind, no whoosh through the pines—only silence. This is the lake she remembers.

"Before I leave, I'll poke around to see if Vac left anything open or running." Mr. Lahti follows her gaze. "But as long as I'm here . . ." He opens the cab tailgate and pulls a fishing rod from under a tarp. "I might as well wet a line."

As she scans the list in her hand she shivers, less from the cold than exhaustion. He's written out numbers for the hospital, the doctor, the office at the art school where the granddaughter studies, and Alpo's own number.

When she looks up, he's already on the dock ready to cast.

At noon she calls the nurses' desk, somewhat revived by her few hours of sleep. There is little change. Thinking she should stay near the phone, she fetches a novel and an afghan from her cabin. Thankfully there's no question of writing—she's relieved of it for now. In the lounge she turns a full circle, but every corner is drafty and uninviting. The kitchen has more promise, with its run of south-facing windows and propane wall heater, but it's musty. She pushes aside the stained curtains and snaps the roller shades up, immediately wishing she hadn't. Dust billows and sunlight reveals just how grimy the room is—Polly can't possibly sit in it as is. The windowpanes are opaque. She locates rags and vinegar and Pine-Sol. A dishtowel around her middle makes do for an apron. While she goes at the windows, she wonders if Vaclav will send for the girl, Meg.

After the countertops and floor are scrubbed the room is vastly improved. She cleans the door of the fridge and puts the list of telephone numbers on it with a magnet before turning to consider the stove. It's dusk by the time she's finished. Yes, she'll sleep, that much is sure.

In the morning, Polly ventures upstairs to Vac's room for things the nurse had suggested—his shaving cup and brush, reading glasses and robe, any prescription bottles she might locate. The second story of the lodge consists of three low, dormered rooms lined with beadboard. One is used as storage, hip deep in boxes. The second is Vaclav's, neat enough with books piled against the perimeter halfway up the walls like sandbags. The bed is made, and his clothes are either neatly folded in the bureau or hung. The stem of a pair of reading glasses marks a page in *Leaves of Grass*. Polly notes the poem and page before tucking the book under her arm to take along. In the hall bathroom she examines the medicine chest, finding Midol and Rolaids, Milk of Magnesia, nail polish remover, aspirin, Mentholatum and Tropicana tanning oil next to the Preparation H. Apparently, Vaclav and the girl did not claim their own shelves. There is only one outdated prescription bottle.

The door to the girl's room (which Polly has no valid reason to enter) has several neon-haired troll dolls nailed to it. She stands with her palm on the wood a full minute before daring to push. Inside, there is a stereo covered with a Corona Beer beach towel, stacks of clothes folded on the bed, and piles of art supplies, oversized art books, and canvases. Every bit of wall is taken up with sketches and charcoal drawings. The closet has a wine-cork curtain. A wire-hanger mobile of pine tree car deodorizers fails to mask the smell of cigarettes, chalky pastels, marijuana, and linseed oil.

Polly pulls up the window shades and stands looking at the girl's drawings for a long time.

At the hospital she steps in from the corridor, relieved to see he's not alone. An orderly is just settling him back onto his pillows. He's a little slumped. She injects cheer into her voice, hefting her basket. "I've brought pajamas."

The orderly faces her. "Vac's just had his bath and a clean gown."

"Oh."

The young man hurries to gather his basin and cloths and glances at the basket. "Maybe he can wear them once he's less connected."

There are an awful lot of wires. He looks better, though. She approaches the bed.

"Hello. You look better."

"Not so."

"Yes, you do." She takes things from the basket and places them about the room, propping the school portrait on a shelf. "This is Marcheta?"

His face softens. "It is."

Either his neck is stiff or he's too weak to turn his head, so Polly stays in his line of sight.

"That was quite a scare you gave me."

"Yes. Myself also. They sent a priest in the night to . . . sprinkle me." He nearly smiles. "I'm clean enough now for heaven."

"Oh. You're . . . ?"

"Catholic? Religious? No. This life is all."

She nods in agreement and they sit in silence until he closes his eyes. Perhaps, she thinks, he is thinking. Not wanting to interrupt, she sits still. But time is passing. She fights to not look at her watch. Finally he shifts. Thank God.

"Mr. Machutova . . . Vaclav. I'm not sure about staying on. I mean, I should leave Naledi, don't you think?"

"Paah," he says, closing his eyes again.

Polly picks lint from the sleeves of her cardigan, looking up every so often, expecting him to start snoring. Just as she is about to find a pen and a bit of paper to leave a note, he does.

It's nine o'clock by the time Polly finally sits in the lodge kitchen, having dragged an armchair from the lounge to wedge near the wall heater. Next to the chair is a shelf of old cookbooks and magazines. Straightening them, she sees a photo album in between *Betty Crocker* and *Bull Cook Authentic Historical Recipes and Practices,* which she opens to a recipe for possum. She will save it to read later.

The album is filled with ruffle-edged snapshots. In one, Vaclav and his teenaged son pose with a trapper's pole sagging with pelts. Another shows them holding Tomas's university diploma, the young man either winking or squinting. She wondered if there were any pictures from Vac's home country, or if perhaps, like her, he had left his past where it lay. So many did during the war, she supposes. Several exterior shots of the lodge and cabins pepper the album, with white ink captions across the bottoms: "Cabin 12," "Cabin 17 in Winter," and so on. One labeled "Maids' Quarters" shows a bunkhouse with three beds made up with such precision the black stripes of the Hudson Bay blankets line up perfectly one bed to the next. An outdoor shot shows Vaclav standing on a timber beam in the roof rafters of a cabin being built, his hand on a large wooden mallet. A beach photo

catches a water skier blurred like a ghost and sinking to a stop
a few yards from the dock where guests lounged in deck chairs.
These would have been the postwar years, Polly thinks, the salad
days of the '50s, when things felt hopeful again. There are two
interior shots of the cabin she occupies. In one, windows hook
inward to the porch ceiling, allowing sun to mirror in from the
lake, and though the print is black and white Polly recalls the
floor, now covered with indoor-outdoor carpet, as it was, planks
painted blue like the lake, with oval rag rugs scattered like islands. A kitchen shot shows the stove with an apron hung next to
it, which Polly remembers as lavender. The glass tumblers were
emerald and the shelf paper red check—memory fills in the color
for her. A calendar advertising outboard motors is tacked to the
open bedroom door, where she and Eleanor had pushed two
narrow beds to make one.

They would lay with their heads together, making shadow
puppets on the ceiling with flashlights, snorting like schoolgirls.
They drank the best wine one could buy in Hatchet Inlet, and
Eleanor taught her camp songs and dirty limericks, replacing
all the hims with hers and all the lumberjacks with lumberjills.
They had tramped, swam, and paddled through their month at
Naledi. When they could be bothered, they wrote silly postcards
to friends, signing off, "Having a time in Vacationland!" or "The
weather is here, wish you were great!"

He's straighter today, propped and eating soup like a child with
his left hand because his right has an IV taped to it. She's brought
the photo album, along with the saltwater taffy he'd asked for,
and all the cello recordings she had with her own cassette player—
much less tinny than the battery operated one in his kitchen.

As he eats, she reports that all is well at the resort, tentatively
adding, "I've begun packing my things."

He lays his spoon aside. She scrapes the chair closer and
opens the picture album and asks him about the photos. He answers as if taking a test, with a hint of impatience. "We trapped

beaver and mink." "That is the girl's mother. Yes, similar hair." "There were two maids, sometimes three, a dock boy." "Yes, when she was three. Marcheta, Meg."

He stops responding, and she looks up to see he's looking at the ceiling, blinking.

"I do not ask for so much . . ."

She leans in. "Pardon?"

"Since already you saved my life, such as it is. But now I ask you stay your time."

"You want me to stay? But why?"

"In some days I will get worse. Then they will call for Marcheta and she will fly home . . ." He meets her eye.

"But you're getting better, not worse."

He slowly shakes his head. When she looks, really looks, she sees the truth in the film dulling his pupils. His bony arms and neck, usually covered by sleeves and collars, are slack, papery, looking slightly deflated. She swallows. "But haven't you any family that might come and be with her?"

"Marcheta's mother had a sister . . . somewhere." He shrugs. "It's best Naledi not be closed up, not empty when the girl comes."

What excuse could she even start with? Staying was one thing, but to wait around for a young woman she's never met, one who will no doubt be distraught when she does arrive . . .

Polly looks at him and inhales. "Yes. Of course."

Back at the resort, driving under the arch, she sees the boy Pete has already attached the Closed for Season sign across the gate. She's agreed to stay on, not just her time, but for a week past the end of the month. Quite probably by then, she thinks, there could be snow . . .

This time she doesn't hesitate to enter the girl's room. The drawings are thumbtacked across one wall—large, sixteen by twenty inches. There are ten drawings, and not one of them is what it appears to be. Margaret, Marcheta, Meg has a light hand but a broad sweep that covers the paper edge to edge. After

Polly's eyes adjust to the dim light she notes again the grace in the drawings of rocks and trees, water scenes, a riverbed, a stand of rushes. At first glance they are beautifully executed nature drawings. Upon closer inspection one can see each contains human elements. The rubble of round stones like a small moraine deposited at the *v* of a cliff is a pile of naked babies curled in sleep. A particularly elegant drawing features slender, translucent nudes trapped within a great fringe of icicles. A series of birch trunks reveal themselves to be barky humans bending their limbs stiffly, at branch-like angles. Most all the drawings make such plays on camouflage.

On a shelf are a number of small clay sculptures. A half-dozen heads of nuns in their black-and-white headgear of veils and wimples, all set atop animal or bird bodies. A skunk, a woodpecker, a beaver, a milking cow with full udders and a rosary around its neck instead of a bell. The nuns' faces are quite distinct. Polly could guess they were taken from life because Meg had been either vicious or kind in her depictions—one with a gentle face had been given the body of a deer. These sculptures were more juvenile than the drawings and not as subtle, but still imaginative. Polly has to laugh—no doubt these nuns had been the girl's teachers. So this is the Meg she'll be dealing with.

Eleanor had never been one to judge others, and the worst Polly ever heard her say of someone was that they lacked imagination. Looking at the girl's work, she sees an overabundance of it, often just as troublesome. But how wonderful, she thinks, to let the mind go to gather what whimsy it will. How simple might it be to do just that, just let go—to create characters and set them onto unlikely stages. Why not in writing? Polly supposes that's what novelists do, just make up people who interest them and set them in places one might yearn to live or explore. To take the opportunities passed by in life and reclaim them on one's own terms on the page, to write the experiences nearly grasped but missed. The pudgy beaver nun statue is still in her hand—the one that looks a little bit like her. She slips it into her pocket with only the slightest flicker of guilt.

Downstairs she drinks a pot of tea, mostly while walking aimlessly around the lodge with her cup in forays from the kitchen to the porch, then back, then to the reception desk, the bar, the hearth. *A novel.* The notion follows her to bed, where she cannot concentrate to read, not even a page from *Bull Cook.*

When Polly arrives at Vac's open door the next morning, he is just finishing breakfast, looking much better. After she clears the tray and gets him a second coffee, she shyly tells Vaclav her idea.

"Good," he says, looking her in the eye, "now you have no hesitation."

She sits and paces in turn, ruminating aloud about possible plots and characters, saying several times, "Of course, it could all change, but . . ." Polly winds down after an hour, only to look over and wonder if he has heard a word. Vaclav shifts his head. "Go. Go be with your ideas. I'm a little tired."

On her way through town, Polly stops at a shop selling dusty office supplies where she splurges on a used Remington and a box of typing paper.

She writes in the evenings and in the mornings. Between breakfast and sitting down to her typewriter Polly calls the nurses' station for news. Just as Vaclav predicted, she has no hesitation. The shape of a story emerges around the structure of a plot, the details come. Each paragraph tapped out seems a brick on which to set the next. Always having thought herself a practical person dealing in facts, Polly is surprised by the reach of her imagination, and lost in fiction she is nearly entertaining herself, more or less daydreaming on paper.

The day usually includes a drive in, nearly an hour commute that provides her time to think on her work. She and Vac spend half their time just blinking through their own thoughts. If he's alert, she'll read the paper aloud or tell him things about Naledi he might not know—that it's perched on the oldest stone on earth, a strata of greenstone marbled with schist and layered with folds of jasper and iron, or that there are six types of wild orchid in his bog alone. She spells out the Latin names to show him. The day of the first frost she explains how inversions in the valley cause the extreme cold the area is famous for. She'd seen a bear rooting out a den at the base of a white pine. The boy, Pete, had stacked more wood and pulled in all the boats.

She has decided on a character for her novel, also a geologist, one who just happens to reside here near these border lakes. As they converse, Polly tries to seem casual while watching for changes. Vac's body may be failing, but his mind remains sharp. Nurses tell her that sometimes he eats, sometimes not. His status is not upgraded, and he sleeps rather a lot. If he nods off during a visit, she'll scribble notes in lieu of good-bye.

At the end of the second week he seems better, sitting straighter. He asks for a bottle of beer and a hamburger, which Polly thinks is a very good sign. He says he would like to call his granddaughter.

After the operator connects them, Polly waits just outside the door. She can detect false cheer and hedging when she hears it. When she steps back in, her arms folded, he waves her away.

Early on Saturday Polly hears the slam of vehicle doors followed by men's voices, good natured and grunting. Outside, Alpo and Pete Lahti are easing a wheelchair from the back of a panel van. Vaclav is wrapped in a jacket and hospital blanket, belted in, a cap pushed down over his eyes.

"Good Lord!"

An hour earlier she'd called the nurses' desk and was told, "Asleep." Pounding down the porch steps she calls, "Just what is going on here?"

"Miss McPhee." Alpo takes off his cap and bows. "We are going fishing."

"What? Have you lost your mind?"

"Fish-ing."

"Are you drunk?" She strides to the chair and peeks under the brim of Vaclav's cap. "Are you all right?"

He shrugs. "Fine. No one is drunk. Beer would taste nice, though."

Pete asks, "Any in the cooler?"

She aims a withering eye at the two over Vaclav's head. He's no better than he was the day before. The irresponsibility, the audacity . . .

Back in the lodge she goes directly to the phone, stretching the cord so she can see out, where Pete and Alpo are carefully maneuvering the chair, lifting it completely along the more rugged parts of the path. At one point Alpo simply lifts Vac out and carries him the rest of the way, the boy following with the chair. She picks up the phone to dial the nurses' station. When they reach the dock they replace him to sitting and tuck the blanket around Vaclav's middle. They roll him to the end and aim him toward the best view. Pete engages the brake. Alpo turns a bucket upside down for a stool and sits close to the wheelchair.

Polly hangs up in mid-ring and goes back outside to stand vigil on the slope. She looks at her watch. If they don't take him back in an hour, she will call.

The boy comes out of the boathouse with three poles and a tackle box. He and his father flank Vac, fiddle with lures and poles, and toss out lines. Vac listlessly holds the rod handed to him, turning his face upward, as if he cannot get enough sun.

The day is a gift this late in the season. Yellow aspen framing the late-autumn sky. Polly has to admit that if ever there was a morning to enjoy Naledi . . .

She watches Alpo lean in to better hear something Vac is saying. Alpo nods and slowly turns the wheelchair to face the span of the hill, allowing Vac a view of the lodge and the few cabins visible on the piney slope. When Vaclav points again, Alpo swings the chair to face the shore and the span of the lake. He shifts him like this several times. Vac is taking it all in, a slow panorama.

Polly walks through to the bar to the red cooler and takes out as many beers as will fit in her apron pockets but doesn't see a bottle opener. But then they are all the sort of men who carry pocketknives.

She shares a beer with them, no one saying much. Then they gently lift Vac back into the van.

Upon waking Monday morning, Polly knows something is wrong. She reaches the lodge just as the phone begins ringing. Vac has spent the night in intensive care.

"Is it . . . ?"

"It's time for Mr. Machutova's granddaughter to come home, Miss McPhee. Mr. Lahti's son has contacted her. I guess a flight's been arranged."

Polly asks what she can do and is told, "Nothing."

He is diminished, sunk into the bed. His voice is airy, like some tube within is punctured.

"Marcheta's coming?"

"Yes. Tomorrow night." Polly tidies the blanket he's tried to kick off. "Peter will go to the airport to pick her up. And Mr. Lahti says he'll try to track down her aunt, Catherine, Cathy? She doesn't fly, apparently, so she could be awhile . . ."

He shakes his head, and Polly understands he doesn't care about such details.

"Tomorrow?" He seems to be calculating something.

"Yes."

After he finishes his thought, he takes a breath. "October is the lovely month. Your cabin will still stand next year. You will come back."

He's talking nonsense. "Of course," she humors him. "Of course, I'll come."

"You think I joke. You're good at Naledi, Polly. You see more than just the skin of a place."

She decides he must mean *surface*. He's never called her by name before. He remains very still as if saving his energy for the next thing. Sitting, she rummages in the cardboard file and shows him the papers he's requested from his desk drawers. She sets a legal pad on her lap like a secretary and waits. After twenty minutes of reading, he motions her to move closer so she can write while he dictates.

Every few minutes the words dry on his tongue and she holds the straw and glass for him. By the time three pages are covered with notes and instructions he's whispered himself to exhaustion.

She rises and slips the legal pad into her bag. "Sleep." She tucks the oxygen tubing back where it's loosened behind his ear. "You don't want to be this tired when she comes."

Touching the skin of his neck, such vulnerable flesh, Polly inhales and averts her eyes so that she sees Vac only from the neck down, at the biology of a body in its last phase. She tries to think clinically, but her detachment is wobbling. If she meets his eye, the idea of a *soul* might come into her head and stick.

And then she'd have far too many questions.

Quickly, impulsively, she leans and does something the heroine of her blossoming novel might do. She kisses Vac on the forehead.

Near the hospital exit she sees the Lahti men climb into Alpo's truck. The pretty girl from admissions, Katie, is looking out the door when Polly reaches it. The girl shakes her head as she pushes the door open for Polly.

"Poor fellas."

"Poor?" Polly turns, the box heavy in her hands. "Have they nothing to occupy themselves? They seem to hang around here quite a lot."

"Hang around?" Katie looks at her quizzically. "Oh, no, Miss McPhee. You see, Mrs. Lahti is here."

"Oh, in hospital? Dear. For how long?"

Katie shrugs. "I'd say not much longer now."

"Oh." She looks squarely at the girl. "I had no idea." And as she says it she realizes that is true of so many things here—she simply has no idea.

In the car, she cranks the window down in spite of the cold and rests her forehead on the steering wheel. The passenger seat holds Vac's folders and envelopes, his final papers. In her hand is the address of a lawyer in the next town, Greenstone. Drive, she tells herself.

It's good to keep moving. At Naledi, Polly has hauled out the cleaning supplies and commenced preparing the lodge for Meg's return. Pete has raked the paths around the buildings and washed the windows. In the afternoon he hoses down the porches, cleans the grates, and lays in firewood, stacking a full cord between the trunks of two pines just steps from the kitchen porch.

They work all day, too busy for more than a hasty meal as it grows dark.

In the morning she does laundry. Never particularly domestic, she now can see how the mindless routines of housekeeping might grow to become a comfort to some—the results are instant.

Pete leaves at dawn for the airport after gassing up his truck at the dock pumps. By noon all the laundry is done, and she's just tucking fresh sheets on the girl's bed when she hears the crunch of tires on gravel. A delivery van rolls to a stop in the gravel loop. In the time it takes to get downstairs, the Italian grocer and his helper are on the porch, loaded with boxes.

Polly insists they wipe their feet and watches as they stock the icebox with eggs and cheese, cartons of milk and half & half. There is bread and packaged cookies and pounds of coffee. They bring in a second load—cases of beer, quart bottles of Aquavit, and a heavy box from the butcher.

"Goodness. Who ordered all this?"

They feign ignorance, each pointing to the other.

The fridge is jammed with white parcels of meat and poultry. The last boxes are light: paper napkins, paper plates, and paper cups. They are stocking the place.

"Wait." When Polly reaches for her pocketbook, they both

shake their heads. Neither will accept a tip. After they've gone she looks at the refrigerator racks bending under the weight of a ham and fat packets of cold cuts. It's enough food for a month. Then she realizes—it's enough food for a funeral.

The afternoon grows gray under a low lid of clouds, and Polly turns on the radio, searching for a weather forecast. She knows snow clouds when she sees them. While waiting for the girl she saws a half-frozen roast into stew chunks, then sits with a Dutch oven between her knees, cutting neat potato squares and carrots that make satisfying thuds on the cast iron. She's far too distracted to write today. Between the stew and putting together a cake mix and cleaning up her messes, she's able to keep busy until dusk, just as the snow begins and Pete's pickup finally pulls in the drive.

Polly pulls off her apron and hesitates near the door, suddenly unsure. She puts the apron back on. Through a part in the curtain she sees the girl slide down from the high cab. Her tinted glasses are round as jar lids. She's wearing a short fake fur jacket and scuffed, thigh-high boots. A huge leather bag is slung from her shoulder. Marcheta—Meg—looks every inch the art student and completely displaced, as if plucked up from SoHo and set down in the wilds. In the halo of the porch light the girl pauses and looks up at the lodge before negotiating the first step. Pete takes them two at a time, hauling her backpack.

Once inside, she drops her bag in a corner and approaches the stove where Polly has stationed herself.

"You must be Polly."

For a moment Polly is struck dumb. Not by the girl or her presence, but of her own. She suddenly cannot fathom how she has come to be standing in this kitchen, awaiting this moment. But she is, very much so, and the girl is reaching out in greeting. Her hand is warm and rough and utterly familiar. A feeling washes over Polly—not déjà vu, not recognition of the girl in any real sense, but that she *should* know her, and that she will.

Her glasses have pale blue lenses. When Meg pushes them up into a mass of curls the color of cedarwood, Polly sees the girl's eyes are puffy from travel, or tears, probably both. She has pale Irish skin and high Slavic cheekbones with a jaw set like Vac's.

Polly inquires about the trip as the fake fur is hung and boots kicked aside. The kettle is set on the hob.

Shedding her things, Meg becomes smaller. As she speaks, her odd accent places her as rootless—raised on Vac's language, with sentences imbued with a nasal Minnesota cadence and a hint of London clip. By the time she's settled at the table, wrapped in one of Vac's baggy sweaters and drinking tea with her knees up under her chin, she seems younger than her nineteen years. She looks breakable, but her gaze is direct.

Polly sits across from the girl and clutches her own cup of tea as if to anchor herself.

"So," Meg meets her eye, "tell me everything."

Without hesitation, Polly takes a breath and begins.

APPROXIMATION

JUST NORTHEAST OF TOWN THE ROAD CUTS THROUGH A
deep ridge of Precambrian rock that once separated remote
from isolated, until timber barons needed to get at the forests
on the other side and blasted through it. The rock walls on either
side of the road are embossed with bore marks, appearing as if
large, stiff snakes had cleaved the greenstone to open the passage. Beyond the ridge, the road ribbons toward the border,
hemmed by dusty spruce and jack pine poking from moss, with
stone erupting from the crust in a dozen stone shades and orange patches of scabby lichen providing an occasional thrill of
color. In the few stands of old-growth pine that escaped logging,
holy-postcard sunlight stabs through, blessing or warning those
traveling any farther north.

Ten miles into the boreal dim, the road makes a drunken
swale around glacial boulders, and Lahti's Hobby is revealed like
a startling pop-up page in a children's book. The Hobby covers
two acres of green wort and fertilized clover, bright as Astroturf
and dotted with dozens of trees of varying heights and shapes—
all meticulously clipped and coerced into tight, conical topiary,
symmetrical as if machined.

Vans loaded with eager campers slow down to cast canoe-
shaped shadows from their roofs as drivers do double takes.
SUVs crawl, passengers wondering if it is a minigolf course, if the
trees are real. Odd as it is, few stop to examine the Hobby or even
photograph it: those headed into the wilderness are road-weary
and itching to get on with their solitude; those on their way out
are hell-bent for soap showers and flush toilets. To locals, Lahti's

Hobby is merely a break in the monotonous drive, a mile marker for the '98 washout.

Alpo Lahti doesn't think much about the Hobby himself. It began as a pastime that has evolved into a daily routine of trimming, shearing, pruning, shaping, and planting. Each year he introduces a few young trees and maybe a yew or arborvitae. When one falls victim to diplodia blight or blister rust, he's more watchful of the others, washing them with botanical detergents or peroxides or vinegar. If a tree doesn't rebound in his care, he cuts and burns it, then grubs the stump to rid all traces.

The Hobby began after Rose passed, just after his daughter convinced him to attend a grief support group. Alpo went, planning to stick his head in so he could claim he showed up without lying. But as the only male, the only widower, and the last and largest person in the door, he was too conspicuous to sidle away. Soon enough he was clutching a Styrofoam cup and a bear claw, a dozen expectant faces canted his way like deer.

The widows urged Alpo to tell Rose's story from the beginning, from diagnosis onward. As soon as he began, they began interrupting—asking how this felt or how that felt, how hearing the word *cancer* felt, how the next five months felt, and then, afterward, how he felt.

Alpo sighed. Things had to be done, Rose had to be taken care of. It was ovarian. He took third shift at the plant. Rose's sister Sharon came from Alberta, parked her Winnebago near the bog, and tended Rose while he worked or slept. Toward the end they both learned how to inject, and a hospice nurse came three times a week.

Hoping honesty was what they wanted, Alpo admitted he hadn't felt much of anything when she died. He wove his fingers into a hammock and told them it was only after, when the bed and oxygen trolley were cleared and the casseroles were eaten up and Tupperware returned—when there were no tasks to fill his hands—*then* it seemed he might collapse into the raw space where his wife had been. But he hadn't.

As if grief were a problem to be solved, the widows faced

Alpo and offered the same solution twelve different ways. What he needed was a pastime, a hobby.

He pretended to agree. "But what?"

Anything! They offered whittling, model planes, bluebird houses, diamond willow walking sticks. Marquetry. Their suggestions were proffered in wistful and annoyed tones, as if recalling echoes of their departed husbands putzing and hammering out of sight in so many basements and garages.

Caught in the small-eyed glare of Ruth Witti, Alpo had the unchristian thought that though Guy Witti's body and ice house were never recovered, he maybe was in a better place.

He cleared his throat. "Those are all fine ideas, ladies." After working indoors all day with tools in the machine shop, none of their suggestions appealed to him in the least. Mrs. Huttala pointed her aluminum cane. "You should read!" she shouted. "The Bible!"

Alpo left in a lighter mood. If it were only a matter of a hobby, he'd find one. And though it was already there in his yard, months would pass before he realized.

In the front yard stood the white spruce Sharon and the kids had planted in Rose's memory. When it set out its first new growth, Alpo thought it looked shaggy, so he clipped away the soft new buds, careful to prune each just a quarter inch from its scaly source. The repetition and rhythm of pruning were pleasant, mindless. When he finished, the ground was covered with delicate buds, so tender he was moved to bite into one—if only to see why the deer were so crazy about them. When the sun started to slide, Alpo realized he'd been at it for hours. Chewing pale needles, Alpo raised a sticky hand to shield his eyes. Not realizing he had felt bad, he suddenly felt better for the first time since Rose's death.

The spruce looked a bit bereft alone in so much yard, so he planted a mugho pine and a Prince of Wales juniper. He ordered a few fertilizers and pesticides. Recalling the taste of new spruce, he surrounded his two acres with wire fence of unleapable height.

When his cousin Gil drove from Blackduck to take him out

for the fishing opener, Alpo was shaping a fledgling cedar he'd planted for Mother's Day and was put out at being interrupted, annoyed by the marks Gil's boat trailer had embossed on his clover. "Lemme just finish this, Gil, then I'll put new test on my reel and we're good to go."

Gil leaned against the cab. "Only God can make a tree, Alpo, but only you would prune one with barber shears and calipers."

Alpo made no excuses for being precise—as lead machinist on his team, he had to be. If one cog on a piece of equipment his crew fabricated was even a cunt hair off, it could mean an OSHA nightmare. Nobody wants dead miners on their conscience.

He customized a few garden tools, welding a pocket level to a small hedge trimmer, and since there would be no more turkeys, refitted the electric knife. He cut extra notches into handsaws to make smoother passes. The height of his trees was conditional—none grew beyond the sum of Alpo's height plus that of his favorite ladder—a sturdy eight-footer he saw no reason to replace. He jerry-rigged an old wood chipper with pliable tubing to make a mobile fertilizer spreader—the fish offal, bones, compost, and ash that went in emerged out the nozzle end as nutritious ooze the color of braunschweiger. When complimented on his green thumb, Alpo would nod at his gore-crusted machine. "Bullhead smoothies, nothing special."

Alpo didn't realize what he did had a name until the Section Three road south of his driveway was surveyed and renamed. He watched as the sign was bolted to its post, green and white stamped letters making it official: Lahti's Hobby.

He tended his trees in the mornings. Around ten-thirty he drives in to fetch his mail, then settles in at Pavola's to have his second round of coffee and read the papers. He might stay for lunch with Chim or Ray; he might not. He listened to the shock jocks on the boom box rattling the glass pie case but left the fist shaking and backtalk to the others. When they weren't slamming plates or pouring refills, Sissy and Laurie kept them up on local gossip. Both were over forty but didn't much mind being called girls, though Sissy took only a certain amount of shit from Chim before threatening to pour the next cup where it mattered, and Laurie refused to serve Big Juri Perla unless he passed her version of a breathalyzer, up on her toes.

In May, a full week went by without Alpo showing up. Ray and Chim assumed he was either busy with spring pruning or down with the flu that was plowing clear so many beds up at the nursing home. When Alpo didn't make it to Bibb Esko's retirement party, Chim called but only got a busy signal. The next morning he drove out to see if Alpo had fallen from a ladder or stroked out. Neither: he was kneeling in the mulch under a loblolly pine, next to a black Japanese globosa.

Chim joked to Alpo's backside: "We thought you might be shacked up out here—that maybe one of them bruisers up at the Klondyke jumped the fence for you. Laurie was all set to pool her tips to buy you a bottle of that Viagra."

Alpo answered through the twine in his teeth. "Yeah, well, shacked up, I'm not." He backed out, holding a cluster of needles. "Godammit."

"What's the problem?"

"Problem is I don't know what the problem is. Think Sissy's cousin down at the library would show me how to use that Internet? I have to look up some blights. There's nothing in my books."

Alpo sat among children in the library and learned to push a mouse. A girl still dragging a blanket showed him how to navigate the Web. In a few days he was surfing and e-mailing without much fumbling. He spent afternoons researching diseases and molds, picking up bits of Latin along the way.

Erv from County Extension came out and they lay on their backs aiming flashlights along the trunks. Erv couldn't guess what might be causing them to ooze a thin, tacky, brown syrup.

"Christ, Alpo, most of these aren't even native species. Probably one of 'em imported something viral."

Within a week, the needles closest to the trunk of every tree in the Hobby suddenly turned yellow. His trees were failing from the inside out.

Kenny Odegaard from the DNR was no help, only offered to spray for pine beetles, which there wasn't a one of. Les Klun, the section ranger, suggested a dendrologist. When Alpo finally located one in Winnipeg, the man refused to speculate over the telephone, demanding needles and core samples. Alpo felled his sickest tree and packed needles and thin rounds of trunk into a FedEx mailer. The results could be either a week, the dendrologist told him, or six—as if there were that kind of time.

Fearing the worst, Alpo borrowed Ray's Nikon and took pictures of the Hobby from several different angles. He wanted a record at least. But none of the shots was frameable. Juri took some wobbly video that wasn't great either.

The three of them were on their elbows at Pavola's when Tom Maki came out of the men's, hitching his belt. "Damn, Alpo, you weren't this long-faced when Rose was sick."

After a taut half-second, Ray swiveled. "Shut your fucking trap, Maki, or you'll be shitting your own teeth tomorrow."

Alpo held Ray's arm down. "You got a plastic hip and twenty years on him, Ray."

"He insulted you."

"He's just got a big mouth and is stupid enough to say what he thinks."

They watched Tom launch out the door to bumble around Meg Machutova just coming in. She managed to squeeze past, shaking her head.

Chim sniffed. "That painter lady. Watch now, two bits says she don't say boo."

Meg waved her dollars at Laurie, set them on the till, and stepped behind the counter to get her *Chicago Tribune* and fill her travel mug. Joe Pavola special-ordered city newspapers for Meg and a number of summer people in hopes they'd order breakfast as long as they were in the café. A few stuck around for a meal, but most only bought a coffee. Those fetching the *New York Times* did neither.

Joe blamed his regulars, sometimes coming out from behind the grill to shake his cleaver. "Jesus, can't you be a little friendly? Staring just scares folks."

Just as she was leaving, Meg nodded at Alpo, saying, "Hey."

Alpo nodded back, watched the door shut, blinked at Chim, and held out his palm.

"For 'Hey'?" Chim set his Zippo on the counter and swept most of the tip meant for Sissy toward Alpo, who pushed the coins back with a disgusted sniff.

"Hell," Juri offered from his corner, "she was downright friendly today. You know her much, Al?"

"Not really. I knew the old man a little. My boy Pete went out with her one of those summers he worked up at Naledi. Never brought her out to the house, though."

Ray leaned. "How's he doing?"

"Pete?" Alpo watched out the window as Meg crossed the street. He hadn't thought of his son in weeks. "Couldn't say. Maybe drinking, maybe not."

He was waiting near her vehicle when she came out of the bank. He pointed to the left rear tire. "Could use a few pounds of air in that."

"Oh, I could. Thanks, Mr. Lahti."

"Alpo."

Meg nodded. "Sure."

"I saw that article—the one with the pictures. And I read that you're living out at the resort now."

"Uh-huh. What's left of it."

"Well, the lodge is solid enough . . . shame, though. You know my Rose passed not long after your granddad Vac."

"Yes. Yes, I did. I was very sorry to hear that."

"Yeah, well, it's what, almost twenty years now, so . . .." Alpo saw she was rushed and only being polite, so he got to the point. "Listen. You're a painter, and I need a picture."

"You do?"

"A commission. You do those?"

"Ah, depends." She sounded doubtful. "On what you want painted."

"My yard. The Hobby, I guess people call it."

Meg's brow hitched. "I've seen it."

"And I've only seen a few of your paintings, but what I'm

looking for is more like an actual picture." He pulled out a battered field guide and opened it to common juniper. "This is what I need, something realistic that looks real."

"Representative?"

"That's right. Thing is, I need it quick. I've got some sort of blight, so I don't know how long . . ."

"You want me to paint your yard?"

He shrugged. "Yeah."

Meg looked at Alpo's vest like she was counting the quilted squares. She nodded across a dozen or so before meeting his eye. "All right. I'll drive up and take a look."

The next morning Alpo watched from his kitchen as Meg meandered figure eights around his trees, standing back to tap her chin before circling again. She clipped across the road where her old Cruiser tipped into the ditch, and he thought, Fine then, go. But she only climbed up the rock shelf and stood staring at the Hobby from there.

He poured a cup of coffee and walked it out to her, easing down the ditch and up the scrabble, careful of his knee.

"Well?" He held the cup up to her.

She crouched to take it. "I'd say you're rather an artist yourself, Alpo."

"Oh, sure."

"I'm serious. Come take a look from here."

She offered a hand, but Alpo hoisted himself. Standing on the ledge, he realized he'd never seen the place from this angle, how the Hobby was set just so, surrounded by the real forest.

"I'd paint it from here. Not just your perfect trees, but how they're framed by the wilderness." She grinned at Alpo. "If this was out East, it'd be on the cover of *ArtForum*."

Once they got her easel up and leveled, she clamped on a drawing pad, set up a golf umbrella, and squinted at Alpo's trees. "They seem healthy enough. I mean, they look fine from here."

He shouldered the tailgate shut. "Rose looked fine, too, damn near to the end."

Meg went in the house once for the bathroom but otherwise kept to the ledge with her spooky dog. At five o'clock she knocked to say she was done sketching and would come back Tuesday with a canvas. She could finish the painting over the next few weeks or so, depending on the weather and the light.

The Winnipeg tree man sent his inconclusive report, half of which Alpo could not make out, along with a bill for two hundred dollars. Alpo couldn't fathom how a painting could take more than a few days, but there was Meg nearly every morning, dabbing away. His trees were in stasis, not getting any better, not getting worse, just the usual brown treacle. A week passed and still nothing died. The sticky weeping baffled him. That it kept coming.

Meg stopped showing up and a few days later called to say the painting was dry and varnished. He asked her to bring it to Pavola's after lunch on Monday. He knew about art openings, that there was food and definitely drink involved, so he asked Ray to pick up a case of Blatz and a few gallons of wine. Joe offered to make his little pizzas and a tray of rye and herring. Alpo was a little embarrassed at the fuss, at everyone pitching in their little favors. Streamers hung from the fluorescents, and Sissy had made tree-shaped cookies. Folks from up and down Main Street came in to stand around drinking beer or sipping Dixie Cups of wine.

The painting was propped on two chairs. Alpo barely glanced, standing just offside, listening carefully to everyone's comments, hoping they might inspire his own when it came his turn to look. "Pretty," the women repeated, predictably. "Just like a photograph." "It does the Hobby justice," etc.

Bertie and Sam left their squad parked with its lights twirling and came in to joke that there must be trouble since the café door was still open past 1:59. Bertie said his aunt was a talented painter, too, but couldn't paint like that.

"It's nice," Laurie whispered, "that she could paint some actual place for a change."

Hal from Lefty's Bait Shop made everyone laugh by giving it a two-thumbs up, holding his good thumb up twice.

The party was nearly over before he dared take a real look for himself.

It was exactly what he had asked for. More, in fact. The artistic license Meg had taken had imbued his trees with bright highlights and deeper shadows—a whole lot of depth—making it seem like you could step right into the Hobby. For sure there was some art term for that.

Alpo dug the checkbook from his coat pocket and motioned Meg to an empty booth.

"I know this isn't gonna be cheap, so don't think you're gonna shock me." He had Googled Meg weeks back, when links to galleries in Chicago and London led him to lists with breathtaking prices. Still, nothing like the doctor bills. "So, what's the damage?"

Meg shrugged. "Nothing."

She was joking, so he joked back. "I might not be from the city, but I know nothing is no price."

Meg frowned and pushed the checkbook aside. He was reminded of her granddad—that look he'd had, she got. When Vac Machutova was roused to say something, it was usually worth listening to.

"It's only a painting," Meg said.

"C'mon, here, Meg, I don't—"

She stopped him by laying her hand over his. "Pete told me what you did for Vac."

"What?"

"After Doc Klun had him in the hospital for good."

Alpo frowned at her hand. "I didn't do anything."

"Yes, you did. You got him in your panel truck and drove him to Naledi for a last look. You took him fishing."

A memory clicked. "Geez, that?"

It had been right after Rose first fell ill—when there were too many reasons to be around the hospital for too many hours at a stretch, hanging around the halls waiting for the results of this test or that scan. Taking the old man for a ride had been a selfish lark, an excuse to escape the green tile. Pete had helped, anyway.

They'd been making small talk in the hall, old Vac pulling his wheelchair along with a slippered foot. Alpo asked after the pike at Crow Point since the winter kill the season before, and Vac grinned a little and said, "Well, go on up there and wet a line."

And then Alpo looked over at Pete and they seemed to get the same idea at the same time.

Out at the resort, he'd carried Vac down the hill while Pete managed the wheelchair. He hadn't weighed much by then, bony as a zipper. Alpo remembered they sat with him at the end of the dock. It was hard to keep everything about those days straight, but yes, maybe he did put a fishing pole in Vac's hand . . .

It had been a pretty day, one of those blue September days still clinging to summer but hinting at what's coming. Vac seemed glad enough to be home, if only for a couple hours. The Canadian lady looking after the lodge had even brought out beers. They cast their lures and caught a few perch. But that was it. When Vac started nodding, Alpo worried maybe they'd worn him out. At the hospital they'd brushed the pine needles off him, plugged him with a breath mint, and snuck him right back through the side entrance—no one the wiser.

"Hell, Meg, that was nothing. Anybody woulda done the same."

"But nobody else did." Meg's gaze swept from the swag of streamers to the empty Gallo jugs and trays where triangles of cheese had begun to curl. "This was nice . . ." She stood.

He supposed it was.

After she'd gone, he stayed in the booth until the party was just himself, Juri, Chim, Ray, and Joe. With the door locked, they aimed themselves at the painting and set to drinking the rest of the beer so Juri could turn in the empties for the deposit.

At home he hung it where he could see it, above the TV. But it did not make Alpo feel the way he hoped it would. It was pretty and worth a lot of money, but like Meg said, it was only a painting. Only an approximation.

Outside, the real trees of the Hobby had begun to rally. Within a month, whatever was wrong with them stopped being wrong. After they'd been examined and reexamined, Alpo stood in the middle of the Hobby turning slow circles with his arms hanging, knowing he should feel relieved.

Over the autumn, Alpo began fly-tying classes at Lefty's. Under Hal's guidance, he hunched over his tying table with scraps of fur and feather and clamped tiny hooks into his vice. By spring he'd mastered the Damsel Nymph and Irresistible Adams. He could tie Woolly Worms in his sleep and even made up a few flies of his own. He ordered a monocle made in Switzerland and paid for it with his tax refund.

The yellow inner needles of the trees had shed over the winter, and in May they were replaced by hale, green growth. Not many noticed that new buds on Alpo's trees went unclipped that spring; few remarked on the Hobby's perfection seeming less perfect—that the trees looked a little fuzzy around the edges, in need of a shave.

A second season passed with the trees growing unchecked. Then another. By the time Alpo tore down the deer fencing, the Hobby was so shaggy not a head turned or a finger pointed from the vehicles barreling north. Branches grew out and up quickly, or maybe it just seemed quickly to Alpo when he compared the view out the east window to the painting hanging near it.

Colorado spruce brushed unruly limbs against Baltic cedar, Baltic cedar elbowed Fraser fir. Volunteer saplings took hold in the wort. The princess pines edged upward and outward, inching toward the property line and over, reaching out cautiously, blindly, to where the wild trees grow every which way.

EG KNOWS THAT NO MATTER HOW SORELY NEEDED or hard earned, vacations seldom turn out as antici-pated. The brochures with Photoshopped come-ons promise tranquility, but two weeks out of fifty-two are not enough to unknot eleven and a half months of stress or exhaustion. There are no blackout dates for unhappiness during high season.

More marriages than her own have ended at Naledi. Inevi-table, when you consider the lifespan of a resort—how many hundreds of couples have vacationed here. Of course, there'd been more happy and contented (or at least ambivalent) couples than miserable ones edging around each other in the small pine-paneled spaces or staring shoreward together through the bulged and mended porch screens.

People tended to have more sex on vacation. She knew that much, having cleaned cabins as a teen, when she would strip and remake cabin beds each Saturday, finding evidence of coupling on stained sheets. Walls just behind the headboards were scuffed by rhythmic conviviality. Pulling along her red housekeeping cart, Meg heard noises coming from various cabins that signaled fresh towels were not the moment's desire. From the time she was old enough to drag along behind the cleaning girls, she knew that husbands who did not fish in the mornings had happier wives, and that cabins emitting the most laughter also had waste-baskets with stiff discarded tissues and odd sausage casings that she realized eventually, appallingly, were not sausage casings.

At that age she had to wonder why sex, why biology was asso-ciated with gasps, giggles, or shame. Vac had seemed so detached and unaware of the carnal facets of life Meg might have assumed he was as asexual and smooth as a Ken doll down there had she not once encountered him—to their mutual mortification—on the short path from the sauna to the lake, jogging and pink, tackle a-bob and skinny legs pumping.

Around the time she'd gone away to school she'd already knit together clues regarding Vac and Ursa, the delivery lady, but she could not imagine what two people that old—Ursa in her sixties and Vac close to seventy—would get up to besides fishing or playing cribbage. Maybe holding hands, so she left it at that. Years later she deduced (with a slight shudder) that they had indeed been intimate, for years. She mused over the notion, wondering if they'd experienced those lovely moments afterward, when warm bodies feel most alive, when for however long that lasts you're not alone. If her grandfather had such moments they surely would have been a departure for him. Vac had steadily, subliminally, and perhaps even unconsciously insinuated to Meg the idea that however agreeable the company of others may be, company is not necessary.

In spite of marriage being a concept hard to get her head around, Meg dived in anyway. Vac would never have approved of Jeremy, in fact would have laid odds on the marriage not outlasting a bottle of Worcestershire sauce. And would have been right. Her deeper feelings for Jeremy had slunk away long before her lucid moment in the lodge kitchen. One of these days Meg might even tell Hal Bergen how he'd unwittingly and quite literally had a hand in her decision—that she had, during one surreal moment holding Hal's hand, promised herself she would henceforth choose what hands she held, deciding that Jeremy's had felt more lifeless than Hal's when she'd packed it up in ice and sent it off.

They'd married in a tiny chapel around the corner from the same Chicago courthouse where the divorce was later granted. It had been a brief exchange of canned vows, followed by a luncheon at the Drake with a handful of friends, and family, Jeremy's jetlagged parents and her own few scraps of family—Polly, Aunt Cathy, and her cousin Patrick, whom Meg barely knew then. Meg drank far too much, which wasn't her habit, but then she wasn't herself that day, bawling when she realized that butter-cream frosting had ruined the fawn velvet sleeve of her little dress, which at that moment she loved more than Jeremy. There are a few Polaroids from that afternoon, as faded and blurred as her recall of it. The face that developed in the pictures beamed more frantically than happily from pages of the wedding album. Never a good sign, Meg thinks, and now she's even forgotten what drawer or box those wedding pictures had been relegated to.

Meg has an old Super 8 reel of her parents' wedding in color but with no sound, so that their mouths only move in silent vows and toasts and smiles. She keeps meaning to show the reel to Deaf Jenny who works at Pamida so she can translate what their lips are saying. In Hatchet Inlet, people's names are often tacked with descriptives not necessarily flattering or at all PC. There is Fat Pat, the librarian, so called because the other librarian is also a Pat, but Thin Pat simply has no ring to it. The formerly flat-chested hygienist at the dentist office was Karen, but postsurgery is now known as Tits, toting an impressive pair that she'd saved for, for very a long time. Meg remembers the first time Jeremy heard Gimp Wuuri answer to his nickname. Gimp must've heard the gasp because he cranked his bent neck to where they stood in the checkout line and shrugged. "Well, I am one, ain't I?"

On the old reel, Meg's parents kiss and wave as silently as the dead would. Vac stands stiff in the background, dapper in his narrow suit, with hair. In the next scene, on the steps of the church, the lens pans over guests throwing rice, the women in white gloves with bouffant hair and Jackie O hats, and the men all smoking and looking like stand-ins for the Rat Pack.

As for Vac's marriage to her grandmother, Meg assumes their wedding was somewhat traditional, only because what is left of the single surviving photograph seems so: the bride in pearls and a spray of white lily and one lace sleeve—just below where her head had been torn away. That hasty editing would have been the handiwork of Vac or Tomas—each had reason enough.

Meg walks the path from the lodge, hoping Polly might have leftover pound cake in her cabin for tea, maybe some of the oranges. The path twines along the shore through a copse of birch, down to the inlet of bald rock where the two remaining cabins stand. Polly's cabin leans on its supports, a little like she does. Meg had convinced her to come early this year, sensing a shift, aware that time is finite and the amount left to her old friend is narrowing. They've had most of the summer together. Next month she will pack Polly's things and the cabin will be shuttered.

Farther out on the peninsula is the outpost, its porch aimed toward the narrows, where a rock can be skipped to sink in Canadian waters. Meg has always thought of the outpost as the little cabin that could—so far from the others, facing north with brave windows as if to say, *Try me.* Vac had always grumbled that it was too exposed, too far from the lodge, always too goddamn something. Sun flaked paint from the trim, spray from November gales weighted the roof with ice. Until a few years ago Meg had intended to tear it down but couldn't quite. Then Jon Redleaf came to fix the lodge hearth and offered to repair the outpost. Ever since, he's been a sort of self-appointed handyman, bartering work for rent. Meg's well aware she's getting the better end of the deal, but he won't accept a dime above the cost of building supplies. The cabin has a new bluestone foundation, a steel roof, and a skirt of fresh cedar shakes that will weather to the same gray as the granite below.

Having done things her own way for so long, Meg didn't think having someone around Naledi would work out, but Jon seems a presence she hadn't known was missing. Days can go by with only a wave or nod from afar, but it's enough that there's another body around the place, someone else breathing to dilute the air of isolation.

There are occasional visitors—one today, in fact. She sees the red bicycle propped near the outpost and the shy masseur, Veshko, on a camp stool fishing from the dock.

Jon says new porch screens for Polly's cabin are next, and

when he mentions a project it usually means the materials are already in his truck. He'll be heading west in the morning to his nephew's graduation party and had come to the lodge earlier in the day asking Meg if she had some ribbon or a leather shoelace to finish off the end of his braid. She's not the ribbon-owning type, but after a search of drawers came up with better, a cheap sterling bracelet bought at a head shop in the '80s, thin enough that Jon could bend it into a coil with his hands.

Meg is secretly proud of her ability to make do, ever ready with a fix—this far from anywhere there are plenty of opportunities to come up short and be in sudden need of a part or ingredient or tool. Back in the day, barely an afternoon would pass without some guest coming into the bar needing something mended, plugged, or patched and vexed enough to ask a girl for help. Early on, she mastered reattaching dolls arms, fixing flip-flops, cutting new straps for snorkels from inner tubes, and fashioning water-wings from motor oil bottles. She graduated to cotter pins, a Dremel, epoxy, and solder. When she'd fixed something in a particularly clever way, such as splinting a snapped fishing rod from the inside with a peeled alder whip, Vac would work his face into that wink that looked like a tic to anyone else and mutter his highest compliment, "See? You're not so dumb."

She could do things with the springs from Bics and papers clips that left guests blinking in gratitude. It pleased her to her core to be cleverer than grown men who usually wore suits and bossed people around or designed bridges or stood in operating rooms with their hands inside people. Meg secretly enjoyed untangling their hopeless nests of fishing line—though anyone watching her might have thought her touched, the more snarled the better, and no odder in her mind than the jigsaw puzzles so many guests labored over in the evenings to distract themselves from the lack of television, trying to ignore the fact they were surrounded by miles of nothing and night, unaccustomed to the distant howling, eerie hoots and the mysterious rustlings, creaks, and croakings of the darkness.

Over the years she's had to consider selling Naledi, but

somehow the money has always turned up, so she's never had to imagine actually leaving. Naledi has always been here and has always been the other side of everywhere else. There's life outside, where one event leads to the next and one is never sure what might happen, and then there's here, where time is cyclical, the seasons defining all, where nothing much besides the inevitable happens.

Above her head, the resident hawk wheels in a dome of sky blue enough to look phony. The top of the dome is fissured by a loop of geese trussed like nuns and migrating in rosary formation. Meg can see Polly on her porch, sunk into the wicker and goggling through a rusted screen at the view, maybe seeing her memory of it. Now that she's growing blinder, she's more attuned to sound and knows Meg's approach before her first step on the stairs. Polly is complaining before the door is even opened.

"It's been a racket all day."

"The geese? It'll all quiet down in an hour, Polly."

"They've ruined my nap."

Polly's having one of her maudlin days. Meg can tell because she's wearing the piper's tam banded with the McPhee tartan. She only wears the Christmas plaid when feeling nostalgic or mortal. The tam is perched oddly on her head, and Meg studies Polly while tapping a tooth, deciding that it's not worth mentioning that it's on backwards.

"What's that tapping?"

"Mmm. Nothing."

Polly, always ready with an opinion, claims Meg has grown taciturn, like Vac, and too quiet. "Awfully like that big Jon over there. You're as oniony as that Chippewa," she says. "Not the easiest to peel."

"Anishinabe," Meg corrects her. "Or Ojibwe—I can't keep straight which is proper. And believe me, I talk plenty."

"To yourself. I could hear you this morning."

"To the radio."

"Same as."

Meg runs a finger along the pine chaff on the sill. "Jon'll be fixing your screens soon."

"Good. This place could use some attention. I can remember when this cabin shone."

"I know, Polly. I used to shine it."

Polly was the last-ever guest at Naledi. Vac saw to it that she would perpetually be the last guest by formally deeding the little cabin to her, which she has occupied nearly every summer for twenty-five years, making the trip even during years when Meg was abroad. Her state upon arriving this year alarmed Meg—her stoop more pronounced, her guesses as to what's in front of her more often wild. Blood relative or not, Meg suffers a loved one's frustration at being unable to make things any easier or more comfortable for Polly. Over time their roles have slowly reversed: she watches over Polly now.

When Meg glances down at the squares of notepaper Polly has shredded into her lap, she wonders if her old friend will be writing anything this month. It's three years since she's published a book, and her laptop sits closed as a clam on the porch table. She complains writing is less interesting than it used to be, and is overrated, like sex. "As if writing is such a noble endeavor. As if what I have to say has weight or meaning just because I'm vain enough to lay it out on a page." She makes such comments more often of late, revealing just how tired she is. Over dinner the night before she'd said, "I'm wrote out. At least what in me is worth writing. See, even my grammar sputters." Most days she's parked on the porch, content with her headphones, listening to cello concertos, audio lectures, or books on tape—sometimes even her own novels. In Polly's stories, forward-thinking heroines embrace carpe diem attitudes and do with their lives what Polly would have if she'd had the courage—travel to exotic places, take risks, come out, challenge the close-minded, make waves. Her characters are adventuresome and diligent and face danger with bravado, and while they do not always prevail, they never completely fail; they never give in.

At the beginning of the visit, Meg was shocked to see an e-mail from Polly's editor printed out with the font set so large each letter was the size of the Jolly Ranchers she's always tumbling against her dentures. They drove to Duluth for new glasses, which Polly complains about no end, saying they weigh her down like ballast in spite of the lightweight titanium frames. Now, when caught by Polly's comically enlarged stare, Meg must press away a grin.

Polly is the age Vac was when he went. When she claims getting old is hell, Meg believes her, unable to imagine which would be worse, losing sight and mobility as Polly has, her still-sharp mind confined in a failing body, or succumbing to the drift and lurch toward dementia. Somewhere in the lodge Meg has a telling memento of her ex–mother-in law Daphne's last months: a deluxe Scrabble board that she'd mistakenly baked one morning instead of her customary tray of scones. The board came out of the oven a Dali-esque droop of terrain like a topographic mold, letters held fast in the melted plastic. A week after the funeral, when clearing Daphne's belongings had commenced, Jeremy had watched Meg fish it out of the bin and wedge it into her luggage. It was simply too poignant a keepsake to leave behind. She'd admired the old woman, and many of the words drunkenly crisscrossing the board seemed so very Daphne-like: DIBBLE, BARROW, TRUDGE, HASP. It had irked Jeremy no end that his mother could still recall all the two- and three-letter words in the Scrabble dictionary (including those with a *q* but no *u*) but could not tell her own son from the man who clipped her privet hedge.

Polly's decline seems doubly unfair, considering how physically active she once was. She used to roam like a goat over the trails and old logging roads, but now when she ventures out at all she sticks to the main road, wearing a knee brace and using a pair of hiker's poles, leaning on one and poking the other ahead to dispel shadows. She's taken to wearing the sort of neon-green vest road crews do so that if she cannot find her way, someone will find her. Meg insists Polly take Ilsa along on her walks, and off they go together, both staring their milky stares. Meg sometimes puts on her sneakers to sneak behind.

Meg plans to invite her to live in the lodge but can almost script what Polly's response will be to that. She must find a way of bringing up Senior Cedars in conversation but is fairly certain Polly will refuse that as well. Those are the selfish solutions, but the less convenient solution is one she is prepared to undertake— accompany Polly back to Nova Scotia and get her settled in some assisted-living facility there. Meg wouldn't mind extended visits to Canada over the next years. She can paint there just as well as here, swap the worst of the Minnesota weather for the worst of the Maritimes.

She will never forget her first meeting with Polly. She'd been summoned home when Vac began dying in earnest, when Polly's presence at Naledi had come as a complete surprise. A stout stranger with an expression that shuttled from trepidation to curiosity cautiously explained the gravity of Vac's condition in her rigid accent. Meg was so jetlagged she barely took in much of the conversation but was struck with the feeling—upon seeing her anchored near the stove—that Polly would somehow remain, had already somehow filled a small part of the void her grandfather's death would inevitably carve. Later, Polly hesitantly relayed how Vac had arranged that she become Meg's legal guardian. It was only to be for three years, until Meg turned twenty-one. So much happened during Vac's last days. With the subsequent wake and funeral and legal arrangements, there'd been little time for everything to sink in, but in the months afterward when each was back in her respective place—Meg at school in London and Polly in her sea-swept province—both knew they had somehow been duped into an alliance. Vac's bid to stitch Polly and Meg into some semblance of family had succeeded, whether they wanted it or not. If Meg possessed any gift for making do, she would have to credit Vac for it—hadn't he simply been working with what he had on hand? Fortunately, the *what* had been Polly.

Meg has only two living relatives, her aunt Catherine and cousin Patrick—a pimply string bean who had spent the duration of Meg's wedding luncheon gulping at Jeremy and clinging to his every clipped word. She'd thought her young cousin was a little odd but knows now he'd only been cripplingly shy. Before marrying Jeremy she decided to track down her only other known relation, her grandmother—the faceless Magda from the torn wedding photo. At the time, Meg felt oddly and suddenly compelled to find her grandmother but later wondered if she wasn't looking for a reason to alter her plans to marry, perhaps hoping Magda would provide one. She'd been right there in Vac's address book, just like that, under *M*. She wondered if he'd contacted her after her parents' crash—he would have at least done that, she reasoned.

Meg was on summer break in Brighton, and Vienna wasn't all that far, so she made the ferry crossing and set off with her Eurail pass, toting along clotted cream and raspberry sponge because they seemed like the sorts of things you'd bring from England.

Magda's neighborhood was a leafy maze of cobbled streets with tall houses and narrow courtyards behind iron gates. As she walked, Meg realized Magda was probably wealthy, and when she located the house, the most elegant on the block, she nearly turned back, worried her grandmother might think she'd come to cash in on her guilt, which only made her more nervous. She had sent a letter, and several weeks later received a tepid response, reading more welcome into it than was there. She had replied to Magda immediately with the date and approximate time of her arrival.

A woman wearing an apron and tennis shoes answered the door. She wasn't nearly old enough to be Magda, and after greetings and a few gestures Meg deduced her to be the housekeeper. Meg spoke no German, and the housekeeper spoke no English, and, surprisingly, no Czech, so they fumbled for some common language, the housekeeper gesticulating with her feather duster until Magda herself crabbed into sight on her cane, jet beads looping toward the floor, shaking her head over their attempts at French.

"You should have called from the station." She looked Meg over. "I would have sent Clara to fetch you."

Magda was a more fashionable, older version of the Viennese matrons Meg had seen in shops and cafés lining the long walk from the station. Her white hair was stiffly waved and sprayed to a chalky shell. She was over ninety and had been a big woman once, but had deflated and hunched so that the slack components of her swayed from shoulders and spine like a suspension bridge.

"Follow," she commanded.

The house was vast and dark and too warm, its many vases of flowers not enough to mask the smell of glue and age. Surfaces and bookshelves were crammed with Limoges figurines and crystal tchotchkes that were likely the bane of the duster-wielding Clara's existence. There were few books. The gilded chair Meg was steered to was somehow less comfortable than her seat on the train.

Clara served coffee and pastries, cutting Magda's into little pieces as if for a child, while Meg told her grandmother about herself, talking too quickly, telling how she'd been teaching in Bath, that she had a very bright, very tall fiancé, and that they would move to Chicago at the end of the semester because Jeremy had secured a post at Northwestern. They would marry in Illinois, spend part of the summer at Naledi, and honeymoon in Paris before the start of fall term. When finished, she clamped her mouth shut—the summation of her life up to that moment had taken two minutes. Magda scrutinized Meg as she spoke but did not respond with her own story.

After coffee, Magda led her through the walled garden, droning on about her flowers as if the garden was what Meg had come for. She seemed astonished that Meg knew so little about domestic garden plants. She urged her to repeat the names she ticked off in Latin or German. Meg casually mentioned that she could identify quite a few wild North American orchids, lilies, or woodland plants in Latin and was given a look for her boasting. Embarrassed, Meg kept her mouth shut and learned the names of Magda's brash, hotly colored blooms, altogether too pungent, too orange. The garden was small, but at Magda's pace and tutelage their stroll took an hour but seemed longer.

Afterward, they sat in the conservatory, where ornate radiators thumped and steamed so that the damp woolen smell of Meg's skirt rose to mingle with her own sweat. She laid open the photo album she'd brought and turned the pages very slowly, explaining each shot to Magda from the beginning, when Vac was just settling in at Naledi.

"And here's Tomas." Meg waited for Magda's reaction. She had carefully chosen the shots of her father and put them in order of age: chubby-cheeked on a tricycle; then a few years older feeding a tame deer; next, in swim trunks as a skinny youth, tanned and afloat on a raft of oil barrels. She moved on, pointedly saying "Tomas" again at another picture and once "My father," though she was able to refrain from saying "your son." There he was as an adolescent, standing with skates flung over his shoulder, his features forming to handsomeness. Next was a college graduation photo with Tomas in his mortarboard standing next to Vac, each holding a corner of his diploma.

They were sitting close enough to touch, but both took care not to. Magda didn't seem at all affected by the images of the family she'd abandoned. As she scrutinized faces in the photos, nothing was revealed on her own. Magda asked no questions—at least none that Meg would be dying to ask if a long-lost grand-daughter suddenly landed on her doorstep. After silently scanning four or five more pages, Magda made a noise like a snort and dragged a fingernail over Vac's face.

"He ceaselessly spoke of going to the north—when he described, I only could picture Finland, even Lapland. I never would have dreamt he meant America, another continent. I could hardly believe when I found out."

Magda's knobby hands either twitched in her lap or raked at her wheezy little lap dog, Henrick. She kept hinting Meg might want to pet him, too, but she leaned well away, keeping clear of his needly teeth. Meg was tempted to tell Magda how Vac determined the measure of a dog: those worth keeping calmly registered gunshots, then waited for the splash before launching from the boat or the duck blind, swimming back with the fowl unbruised in its mouth. A respectable dog could pull four times its weight over ice and never growled or barked without good reason. When Magda wasn't looking, Meg bared her teeth right back at Henrick and silently snarled. A dog discovered indoors sitting on furniture wouldn't have known what hit it.

"Why did he choose America, do you think?" Meg knew it was a loaded question.

Magda's eyes narrowed. "He had sabotaged his own prospects in Prague by then, you see? Refusing to work on bridges or buildings because some other engineers weren't Czech."

"You mean German?"

"Yes, German. He turned down security . . ." she leaned in, "and a good living for his family."

Her grandfather had never stopped hating the Germans—at least not since she could remember. When she was young, Vac would take her along to his rare evenings at the Sokol Hall, where she'd be given her own table to spread out her elbows and colored pencils, within earshot of Vac and his few cronies. Mr. Danacek from the boat works, Evon the baker, and the Polish pharmacist whose name was so fraught with the consonants *c, w, y,* and *z* everyone just called him Uncle Doc. The lot of them all jokingly identified themselves as bohunks, claiming that in America their bloody histories didn't matter—forget that the sundry ancestors of one would have brutalized or killed the ancestors of another. Meg listened and sketched and drank ginger ale with waxy cocktail cherries while they knocked back shots, tapped their toes to mazurkas, and grumbled about the state of everything. She recalls the evening Vac suddenly held up a bottle asking his mates, "You ever see a German wear a baseball cap?" They'd roared at that one and proceeded to speculate on how history might read differently if the Nazis had only embraced the game of baseball. Amid snorts and wheezy laughter they recruited rookies from among the defendants at Nuremberg and assigned them positions—Goering as an outfielder, Keitel the pitcher. They chortled over the image of Mengele as catcher and demoted Hess to lowly batboy while wiping tears of mirth. Evon, who'd lost two sisters in the camps, did an imitation of Hitler as the announcer, holding a finger where a mustache would be, speaking into his Schlitz-bottle microphone: "Und zee bettom of zee eighth innink, it iss a hit . . . und a run . . . und a score!"

The others whooped and cheered.

"Und now, zee pitcher shall be *shot!*"

Humor, Vac would insist, can anesthetize the worst.

Meg knew instinctively to not expect anything approaching humor or irony from Magda, but she didn't think it so far fetched to expect a bit of warmth, maybe a revelation or two. Magda seemed unwilling to acknowledge even the fact of Meg, her own flesh and blood sitting inches away.

"Yes," she continued, "Vaclav was always speaking of the woods, the nature. A better place to raise a family, he would say. Better than Prague? Better than Vienna? To raise what sort of family—creatures, I would ask him, wolves?"

"*I* was raised there." Meg couldn't help her tone. She'd only been half-raised at Naledi; still, it wasn't as if she or her father had been brought up feral. She knew when to pick up which fork and could recite the compulsory poems.

Meg raised the album closer to Magda's face—a family photo with Tomas smack in the middle, her mother next to him, and Vac standing behind with his hand on his son's shoulder. Meg was leaning on her father's knee, all sprung curls and freckles. "That's the last photo taken of him. Of us."

Even that didn't seem to crack her. When they reached the page, the newspaper articles and obituaries, Magda dug a tiny pair of glasses from the depth of the bosom of her dress and bent over to read, her mouth hard. When finished, she made no comment. A chime tinkled from the back of the house and Magda quickly closed the album.

"It is dinner."

For someone so bent over, Magda could move very quickly. Meg tucked the album into her knapsack, mumbling to Magda's back, "Right. Saved by the bell."

The table was too elaborately set for the meal. There was soup and dry chops and a few salad greens swimming in mayonnaise—probably what Magda would've eaten had she been alone. Meg interpreted the offerings as a declaration that her visit was nothing special. The dessert of stewed prunes in yogurt exclaimed it.

After the dishes were cleared, Magda surprised Meg by hauling out her own photos to spread on the tablecloth. Within minutes, Meg began to think she might understand some of her grandmother's self-absorption. Magda had once possessed the sort of beauty you could not turn away from: flawless skin, a mass of black hair, and deep azure eyes set in a face like Greek marble. She'd been an only child, she said, and Meg could guess she'd been spoiled, given advantages and set apart like something precious. As a young woman she'd had a figure that would have been in vogue then. But looking from the photos to the real woman, Meg saw no remnants of beauty, inside or out; the once-majestic bosom had gone south, ready to topple her with its weight. Her formerly smooth cheeks swagged into the crepe of her neck, and her eyes were shrunken and faded like something washed too often, the lower lids fallen open like a coin purses. She was wholly unrecognizable as the same person, her entire being decidedly unlovely.

Meg was unable to imagine Vac in Magda's once-luminous presence. He'd always seemed immune to beauty and perhaps Magda was the reason why. He might admit a sunset or a speckled trout was good-looking enough, or, if Meg brought him a drawing or painting she'd worked particularly hard at, he might even nod and claim it "wasn't bad." Such measured praise never injured Meg. It was unspoken but understood that praise didn't matter—doing something worthy of it did.

Faced with Magda, Meg wondered if maybe someone else might be able to find the good in the old woman. Even though she'd traveled so far, Meg was not offered a bed. At the end of their visit Magda led her to the door, giving directions to a nearby hostel. As Meg wriggled into her backpack, Magda's gaze went over her shoulder as if toward some passerby, but there was no one on the dusky street, just a sodium lantern flickering to life. She spoke very deliberately: "I went back for the boy, you know. As I meant to, as Vaclav well knew I would, only a week later. But in Prague I find the flat empty—he had taken Tomas. I didn't know where . . ." Magda leaned so heavily on her cane Meg was afraid she'd have to prop the old woman up. "Nothing for thirty years. Then one telephone call to say the boy was dead." She blinked her dry eyes. "I can guess what he told you—that my lover was a Nazi, no? He was German, yes, but had left the party. He was civilian, only worked for the regime." Her grandmother abruptly went still and looked Meg fully in the eye for the first time. "We were married thirty-seven years." She nodded as if that explained everything.

"Yes?" Meg let her hand fall from the doorknob, imagining Magda might possibly be having some change of heart, would invite her back in, tell her the whole story, but Magda only knit herself as upright as she was able and cleared her throat. "I do not know what I can offer you, young lady. It is regrettable you have so little family, but I have no need for such reminders as you." In case that hadn't driven home the message, she added, "I already have grandchildren."

Meg looked into the faded eyes to see that indeed there was nothing for her there. "Do you?" she asked, opening the door, letting a gust of cold air in as she stepped out. All she could think to add was, "Well, aren't they the lucky ones." Wind pushed the heavy door wide, too far for the old woman to shut it without stumbling out into the cold herself. Without turning to watch Magda wrestle it shut, Meg opened the gate and swung it wide on its hinges before turning onto the cobbles and walking away.

She found a hostel near the station and in the morning was on the first train. All the way back to France, she stared at her reflection rather than the landscape, blind to the scenery, intent on what a face reveals. Meg realized Magda was so one-dimensional she might have been a character in some made-for-TV movie and was perhaps the first truly uncomplicated adult Meg had ever met. Her grandmother was not totally bad, just not very good, with not a shard of insight. Vac never bothered with put-downs or insults, but when roused by someone contemptible, he might accuse them of lacking introspection—the most objectionable trait he could think of. On her own face, masked over the speed-streaked landscape of the Austrian countryside, Meg saw some of Vac's guardedness settle into her eyes.

Months later, during her honeymoon, when Jeremy was suffering indigestion from the Parisian food he wouldn't stop eating, she occupied herself painting Vac's portrait from memory, pinning the source of his perpetual look of distrust, knowing who put it there.

She reaches for Polly's hand and squeezes. "You want some tea?" She had not told Polly about her meeting with Magda until years later, because she's grown to consider Polly family, and in her mind the trip to Vienna felt disloyal. She only wishes in hindsight that she'd left Madga with more presence of mind so that she might have replied, "And I already have a grandmother."

Meg stands in the cabin, looking around. A cushion on the wicker settee needs punching. She scans Polly's shelves for anything new, but there are only a few large-print reference books, novels and stories by Canadian and Irish authors. Copies of Polly's books, some reissued as a set with corresponding covers and matching fonts. *The Salt Cliffs* next to *Water Notes* next to *Tango for Cello* and *The Pebble House*. Meg picks up *The Salt Cliffs* and looks at its title page, and the dedication she's read a dozen times. Unsure of its meaning, she's been tempted to ask Polly, though surely it was some message between Polly and Vac alone: "In gratitude for words unforgotten, 'Live without hesitation.'"

Nothing she'd ever heard her grandfather say. But then what do children really know of the lives of adults? Putting the kettle on, she finds a plate for the cake, and when she peels the oranges carefully sets the segments in a spiral pattern like a nautilus—it doesn't matter whether Polly can see it or not. What matters is that it's done.

ASPIRING STUDENT REPORTER TIFFANY SWIFTHAWK IS IN THE honors program at Hatchet Inlet High School. Her radio interview assignment is worth a third of her grade in Media Today. She hopes to plump up her digital audio résumé because she's applying for the summer session at the School of Broadcast Journalism down in Minneapolis, which holds a three-week camp for juniors and seniors. Mr. Maki had instructed students to seek persons with interesting occupations, histories, or talents, interview them, edit the piece, and post it on the school's podcast, the best of them to be aired on the local public affiliate, WSQW.

Unfortunately, while other students were off scrambling to line up interviews, Tiffany was down for two days with strep and a fever, and by the time she was back on her feet pickings were slim. It's not like Hatchet Inlet is a hotbed of notable individuals—there's the oldest living resident, Ursa Olson, who has a mouth like a sailor and so not great for radio; the topiary man kids call Alpo Scissorhands, who hardly talks at all; the identical Kapalanen twins out at the Musher dogsled resort; the stump-sculptor-bartender Chainsaw Sally; and Annie Littlebow, the medicine woman and old-timey midwife. By the time the antibiotics had kicked in, all were taken, even creepy Wolfman Willie, which left the sheriff, the mayor, and others even more uninteresting. Anyone from the reservation is out of the question— Tiffany isn't about to interview some creaky, slow-speaking elder on the air. She wants out of Hatchet Inlet, not deeper in.

Tiffany clomps into Pavola's, shedding snow from her mukluks. There was Meg the painter sitting at the counter, the lady her uncle rents a cabin from up near the last boat launch everyone calls Bumfuck Narrows. Tiffany unzips the top of her banana-yellow snowmobile suit and slides half-peeled onto a stool next to Meg. Meg, nice as always, asks how she is. Tiffany tells, describing the assignment, dramatizing her failure to procure a decent interviewee and the unfairness of it all, so distraught that a little projectile of spit punctuates her complaint, the wet BB arcing over the crust of the meat pasty Meg is fortunately just finishing. Without missing a beat, Meg lays down her fork and takes up a knife to cut her wedge of cake in half, pushing the dessert plate toward Tiffany.

After a Coke and the cake, Tiffany revives some. Looking at Meg anew, she pauses.

"Hey. *You* were someone, right?"

And now Meg sits staring at her laptop at the Minnow Bucket, which has WiFi and espresso but no minnows. Tiffany has e-mailed a list of preinterview questions for her to "practice" for the real thing. Later, they will meet at the high school computer lab to record the actual interview. Tiffany's plan is to add music and narrate parts in a sort of *This American Life* monotone. She's also asked for some JPEGs of Meg's art to post on the home page for extra credit. With luck, it will air next Friday on WSQW right after the Polka Peggy show.

Meg scans the list. She has all morning.

"What was it like growing up at a resort?"

"How come you only paint water?"

"What other artists aspire you?" Meg assumes Tiffany means "inspire."

"What advice would you give a young artist?"

"You lived other places—Chicago and England. What did you miss the most about home?"

"Now that you're back in Hatchet Inlet, what do you miss about real life?"

"If you could live during any time or era, when would it be?"

~ ~

Just out the window, chickadees crowd the feeders. When a flicker swoops in, they all fall like scraps, pulling tiny avalanches of seeds with them. Back in debate class at St. Agnes, Meg learned that to improve any answer you first wrote it out, then read it aloud—a rare nugget of her mostly forgotten education dredged forth. She taps out her first answer in a few minutes, then not quite aloud but moving her lips, she reads, glancing around at the other two customers, both wearing earbuds, eyes bolted to their own screens:

"It's no vacation, like some might think. Anybody who wasn't visiting was always working. Every day between fishing opener and Labor Day we took care of the guests and the place, then fell into bed and slept like rocks, then got up and did it again. The rest of the year was school. I never thought much about what it was like, time went too fast.

"Sometimes rich families brought their nannies or mother's helpers. That's how my parents met. My mother had a summer job as nanny to a bunch of boys who came each year, and my father was working the docks and guiding.

"We all did our summer jobs like everyone else; we just had a nicer view."

Naledi wasn't fancy, or convenient, being so far from town. It wasn't modern, as in "modern housekeeping cabins"; in fact, not every cabin was even wired for electricity. Some had propane light fixtures and suspect refrigerators the maids called "death by Servel." But the resort was inexpensive and obsessively well kept. Meg seemed always to be holding a rag or mop or sponge, mind-lessly polishing or wiping even what surfaces she'd happened to pause near—a car fender, or the aluminum arm of a lawn chair, or some slope of stone if that's where she'd happened to plunk down. Naturally, her own room under the lodge eaves was a con-trast in chaos, where under each grungy layer of what Vac called her "strew" she knew precisely where everything was.

"It wasn't very exciting, though we never knew who might

show up—an opera singer, a senator, a defrocked priest, a teen-aged nymphomaniac . . . ."

She deletes "nymphomaniac" in favor of "homewrecker," then deletes that deciding both are too outdated and types "slut." "Once we even had a private detective following a man whose 'niece' was not his niece."

Meg sits back. The guests did make it more interesting—you never knew who would show up or what they would be like. Some had crazy pasts or were funny or awful or weird or had dragged some built-in drama or hysteria along to ruin the vacation for their entire family and sometimes those in neighboring cabins. Occasionally one of the mothers would discover Meg was an orphan and set out to somehow make that right in a way that meant right for them. Sometimes they mothered, or smothered, or were overgenerous or sappy like they'd found some injured bird. A few simply paid attention to Meg, more curious about her than her orphan status, or just listened when she spoke. Those were the ones she didn't mind.

Most guests were regular folks and very relieved to be not working their boring jobs or toiling around the house—just enjoying themselves, which rendered them completely forgettable. What most everyone shared in common were their fairly predictable reactions to the place itself. Some were overwhelmed by the quiet, others went a little stir-crazy with their own idleness or experienced a sort of overload. Some lit into the flora and fauna like amateur Darwins, or got claustrophobia with so many trees, or agoraphobia with too little of the familiar. Quite a few arrived unprepared for the swings in weather: in June it could snow or swelter, but few thought to pack both bikini and mittens. Meg did a brisk business in the little retail corner of the lounge where they stocked crew socks and knit headbands and hooded sweatshirts embroidered with the Naledi pine tree logo and its motto, "The Last Resort."

Weather was one thing and could be prepared for, but insects could break the toughest guest, particularly during black fly hatches. Though she'd been quite young, Meg remembers a

Marine just back from Saigon, showing up in his uniform straight from the airport. For the previous year in Vietnam he'd dreamt of nothing but going fishing and promised himself that if he made it out alive he would do just that. But whether in his cabin or in his canoe, peace eluded him—there was too much quiet. All he could hear were the flies—not just the buzzing, but the beating of their wings and their breathing. He'd survived two tours of combat, but after three days at Naledi he had to be fetched by his high school hockey coach and driven to the VA hospital at Fort Snelling.

Tick season always provided plenty of slapstick in the lounge—guests jigging to their feet and barely out of sight before hands were deep in their shorts or swim trunks, burrowing blouses and bras, searching out the little bastards. People ran their hands through their hair so habitually the place appeared populated by deep thinkers. The only thing worse than suspecting a tick was finding one attached. Meg had several methods for removal and raked in decent tips doing it, though if Vac caught her accepting money for such a service he would simply look at her until she gave it back. He was forever making her return money rightfully earned.

During the mosquito heights of July, everyone suffered, swatting and scratching, waking on sheets checkered with their own blood. Dousing with DEET was the only relief, but too nasty for little kids or anyone sunburned or already raw with bites. Meg took a cue from the nuns down the shore at Camp Gummy and made wimples of mosquito netting attached to Twins baseball caps with a few grommets. She displayed these above the reception counter, which also did duty as candy case, complaint department, lost and found, and first-aid station. The souvenir corner had a dusty stock of beaded key chains, cedar boxes stamped "Vacationland," and miniature canoe paddles. The mosquito wimples sold fast, eclipsing her boiled fisheye jewelry and the mobiles she fashioned from snare wire and old fishing lures.

To guests, slimy creatures were as bad as bugs. On the beach once Meg watched an obese sunbather faint after lifting one of

her rolls of stomach fat to discover a small colony of leeches settled there. Meg wondered where a person could even buy a two-
piece swimsuit in that size. When the fat woman woke up, she
went practically mental searching her many creases, hadn't even
said thanks when Meg handed over the saltshaker.

She leans over the keyboard to tap, "Nature could be a
challenge."

If growing up at a resort was any different from growing up
anywhere else, how would she know? Other than the summer her
parents got on the plane that didn't land where it was meant to,
each summer was just like another.

In the months following the crash, Meg puzzled over Vac's
odd story about the other, bigger lake, where her parents were
"at resting" underneath. At seven she naturally wondered, if her
mother and father were underneath, who else might be? Was "underneath" another world? Her snorkel mask revealed little more
than the murky bottom, schools of minnows like animated beer-
can tabs, the slime of frogs' eggs, and the detritus of stuff lost
or dropped from boats. But nothing as impressive as a broken
fuselage, nothing so bright as a mother's bones.

She reads the next question and gets a refill for her coffee and
a scone while pondering it.

"In my mind, I paint everything *but* the water. I report what
is captured over the surface, reflected in its mirrors, sometimes
still and sometimes fluid and unpredictable or warped, like life.
The surface separates halves of above and beneath, the known
and unknown." Meg rereads and sighs. It sounds like art-speak
and only approaches what she wants to articulate. She's often
struck by the absurdity that visual artists are even called on to
explain or justify their work in words when words are so often a
second language for them. Can't folks just look at art and take it
for what it is, or be content with their own interpretations?

If there is one constant threading through her life, it's been
water, and she rarely strays very far from it. Even at St. Agnes in
Chicago she was only a bus ride from the shores of Lake Michigan. In the early years, Vac migrated to live near the convent for

part of each school term, spending his days haunting the library or pier or huffing along the streets against that sort of Chicago wind that always felt more vicious than any at Naledi.

Their weekends were spent in the Field Museum, Shedd Aquarium, and farther south along the lake shore, just sitting or fishing or combing for rocks or flotsam. Sometimes she gazed over the span of the body of water that had taken in her parents and tried to remember them. Hers was a curious loss. At first she mostly missed the physical, often crawling into bed with her little dorm mates at night, or appearing next to Vac's snoring form like a sleepwalker, retaining no memory of the ritual in which he wrapped her mummy-style in the blanket she'd dragged along and then pulled her in, laying his hand over her small back until they both dreamt again. She was too young to properly mourn, and for the first year or so half-expected her parents might reappear, until eventually that expecting slowly wore away.

Meg retains static memories of her parents on their last day, though is uncertain of those few memories for surely her imagination has filled in the details: her mother holding a carry-on bag, her free hand cradling the ever-larger bump that never got the chance to become her little brother or sister. Anne's red hair was held at bay by a leather oval pierced by a wooden stick, and copper freckles swarmed her arms like ants. Her ankles had lost their shape under the weight of the baby so that Tomas had teased her as she lumbered up into the VW bus, saying something about "cankles," which Anne refused to laugh at.

They had planned on bringing Meg, but at the last minute Vac suddenly insisted she stay with him. If her parents had any real objections, they were so surprised at his rare imperative they thought it best to simply comply. Vac plucked up her 101 Dalmatians suitcase and tucked it under his arm; he hadn't merely held Meg's hand, he'd seized it.

Before getting in behind the wheel, her father pried her from Vac and swung her up in the air while they sang the airplane-moon song they'd made up together. He'd smelled of newsprint and grease from changing the oil. She'd been annoyed at him for leaving yet again, he'd been gone too much already; all summer he'd traveled back and forth to his small engineering firm in Elmhurst. Her mother had already cut back to half-time at her own job and was only going along for a doctor's appointment.

The VW made its laboring whine, and from her perch on Vac's shoulder Meg watched the back end of the bus bump up the drive. The scene had grown in her adult mind to cinematic proportions: a small child waving a pudgy hand as tail lights recede down a ribbon of gravel into a tunnel of summer-green trees. The last she would ever see of her parents.

Later in the day, the sheriff's car came, eliciting much curiosity from the guests. She recalls being carried inside and placed on the couch as if she were an object. Vac paced between the lounge and the wall phone in the kitchen for what seemed like hours and probably was. It was odd for him to be inside during the afternoon, but she played with her dolls because she hadn't gotten the erector set she'd asked for, changing out legs and arms so that brown Barbie had a white torso and white Barbie had one brown leg sticking out from her minidress. Heads were taken off and filled with ashtray sand and switched. She had made a doll hospital under a table in the lounge, later regretting having rendered Skipper bald with a nail clipper. Many arms and legs had been amputated, reattached, and bandaged with masking tape, so that by the time the phone finally rang and Vac pounced on it, her little ward under the table resembled a MASH unit.

Years later she realized those hours spent doll-doctoring would have been the hours between the beginning of the search and the discovery of floating wreckage and bodies. Vac packed a bag and left Naledi then, carrying a wedding photo of her parents for the coroner. For three days Meg was looked after by Ursa, the beer delivery lady, who was nice enough but swore quite a lot, so that when Vac returned he was irritated to find Meg's vocabulary had expanded to include obscenities delivered in a Swedish lilt.

For a long time Vac's jaw moved like the Tin Man's and he was more silent than usual—it was days before he could pull her into his lap and stutteringly explain why her parents had not come back.

Later, when she was installed as a proper schoolgirl at the convent academy, Vac came to Chicago less often, staying in a sublet a mile from campus, sometimes in a cheap boardinghouse. On their trips to Lake Michigan they carried fishing poles and loitered on the piers with no plan, idly casting for fish they would never eat themselves. The Chinese immigrants fishing beside them would ask politely for their catches, laughing when Vac warned them of mercury and other pollutants. Using gestures and raw English, they would boast how much filthier the rivers in their homelands were, where the goal was not to stay healthy but to stay alive.

They sometimes all fished in a row, a line of old men and a girl, all absorbed in their thoughts, all wave-watching the gray expanse.

Meg's aunt Catherine believes, as the Chinese do, that individuals have an element. If that's so, then Meg's is undeniably water.

She finishes: "I paint water because it's the one thing I can count on to change."

Next is Tiffany's "Who aspires you?" She'd prefer a simple "what inspires her." To Tiffany Swifthawk or listeners of WSQW she might answer Monet or Turner because those names might ring familiar and Frederic Church might not. Meg doodles in the margins of the page. Her real answer includes obscure painters she learned of only well after arriving in London. The first year there had been spent feeling green among academy students who had already taken color theory and life drawing. She'd been wholly unprepared, feeling every inch the hayseed after her silly landscape and watercolor courses at St. Agnes, where most art books had been victim of Sister Marie's coupon clipper—any depiction of nudity or actions considered unchristian, carnal, or violent were razored away by Sister. The Italian masters suffering in particular.

It took a full year at the academy for Meg to shake off her

trepidation—a year of watching, listening, drawing, keeping her mouth shut, and feeling homesick. Recalling those long months always make Meg's shins ache. When she hadn't been standing at an easel on a cold studio floor, she'd be shifting foot to foot on the marble of the Tate or the National Portrait Gallery, drawing everything, scrapping it all, then drawing it again.

She had not been inspired by one particular painter, or even a teacher, and so took her own direction. Vac might once have had practical opinions about Meg becoming an artist, but he'd died before invoking them, leaving her to Polly, who hadn't seemed alarmed in the least that she was set on painting. Polly had grown up in some God-fearing cult, and her response to such harsh judgment was to develop a fierce live-and-let-live attitude. And no wonder. Polly had been herded toward the narrowest future possible, veering away just in time after winning a scholarship to study biology. For choosing science, she was banished from her family and rendered an orphan in her own right. Polly says that had they known she was a lesbian to boot, they might have never recovered from the shame and would quite possibly have been banished themselves. And so Polly never steered Meg, only guided. Besides, as a college professor she knew well enough how nineteen-year-olds respond to advice. Meg became an artist be-cause it did not occur to her that she could be anything else, though she did have enough sense to get a teaching certificate along with her degree. Her answer is terse but truthful: "I'm not inspired by any artist, only by what I see. I just paint."

Meg chews her lip. She really doesn't have a better answer. She is a terrible choice for Tiffany's project, now that she thinks of it—a painter as a subject for radio?

When pitching the interview, Tiffany had actually used the term *hermit,* making Meg laugh. Maybe she can seem antisocial, but the truth is she simply finds it difficult to be at ease around people who themselves are not. Rumors here are often seeded by what one *doesn't* do: she's likely a lesbian since she hasn't re-placed Jeremy, might have "gone Jewish" because she doesn't attend church, must be rich since she hasn't yet sold Naledi, and is probably a vegetarian for not buying any meat raffle tickets. Lord knows what they'll come up with after the interview. She underlines the next question: Advice to a young artist?

"Avoid detractors. Try several mediums before settling on one. If you paint clouds, try metalwork. If you make ceramics, try etching or oils. Challenge yourself to create things you think you cannot do or probably won't even like." Her fingers scurry over the keys. "If you really are an artist, you'll have no choice."

Before he grew to find her painting tiresome, Jeremy actually encouraged her. When they met, he'd described her as "a fringe girl" to his friends—very unlike the twin-set-sweater-and-pearls type his mother, Daphne, might have preferred. To him, Meg was a female version of a bad boy, and an American to boot, making her doubly unsuitable. Jeremy was already aimed toward academia and a fairly certain and boring future and so naturally he was up for a bit of diversion, and Meg had more than provided one. She remembers his alarm when she dragged him to alternative galleries in seedy parts of London or rough, cheap pubs near the academy or hole-in-the-wall restaurants in the East End, seeking vindaloo and jerk and other alien foods. Hygiene, personal safety, culinary and artistic tastes ranked differently on their respective scales, none of which seemed obstacles in the beginning: each just assumed the other would eventually see the stupidity of their ways and change. The "novelty" of Meg's work was not sustainable in Jeremy's opinion, and the non-English-ness that made her stand out in the beginning eventually prevented her from fitting in. If Meg were asked at gunpoint why she stayed with Jeremy for as long as she had, she wouldn't have an answer. There were numerous reasons, she supposes. Daphne, for one, who set her priggishness aside and allowed herself to love her daughter-in-law—a surprise to Jeremy, who'd semiconsciously meant to make some statement to his mother with Meg or at least shock her somehow. Meg was buoyed by the attentions of her smart, bitterly funny mother-in-law, who was frightfully English in the best ways, self-deprecating and wry, polite and well read but modest. Any inklings of leaving Jeremy simply weren't as strong as her inertia, her admiration for Daphne, and visa concerns. She is ashamed now to admit that money played a part in her staying. Her income never approached Jeremy's, handsomely subsidized by an inheritance from his grandparents. His lifestyle was always a notch or two higher than she was able to manage, so she was always behind. When the resort began to deteriorate, she'd had to hire a caretaker couple, and as lakeshore taxes soared every year, her insurance settlement from the airline shrank to nothing, and Meg found herself having to ask for help that was not in Jeremy's nature to give. It was only after Daphne died that Meg realized Jeremy alone wasn't quite enough. In the end, after their years together in Chicago he was as relieved to go back to England as she was to retreat north.

Meg likes to imagine Jeremy back where she found him, drinking brown ale in a pub with his futsy, tweedy fellows from the university. She can almost imagine him happy, remarried to someone more suitable, more academic, maybe even having the children Meg had put aside in favor of her career.

Advice to a young artist?

"Don't expect everyone will understand."

The last questions were simple.

What had she missed about Naledi?

"The quiet and solitude."

What did she miss about the real world?

"The noise and the people."

If she could be born at any time in history?

"The future."

Tiffany meets Meg at the computer lab. The actual interview goes well enough, with Tiffany e-mailing afterward to say it made the cut and will be aired on the weekend, wedged between Wolfman Willie and the Musher Twins.

Meg is expecting company; her Aunt Cathy and the very grown-up Patrick are driving up from Minneapolis. Meg will buy some wine and maybe try cooking something, and they can all listen to the broadcast together, maybe have a few laughs.

As long-gone as Vac is, Meg sometimes senses him in places where he used to pop up. Not quite a ghost, more like a peripheral glitch—an amorphous scrap of plaid, the blurred streak of a gesture, a whoosh overhead like the cast of a lure, or the swift fall of an ax. She knows the notion is ridiculous and shrugs him off, sometimes laughing or saying "Shoo!" aloud and ridiculously. She's tentatively mentioned these pockets of saturated air to Jon Redleaf. His people believe in spirits, but he claims to be a lousy Indian that way, a realist who insists the lore is only lore and a ghost is only what we make it, though he thinks he might know what she senses out there, chalking up her sightings to some hangover of collective energy. Meg's amused by the notion, because if a fraction of the fifty years of Vac's cumulative energy working around Naledi took form, great drafts of him would ricochet off trees and scour eaves and scoop into the bows of boats and froth the lake to funnels.

If he were here, she'd know it.

Ninety percent of visitors to the resort couldn't pick Vac out of a lineup any more than they could spot a grouse in the brush. Meg would often give Vac grief about his clothes in all-terrain colors and his wolverine elusiveness, especially when sought out by guests with inane complaints or requests. He rarely showed anger; his temper was the long-suffering, low-simmering type that erupted in rare, showcase moments.

Some weeks after the plane crash, her father's VW bus was returned from the airport and stowed behind the woodlot. Since no one drove it, it became a playhouse and catchall for Meg—the one place she could be coaxed into napping. When Vac tired of having to go all the way around the sea of cordwood to check on her, he parked it closer, just off the circular drive where he could see it while sitting at the kitchen table. Eventually she outgrew naps, and the tires of the bus went flat, one by one, its bright aqua finish fading to a chalky robin's egg blue. The roof slowly disappeared under layers of pine needles and chaff that eventually hosted tiny ferns. Vac towed it back to the tractor shed where it sat for years, Meg using it mostly as a cache for things she wouldn't want found in the lodge. She took a few vacation boys to see it, where they kissed her with bad breath or braces on their teeth, or jutty tongues, or nice melty lips. While she was away at St. Agnes, Vac finally sold the van to some guest, a car nut keen on restoring it. She blanched when she got the check in the mail with its notation "Meg's VW." Yes, it was hers, she'd fumed. He'd had no business selling it. Even now Meg feels old shame and anger, feels trespassed upon when she thinks of Vac cleaning out her bus, all the little compartments and crannies, boxing up her private life, handling all her little mud sculptures, syrupy notes from boys, her beer coaster collection, the family of troll dolls made anatomically correct with little add-on genitals and nail-polish nipples, a long-forgotten pair of bloodied panties crammed under the dash from when she got her first period and was so ignorant and scared she reasoned that if she hid it away it would go away. There were jars clanking with the keepsakes stolen from the resort mothers she liked; she only took from the interested ones, never the pitying ones. Mementos—always only one earring because two would arouse suspicion, two would have been theft. Vac found her collection of house keys, though less valuable, to be a more malicious matter. She'd eased them from the key rings of guests who'd been in some way awful, so she might have the deep satisfaction of imagining them finally arriving home after the long drive and dying to get inside their houses, needing to pee, frustrated and hopping—they'd be fumbling, locked out, keyless, and clueless. Home, but not quite.

The keys nearly filled a fruitcake tin. Vac had spread them out along with the single earrings and roach ends and a little square of hash over the quilt on her bed. He did things that way, let her know he knew, then shamed her with his silence. But the theft of keys and earrings eventually roused him to words. He made her go through the guest books, identify her victims, and write them notes to send along with the returned earrings, not caring that most would be sent the wrong one. He would have made her do the same with the keys if he could, then threatened to send her down the shore to Camp Gummarus for the rest of the summer. She reminded him he'd then be short a Saturday cleaner *and* an afternoon bartender, so Vac scratched his stubble and decided instead to take the battery out of the old jitney so that all she had for transportation the whole summer was a runabout with an ancient Evinrude, and a too-small bike with a banana seat.

Since neither she nor Vac took tears very seriously, she'd acted out the way a boy might—filling a dozen Mason jars with gasoline, half-burying them into the sides of anthills, setting them on the bald rock slopes, making little twig fires around them, then backing up to aim a .22 from just out of range of flying glass and flame, and blowing up the jars in satisfying little Hiroshimas, one after another. That got to Vac, it being a particularly dry spring. They had a real face-to-face then—a first for both of them, with heaving shoulders and her nose running and his words glittered with spit, the scene evolving into much more than just an argument about dishonesty and theft or doing dangerous, stupid things. It dredged forth ten years of reticent grief and self-pity for both of them. After seeing him break after so many years, Meg finally fully understood that her loss had been Vac's loss, too.

She invites Tiffany to tour her new studio. With a view like an aerie, it's built on the highest point of the property, a high plateau one would only consider scaling because the sunsets are worth it or to stay in shape.

Between helping to finish the studio and her recent trips to Nova Scotia, she's barely had time to settle in and unpack the studio, let alone paint in it.

Polly is in Halifax for good now, however long "good" will be. She is, by her own admission, blind as a worm and on a bad day will complain over the phone that her knees burn, or that the people in her wing of the facility are just all so bloody old, or that she doesn't know which is worse, the symptoms of Crohn's disease or having a disease with a name that shouts from the rooftops that she is old and gassy. She has told Meg that for the first time in her life she prays—to be taken. "Beam me up, Scotty," she jokes. When serious, she claims to be looking forward to the void and the absence of feeling, to be relieved of her body. She's had enough, thank you.

But mostly she's positive and, surprisingly, has begun a new book, dictating it into a recorder. Polly won't say what it's about, only that she's nailed the title. Meg is almost certain it must be the memoir Polly came to Naledi to write so long ago but never could. She hopes her old friend will have enough time to finish.

When the studio door blows shut, the young dog at Tiffany's feet twitches in its sleep, her thick paws moving in some fantastic pursuit. Iris is half-husky and at six months is already larger than Ilsa, who had crawled under an overturned skiff on Thanksgiving afternoon for her very last nap. The new dog's icy-blue eyes are a jolt after Ilsa's muted cataract stare; Meg had forgotten just how much a dog watches, and this one seems almost neurotically alert, though like Ilsa, Iris only barks for a reason, and she is learning her commands. So while Meg's thankful for that, she's forgotten the tedium of training a dog, the repetition, the frustration, pockets always gritty with kibble, the shoes chewed. But she and Iris are slowly learning each other. She shows Tiffany how Iris will sit, stay, fetch, and hold with the treat perched on her nose until Meg gives the signal.

The foundation of the studio sits only a few feet from the cliff face, and Meg's easel stands just inside the wall of windows. The building is a three-sided wedge, a slice of glass pie with greenstone blocks forming the crust of the back wall and foundation. The only approach is the zigzag of stairs cut into the pillow-rock incline, an endeavor that took Jon months with frightful saws and epic noise, prompting Meg to dub it the Inca Trail. At the base of the steps brush is filling in where the crane had been parked and trees cleared. The muddy ruts have settled and have greened up with spring growth. The earth heals quickly here; clearings where old cabins once stood are grown over with birch, paths have grown closed, and docks have fallen away board by board like rows of rotting teeth. The old gas pumps are gone. You wouldn't know the place was ever a resort. She's had a surveyor out to mark off four large lake lots near the property line bordering Camp Gummy in the event she ever decides to sell and has considered deeding the inland wetlands to the convent to avoid the taxes—forget that Vac would rise from the dead if he knew she'd given even worthless land to a church. She'd once asked why, since he hated religion, he had sent her to St. Agnes. "Because they could teach you Latin," he'd replied, "and I knew you were too sensible to swallow the rest." Only half his hopes came to be. By the end of her catechism she was amazed and shocked how little the religion had progressed since the Middle Ages—that people still bought it. She could barely recall a word of Latin.

After working in the lodge porch for so long, hemmed by knotty pine and heavy shade, Meg had craved light and space but hadn't counted on quite so much of both. Or such drama. She can only imagine what the bush pilots above might make of the studio. The local hawk, circling, seems curious and wary at his own reflection. She can watch him through the wide pane but still cannot look down to the lake without some tug of vertigo. Meg has never been to the top of the Hancock Building, or the Eiffel Tower, or even the fire lookout near town, and should have mentioned as much when the Perla brothers suggested the cliff as a building site, when she'd only been imagining unimpeded north light, not this view that begins at the clouds and spirals lakeward. On a clear day visibility is twenty miles, thirty when it's cold and the air is crystalline, when the lights of Hatchet Inlet can be glimpsed. The north view is of the jagged Ontario shore, which gives way to forest that peters out into bog land where a dozen small ponds glint like strewn scraps of tin. Along with the view and the stars and clouds also comes some danger of lightning strikes, so after imagining herself flash-broiled, Meg had a sixty-foot conductor rod erected on the adjacent ledge.

It's been a tentative start, and she's not quite gotten her legs in this high place but feels some slow inspiration is coming for her: her eye is changing some, her gaze lifting, aiming skyward. A new perspective from above the shaded slopes of Naledi and the shore, above the canopy that shields it all, things feel different.

When she had described the studio to Polly, saying how it reminded her of a boat, Polly clapped and suggested Meg christen it. In fact, Polly loved her own idea so much she's promised to send champagne. She reminded Meg that christenings require witnesses, meaning people, meaning a party. Polly would naturally be the guest of honor in absentia. The studio has been the gift she'd insisted on, dearly wanting to give something she can enjoy giving while alive, or, as she says, "on the hoof"—something real besides the after-the-fact impersonal inheritance of her estate, the piles of papers and bonds and royalty accounts and manuscripts she imagines will only become as burdensome to Meg as they have become to her.

Meg can't think how to approach a guest list so simply ends up inviting most everyone she encounters, encouraging them to bring friends, handing over invitations from her deep shoulder bag as if there is a bottomless supply. She'd given a dozen to Tiffany saying, "Whoever you think." She's shown the girl the burial mounds that her uncle now tends, the groomed path and the shaded glade. During their radio interview, Meg talked at length about the burial mounds, avoiding most of Tiffany's original list of questions. Many visitors have come out since: a few school groups, a pair of cultural anthropologists, and a clutch of elders proposing a plan for reappropriation of the land, which Meg has gladly agreed to sell for one dollar, having always felt uncomfortable with the perceived responsibility of owning a place that isn't ownable, as if one could casually say, "Oh, and down this path lies our little patch of sacred ground."

The party sneaks up on her, and before she knows it's nearly June and she's standing on the lodge porch and looking out over the gathering. There are the few people she might call friends, but most are acquaintances, some she knows only in passing by name or face: the barista at the Minnow Bucket; the new Sheriff Janko everyone calls Janko Junior, whom she'd met while being tick-eted for Iris's lack of dog tags. Polka Peggy is wearing something like a square-dance dress, looking exactly like she sounds on the radio. Gimp Wuuri has brought his mother, Ma Gimp. There are a few of the staff from the casino, and the Perla construction crew along with most everyone from Pavola's and Chainsaw Sally's. Pat and Fat Pat the librarians have arrived together.

Meg pinballs among them all, greeting, directing them to the buffet and bar, where both kegs have been tapped. She's not re-ally able to talk or linger much, but then isn't that the way of hosting a party? There's never been a real party at Naledi, she realizes, thinking out loud.

"Then it's about time, right?" The man responding is new to Hatchet Inlet, Granger-something, who works over at the res-ervation as a counselor. Meg had been surprised earlier to hear him giving directions to the bathroom in the lodge as if he knew the place.

"I guess." She looks at him curiously.

"I knew your grandfather." Everything about the man is broad—he's built like a bulldog with a wide face and wide smile. Just as he's about to say more, something metallic clatters behind them at the barbeque, a steel tray lid fallen to the flagstones. Jon, wearing an apron, is already picking it up. Most of the party is being catered by Joe Pavola, but Jon had wanted to contribute. He's taped a few recipes sent by his nephew Bear above the grill and is slow-roasting ducks in a glaze, not looking entirely com-fortable with the basting brush in his hand. Most guests already have appetizers, nibbling on walleye fingers and mallard pâté. Lenny Blatnik is serenading with his accordion, and with both hands occupied he accepts tidbits open-mouthed, like a seal tak-ing tips.

After the meal—declared a great success—gusts of wind whip up an impressive mess, sending napkins aloft while liquor-slowed hands try to snatch as scraps flip and flap past the tiki torches and into the dark woods. Stained paper plates skitter and roll and are shouted at, stepped on, trapped.

It's well after eleven when Meg realizes it's now or never if they're going to christen the studio. It's a challenge to round up so many full and slightly tipsy guests, either deep in conversation, dancing, in midjoke, or ready to topple. She elicits help from her cousin Patrick and his partner Kevin. It takes a while and some good-natured grousing, but eventually everyone is herded away from the tables and circles of camp chairs to assemble at the base of the Inca Trail. Cassi Olson had suggested the invites include BYOH, Bring Your Own Headlamp, and most have, so that when they start up the hill they make a sort of glittering conga line, Meg in the lead.

Hal Bergen climbs just behind, pretending to huff and puff until she turns around, and says, "Meg, can ya gimme a hand?" He never seems to tire of his joke. Each Thanksgiving since the sawmill accident, he has sent Meg a gift card from his outdoor gear and bait store, Lefty's, the venture he seeded with his insurance money. He has kept Meg in polar fleece and lures for several years now.

Pete Lahti, fresh from treatment and looking less puffy, walks next to Granger. Coming up behind slowly is Alpo, propped up by his fiancée, Sissy, and Veshko, the masseur from Sarajevo, who's been helping Alpo since he broke his hip in Pavola's slipping on a butter pat, which he will never hear the end of. Veshko works part-time at Senior Cedars in physical therapy and has just opened his own hot stone massage spa, Pebbles & Bam Bam.

Aunt Cathy is whispering some encouragement into Cassi's ear, urging her forward. Cassi's been installed in Polly's cabin most of the summer, studying for the SAT, avoiding her family, and mourning her great-grandmother. Meg was barely able to coax Cassi out for the party by insisting that Ursa—Bana—would want her to carry on, to "party on," which only fell flat since Cassi's too young to remember *Wayne's World*. Ursa, driving home from a particularly spectacular fire at the Skevold's lumber mill, had hit a yearling whitetail and careened into a bridge abutment, flying headlong through the windshield of her Oldsmobile and into the current of the Wikawashi. Cassi suspects her great-grandmother had been aiming for the deer, making the accident that much more tragic and senseless. Meg has not mentioned Ursa's disdain for seatbelts, that her famous lead foot might have contributed to that senselessness.

There are smatterings of "Oohs!" and "Ahhs!" as people reach the ledge and extinguish their headlamps. The building and its expanses of glass reflect the entire party in silhouette with a full moon behind them. The stone appears light and chalky and the moon washes the treetops an ashy gray. Patrick and Kevin ease through the gathering, filling the plastic champagne flutes.

Meg steps up onto the milk crate placed at the hard front angle of the studio. The champagne bottle wrapped in a towel is already on the window ledge. The Perla brothers and Jon should by rights be standing next to her since they built the studio, but they hang back behind the group, either shy or keeping an eye on those guests near the cliff edge.

She's thought hard about what to say, had written down a few sentences, and even memorized a line from one of Polly's favorite Sara Teasdale poems, but upon looking out over the faces, she realizes it's much too somber for the occasion and the crowd.

> Like barley bending,
> In low fields by the sea,
> singing in hard wind,
> Ceaselessly . . . .

Almost everyone is talking, some are laughing. Comments float good-naturedly from alcohol-loosened tongues: "Would you look at that?" "Good luck washing those windows." " 'Spose she'll be staying now?"

She reaches into her pocket for her scrap of paper and clears her throat, but no one has heard. To get their attention she grabs the bottle of champagne and holds it high, calling, "It's time!"

Just as she has them, the instant she opens her mouth to begin, the bells at St. Gummy commence with a single ring, the wind delivering the sound to the ridge as if by a great megaphone. Laughter accompanies the interruption through the first few peals, then trails off under the resonance, and everyone goes still, their faces naturally turned toward the sound as the deep tones expand the night sky, slowly.

Seven, eight, nine . . .

Everyone is smiling, all suspended in the same moment . . . *ten . . .* they are all in it together . . . *eleven . . .* and, wait for it . . . *twelve.*

After the last echoing toll dissolves, they are all enveloped in silence and residual awe. Meg has forgotten her few lines, not that they were all that, but even eloquence would fall flat and forgettable after the bells, the tintinnabulation. Looking out over the quilt of faces, she swallows and thanks everyone for coming, feeling a sting behind her eyes for how much she means it.

There's applause and hoots as she smashes the wrapped bottle against the foundation, and plastic champagne flutes are held high. Someone hands one to Meg and she lifts it to the gathering.

A toast, of course. She'd forgotten there would be a toast.

"To . . ." Meg sees they really are expecting something from her. Chatter rattles to silence, then after a few beats the silence begins to grow twitchy with expectation. She scrabbles and grubs, but the bells are an impossible act to follow, and she is lousy with words. Instead, Meg tips her champagne, first to the moon, then to the faces of those who have bothered to make the climb, some still a little wheezy.

"To . . ." She makes the sort of toast Vac would make, admitting that it is indeed "a good-enough midnight."

The writing of this book was supported in several ways, especially by the encouragement and space to work provided by many generous friends and relatives. Thanks to my editor, Todd Orjala, for taking this book on, and to the staff of the University of Minnesota Press for their forward thinking in publishing *Vacationland* as a paperback original. More thanks to editors Louisa Castner and Laura Westlund for scrubbing this manuscript clean. Appreciation to Carol Connolly for her tireless encouragement and support over the years to all Minnesota writers, and for providing an opportunity for early readings of these stories. Thanks also to intern Elaine Kenny for all her hard work and sass. Bottomless gratitude to Jon—you had my back while I wrote this book.

Reading Group Questions and Topics for Discussion

1. Meg claims that Naledi Lodge seems nearly alive. Can a place or setting become as essential to a story as the humans inhabiting it?

2. As the philandering ad man in "Reparation" maintains, each eye has its own lens to the past. Ed appears to have lived guilt-free for decades. Is he buying redemption by giving Meg a set of paints and purchasing her most expensive painting?

3. Improbable scenarios might seem more plausible at a distance. When Estelle and Miriam set out on the mission to hasten their sister's death, each has gone to the trouble of procuring drugs, but has either thought things through?

4. Refugee Veshko struggles to adapt to his new home of Hatchet Inlet. Do his observations fairly portray the rural culture where he's landed?

5. In "Moderation," chemical dependency counselor Granger settles old battles he had with his father, but there are other loose ends in his past. What might his intention be in returning to Naledi?

6. Cassi, the lost teen in "Navigation," can control her own ADHD but feels helpless before the threat her family poses to her great-grandmother, Ursa. Does she understand that

she has become lost on purpose, or does that understanding occur only when confessing to Meg?

7. When Rob Perla becomes caretaker of Naledi, he gets a different view of his own region and its attraction to outsiders. How does his year at the resort change him? How does it change his relationship with Katie?

8. Jon Redleaf seems deliberately out of touch with his Ojibwe heritage and culture. Does his walk among the burial mounds or his moving to Naledi suggest that might change?

9. Ursa Olson is cantankerous and short-tempered with most people, preferring trees to relatives, but Vac and great-granddaughter Cassi are exceptions. Did her relationship with Vac come as a surprise?

10. Patrick is not open regarding his sexual orientation, despite Cathy's nurturing. Does he still carry the shame his father heaped on him when he was a boy? How does his trip to Naledi affect his long-held apprehensions?

11. As the airplane loses altitude, Tomas Machutova mourns all he has not done and all he will miss in his daughter Meg's future. Are his memories and ruminations believable in a portrayal of a person facing sudden, unexpected death?

12. Recognizing that her family is cowed and isolated by their cultish religion, Polly turns to facts and science. Even so, she pulls a puritanical thread later in her life, preventing her from completely embracing her relationship with Eleanor. Does writing fiction finally give her the opportunity to live how she might have, had she been braver?

13. Alpo Lahti's Hobby has kept him too busy to think much about the death of his wife, Rose. Will letting his once-

beloved trees go untended mark the beginning of his grieving process—or the end?

14. Occlusion: the word mirrors Polly's failing eyes and Magda's lack of insight. Polly has been Meg's true maternal figure, while her biological grandmother dismisses her. How has Meg's motherless condition exhibited itself?

15. Asked about her life by Tiffany Swifthawk, Meg muses about how much of it is inexorably twined with the resort, yet she has mixed feelings about Naledi. Will she ever be able to leave?

In resort communities, there is often tension between locals and tourists, with stereotypes assigned to both. How do the characters in *Vacationland* fulfill or break such stereotypes? What might the tourist and the locals in the novel discover they have in common?

Many vacations are stand-alone nuggets in time and memory, bookended by beginnings and ends: the journeys to and from. What is your most enduring vacation memory?

Each story has a connection to another (besides the shared settings of Naledi and Hatchet Inlet), mainly through characters. Were you able to follow these connections in a way that pulled the book together for you? Did these interrelations among the stories contribute a sense of unity to the book, making *Vacationland* a novel rather than several short stories?

If you could ask the author one question about this book, what would it be?

SARAH STONICH is the best-selling author of *These Granite Islands*, translated into seven languages and shortlisted for France's Gran Prix de Lectrices de *Elle*; the critically acclaimed novel *The Ice Chorus*; and a memoir, *Shelter*. The founder of WordStalkers.com, she lives in Minneapolis and spends summers in northeastern Minnesota.